Praise for Colin Barker's murder mysteries

PRAISE FOR *FALSE PERSPECTIVE*

"Well written, exquisitely structured mystery that kept me guessing till the end. Introduces us to a score of well-developed characters, all participating in some way in art, its collection, and its provenance."

—BRUCE MERCHANT, author of *Moonkind*

"The book is beautifully written, and informative about stolen art, which makes the book a fascinating read. Barker (a professor like his protagonist) is an excellent writer and takes us on a ride through academia at a small New Mexico university."

—M.B. GRANA, author and winner of the
2000 Willa Cather Award for 'Begoso Cabin.'

"The mystery's characters are vividly portrayed. I am a fan of mysteries (and) look forward to Candrew Nor's next mystery."

—STEPHEN JONES, poet, author, and Amazon reviewer.

"A hidden gem. A great "who dunnit" that will keep you guessing to the end. I loved some of the characters."

—HOPEYOUHAVEBETTERLUCK. Amazon reviewer.

"Captures the northern New Mexico landscape and culture . . . while giving the reader a glimpse into the Santa Fe art scene"

—SUSAN CUMMINS MILLER, author of
the Frankie MacFarlane mysteries.

seem credible even though they are fictitious. . . . Barker integrates his knowledge of his science with the plot in a plausible manner. The result is a novel that moves quickly and has a cast of characters that are very human. Some are very likable—others less so. There are twists and turns throughout and a few dead ends and wrong turns that seem OK at the time they are introduced.
If you are looking for a novel with a different twist, you may well like this book.

—R. BROADHEAD, Amazon reviewer.

"T. Wrecks is more than a skillful, entertaining whodunit (although the cleverly constructed plot will have the reader guessing). Barker's strength is dialog, and 'T. Wrecks' is about people—not flat stereotypes who speak and have reasons, good or bad, for what they do. As Candrew Nor learns, people live in the area of human motivation where everything isn't black-and-white.
Barker reaffirms that he has carved a unique niche in the American mystery genre.

—STEPHEN JONES, poet, author, and Amazon reviewer.

Barker's writing is rich and almost poetic; he displays a love for the desert and hills where this mystery takes place and is able to evoke the feeling that you are there as the action unfolds.
Don't miss this one! As I said before, "It's a Duzzy."

—FRED CHURCH, Venice.

As with Barker's previous mysteries, T-Wrecks is set in the academic world of a small university in northern New Mexico, . . . again as with all Barker's books, this one is extremely well written, full of surprises and exciting twists of plot. T-Wrecks is a fun read.

—M.B. GRANA, author and winner of
the 2000 Willa Cather Award.

MURDER LOVES DIAMONDS

Candrew Nor Murder Mysteries

False Perspective
Murder in the Art Department

Icy Moon
Murder in the Astronomy Department

T. Wrecks
Murder in the Geology Department

Murder Loves Diamonds
Murder in the Minerals Department

Smoke And Mirrors
Murder in the Archaeology Department

Double Negative
Murder in the English Department
[*In preparation*]

MURDER LOVES DIAMONDS

Murder in the Minerals Department

COLIN BARKER

Printed in the United States of America
ISBN 979-8-8693-8359-4 (paper)

Acknowledgements

Novels are written with support and inspiration from friends and colleagues. I particularly want to thank Bruce Moss and Jim Roghair for their word-by-word support in the Santa Fe writers' group, and also David Blaisdell. I'd also like to thank my son Conan, Dave Wavrek, Harry Bockmeulen, and David Lord who were with me on the San Juan River trip and the visit to the Mule Ear diatreme. These visits inspired the novel's plot.

My wife Yvonne patiently put up with my hours at the computer. And the book was written under the watchful eyes of our two dogs—Chile and Jack.

CHAPTER 1

THE MUDDY SAN JUAN River, with the Navajo nation on its south bank, flows through southern Utah, joins the Colorado River, and pours into Lake Powell. It cuts through the uplift known as Comb Ridge, making its way between high cliffs of ochre-colored sandstone.

On one Spring day, the river carried along two inflated rafts, each with a professor and half a dozen geology students. They were all from the University of Northern New Mexico.

In the leading raft, Professor Candrew Nor was pointing out details of the geology, explaining the sandstone structures to the students. He'd been taking photographs and enthusiastically describing the sloping sandstone bedding characteristic of the original wind-blown sand dunes. Sandstones were Dr. Nor's academic specialty. He had lectured widely, developed a well-earned professional reputation, and had many academic publications to his credit.

The professor in the second raft was Mark Kernfeld, one of Candrew Nor's faculty colleagues. This Assistant Professor was a specialist in the chemical analysis of geological materials—a 'geo-chemist.' Not experienced in field geology, he was, however, an old hand river runner and had come along to help with the logistics of this geological field trip.

The river outing was early in the year, the weekend before Spring Break, and it was still quite cool. There were no other rafters floating the river. At the end of the day, the students hauled the rafts up onto a short stretch of sandy beach on the south side of the river. This was in fact part of the Navajo Indian reservation which stretched many miles from the river down into Arizona.

As the sun set and it got colder, and the students were eager to eat hot meals. While several helped get cooking underway, others set up tents. After wolfing down their dinners, in the chilly evening they huddled around a driftwood fire for a couple of hours, trading yarns and swapping lies, before turning in for an early night.

Next morning, after breakfast, they floated a short distance down river before pushing ashore through dense tamarisk. Near where they landed was the start of a poorly marked trail that led up to the prominent Mule Ear, the highest point on Comb Ridge. They hiked for more than an hour, taking the steep, rocky path to the top. The view there was spectacular.

Mark Kernfeld, the geochemist, turned to Candrew and said, "I've floated this part of the river on several occasions, but this is the first time I've made the effort to hike to the top of the Mule Ear." He was busy taking photos of the sweeping view with his cell phone. "Out here, this is about all my cell phone is capable of. But the good news is, I don't get any spam." He grinned. "And I guess the other interesting news is that in the past this area was mined for gold."

"Really?" Candrew had heard that, but didn't know the details.

"Yeah, in the late eighteen hundreds there was an influx of miners panning for gold."

Candrew led the group of students to an area just north of the Mule Ear peak where the exposed rocks were not sandstones but dark igneous rocks. The top of these had been weathered, and the students were excited to find scattered red and green sand-sized mineral grains.

"So, what are you looking at?" Candrew quizzed the students, standing with his hands in his pockets, his hair tousled by the breeze.

"Well, the red minerals, I think, are maybe garnets." The girl's inflected voice made it sound more like a question than a statement. She was dressed in a heavy anorak, had long blonde hair, and was wearing sunglasses. Taking a plastic bag from her backpack, she scooped up a handful of the sand-sized grains and dropped them into the bag.

"What do the rest of you think?" Candrew asked looking around at the group. Several were holding notebooks and one was taking photos with his cell phone.

A short, plump guy with holes in his faded jeans and a baseball cap on backwards, put down his water bottle and said, "I agree. I think Annie's right. They're garnets."

"Yeah. And what are red garnets called?"

The quiet girl, who rarely spoke but was probably the brightest student in the group, said, "Pyrope."

"Good. That's right. And how about the green minerals?" Candrew asked.

"Could be olivines," one student suggested.

Brandon, a graduate students and somewhat older than the others, was currently the Teaching Assistant. He pointed out, "There are quite a few green minerals." Looking around the group to be sure they were all paying attention, he asked, "Could it be diopside?"

There was silence for a moment while they thought about that. Then Brandon said, laughing, "We got here just in time."

"We did?" asked the girl with the pony tail, clearly surprised.

"Yeah. All these mineral grains are going to be swept off the hillside and down into the river by the next heavy thunderstorm."

"So, I guess they'll get dumped in together with all those other sand grains in the river bed," one of the students said.

"Yeah, and in a few million years they'll end up part of some future sandstone." The student in the polo neck sweater turned to Candrew and, grinning, said, "They'll become those 'heavy minerals' you lectured us about."

Candrew was pleased that at least one of his students had understood—and remembered—his explanation.

After spending an hour examining the Mule Ear diatreme, and collecting samples of the sand-sized grains in plastic bags, they hiked down to the river, the rafts, and their campsite.

The geology students ate dinner and Candrew and Mark sat on a couple of large boulders apart from the chattering group.

Mark Kernfeld was tall, slim and athletic, and wearing round-rimmed glasses and a baseball cap that said 'Geochemical Society.' He had wide-ranging academic interests. "Tell me about this Mule Ear thing," he said. "To my untutored eye, I can see it's quite unlike the sandstones along the river banks. For one thing, it's a lot darker in color."

"Well, the Mule Ear itself is sandstone, but that dark area to the north is something completely different. That's where I took the students and they collected mineral samples. It's a type of rock structure called a *diatreme*. What you were looking at was the top of a rock pipe that's maybe a mile or two across and extends many miles down. It punched its way up from deep below the Earth's surface when the rocks were hot, almost molten, but viscous—and it moved fast. It's not my sort of geology, and I'm no expert, but geologically speaking these pipes seem to form almost instantaneously," Candrew paused, grinning, "At least on a geological timescale." He glanced at the geochemist who seemed to be interested.

"These things common?" Mark asked.

"There's an estimated three hundred of them in the Four Corners area," Candrew said. "Some rocks of this type are called *kimberlite pipes*." He went on to explain, "They're like the ones the De Beers company mines in South Africa, near the town of Kimberly. Many of those pipes are similar to the Mule Ear diatreme and also contain garnets and diopside—what explorers know as *indicator minerals*."

The geochemist tilted his head to one side and frowned. "And what do they indicate?"

"Diamonds."

"Really? And how do they manage to indicate those gems?"

"It's now well understood that when these minerals have high trace amounts of chromium it shows they're associated with diamonds."

"Chromium? That's something we analyze routinely in my laboratory," Mark said. "So we could check these red garnets, the pyrope garnets, for you. See if they're rich in chromium." He laughed, "See if you're on to anything."

"Well, thanks for the offer, but no diamonds have been found in this diatreme—yet. Although as far as I'm aware, no one has analyzed the indicator minerals for chromium."

CHAPTER 2

THE GROUP OF STUDENTS and their two professors spent the morning of the third day on the river, with just a couple of brief stops to examine outcropping rocks. The geologic float trip ended early in the afternoon—reluctantly for some, but gladly for others. The students pushed through the invasive tamarisk on the river bank and hauled the rafts up onto a sandy stretch. Candrew had arranged for a bus to be brought to the site. They loaded the camping gear and scrambled into their seats for the long drive back to the university.

Later that day the bus arrived at the University of Northern New Mexico and parked on campus outside Kinblade Hall, a neo-Georgian building that housed the Geology Department. There the students unpacked camping gear and other equipment from the trip, and retrieved their own belongings including the rock samples they'd collected. Amid a great deal of noisy kidding around, they dispersed.

Candrew made sure all the department's equipment was accounted for, unloaded, and stored. He then went in through the ground floor door and took the stairs up to his office. A quick computer check confirmed nothing critically important had transpired during his three-day absence.

It was dusk when Candrew drove a couple of miles east of the university to his home in the foothills. He lived alone in a house that was an architectural compromise, part traditional rounded adobe walls, part large contemporary glass windows. After being away for several days, he was enthusiastically greeted by his dog, Chile, and aging cat, Pixel. He'd arranged with Michelle, one of the graduate students in his department, to feed them while he was on the river. 'Shell, as she was usually called, had done this for several semesters and he knew he could rely on her.

Chile had licked his bowl of food clean and was now standing by the door to be let out. Candrew stood on the patio looking at the constellations and bright Venus in the clear western sky while his dog took care of business, then retreated to the warmth of the house. Candrew himself slumped onto the sofa in the warm sitting room and relaxed with a generous scotch, casually watching the local PBS television channel. It was at times like these that he missed his wife Penny the most. After ten years of marriage, she had succumbed to cancer. That was half a dozen years ago. Now, coming home from his geological trips without her loving greeting was always hard to take.

The field trip on the river had worked out well, and now Candrew was pleased to shower, shave, and get into a real bed—to feel normal again.

Late the next morning, Monday, Candrew drove to campus, parked in his usual spot behind Kinblade Hall, took the stairs up to the third-floor and walked down the passage to his office. He leaned back in his desk chair sipping hot coffee from the insulated mug he'd brought with him. He phoned Renata Alcantara who was a colleague at the university but also a very close friend.

"I'm back in civilization after the rigors of working out in nature," he jokingly told her.

Renata, herself a field archaeologist, was very familiar with the rigors of field work. "I probably can't compete with all those al-fresco, riverbank meals that were served on your float trip." He heard her laugh. "But come to dinner tonight and I'll see what I can rustle up, and you can tell me all about life on the river."

"You make me sound like Mark Twain," he joked.

Candrew spent the rest of the day working, catching up on student assignments and other accumulated items. That done, he went over to his backpack and retrieved the plastic bag with the mineral samples he'd collected at the Mule Ear diatreme. He shook them out onto a sheet of white paper. Moving them around with his finger, he spread the grains out, and took a closer look with his X10 hand lens. Although he recognized most of the minerals, this casual examination left several grains he wasn't sure about.

Eager to learn more details about this mineral assemblage, he called Anton Zabriski, the mineralogist on the faculty. When he described his situation, Anton said, "Why don't you come by my office. Right now's a good time—if that works for you. I've just gotten out of my afternoon lab session. The TA'll take care of the rest of it."

Candrew scooped up the mineral grains and went to see Anton in his office down on the second floor. He ushered Candrew in. The office was basically neat, but with organized piles of papers and folders stacked on almost every horizontal surface. The remaining spaces were occupied by atomic models of minerals, the structures assembled using colored wooden balls fixed in place by short rods. These attractive models were almost like pieces of modern sculpture.

Anton welcomed Candrew, took his mineral grains and studied them for a while with his hand lens. Then, reaching over, he took a low-powered microscope from one of his shelves, pushed up his glasses, and spent time peering at the crystalline grains, getting more familiar with the details. He adjusted the focus. "Interesting mix," he said after a while. "Where did you say you got them?"

"Mule Ear diatreme," Candrew told him. "Out by the San Juan River."

He smiled in recognition. "Oh, yes. That's a classic diatreme location, a kimberlite pipe. One of several places we take our students to get experience. It's 'classic' because it's got a suite of indicator minerals that have been used to show the possible presence of diamonds."

Candrew nodded his head, showing that he was already aware of this.

Anton examined the Mule Ear grains for several minutes with renewed interest. "You've certainly got a few red garnets as well as a group of diopside grains. Also, some ilmenites and spinels. But I don't see any diamonds in this mix, which isn't surprising since I've never heard of anyone finding them in this particular outcrop." He laughed and said, "You'll need to go to Murfreesboro, over in Arkansas, to get your carats. They'll charge you an entrance fee, but you can cart away all the diamonds you find." Anton went on to say, "Diamonds—to most people that means wealth!" He glanced over at Candrew. "If I were you, I'd go and talk to Wilfred Pengelly—he's in the Economic Minerals Department. Valuable minerals and money are his forte."

"Good idea," Candrew said. "I don't know him well, but I'll give him a call."

Candrew was pleased to follow up on Renata's invitation to dinner. A little after six he arrived at her house, got out of the car, zipped up his sweater, and walked to the front door. He was greeted with a hug and a generous kiss.

"Good to have you back." Renata had made a pitcher of margaritas and they sat in the living room drinking and chatting. After a while, Renata said. "I need to check the oven," and disappeared into the kitchen.

Left alone, Candrew sipped his drink and glanced around the room. The fire crackled and the flames gave the room a warm flickering glow—but hardly any aroma. Although the burning pinon logs produced a delightful smell, he realized that most of that went up the chimney. It was ironic that when it was too cold to sit outdoors, that's where you could have enjoyed the most intense pinon aroma.

It had always been obvious from the room's contents that Renata had excellent taste as well as wide experience. There was a mix of Navajo rugs, Costa Rican ceramics, and New Mexican pueblo bowls. A couple of stunning black-and-white photographs of Mayan archaeological sites complemented several contemporary watercolor paintings.

Candrew knew the reason for this eclectic taste. Her mother was Costa Rican, and steeped in that country's culture. Renata had gotten the South American laid-back approach to social events—half an hour past the scheduled time for a get-together was not uncommon, and required no explanation. Also, Renata had inherited her mother's long dark hair and brown eyes. But it was her German father who gave her the precision that dominated Renata's professional life. Her research team was excavating a Mayan ruin in Guatemala and every aspect of that work was carefully and precisely described. The written reports were models of concise, accurate and thorough documentation.

Renata strolled back from the kitchen. "Five minutes," she said. "You want a refill while you wait for dinner?"

"No. I'm fine. I'll just have some wine when we eat."

They chatted casually about university affairs and then moved into the dining room.

"So which way did information flow on your river trip?" Renata asked. "All from you to the students—or did you learn anything new from your field excursion?"

"Yes, I did. Got a new perspective on diamonds."

"Diamonds? Really?"

"We climbed up to the Mule Ear and across to the diatreme. Earlier this afternoon I took most of the samples I'd collected down to the mineralogist in our department. He told me about the well-documented association of some of those minerals with diamonds."

Candrew shook his head. "But none of the materials we picked up had any diamonds in them."

"Your students are lucky to have important geological sites so close." She shook her head. "My students have to go all the way to another country, Guatemala, to do their graduate research."

They ate in silence for a few moments and Candrew sipped his wine. Renata asked, "Have you thought any more about our possible trip to England this summer?" She drank some of her wine. "Which end of the island do you favor, northeast or southwest—Scotland or Cornwall?"

"Don't forget there's always Wales and Ireland if you want to stay in the 'Celtic fringe'."

Renata smiled. "The whole country is only the size of Oklahoma, but there's such a lot to see. We'll have to plan our route pretty carefully." Looking sternly at Candrew, she said. "And remember, it'll be about culture and history. We're not going there just to see rocks."

"Of course," Candrew said with a wide grin. "And archaeology?"

"Well, maybe Stonehenge."

"Of the possible choices, I'd prefer Cornwall," Candrew said. "Long coastlines. It'll be a nice contrast to our land-locked university here in northern New Mexico." He thought about that for a moment, then added, "And Cornwall's well known for its art colonies. Also, some impressive stone age monuments dot the moorlands." He laughed. "I figure I could trade you visits to some Neolithic stone circles for trips to the classic old tin mine sites."

CHAPTER 3

DURING THE SPRING SEMESTER Candrew was teaching a single three hour course. A mere three hours a week—that didn't seem like an onerous chore to most people. But there were, of course, lectures to prepare, student assignments to grade, and he also had laboratory sessions where the geology students learned how to recognize different minerals, rocks, and fossils. In addition, numerous university committee meetings took far too many hours of his time.

And then there was research. It was critical that he generate enough external funding to support his graduate students and their geologic projects. He also needed salaries for research associates and the 'post-docs.' Although he had some discretionary money from his endowed chair, it was also important to submit well-documented, carefully-written proposals to funding agencies. Research itself, especially if it involved field work, could be time consuming and expensive. The eventual results from each supported project had to be meticulously documented, and manuscripts submitted to respected journals for peer review. This was an important step in impressing colleagues and developing a professional reputation. It, of course, provided input for the next round of funding proposals.

At the moment, Candrew was revising an important section of his current manuscript. He usually chose to work at his desk with the office door open—to be part of the department, not isolated in some academic enclave. As he was rewriting a key part of his manuscript, a student appeared in the doorway.

Wearing jeans, a college tee-shirt, and a black captain's hat with her glasses perched on top, the young woman tentatively asked, "Do you have a moment?"

"Yes, of course. Come on in." Candrew always felt his primary obligation was to the students. Although he had office hours posted on the wall outside his door, he was usually prepared to talk to students at almost any time of day.

She stepped through the doorway. "I'd hoped to take your geology course next semester." She paused. "I'm a history major, you know. I don't understand much about science."

"But you have to satisfy a science requirement?" Candrew guessed.

"That's right." She hesitated, then said, "I've always liked Nature, you know, mountains, and rivers, and rocks, and stuff. They're real, not like physics or chemistry that have so many abstract ideas." She smiled at Candrew. "I wanted to know if I could, like, take your introductory geology course Pass/Fail?"

"You want to go for the "Heaven or Hell" option?"

She smiled, humoring the prof's joke. "Yeah, I'd like to take it that way."

"What's your grade point average?"

She told him, "It's a little over three."

"No problem. Just be sure you make your choice clear when you sign up."

Obviously relieved, she smiled, thanked him, turned, and left.

Candrew was always pleased to be able to talk about rocks and the Earth. He knew that over the years quite a few students had taken the freshman geology course and become excited enough in the topic to change their major. So it was well worth his time to encourage other freshmen to enroll in the *Introductory Geology* course.

Candrew leaned back in his desk chair, hands behind his head, and his feet resting on a half open desk drawer. He'd lost his train of thought with the manuscript he'd been working on. Glancing at the clock on his bookshelf, he saw it was close to lunchtime.

Although chilly, it was a bright sunny morning. He made his way across the campus central plaza to the Student Union building where he frequently ate lunch in the Faculty Lounge. The dining area was on the top floor, the fifth floor. On the way up he shared the elevator with two students. Neither noticed him, both engrossed in the cyberworld of their cell phones.

Most days a diverse group got together for lunch, a 'lunch bunch' that included administrators as well as academics. Their various backgrounds led to a wide range of viewpoints, and for Candrew, this was one of the attractions of lunching in the Lounge. He walked over to the large table by the floor-to-ceiling plate glass window that had a spectacular view of the mountains to the east. He pulled out a chair as Rosita, their usual waitress, came over to take his order. He was quite familiar with the menu, but after the many peculiar meals he'd eaten on the river trip, he opted for the *Special of the Day* which was meatloaf.

"Hi Candrew." Ted Devereau from the Business Office greeted him. "What are you up to these days—apart from teaching?"

"Ah, but teaching has just included a three-day float trip on the San Juan River. That got me interested in mining projects, not my normal things."

"So, you going to spend Spring Break panning for gold?" one of the archaeology profs asked. He'd just been reading about South American copper mines, and told Candrew, "With the large-scale mining going on in Chile, they're stumbling on some fascinating archaeological sites. Quite amazing what they're finding."

Candrew couldn't resist explaining some geology. "Chile's being created as the East Pacific gets buried under the South American tectonic plate which is drifting westward. It's what's building up the Andes and stewing out mineral-rich fluids, ones that make ore deposits, like those with copper you were reading about."

"That all happen fast?" Arlan Dee asked. He worked with budgets in the Business Office and his comments were always centered on speed and efficiency. "I know everything in geology takes millions of years," he said, implying: *but who can wait that long?*

"Well, the tectonic plates are churning toward each other at roughly an inch or two a year," Candrew clarified.

Evelyn Snowparski, a biology prof, sitting across from Candrew, nodded her agreement. "Interesting." She went on to explain. "To put things in perspective, that's about the speed your finger nails grow."

Most of the faculty at the table were in the humanities, but they seemed to be fascinated by all this science.

"Talking about copper mines," Jake, one of the sociology profs, said, "I've just been to a conference in San Diego. On the drive back, I detoured to look at some of those copper mines in Arizona. They sure do a lot of environmental damage." He told the group he'd walked out onto one of the observation platforms and looked into a gigantic mining excavation. "The trucks way down at the bottom of that enormous hole in the ground looked like ants. I stood in awe."

"Was it 'awe-some' or 'awe-ful'?" somebody asked.

Grinning, he said, "Just awe-inspiring." He glanced around the group that was listening quietly. "And as Dr. Johnson put it to Boswell: *It was worth seeing, yes, but not worth going to see.*

Professor Lubinski, generally known as 'Lubie,' pointed out how important mining is to the way we live. "We think of metals," he said, "but they're also digging up huge amounts of sand, gravel, fertilizer." Lubie and his parents had come to the U.S. as immigrants from Hungary when he was a young boy, and he still spoke with a slight accent.

"That's right. But don't forget to mention gems," Arlan Dee added. "Just think of the value of diamonds." Again, for him financial considerations were paramount.

"And we all know a diamond is just a lump of carbon, right?" Evelyn said, heads nodding in agreement. "Well, this morning I got my own private supply." Smiling, she explained, "I burnt my toast at breakfast. I had black carbon, my personal proto-diamond."

"Next you'll be telling us about the lead in your pencil," Ted Devereau said. "That's graphite isn't it? Made of pure carbon atoms, just like diamonds."

"True. But there are several ways of grouping carbon atoms," Lubie broke in to say. "You can arrange sixty atoms to look like a soccer ball." Although a history professor, Lubie was highly intelligent and widely read. His views were respected by the rest of the lunch bunch.

"Yeah," Candrew said. "And those sixty-carbon molecules are what they call "*buckminsterfullerene.*"

"Really? What did an architect, like Fuller, have to do with carbon and diamonds?" Arlan Dee wanted to know.

Candrew explained. "The structure of the molecule looks just like a geodesic dome, the sort of thing Buckminster Fuller was famous for. So, conversationally those sixty-carbon, spherical molecules are called *buckyballs.*"

The woman professor at the far end of the table spoke up, "But diamond is still the carbon queen. The ultimate gem stone, and the hardest material known."

"Not quite. Did you ever hear of *longsdaleite?*" Candrew asked. Not surprisingly, none had. "It's pure carbon, but quite a bit harder than diamond."

"Do they dig that stuff up in mines?" she asked.

"No. It arrives on Earth in some meteorites." He went on to say, "Like the Canyon Diablo meteorite just down the road in Arizona. And that meteorite's associated with diamonds."

"It's got a strange name. How did it get to be called that?" she wanted to know.

"Because the scientist who discovered it was Kathleen Longsdale. It was named in her honor." The group seemed interested, and Candrew went on to tell them that a newly discovered mineral is usually called after some appropriate person. "But rocks with a novel combination of minerals are frequently given the name of a place. I'll give you an example: the area around the town of Kimberly in South Africa is important for diamond mining," he said. "So, the rock the diamonds are found in is called *kimberlite.*"

Eventually the lunch group broke up. After his pleasant meal and wide-ranging discussions

Candrew felt it was time to get to work. And for him, work meant research.

He enjoyed the walk back across campus in the warm sun and went into his laboratory in the basement of Kinblade Hall. There Dr. Judy Westerlund was sitting in front of a high-powered microscope.

Judy was a post-doctoral Research Associate who worked under Candrew's supervision on his sandstone research projects. She was tall, athletically built, with auburn hair cut short. She exuded a no-nonsense practicality. Judy picked up her glasses and put them on, then pushed her chair back. "Hi Candrew."

Candrew pulled a stool out from under the wooden bench and sat there telling her about his float trip on the San Juan River. "I think the students learned a lot. There's not much white water, but they had a good time." He got up and went over to the cupboard, took out a mug and filled it from the coffee pot.

"Floating the San Juan is on my list of things to do," Judy said. "but I'm not going out on that river 'til it gets a lot warmer. Maybe I'll do it this summer."

Candrew knew she had studied in Florida where warm water was the norm.

Although her research with Candrew was primarily laboratory-oriented, she'd often gone with him to their sandstone research areas. Most of their projects were focused in the Four Corners area where Colorado and Utah meet Arizona and New Mexico. On the wall opposite the window Judy had pinned up a large geological map of New Mexico and a smaller one of the Four Corners.

At the far end of her work bench was a framed photograph of her boyfriend, Dorian. He was working with the U.S. Geological Survey in Las Vegas, Nevada. She'd enjoyed teasing him that he lived in the newer Las Vegas, because the town with that name in New Mexico was much older.

Candrew was particularly eager to tell Judy about the importance of the so-called 'indicator minerals' he'd collected from the Mule Ear diatreme, and how they might show the presence of diamonds.

"Diamonds? You trying to get rich? Not able to pay for your exotic life style on a professor's salary?" She chuckled and Candrew laughed.

"Pure science," he quipped. "Just like what you do with the heavy minerals that got caught up in the sands we're researching."

"I gather you're going to get me dragged into this new project." She was grinning. "Sounds like fun."

"I hope so. But we won't be looking for the zircons and tourmalines you usually document."

"So, what are these 'indicator minerals' you'll have me hunting?"

"Well, the classic pair are red garnets—you know, the ones called pyrope—and diopside. Maybe also some ilmenite."

"And you're proposing to employ our usual processing techniques to get the indicator minerals out?"

"Not quite. The garnets and diopsides we'll be looking for are probably quite a bit smaller than the heavy minerals you're used to working with."

"I guess I'm going to have to learn some new techniques." Judy smiled.

To Candrew, that seemed to be something she was looking forward to.

CHAPTER 4

TUESDAY MORNING DAWNED CLEAR and cool with a slight breeze rustling the budding trees. Candrew let Chile out and watched the birds around the feeder. The electric heater in the water bowl on the ground was plugged in to keep the water from freeze overnight. It gave the birds something to drink, but Chile took advantage of this setup and lapped up a generous share.

Candrew strolled down the gravel driveway and picked up the morning newspaper. Chile loped along beside him most of the time, but took exploratory forays into the adjacent bushes. Back in the kitchen, Candrew spooned granola into a bowl, added blueberries, and topped it off with kefir. As he ate, he read the headlines, then the comics. His morning *Introductory Geology* class for non-majors was scheduled fairly early, and soon after downing his coffee he drove to the university.

In his office, Candrew pulled out the three-ringed binder with his lecture notes and reviewed the material. Not that he had anything new to teach—nothing much had changed significantly in the geological world since he'd taught this freshman class the previous year. But he wanted to be sure all the topics were in the correct order, he had the timing right, and didn't overwhelm students with too much detail. The introductory class included students majoring in subjects from art to zoology, and careful organization was critical. He set off down to the classroom on the ground floor.

The previous day Candrew had e-mailed Professor Pengelly in the Mining Department and set up a meeting for this afternoon. Pengelly's office was in the far wing of the Engineering Building on the northern side of campus, and after lunch Candrew walked over there. The office, on a corner at the end of a long, second floor corridor, displayed on the door a plastic strip giving the professor's name: *Dr. Wilfred Pengelly*. Under it was taped a sturdy piece of card that proclaimed "*DAMNATI AD METALLA*" and below that—for those who lacked a classical education—was stuck the translation in small print: *Condemned to the Mines*.

Candrew got a friendly greeting. Wilfred Pengelly was solidly built, well-muscled but a little overweight. He made up for his balding forehead with a lush, white beard that surrounded most of his jowly, square face, a face with fleshy eyelids that extended down over much of his eye sockets. He wore steel-rimmed circular glasses. Candrew was sure the Professor was quite a bit older than he was.

"Come on in." Pengelly shook hands and indicated an empty swivel chair.

The office had large windows and was pleasantly sunny. It was a typical academic's lair with piles of papers, stacks of books, and the inevitable computers. There were also several large lumps of rock on the floor. As Candrew sat down he thanked Pengelly for taking the time to talk.

Wilfred Pengelly settled into the chair behind his desk and rocked back. "So, you're planning to get into the diamond mining business." It was more of a question than a statement.

"Not really. My interest in diamonds is purely academic."

Pengelly sat rigidly upright. "So why are you in the Mining Department talking to me?"

Candrew was taken aback. "Well . . . I . . . I thought you might know something about the exploration process. About how indicator minerals lead to diamondiferous kimberlite pipes."

Wilfred relaxed. "Sorry to be so blunt." He readjusted his chair. "We get overwhelmed with amateur prospectors wanting us to tell them the best places to pan for gold, or to explore for copper, diamonds, even meteorites." He leaned over to the shelf under the bookshelves where there was a pitcher of water and poured a tumbler full. He glanced questioningly toward Candrew, who raised both open hands and declined the offer.

"In your e-mail you said you'd found so-called 'indicator minerals' in the Mule Ear diatreme," Wilfred said. "As far as I know, nobody's discovered any diamonds there. We've had several prospectors contact us about other diatremes, both here in New Mexico and over in Arizona. There's lots of pipes, but I've not heard of anything commercial in them."

Wilfred paused, frowned, and glanced around his office. Candrew said that was what he'd heard. "Even one or two of the big mining corporations have sent their exploration geologists to see what we've been up to," Wilfred said, "see if we've stumbled on anything significant. I tried to get them to fund a student or two, but no luck with that." He shook his head. "But the big boys don't worry too much about exploration. They let the smaller companies do the work and make discoveries—then buy them out. So the fierce competition is among the mid-size and smaller outfits. Some real small groups get involved, you know, two guys and their dog out looking for that major find."

As Candrew sat listening, Wilfred went on to say, "The main emphasis in our department is on copper, partly because we can take students to active mining locations, and partly because that's the industry where the jobs are. But we also cover the less sexy materials, like gravel and limestone for cement. Lectures, of course, deal with most mineral entities, and that's when we talk about economic minerals worldwide—which is where diamonds come in." He gulped some water, then added, "And we also cover gold, silver, lead, tin, cobalt, lithium—anything you can dig up and make money on."

"Turquoise?"

"Artisanal." Wilfred laughed. "Opposite end of the scale from your diamonds. I'm sure you know turquoise is an alteration mineral that forms near the surface. Easy to mine, which of course the Indians did. But diamonds, they form hundreds of miles below the surface. We have to rely on dramatic geologic processes to bring them up where we can get at them." He grinned. "And bring up the indicator minerals to tell us they've arrived." He stroked his beard and thought about that. "I can lend you some reference materials if you like."

When Candrew accepted, Wilfred reached up to one of his top shelves and grabbed a couple of books. Then he went over to the row of filing cabinets, and after several minutes searching produced a number of technical publications and two notebooks. He handed them to Candrew.

"Thanks so much."

Candrew sat, obviously interested, while he was told more about the mining industry and the department.

"And speaking about digging things up," Wilfred said, "we do have a couple of professors in the department who teach everything from open-cast mining to planning and excavating underground mines."

Wilfred sat back in his chair, staring at Candrew, and said, "From what you said in your message your specialty is sandstone rock."

"Right. That rarely involves anything minable, however. Oh, maybe, occasionally, uranium, like down around Grants. The main economic role for sandstone is as a subsurface reservoir for oil and gas."

Wilfred was easy-going and happy to talk about his work at the university. For the next half-hour they discussed their academic interests.

At one point, Wilfred did say that a few years ago an incoming Ph. D. student had completed his Masters at the University of

Nevada in Reno, and while there he'd gotten involved in diamond exploration and indicator minerals. "He'd brought his samples with him and was eager to get more detailed analyses. In particular he was interested in the chromium content of diopsides, though he thought the calcium content of the pyrope red garnets could also be interesting. We don't often need that much detail in our work. If we do, we get Mark Kernfeld to do microprobe analyses." He smiled, "As I recall, he's in your department."

"That's right. I got to know him well on the float trip to the Mule Ear diatreme. He'd done some analytical work for a friend of mine in the art department. That involved getting the chemical compositions of several paint fragments from an alleged old painting, and he was able to show that it had to be a fake."

"Quite a useful skill," Wilfred acknowledged.

Above Wilfred's desk was an antique map of the county of Cornwall in the U.K. Wilfred saw Candrew glancing at it and said, "That's where my ancestors came from." He elaborated, "When the Cornish tin mining industry collapsed in the eighteen-hundreds the miners scattered worldwide, quite a few ended up in America." He glanced back at the map. "Including my grandfather. He went to Butte, Montana. Later my father started mining in Colorado."

"The reason I was interested in your map," Candrew said, "is that I'm planning to visit England with a close friend of mine later this year. And Cornwall will almost certainly be on our itinerary. I haven't been there before."

"Then I need to inflict the benefit of my vast experience on you." He laughed. "And my wife can certainly provide lots of suggestions." He stroked his ample beard and stared into the distance for a moment. "Why don't you and your girlfriend—I assume it's a *girl* friend—come over to dinner one night?" He thought for a moment. "How about this Friday, if that works for you. Though I will need to confirm it with my wife." He grinned, "She's my social secretary."

"Thanks. That would be great," Candrew said. "You may know my *girl*friend—actually woman friend—since she's a faculty member here on campus in the Archaeology-Anthropology Department: Renata Alcantara."

"Oh yes. I've run into her once or twice at committee meetings, but I can't say I know her real well. I'll look forward to seeing her."

CHAPTER 5

CANDREW'S LEISURELY SATURDAY STARTED with a breakfast of fried eggs, bacon and toast. Most of the rest of the morning was spent drinking coffee and catching up reading through the pile magazines he'd accumulated over the last couple of weeks. But what he was really doing was procrastinating—putting off the household chores that needed to be done. After a nominal lunch of crackers and a chunk of gouda cheese, he eventually got around to loading a pile of dirty clothes into the washing machine. That done, he took the cups, plates, and cutlery out of the dishwasher that had run two days earlier. Next, he vacuumed the living room and finally got round to changing the bed sheets and pillow cases. Then he, and went back to reading his magazines.

Later he spent an hour going through the reference material Wilfred Pengelly had provided, which prompted him to Google several items relevant to diamond exploration. He was amazed to read that on average it took two hundred and fifty tons of rock to produce a single carat of diamond. Candrew was mainly interested in technical issues, but one of the books Wilfred had lent him gave considerable historical background. He became fascinated by the early discoveries of diamonds in India and later in South Africa. The accounts of falsified mining claims in the U.S. grabbed his attention. It was more than an hour and half later when he realized what time it was.

He left the books on the sofa and quickly showered, shaved, and put on some respectable clothes. A little after six he drove over to Renata's house, getting there only fifteen minutes late. She was waiting for him. As they drove to dinner, Renata told him, "Yesterday, I talked to Professor Pengelly's wife. She seemed very nice and was calling to make sure that Saturday night would be okay with us. She told me we're having *tiddyoggies* for dinner." Laughing, she said, "Whatever they are."

Wilfred Pengelly greeted them at the door and ushered them in. He introduced his wife, Allison, a tall woman with auburn hair caught up in a bun. As they took off their coats, Renata paused, tilting her head to one side at the sound of the music.

Smiling, she turned to Candrew and said, "*The Beatles*." He looked puzzled as to why she would want to tell him that. "*Lucy in the Sky with Diamonds*," she explained.

Wilfred chuckled, "I thought that would be appropriate, given your current research interest in those gems." His wife gave a slight smile, tolerating her husband's sense of humor.

Candrew agreed the song was appropriate. Grinning, he said, "I know there are diamonds in meteorites, but I hope to find the diamonds that are on the ground, not in the sky."

The four of them sat drinking and chatting in front of the living room fire. The space was carpeted, comfortably furnished, and more contemporary than southwest in feeling. On the cold Spring evening it was cozy.

"Wilf tells me you're interested in diamonds," Allison said, smiling. "A girl's best friend."

"And as Zsa Zsa Gabor said, *I've never hated a man enough to give his diamonds back*," Renata joked.

"I guess *Diamonds are Forever* only applies to the recipient," Candrew mused.

Wilfred got up, tossed another log on the fire, and went over to push a button on his audio system. The music changed and Renata immediately recognized the singer and laughed. "*Neil Diamond*," she said.

"My, you do a great job of picking relevant songs." Candrew, grinned and complimented his host. Leaning over to Renata, he said, "I'm impressed you recognize the titles."

"Well," she replied, "if you'd done a more thorough job of partying when you were in college, you would have recognized them too." She tapped Candrew on the arm. "You know what song this is?" When Candrew shook his head, she said, *Love on the Rocks*. I'm sure it had to be specially dedicated to some geology prof."

"Time to eat," Allison said, easing herself out of her armchair. With the Pengellys personable and easy-going, dinner promised to be a pleasant meal.

Sitting around the table, Wilfred said, "I think beer will go best with the Cornish pasties" (which he pronounced in the usual way, as *Past-eez*). "But there's wine if you prefer it."

They settled for beer as Allison brought in the plates of pasties. As she served them, Wilfred said, "We're cheating a bit because the EU, the European Union, requires that anything labelled a "Cornish Pasty" has to have been baked in Cornwall." He grinned. "So, we'll just label it an 'oggy.'"

"A what?" Candrew asked, frowning.

Renata reminded him of what Allison had said to her on the phone, "A *tiddyoggie*," she told Candrew.

As they ate the semicircular meat pies and drank their beer, Wilfred joked, "My name, Wilfred, is really a corruption of Well-Fed." Given his generous paunch that seemed appropriate.

"I'm not surprised," Renata said. "These meat pies are delicious."

"And easy to make," Allison said. "You just take a circle of pastry, load one half with beef, potatoes, onion and turnip, then fold it over. Crimp the semicircular edge, put it in the oven, and you're done." She glanced around the table. "Traditionally, this was the meal the Cornish tin miners ate underground. Where the pastry was crimped and crusty at the edges, it gave them a disposable handle for dirty hands."

"Probably a myth," Wilfred said. "They wouldn't want to throw any food away."

Wilfred turned to Candrew. "I wanted to tell you about our student group—they call themselves the "Major Miners." Chuckling, he obviously approved of that title. "Although they're mainly a social organization, they do schedule visiting lecturers, and occasionally have a field trip." He drank from his tankard of beer. "The reason I mention this group is because they're planning to visit some diatremes on Monday. Since its Spring Break, they don't have classes."

"Sounds interesting, You know which area they're planning to go to?" Candrew said. "Not that I'm particularly knowledgeable about local diatreme locations," he quickly added.

"Well, I'm not sure exactly where they're going, but there's quite a few kimberlite pipes, those diatremes, on the northwest edge of New Mexico and over the state line into northeast Arizona. I believe you geologists call that area the *Navajo Volcanic Field*."

"Which means, of course, they're on the Navajo reservation," Candrew said.

"Right. Anyway, I've been invited to go with the students and wondered if you would like to come along."

Candrew didn't hesitate. "Sure. I'd love to join you."

After downing more beer, Wilfred said, "It'll be a one-day trip. Just pack a lunch—and bring your rock hammer! We'll be leaving from outside the Department real early on Monday morning."

While Candrew and Wilfred talked science, Allison chatted with Renata. "I grew up in Maine," Allison said, "Our side of the Atlantic. But with my transatlantic marriage to Wilf I got caught up in Cornish culture." Allison grinned. "That's why our younger daughter got christened *Brialen*—the Cornish name for *primrose*. She's away at college majoring in boys."

Renata laughed. "I hope she's making good grades."

"And our older daughter," Allison said, "is *Borlewen*. And that translates to *morning star* but everybody just calls her *Lewen*." She ate another forkful of pasty. "We're only following the trend since even David Cameron, the U.K. Prime Minister, gave his daughter a name of Cornish origin—*Endellion*—which translates as *Fire Soul*."

Wilfred broke in. "And I wonder if that politician knew there's even a Cornish mineral with the same as his daughter. It's pretty rare, a very minor copper and lead ore."

"We're looking forward to visiting Cornwall," Renata said. "I just want to keep Candrew from spending the whole trip looking at tin mines."

"There's certainly some dramatic scenery. I don't mean big mountains," Wilfred said, "but high sea cliffs, gorgeous beaches, and charming fishing villages."

"Also moorlands," Allison added. "And don't forget the art colonies."

Much of the rest of the evening was spent talking about the specifics of visiting the Duchy of Cornwall.

Both Candrew and Renata had drunk quite a bit, and when they left the Pengellys late in the evening, Candrew drove very carefully, making sure to muster total concentration. At this time of day there was almost no traffic and they arrived safely at Renata's house. "I think you need to come in for some strong coffee," she said. "I could certainly use some."

Candrew focused carefully, and slurring slightly, said, "That'd probably be a good thing to do."

They sat in the kitchen talking about their evening with the Pengellys. "You certainly seemed to get on well with Wilfred," Renata said.

"True. Besides all the scientific stuff, he had some good ideas about visiting Cornwall."

"And so did Allison."

After drinking a couple of cups of coffee, Candrew had sobered up somewhat.

But Renata said, "You're still looking a little groggy, I think it might be a good idea if you spent the night."

"But I don't have any pajamas," he said smiling.

A slight smile flickered across her face as she peered at him. Her tongue licked slowly across her lips. "I don't think that's going to be a problem," she said quietly.

"At least I have a good precedent," Candrew said. "That Nobel prize-winning Albert Einstein claimed: *When I retire, I sleep as nature made me.*"

She took his hand. "A precedent I fully approve of."

Renata turned off the living room lights leaving just the glow of the lamp in the bedroom. She put her arm around his shoulders as they made their way to the bed. Under the sheets, the warmth of their intertwined bodies made the need for nightclothes moot.

"Hard as diamond," Rented joked. In the darkness Candrew didn't see her grinning.

CHAPTER 6

CANDREW HAD SET THE alarm on his cell phone for early Monday morning. When it woke him, he was unenthusiastic about getting up, but the thought of seeing a couple of kimberlite pipes that day tipped the balance. He stumbled out of bed, dressed, fed his cat and dog, and ate a quick breakfast. Then he dropped a couple of bottles of water and a packed lunch into his field backpack and drove to campus. He parked in the faculty lot beside the Economic Minerals Department where Wilfred was already talking to a group of students.

The row of half-a-dozen cars and SUVs, with the students and professors, headed north from the university to Chama. There they turned west, and drove only a little over the speed limit through Farmington and on to the town of Shiprock. Turning south, they made their way down Route 491. Brandon, an older and more experienced teaching assistant, was driving the lead car. A few miles down the road he slowed, waved his arm out the window, and signaled to the other drivers to pull off on the side of the road. When they'd parked, Wilfred, who was riding with him, got out and corralled the students. He pointed to the prominent, steep-sided mountain off to the west.

"That's Shiprock peak," he told them. "It's the igneous rock feeder pipe that formed the interior of an old volcano about thirty million years ago. Since then, all the softer rocks surrounding it have been eroded away leaving the tougher rocks that form the dramatic peak we see today. It's similar, but not quite the same, as the kimberlite pipes you're on your way to explore."

Several students took photos with their cell phones. Carlos Nez, tall with dark curly hair, was the only Navajo student in the group. He stressed that the mountain was on Navajo land and a spiritual place for his people, the Diné—he used the indigenous name for the Navajo Nation. "Ever since I was a young kid, I've heard stories about that sacred mountain, the *Rock with Wings*." He looked around the silent group. "Our history says it was the giant bird that brought the Navajo people from the far north to our present desert home."

The students listened to him with interest, then tumbled back into their cars and the convoy set off, continuing south.

Further along the road Brandon stopped again, got out, and told the other drivers they should follow his car along the poorly-marked gravel track that angled off the main road to the right. Half an hour of slow, rough driving took them across a dry arroyo, over a ridge and down into another arroyo. There they pulled onto a flat area and parked.

Brandon got out, slammed the car door and locked it. "This is as close as we can drive. From now on its human muscle power."

Candrew was impressed by Brandon's knowledge of the arid, isolated area. He'd obviously had more field experience than most of the other students and Candrew had been told he'd worked in the mining industry for a few years after earning his Master's degree. Recently, he'd decided to come back to school to get a doctorate. To achieve that goal he'd enrolled in the Economic Minerals Department at the University of Northern New Mexico.

As the students pulled out their backpacks, cameras, and hammers, there was a good deal of friendly joking.

"The only things here are rabbits."

"Where are the gold nuggets?"

"Can't see any emeralds."

"No diamonds here at the surface."

Wilfred liked their humor.

Brandon shouldered his pack, pulled on his peaked cap, and said, "Okay, let's get moving." They hiked along a poorly defined path that wound slowly upward. After about fifteen minutes Brandon stopped the group.

"Why are we stopping? I don't see anything," one student said, and several others were obviously thinking the same thing.

"Come on. Good scientists—good mining geologists—need to be observant," Brandon admonished.

"But there's nothing to see."

"Look harder," he cajoled.

With no suggestions volunteered, Brandon gave in, and pointed to a cone-shaped, sandy pile a couple of feet high. "Go examine that," he told them.

The student closest to the pile knelt and looked closely. He was joined by two others. They were rewarded by seeing not just quartz sand grains, but a few very different minerals. Carlos Nez in particular, seemed to be very interested in what was clearly an ant hill.

"Ants as miners—*mini-Major Miners*," Brandon quipped. "They excavate all sorts of mineral grains."

Candrew recognized some of the heavy minerals and told the students, "The darker grains are probably zircons and tourmalines." He knew they were similar to the ones Judy was studying in his lab as one facet of their sandstone research projects.

The group continued up the rocky path on the hillside that paralleled the dry arroyo. Several male students, hiking fast, leapt from boulder to boulder, trying to impress the couple of females in the group. For the next ten minutes they all followed the sinuous trail along the hillside.

They hiked around a sharp bend, and Candrew asked the group, "When the arroyo was in flood where was the water flowing fastest?" And then he added, "And where did it flow the slowest?"

"Slowest on the insides of the bends," several students said at once.

"Right. I'm pleased you remembered something from your sedimentology class. So that's where some of the heavier minerals will get dropped out."

To Candrew the conclusion was inescapable. These heavy minerals were being swept along by flowing water and a few of these grains were going to be deposited from the slower-flowing currents—which were on the inside of the bend. This meant, of course, that their source was upstream. And in this particular case, what was upstream was the outcrop of the kimberlite pipe—a possible diamond-bearing rock.

As they continued hiking up the trail, a tall student with his ball-cap on backwards jumped onto one of the big boulders. It rocked to one side, rolled when he landed on it, and he lost his balance and fell. Tumbling down the slope, he banged his head, cut his leg and ended up flat on his back at the bottom of the arroyo.

Several of his buddies hastily scrambled down. "You okay?" they all wanted to know.

"Yeah. I'm fine. Just a little shaken up."

"Macho man," Jessica Rylander mumbled under her breath. The attractive tall, blonde girl quickly knelt beside the prone student. Looking at his left calf, she told him, "You need to stop that bleeding. I've got some bandages."

As she rummaged around in her backpack, Wilfred said, "The main medical emergency kit's down in the car."

"I'll get it," one of the students volunteered, and Brandon fished in his pocket and tossed him the car keys.

The injured student lay still, looking straight up. Wilfred pulled out his cell phone and flicked on the flashlight. He shined it into the student's left eye, watching for a reaction.

"That's good," Jessica said turning to Wilfred. "Doesn't seem to be any sign of concussion."

"No, you're right. But he should probably lie still for a while."

The students milled around, uncertain, waiting.

Candrew noticed that a smaller, dry stream bed led in from the far side of the big channel where the injured student was now lying, the one they'd been following. He went over and quickly filled two of his Ziploc plastic bags with sand from the inside of the arroyo's closest bend. He labelled them *S1* and *S2* and dumped them in his backpack. With his cell phone, he took several photos of the location. That's when he noticed another large ant hill. He clambered over and scooped off some of the sandy gravel and labelled this sample *S3*.

A chubby student with a pony tail standing with the group shook his head. "I guess this is the end of our expedition to the diatreme."

"Not at all," the injured student shot back. "I'll just lie here and recuperate for a while and you guys can continue on up. You'll be able to collect me on your way back." He smiled. "But make sure you bring me a nice chunk of kimberlite."

Hesitating, Wilfred looked at Candrew. But before he said anything, Jessica broke in. "It's okay. I can handle this. I'll stay here with him. I think he'll be fine when he's rested for a bit, and I'll make him comfortable." She slipped off her jacket, rolled it into a pillow, and put it under his head. "The medical kit's got painkillers and I'll get some water."

Not sure what to do, Brandon seemed to agree that she should remain with the hurt student, but not by herself. "I'll stay here with you," he said. "It's not good for you to be out here alone."

"Not a problem." Jessica stared at him. "I can look after myself. You need to go and see that rock outcrop. I'll be fine."

Reluctantly, Brandon accepted her suggestion, but felt dismissed.

Keeping in mind Wilfred's demand that they hike more carefully, the group set off up the gravel path. It was not too arduous and they continued toward the rocky outcrop, their trudging feet kicking up a cloud of dust. The Spring breeze blew it to the side. But breeze was a mixed blessing because the wind also made it very cold. It took the group about thirty minutes to reach the top. There, enthusiastically wielding rock hammers, the students collected their samples of the kimberlite.

"It's almost like we know what we're doing," quipped the sole remaining girl in the group. She was the one with green streaks through her red hair.

At the outcrop, Candrew sat on a boulder, pulled up his jacket collar, and stared across the mass of dark rock. He imagined it as a hot viscous melt punching its way through many miles of overlying rocks. Glowing red, it had cooled with crystals—minerals—forming. Even the denser ones, slowly settling in the mix, would have been swept up by the explosive gas-charged melt. The fast-moving mixture would have ripped chunks of rock off the sides of the channel and dragged them up. Now Candrew could see some of these huge lumps of the host rock, so different from the intruded mass of kimberlite that was dark-colored and studded with crystals. He hammered off a chunk of the intruded rock and peered at the broken surface with his hand lens. Then he dropped the piece of kimberlite into his backpack—a pack that was getting steadily heavier with all the rock samples he was accumulating.

As the group hiked back down the trail, Wilfred told them they would not be visiting any other kimberlite diatremes that day. They needed to get the student with the abrasions and cut leg to some proper medical care as soon as he seemed well enough to travel.

When they arrived at the arroyo, the injured student seemed to be in good spirits, but it took two sturdy colleagues, one on each side, to help him slowly down the rocky path. His main injury appeared to be his left leg, and he was having trouble putting weight on it. They supported him as he slowly hobbled his way down to the cars. Brandon helped Jessica by carrying the medical kit.

As they all moved slowly along the gravel path, Candrew stopped several times to scoop up more sample material from the sandy stream beds. By now he could barely lift his loaded pack.

Eventually they made it to the parked cars. Jessica tilted back the front seat in her pale blue Lexus until it was almost horizontal so the hurt student could stretch out for the drive to the university.

A tired and subdued bunch of students dozed in the back of the other vehicles as they made the return trip to campus. When the convoy arrived, they took out the rock samples they'd collected, and retrieved their personal belongings. Pleased to now have cell phone service, they were all eagerly calling friends.

Candrew walked over to the faculty parking area at the side of the building and climbed into his Explorer. He backed up to the car he'd been riding in and struggled to haul out his overloaded backpack. One of the students helped him lift it into the truck. As Candrew drove away past where the student cars were parked, he passed Brandon loading his battered truck. Dark green, it had several lighter paint patches where the dents had not yet been repaired. Brandon raised his hand in acknowledgment as Candrew went past on his way home.

CHAPTER 7

SINCE THE TRIP WITH the *Major Miners* club had been cut short, Candrew arrived home sooner than he'd anticipated and was greeted by an excited dog. After a cold beer and dinner of leftovers from the fridge, he had an early night, slept soundly, and got up for a leisurely breakfast.

Before leaving for campus, he went into his living room and retrieved the books and papers he'd left on the sofa, the ones Wilfred Pengelly had lent him. Candrew wanted to take another look at the article that described how diamond indicator minerals could be separated from all the other grains in a sediment. After the previous day's excursion, he certainly had plenty of grains to work with. He'd read how these techniques had become an important part of diamond exploration around the world, and had recently been a key factor in locating an important mining area in the Canadian wilderness.

At the university, Candrew parked in the almost empty lot behind Kinblade Hall. He struggled to lift his backpack, heavy with sediment samples, out of the Ford *Explorer*. He realized it was going to take serious effort to get the samples into the lab. He solved this problem by getting three cardboard boxes and distributing the Ziploc bags of sands among them.

When he stumbled into the sedimentology lab, dragging the heavy but manageable packages one at a time, Judy greeted him with a broad grin. "I think you've earned some coffee." He slumped down on one of the wooden stools, and handed her his mug. She filled it. "And you're in luck. I still have a couple of donuts left." She flipped the lid on the box and Candrew took the last chocolate-covered one. As they drank their coffee, he told her about the field trip and the reason it had been cut short.

"I'm sorry to hear one of the mining students was hurt," she said. "And it's a pity you could only make it up to just one of the kimberlite outcrops."

"Yeah, but I did manage to get a pretty good suite of samples from that area."

"So I see." Judy glanced at the three boxes on the floor that had the Ziploc bags full of sand.

She helped him lift the boxes with the sample bags off the floor, and they put them on the side bench. Data from his field notebook let him line up the ones with an M label in numerical order. Candrew excluded a couple, telling Judy, "You don't need to worry about these. I don't think they can tell us anything useful."

They put the other samples, the ones numbered $S1$, $S2$ and $S3$, into a separate group.

"How do you want me to process all this stuff?" Judy asked.

"Well, the indicator minerals I'm looking for are going to be small," Candrew said. "So, the first step will be to sieve the sand samples and get rid of the larger grains."

"Which is pretty much what we do with the sandstones from our ongoing research projects," Judy said.

"True. But this time you need to take one of our big magnets and pull out anything magnetic. The garnets and diopsides I'm after are not magnetic and they'll get left behind."

"And I know what's coming next—those smelly liquids." She grimaced.

"Yeah, sorry about that."

"Let me see if we've got any left." Judy went over to one of the end cabinets and sorted through the bottles and cans. "Yep. Here we are." She held up a large glass bottle containing a murky brown liquid. She read the label: *methylene iodide*.

Candrew knew that the quartz grains and most other minerals would float in this very dense liquid, but both the garnets and diopsides he was after were dense enough to sink. So, this provided a way to separate them.

Usually on a Tuesday morning Candrew would be teaching his class. But not this week—it was Spring Break. He sat at his desk and pulled out the draft of the manuscript he was rewriting. After a little over thirty minutes work, he took a break, pushing back his chair, and with his hands behind his head thought over the previous day's visit to the kimberlite pipe. This prompted several questions. On impulse he got up and headed over to see Wilfred Pengelly.

Wilfred's office door was open, and Candrew saw him standing beside the desk talking to a student. After Wilfred handed him a paper folder, the student turned to leave. As he came through the doorway, Candrew realized it was Carlos Nez, the Navajo student who'd been on the previous day's field trip. But Carlos showed no sign of recognizing Candrew.

"Come on in." Wilfred said, lifting a pile of papers off one of the desk chairs and gesturing Candrew toward it. "You recovered from the exertions of searching the kimberlite pipe for diamonds?" he asked, grinning.

"Yeah, I'm fine." Candrew took on a more serious tone, "How's the injured student doing?"

"When we got back, the infirmary did a detailed check, gave him a thorough going over. They didn't find anything too serious. No broken bones, just a bad sprain, although there were quite a few cuts and abrasions. They patched him up, gave him some pain-killers, and sent him home."

"I'm glad to hear it wasn't serious," Candrew said. "Field work always has its risks."

"Well, we took the most direct route to the rocky outcrop." Wilfred stroked his beard and nodded. "We have Brandon to thank for that. It was good he'd proposed the Spring Break trip." He smiled and went on to explain, "He's my Teaching Assistant this semester and he's been really helpful. With his industry experience, and his earlier degree from the University of Nevada, he's been invaluable." Wilfred paused. "He's bright and personable—I've gotten to like him."

"You're lucky to have someone with lots of experience." Candrew thought back to Brandon's role on the field trip. Smiling, he said, "He seemed to be quite smitten with that attractive blonde girl."

"Jessica? Yeah, but I feel she might be out of his league." He leaned toward Candrew. "How many undergraduates do you know who drive a brand new Lexus? She comes from quite a wealthy family in California." He shook his head. "Maybe pretty, but she's a spoiled brat. Everything has to be done her way. Won't ever take 'no' for an answer."

"With a background like that, it doesn't seem she'd choose a career in Mining Engineering," Candrew said.

"No, it doesn't. I'm not sure where the family money comes from." Wilfred stared into the distance for a moment. "I've met the father once, and then only briefly. He had been at a financial meeting in Denver and on the way home came by the university to see Jessica. He was here only a couple of hours. I think he's involved in investments, maybe real estate."

"I'm surprised Jessica isn't doing a business degree." For a moment Candrew thought about the two women now in his life—both were in the sciences. "Judy, my Research Associate, is processing some of the sandy samples I collected when we were out at the diatreme," he said. "I'll be interested to see what she finds."

"And Renata?" Wilfred asked. "How's she doing?"

"Like us, she's enthused about research, but also a conscientious lecturer."

"I certainly enjoyed meeting her at dinner last week. We had a most enjoyable evening."

And a most enjoyable night, Candrew thought, although he didn't say anything.

"If you've got the time, Allison and I would like to have you and Renata to lunch next week." He threw up his hands, "I can justify it as a technical get-together, since I find I'm more productive with coffee and lunch than I am with drinks and dinner."

Pleased by the invitation, Candrew said, "I'm sure she'll be happy to come."

"Next Tuesday?" he asked.

"Sounds good."

Candrew left Wilfred and walked back across campus. The rest of the day proceeded smoothly—he worked on his manuscript, coped with a couple of interruptions by students outside of office hours, and read several technical publications. But his mind kept drifting back to the samples he'd collected in the arroyos. He was tempted to go down to the lab and see what progress Judy was making in separating indicator minerals. But since she was competent, hard working, and well organized, he felt it best to leave her alone. Eventually he gave up on serious work and drove home.

After his usual microwaved dinner and a beer, Candrew watched television sitting on the sofa with a cat on one side and a dog on the other. When Candrew moved his dog out of the way to reach across, get his cell phone, and call Renata, Chile clearly considered it an imposition.

He gave Renata a brief outline of the trip with the *Major Miners*. "We had to cut our field trip short," he told her, "One of the mining students fell and got banged up. Cut his leg."

"I'm sorry to hear that. Nothing too serious, I hope."

"No. I just talked to Wilfred Pengelly. He's going to be okay, although the accident did mean we only had time to visit a single diatreme."

"Too bad. And so you only got a few rocks, not overwhelmed with samples?"

"Enough to keep me going." Candrew laughed. "At least enough to keep Judy going. I've already taken them down to her."

Candrew told her that Wilfred said he and Allison had enjoyed dinner the other night. "He asked if we'd like to have lunch with them next week. He suggested Tuesday."

"That's fine with me. I can never resist a free meal—especially when the food's good."

After fifteen minutes or so of chit-chat, he clicked the phone off. It was getting late. He was about to get a mug of hot chocolate, go to bed, and read, when the phone rang.

"Hope I didn't wake you." It was Judy. "I know it's late, but I thought I'd bring you up to date with my progress separating your sediments. I've gotten the heavy liquid separation technique worked out. So far, half the M series sands are done, although I don't have much good news."

"You don't?"

"No. Most of the samples I studied had almost none of those indicator minerals you were searching for. Only one of the group had any at all." There was a pause. "I've e-mailed you the details."

Candrew was disappointed, but not surprised. "That's a pity," he said. "I suppose it's to be expected since nobody has found any diamonds out there."

There was a moment's silence. "I actually claimed, '*most of the samples*,'" Judy said chuckling. "Two of them, the ones you'd labelled *S1* and *S2*, did have quite a few of the red garnets as well as some green mineral grains I assume are diopside. But the real star was *S3*, it was loaded with the two minerals."

"Wow. That's encouraging." Candrew was delighted.

"Anyway, what's so special about the *S* series?" she asked.

"All three came from the same stream bed, although I scooped *S3* off an ant hill on the bank. But then ants are well known for excavating stuff from the subsurface." He readjusted his position on the sofa, which meant pushing Chile back. "That side stream is small and drains a different area. It cuts into the far side of the main arroyo. Of course, now the main problem is to figure out what's upstream from the arroyo I sampled." He thought about that for a moment. "It strongly suggests there's a kimberlite pipe up there."

"Well, I'm glad I had some good news for you," Judy said. "I worked real late to get that data." Candrew laughed, "So do I get paid overtime?"

"'Fraid not," Candrew said. "But you're free to keep all the diamonds you can find."

"Generous."

"I really appreciate the amount of work you've done—even if you don't get paid extra," Candrew said. "I'll come by the lab in late morning and pick up the concentrates."

"That's good. I should have more separates by then."

"I'm planning to take the samples over to Mark Kernfeld. He's the geochemist in our department and was with me on the San Juan float trip. His lab's got a fancy machine that can do detailed analyses of minerals. I really need that extra compositional data." He was thinking about the article Wilfred had lent him, and its ideas about chromium and calcium concentrations in indicator minerals.

After thanking Judy for her efforts in getting key minerals separated, Candrew pulled out his cell phone. He quickly located the photos he'd taken of the small dry stream bed. They definitely showed it fed into the adjacent gravelly arroyo, the one they'd followed up to the diatreme. Other photos showed the sharp bends where he'd gotten his sandy samples. Although he had taken quite a few photos, none gave a good image of the upper part of the side stream. And he wanted to know what area that stream drained.

At that time of year both stream beds were dry, but he was well aware that flash floods, especially after summer thunderstorms, sent water pouring down the channels. Those currents could have transported eroded minerals from exposed and weathered rocky outcrops. Included among them might have been some critical indicator minerals—and those would have become part of the samples he'd collected and could be showing the presence of diamonds.

CHAPTER 8

AFTER A SIMPLE BREAKFAST, Candrew slipped on his padded jacket and sat out on the cool patio in the early morning sunshine. Usually he'd be rushing off to campus, but the week of Spring Break gave him a chance to relax. While the morning's intense, clear blue sky was classic, he preferred the interest provided by cloud formations—even if they were only aircraft contrails spread out by the wind. He read through the day's newspaper, and having absorbed the ills of the world, turned to the Sudoku puzzle. This morning it was rated "bronze," and he had no trouble completing it. His aging cat Pixel sat in the open doorway, watching the birds, apparently trying to decide whether to venture into the cold garden. But Chile hadn't hesitated, and had already bounded out, searching through the bushes, sniffing for evidence of nighttime visitors. Finding none, he'd come and sat on his haunches beside the patio chair. With his crumpled ear, he had his usual quizzical look. Candrew got up, went into the kitchen, found a chewy treat, and tossed it to Chile. Pixel had retreated to the warmth of the living room.

Late in the morning Candrew grabbed his unopened briefcase, tossed it in the car, and drove to his office on campus. After briefly checking e-mails, he was eager to get down to the sedimentology lab and talk to Judy.

Apart from one graduate student carrying an armful of books, the halls were deserted—after all, it was Spring Break. Candrew pushed open the basement door to the lab. "Good morning, Dr.

Westerlund, my fantastically hard-working associate," he said, kidding her.

"I'm feeling tired this morning," she sniffed. "After your project kept me working until the early hours of the morning. I went to bed way after my usual bedtime."

"Such a sad tale," Candrew said. He knew where this was going and shook his head. "But academic research labs don't pay overtime."

Grinning, Judy shook her fist at him. Then she turned and poured freshly-perked coffee for both of them. "I need this to wake me up. But be careful, it's hot," she warned. "Oh, and there aren't any donuts today."

"Joking aside," he said, "I really appreciate your doing those mineral separations—and getting them done so quickly."

"Always glad to push back the frontiers of science," she said, sipping her coffee. "Though I'm beginning to think it may be the frontiers of mineral economics that are going to get pushed back," she laughed.

Getting more serious, Judy readjusted her glasses and asked, "So you think these mineral separates are going to be helpful?"

"Well, the fact that it's actually possible to make separations is definitely an encouraging first step. Also, that you found both red garnets and diopsides—and that they were especially abundant in the S-series sands."

Judy sipped her coffee and smiled, obviously pleased she'd been able to help. "So, what's the next thing I need to do?"

Candrew pondered the question for a moment. "Let me look at what you've got."

Judy handed him the vial that had the most mineral fragments and Candrew poured them onto a sheet of white paper. He pulled out the ten-power hand lens he always kept in his pocket, and used it to examine the garnets and diopsides.

A few minutes later he looked up. "Do you still have that low power microscope?" he asked, "That fifty-power one."

"Yeah. I'll get it." She went over to one of the cluttered shelves, found it, and handed it to him. "What are you looking for?"

"Looking *at*. I want to see the surface textures."

After examining the grains for several minutes, Candrew straightened up. "I've been reading about surface textures, and now I know these grains can't have travelled very far. Which means, of course, the source of the mineral indicators—and any diamonds—would have to be fairly close."

"That's quite a conclusion."

"Certainly is," he said, chuckling and obviously excited. "It'll be important to go back to that area and see if I can track down the source. My guess is, it's probably one of the exposed kimberlite pipes." He poured the mineral separates back into the vial and sipped his coffee. "I'm already planning the trip."

"And you'll just scoop up the diamonds?" Judy grinned, sipping her coffee. "You going to get yourself a mule, a floppy hat and a pickaxe and become a real prospector?"

Candrew laughed. "No. It's going to be a lot more high tech than that."

"Really?"

"Yeah. My next step, now that you've separated the garnets and diopsides, will be to get them analyzed. I'm planning to take them over to Professor Kernfeld. He's got a fancy—and expensive—machine that can do that."

For the next half hour Candrew and Judy drank coffee and turned their attention to the sandstone results she'd gotten for one of their ongoing, funded research projects. The area near the Four Corners had nothing to do with diamonds. She had made good progress, and Candrew was pleased with the results.

"We may have to go back and get more sandstone samples from our study area in southeastern Utah," he said.

"Given a choice, I'd wait for warmer weather," Judy said grinning. "But as long as you're going to be more involved in mineral exploration you should take some field excursions to the classic mining areas in the state: like Questa, the Lordsburg area, even Silver City. And there's always the Cerrillos Hills, they're pretty close."

"You mean that mining area a few miles south of Santa Fe?"

"Right. A couple of weeks ago I went down there with Mindy, the friend I play racquetball with. We hiked most of the trails and had a good time." She got off her wood stool, fetched one of the brochures describing the area, and handed it to him.

Candrew glanced at it and asked, "What are they mining there?"

"Nothing now. It used to be a major source for lead, and some silver, as well as a few other things like manganese."

"No gold?"

"No. Apparently there was some in the adjacent Ortiz Mountains, but not a lot." Candrew seemed interested. She told him that in the past there wasn't any iron ore in the area. "So, iron was quite valuable—as valuable as lead," she said. "It had to be carted in until the railroads were built and could deliver it cheaply."

"You learned quite a bit of history."

"And geology," Judy said. "Both the Cerrillos Hills and the Ortiz Mountains are what's left of the feeder systems from thirty-million year old volcanoes. We're seeing the old plumbing of those eruptions."

The similarity to kimberlite pipes was not lost on Candrew. He thought back to the well-exposed Shiprock they'd seen on the diatreme trip. He realized it was a rock of similar age.

Judy glanced at the vials with the mineral separates she'd prepared for Candrew. "What elements are you going to ask Kernfeld to analyze for you?"

"Chromium and calcium."

Dr. Kernfeld's microanalytical facility was in a low, one-story building that had been constructed as an annex to Kinblade Hall, the geology building.

Unusual for him, but he was in a hurry, Candrew took the elevator down to the first floor, then made his way along the hallway to the analytical laboratory. He had with him two dozen plastic vials containing the minerals Judy had separated from the sands he'd brought back from the previous weekend trip.

Candrew knocked on the lab door and went in. A tall, slightly overweight, youngish man in a black tee-shirt was seated in front of a computer terminal typing commands onto a keyboard. His glasses were perched back up into his long ginger hair. He paused, glanced at the screen, then pushed back his chair. "You need help?"

"Yeah. I'd arranged to see Mark Kernfeld this morning. Is he available?"

"Hold on a minute. I'll see if I can find him." The researcher shuffled out of his alcove, across the lab, and down a passageway on the opposite side.

Candrew stood waiting. He had no doubt Professor Kernfeld would be there—he had a well-earned reputation as a workaholic. And, anyway, Spring Break was for students, not research-oriented faculty. Candrew had been left alone in a large, almost square room. In the center was a huge analytical instrument that appeared to be a combination of a stainless steel, high vacuum system wired to several cabinets of electronic gear. A row of LED lights was flashing, and so was the computer screen. Candrew assumed from his morning phone call to Mark Kernfeld that this instrument was their ion microprobe.

The lab was well lighted, stark white, and pristine, although there was a low hum of vacuum pumps and cooling fans. 'Sterile' was how Candrew thought of it. So different from his lab with all the dusty cardboard boxes, piles of rocks, and stacks of field equipment lying around.

Mark Kernfeld came across to greet him. Tall, with a shock of unruly blond hair, he was lean, obviously getting plenty of exercise. Mark wore slacks and a V-necked sweater over a buttoned-down blue Oxford cloth shirt. His dark brown eyes had a focused intensity.

"Hi Candrew," he said. "Come on over to the office." He glanced at one of the gauges on the instrument panel, then led the way through the lab and down a side passage that ended in a glass cubicle.

Kernfeld was intrigued by Candrew's interest in diamonds and remembered their discussion on the San Juan River trip. Candrew told him about the visit to the kimberlite pipe with students from the mining department and handed him the box of plastic vials. "Here's the indicator minerals my Research Associate separated." He smiled. "None of them are from our river trip."

When he'd finished explaining their analytical procedures, Kernfeld stroked his chin and frowned. "We've got several major projects ongoing, so there's quite a backlog of work. I'm afraid it may be a while before I can get to your samples." He pushed back from his desk and shook his head regretfully. He asked Candrew, "Are any of your samples especially high priority?" He tipped his head to one side. "Any you'd like us to analyze first?"

"Well, yes," Candrew said. "I'm particularly interested in data for the ones labelled with an *S*. There are only three of them." Disappointed, he had no choice but to expect data for the others to come much later. At least Kernfeld said he'd e-mail the analytical data as soon as they had it.

Kernfeld unscrewed the lid of one of the vials and casually glanced in. "They all look pretty small—but that's not a problem. We'll have no trouble mounting them for analysis in our microprobe."

Although searching for diamonds wasn't a high priority for Candrew, and not one of his funded research projects, he regretted that things were not going to move very fast.

Candrew sat in the only padded chair in his office thinking about the morning meeting with Mark Kernfeld. He was pleased Mark would be analyzing his garnets and diopsides, but disappointed that this was probably going to take a while. But did this matter? He had no deadlines and no commitments.

He began to wonder why he'd become so interested in tracking down diamonds. What was his motivation? Certainly not their monetary value—he was unlikely to find any huge deposits and get real financial rewards.

For prestige? To impress his friends and colleagues who would certainly respond to the discovery of a new 'diamond patch'? But he was sure he didn't have that much ego.

Was it for science? Generating additional information was always important. But a novel find of diamonds in the area's kimberlite pipes wasn't likely to lead to major new geologic concepts.

Candrew had always been a problem solver. It had always been his main motivation, his driving force, even when he played games as a youngster. Now it was science that posed the problems, and he had no illusion about the satisfaction he felt when he worked out something that no other scientist had been able to. Peer-reviewed, published articles were a way of keeping score—and he had an enviable track record.

But problem solving usually involved competition. Were there others evaluating the kimberlite pipes he'd been sampling? Who else was trying to find diamonds?

CHAPTER 9

With few students around, and no course to teach, Candrew's day was more relaxed than usual. He rocked back in his desk chair and phoned Renata, who he knew was working at home. They chatted about the small inconsequential things that only close friends can. He told her that Judy had successfully separated the indicator minerals from his sand samples, and he'd taken them over to Mark Kernfeld's lab for analysis.

"What sort of detailed information about mineral composition do you want from him," Renata asked, not having a strong geochemical background.

He told her, "Concentrations of the elements chromium and calcium."

"You're lucky to have colleagues who've got the fancy machines that can do those sophisticated analyses," Renata said. "I wish we had some people in our department who could work out the age of artifacts. Even carbon-14 could be very helpful."

"Yeah. But with Mark Kernfeld's unique instrument there's lots of other researchers wanting analytical work done. I'm going to have to wait in line."

"Poor baby."

"Thanks for the sympathy."

Shortly before noon Candrew made his way across the quiet campus to the Faculty Lounge. He joined his colleagues, taking a seat facing the picture window and looking out at the mountains. There was still a dusting of snow on the highest peaks, most of which were above the tree line.

The lunch regulars knew Candrew had gotten interested in the search for possible diamond deposits. As he ordered his lunch from Rosita, their usual waitress, there was a barrage of questions.

"How did your weekend mineral exploration go?" Ted Devereaux from the Business Office asked.

Before Candrew had time to point out it was only a student trip, Arlan Dee was asking, "You haul back a bag full of diamonds? Find enough gemstones so you can retire?"

This was clearly said as a joke, but it made Candrew wonder. Retirement was way off in the future, and he'd never given it any serious thought. He enjoyed teaching and the interaction with students, as well as his research projects with Judy. He had no plans to quit anytime soon.

"No diamonds," Candrew said. "I only brought back some garnets and other minerals that can be used to show whether diamonds might be present. Sort of pointers."

"Garnets? They're gemstones. You diversifying?" somebody asked.

"Unfortunately not. These are way too small to be used in jewelry, although they are bright red. Same with the diopside minerals—good green color, but tiny."

The overweight man with heavy horn-rimmed glasses at the far side of the table was a rather humorless mathematician. "Diamonds can be made synthetically," he snapped. "Why go to all the trouble of tramping around in the wilderness looking for them, and then go to the expense of digging them up?"

Lubie butted in, smiling. "The usual reason—money. It costs more to grow gem-quality diamonds in the lab than to mine them. And I'm sure you realize that high-end jewelry wearers will want something 'genuine'—something from Mother Nature, not a synthetic bauble made in a lab."

"It's a different story with small, imperfect diamonds," a bald engineer at the far end of the table said. "Diamonds that aren't gem-quality get used as abrasives—and most of those are made synthetically. Cheaper than mining them."

There was silence for a moment, before Ted said, "Gems are okay, but they're luxuries, just for the wealthy." His viewpoint was always financially oriented. He pointed a finger at Candrew. "You ought to get into things we really need, like lithium—the metal we've got to have for our cell phones and car batteries."

"You could talk to your friends in the Mining Department and branch out," Lubie suggested. Smiling, he added, "Do some geology with economic consequences." He paused to take several gulps of his black coffee. "Think about the four corners of the Earth—not just our Four Corners."

"But don't stay on land, go offshore and scoop up some of those nodules lying around on the ocean-floor." The advice came from Evelyn Snoparsky, a red-headed professor in the Biology Department. "They're loaded with manganese, nickel, and lots of other valuable metals." She glanced around the table. "Maybe you could rent the 'Glomar Explorer.' It was supposed to be designed to dredge up manganese nodules."

Not surprisingly, the lunch bunch had never heard of this ship, but Lubie had pushed back his chair and was laughing. He told them, "Nodules were merely a cover story for that ship. It was actually built by the CIA, with help from Howard Hughes, and was intended to recover a sunken Russian submarine." There was a fascinated silence. "They were only partly successful, just got half of it."

"If you're going offshore, Candrew, you'll have to get political support," someone noted.

"But President Hoover is long gone."

"What the hell are you talking about?" the mathematician wanted to know.

"Our past president was a mining engineer. That's how Herbert Hoover made his fortune."

And Lubie was quick to note, "He even translated the Medieval mining treatise, *De Re Metallica*, from Latin."

"But be fair," Evelyn said. "His wife had a major role helping with that. They both had geology degrees from Stanford."

Discussion rambled on with most of the group unaware of the details of mining.

Lunch over, Candrew spent the rest of the afternoon at the cluttered desk in his office reading technical articles and working on his manuscript. The day had evolved into a low-key time for catching up. His thoughts, however, drifted back over the lunchtime discussion of mining and its importance for our way of life. He couldn't help realizing that the availability of metals like lithium, cobalt, and even copper, would have a major impact on our future life style. But if no more diamonds were discovered it would have virtually no effect. Yet as an academic, he was well aware that detailed studies of these rare gems could provide critical information about conditions deep in the earth.

At the end of the day, Candrew gave the filing cabinet drawer a push and watched it slide shut. He turned off his computer, slipped on his jacket, and took the stairs to the parking lot. On the way he went by the basement lab to visit Judy, but, unusual for her, the door was locked and she was not there.

Late in the evening, Candrew sat in his living room, Scotch in hand, with the last of the burning logs dying in the fireplace. He was watching the end of a film on television. Although he'd seen this favorite several times, and knew exactly how the plot played out, he was always prepared to enjoy it one more time. He liked the sense of continuity it gave.

The phone rang. He was curious to know who would be calling at this late hour. Renata maybe? He hustled into the kitchen and grabbed the receiver—it was Mark Kernfeld.

"I hope you don't mind me calling you this late, and at home," Mark said.

Candrew smiled to himself. For Mark, research was a twenty-four hour a day occupation. "No. Not at all," he replied. "I'm delighted to hear from you."

"I've just got some of the results you wanted. But only values for the minerals in your high-priority *S-series*."

"That's great. I'm surprised you could get the analyses done so quickly."

"Yeah. I was helping our new post-doc become competent using the microprobe. We have to get our incoming researchers familiar with it, trained, and up to speed. I think he's going to turn out to be an excellent analyst." He hesitated. "I hope you don't mind, but we used your mineral samples as the study suite. They were a good group for what was needed. We ran them multiple times, so you're getting a really first-rate data set. Lots of duplicate analyses." He paused.

When Candrew said nothing, Mark continued, "Garnets can be complex and have quite a range of compositions. The chromium values you wanted came in rather high. Was that what you were expecting?"

"What do you consider 'high'?" Candrew asked.

"In most cases, pushing a hundred parts per million."

"That's right in the range that's been documented for pyrope garnets associated with diamonds," Candew said, pleased with the numbers.

"Interesting. I need to get some of those references from you. Let me jot that down." There was silence for a moment. "Since detailed analyses of your samples were being used as a training exercise, we got data for a wide range of elements. Are there any others you're interested in?"

"Well, yes. Do you have data for calcium?"

"Sure do." Candrew heard classical music in the background as Mark was flipping through some papers. "The values seem to be pretty low. From what I know about garnets and diopsides, I would say they're extremely depleted."

"Again, consistent with what's been published for diamond indicator minerals," Candrew said.

"I'll e-mail you all the information," Mark said, "Sorry about the delay processing your other samples—that *M series*. We'll do them as soon as we can."

"Now that I've got this amazing *S-series* data, there's not quite such a rush."

"Okay. If you want more details about what we're doing, I'll be in the lab all day tomorrow," Mark said. "Come on over any time after nine."

Candrew wasn't surprised. As the last day of Spring Break, most of the faculty would be taking the day off, making the Friday part of a long weekend. But Mark Kernfeld was living up to his reputation as a dedicated scientist and would be in the lab working.

Both Chile and Pixel were curled up asleep on the bed. Candrew lay there, but didn't sleep. He was mulling over the information he'd just gotten from Kernfeld on the mineral compositions. The chromium values for the garnets were in the classic range indicating proximity to diamonds. And the calcium values also fitted in nicely.

His plan was crystallizing rapidly—he was scheming to go back to the stream bed where he'd found the *S-series* indicator minerals. He'd collect more sand samples. But his main objective was to follow the arroyo all the way up to the kimberlite outcrop.

What would he find there?

CHAPTER 10

MARK KERNFELD'S ANALYTICAL DATA had left Candrew in no doubt. He had planned exactly what he was going to do.

But first he needed to tell Wilfred about the new results he'd just gotten for the samples collected on the Major Miners' field trip. It was mid-morning when he called, but the phone rang several times, finally switching to take a recorded message.

He's probably off in his laboratory, Candrew thought. He hunted around, found a university directory, and looked up the number for the lab. This time the phone was picked up promptly—but not by Wilfred. It was Brandon who answered.

Not recognizing his voice, Candrew asked, "Is Dr. Pengelly there?"

"Sorry. I don't think he's in today." He paused, "You want to leave a message?"

"Yes. This is Candrew Nor. Would you tell him that I've got some interesting analytical results for the samples I collected last week on the trip to the kimberlite pipe." He paused, "The one where that student fell and hurt his leg."

"Yeah, that guy seems to be recovering okay." There was a moment's silence. "This is Brandon you're talking to. Remember, I organized that trip for Dr. Pengelly?"

"Oh, yes," Candrew said. "You did a great job."

"I'm in his lab now trying to pin down the silver content of the copper ores he's interested in. What message did you want me to give him?"

"Well, Brandon, let him know I've just got analytical data for some of the sands I collected on our trip to the diatreme. They're intriguing."

"Anything specific you want him to know?"

Candrew hesitated. "Yes, there is. The smaller side arroyo—not the one we followed up to the kimberlite outcrop—had abundant indicator minerals. Tell him that the garnets were chromium rich which is, of course, a clear indication of associated diamonds."

There was a short silence before Brandon said, "That's really quite astounding."

"And you can tell him I'm planning to go back there for a more detailed look. I'll check with him when I get back."

There was another silence. "You going alone?"

"That's what I was planning."

"Then be very careful. Make sure *you* don't fall like that student did," Brandon said.

The phone call ended, and Candrew sat for a moment thinking about his upcoming visit to the arroyo. Then he called Renata.

"We'd talked about getting together for brunch tomorrow," he said. "Sorry, but I'm going to have to postpone that."

She didn't seem too upset, and as usual was tolerant of Candrew's last minute changes in plans. "I can tell where your priorities lie." She laughed. "So, what's the urgency this time?"

"I'm going back to visit the area I went to with Wilfred Pengelly and the students last week. You're welcome to come along."

"Thanks for the offer, but I think I'll pass on that generous invitation."

"Remember, I told you I was getting some minerals analyzed. I got the data much quicker than I expected—and it seems to be really significant. I'm excited and going back to check the area one more time. I'll get additional samples."

"So, you're still pursuing your diamond quarry?"

"Sure am."

"Well, good luck with that."

Candrew spent an hour that evening packing for the next day's trip. Chile sat watching, his crumpled ear giving him the usual quizzical look. As Candrew put his tools, camera and notebook into his backpack, he glanced across at Chile. This prompted a call to Michelle, or 'Shell as everyone called her. She was the graduate student who looked after Candrew's dog and cat when he was out of town. She was reliable and had had that role for more than a year, and was always quite happy to come by the house and feed the animals—even take Chile for a walk.

Shortly before dawn on Saturday, Candrew pulled out of his driveway and set off west. It was cold and just getting light with the sun still below the horizon. With little weekend traffic he made good progress as he followed the familiar route toward Farmington before turning south. He stopped only once and that was to stretch his legs, sip his coffee, and admire the vista of Shiprock. The exposed throat of this old volcano dominated the landscape, standing tall above its flat surroundings. Candrew was certain that in some ways the prominent rock was similar to the kimberlite pipes he was on his way to explore.

Candrew knew dramatic rock formations always intrigued geologists and prompted them to find explanations. So, this was nothing new. Since prehistory, humans have wanted to understand why some rock forms are unusual, and this often invoked the need for a religious interpretation. Candrew thought of *Devil's Tower* near the Black Hills where the sacred narratives of several nearby tribes involve a very large bear. No indigenous myths, however, seemed to include diamonds, although a few did try to explain attractive minerals like turquoise.

Candrew knew Shiprock had its own myths and recalled the one recounted by Carlos Nez, the Navajo student. While archaeologists had shown that the Navajo (and Apache) had migrated from the Athabascan region of western Canada, the Navajo's own myth attributed their arrival to a huge bird that transported the tribe to their present location. This was why their name for Shiprock is *The Rock with Wings.*

After leaving Shiprock, the rest of the route toward the kimberlite pipe—the diatreme that he'd visited with Wilfred, Brandon, and the Major Miners—was quite straightforward. When he turned off the main road, a gravel section soon gave way to a rugged, dusty dirt track with abundant potholes. After bumping along for quarter of a mile, he parked in the same flat spot used on last week's field trip. This area was close to the intersection of the big arroyo and the adjacent smaller one he planned to hike up. Candrew glanced along the main arroyo. Judy had found very few indicator minerals in the samples he'd collected there, but so far he had not gotten any analytical data from Kernfeld. Candrew was well aware that nobody had reported diamonds from the diatreme they'd visited.

Candrew turned toward the side arroyo, and as he hiked along the dry stream bed he recalled looking at the garnets and diopsides under the microscope when he was showing them to Judy. The surface textures he'd seen were consistent with those minerals having moved only a relatively short distance. He felt a sense of excitement. Instinctively he started hiking faster—he was eager to get up to the outcrop.

The sunny blue sky was cloudless, but it was still cold. There was no wind and the only noise in the calm air was the cawing of a pair of crows cruising overhead. When the indistinct trail became too difficult to see, he just picked the route with smaller cobbles, staying for the most part in the dry sandy arroyo and avoiding big boulders. The slope was initially gentle, with just a few scattered plants and stunted bushes on the arid hillsides. After about an hour's hiking it became much steeper, and he scrambled up, slipping and sliding on the gravel—but the clearly outlined outcrop ahead encouraged him. Finally, he arrived at the top. There was no doubt this was kimberlite. The bare surface of the exposed broken rock stretched away about thirty yards in each direction outlining a roughly circular area. He sat down, recovering from the climb, and drank a copious amount of bottled water.

After his brief rest, Candrew went to the edge of the outcrop, took a series of photographs, then walked back across the rugged surface and examined several broken, weathered pebbles. He dumped a couple into his numbered plastic bags. Laying his hammer down, both for scale and as a place-marker, he took more photographs. Then he used the hammer for its real purpose—chipping off lumps of rock. These pieces also went into labelled plastic bags.

Pleased with the material he'd collected, he squatted down and examined the contact between the sandstones (which were his research specialty) and the dark kimberlite. Candrew took off the heavy backpack and sat on a convenient boulder to jot information in his field notebook. He wondered what the collected samples would show when Kernfeld analyzed them. Any indicator minerals, especially high chromium garnets, would be a major find. But a diamond or two would be the ultimate discovery. *Enough fantasy*, he thought, time to head home.

Candrew peered over the far side of the outcrop to see if there was an alternative route back to his parked car, and noted one possible way down. It was steeper than his original trail, but he was sure he could make it—and it would give him a chance to study other rocks.

Although challenging, the first section of the route was passable and led across picturesque, vertical sandstone cliffs. About a third of the way down, Candrew faced a near-horizontal narrow ledge where several trees had gotten themselves established. As he pushed his way through the branches, he saw that there was a cave partly obscured behind one of the thicker clumps. When he got closer, he realized the opening was not natural. Rectangular, and almost certainly man-made, it was roughly six feet high and a couple of feet wide. It seemed to be a narrow entrance to a tunnel. Further inspection convinced him that the rock debris he'd seen on the sloping rock face wasn't a natural scree, and had been dumped there, probably when the tunnel was being excavated.

Candrew slipped off his backpack and took out his cell phone. He left the pack near the entrance, switched on the phone's flashlight, and went into the tunnel. The first thirty feet or so was dead straight through sandstone. Then it transitioned into dark kimberlite rock. The rock surface reflected light from his cell phone, and showed tool cut marks where it had been deliberately worked. Candrew immediately realized that this tunnel had been dug directly through the area's sandstone rock to reach the deeper part of the kimberlite pipe he'd just been sitting on top of. But who would want to do that?

The cell phone light was dim, and at one point he stumbled and almost fell. Regaining his balance, he shone the light down, and saw he'd tripped on a shovel. He kicked it out of the way. But a pair of parallel eroded ruts was obvious in the floor of the tunnel, Candrew realized that quite a few carts must have been hauled along this passage to have made these tracks. Were they motorized, he wondered? A short distance farther along, the tunnel widened considerably, not only from side-to-side but also above. He pointed his cell phone up, but the beam faded into the distance, not strong enough to light the high roof.

Clearly, an enormous amount of rock had been mined out to produce this huge cavity in the kimberlite pipe, much more than accounted for by all the broken fragments littering the hillside. *Why had anyone gone to all that trouble?* Candrew wondered. *And where had the rest of the rock been taken?* He knew kimberlite had no commercial value—unless it had diamonds in it.

After thoroughly studying this mined-out cavity, and taking more flash photos, Candrew headed back to the entrance. He stepped out into the daylight, paused to let his eyes adjust to the bright light— and was stunned to hear a man's voice.

The man leaning back against the rock face demanded, "What the hell do you think you're doing?"

CHAPTER 11

CANDREW STOPPED DEAD IN his tracks. He hadn't expected to meet anyone near the kimberlite pipe, and certainly not someone so aggressive. Speechless, he stared at the man.

He was tall, wore a sleeveless leather jacket over a denim shirt, his jeans tucked into heavy work boots. A long, dark-haired ponytail hung from under his cowboy hat.

Candrew peered at him in surprise. His first reaction was that he was probably American Indian, most likely Navajo.

The thought fitted with the man's demand. "You aware this is Navajo Reservation? You know you're trespassing?"

Candrew did know this was Indian land, but with no warning signs and no fences he assumed you could hike across it. Besides, the *Major Miners* group had been in this area only a week ago—and one of those students was Navajo.

Before he could frame a reply, the Navajo stepped away from the rock surface and leaned toward him. He hooked his thumbs in his belt and demanded, "What you doing here?"

"Well, I . . . I'm a geologist," Candrew said. "I was just looking at the sandstone rocks." He thought it best not to mention his interest in kimberlites.

"Geologist, eh?" He glared at Candrew. "What company you work for?"

Candrew realized that he'd been subjected to a barrage of questions since he'd left the tunnel. But he knew nothing about the man in the cowboy hat who was asking them. He replied. "I'm a professor at the University of Northern New Mexico."

"That right?"

"And you?" There was silence. Candrew didn't get an answer.

"You come here with the bunch of students last week? The ones who climbed up that other hill." He nodded toward the distant diatreme. "Probably collecting kimberlite rocks to see if they had any diamonds in them." He chuckled. "Or maybe looking for those garnets that tell you if you're close to the gems." He nodded and stared at Candrew. "I guess they all got educated, and had a good time." He grinned, "Except for the guy who fell and got hurt. He had a cute girl take care of him, though."

This man was surprisingly familiar with what had been going on in the area—and also seemed to be quite knowledgeable about diamond exploration techniques. Candrew wondered where he'd gotten his information. Had he been spying on the students when they hiked up to the kimberlite outcrop?

Candrew picked up his backpack, tossed in the lump of kimberlite from the mine, and pulled on his cap. The man watched him carefully.

"You collect mineral samples to show your students?" His attitude was slightly less aggressive, more friendly. "Or even get some for yourself? Most geology profs I know . . ." The tall man abruptly stopped talking, tilted his head to one side, listening.

Candrew heard it as well—the sound of human voices.

A moment later two young men appeared over the edge of the arroyo. Amazed, Candrew recognized both of them—Brandon and Carlos.

Brandon waved to him and yelled, "Hi, Dr. Nor." He didn't seem in the least surprised that Candrew was at the outcrop.

But it seemed like too much of a coincidence for Candrew. As Brandon walked over toward him, Candrew remembered that yesterday he'd called Wilfred and left a message that included information about his coming out to this site. Although Brandon took the message, it left unanswered the question of why he needed to be here now.

Carlos went across to the other man, nodded, and said, *"Ya'at'ééh."* Candrew knew this was the traditional Navajo greeting. It confirmed his suspicion that the tall, dark-haired man was in fact Navajo.

The four of them grouped together. Carlos acknowledged Candrew, and then introduced the other Navajo as '*Raven*.'"

"Popular place," Brandon quipped.

"So why are you here?" Candrew wanted to know.

Brandon glanced from Carlos to Raven. "There's lots of interesting geology out here. I've some mining experience and have been advising them."

"That's right," Raven said. "Our reservation covers twenty-five thousand square miles—lots of rocks. You're a geologist, you must know that."

"And they're *our* rocks," Carlos said with a contentious look. "Anything valuable is going to stay with us."

Diamonds, Candrew thought? Is that why they were here, to watch what he might discover? To be sure they knew what he was doing?

Now that Carlos and Brandon had arrived, Raven appeared more cooperative. He glanced over at Candrew's heavy pack. "We have lots of amateurs poking around out here, looking for pretty crystals. My guess is, most of those minerals end up at the *Tucson Rock and Mineral Show* and get sold. I know you professors like building up your own collections." He grinned, "And some of you generous professors even collect interesting rocks to give to your students."

"But rocks aren't all that gets 'collected'," Carlos said. "People steal, like, anything of value. They'll even haul away cactuses. Sometimes real big ones. And, of course, if they can find an old Anasazi ruin, they'll cart off all the pots they dig up."

Candrew was not surprised. He'd heard lots of stories of looting. While he found kimberlites geologically interesting, he knew they didn't have spectacular crystal clusters that ended up on coffee tables or in display cases. This was certainly not a prime prospecting area for large crystals.

It was almost as though Raven, in his pushed-back cowboy hat, was reading his mind. "These are not the best locations," he said, "but there are a couple of old abandoned mines east of here that still have some amazing mineral veins, big crystals. You could get some great mineral samples out there." Staring at Candrew, he was obviously gauging his interest. After a moment's hesitation, he said, "We'd be happy to take you over and show you."

Brandon was nodding in agreement. "Yeah, he's right. There's still some nice mineral clusters over there. It's well worth a visit."

"You going to be around tomorrow?" Raven asked. "I can get one of our drivers to run you over. You can see for yourself." He paused trying to gauge whether Candrew was interested. "The mine's abandoned. You can chip out some nice crystals for your own collection, even pick up a few for your favorite students."

Candrew thought of Judy's advice that he should get more familiar with the New Mexico mines and the mining industry. Anyway, he was always ready to acquire more rock specimens. He also realized he didn't have class until Tuesday, so it gave him a couple of days free. "I guess that's a possibility," he said. "It's a generous offer."

"Okay. Why don't you check into the *Route 66 Highway Lodge* down in Albuquerque, it's on Central, and I'll get someone to pick you up tomorrow. He'll know all about the mine." He considered that for a moment. "It's going to be early afternoon before the driver'll be able to get there."

They talked more about the geology of the area, and after a while Candrew grabbed his loaded backpack and left, slogging along the gravel trail back down to his car. He took Route 491 into Gallup, and went into one of the truck stops for a blue corn enchilada and a piece of pie. Then he took I-40 into Albuquerque.

Although it was getting dark, he found the motel on Central Avenue easily with its prominent neon sign. He parked in the gravel forecourt and checked into what was obviously a typical sixties motel. The room's carpet was stained, the only chair sported well-worn patches, and the tap in the bathroom dripped continuously. In his field work out west, Candrew had spent more than his fair share of nights in decrepit motels. The room was warm, however, and it did seem that the bed was large and comfortable.

He plugged his cell phone in to make sure it would be fully charged, then lay on the bed thinking through the events of the day. Finding the tunnel that led into the deeper part of the kimberlite pipe had been an amazing discovery. He was convinced he'd stumbled on a kimberlite mine—which almost certainly meant it was being worked for diamonds. But where did Raven, the Navajo man at the tunnel entrance, fit in? Surely the meeting wasn't purely accidental? Or did he know that a geology prof was going to be showing up? Candrew had left a message for Wilfred Pengelly with the plans for his trip, although it was Brandon who'd answered the phone.

Brandon—what was he doing at the mine? Was he really working with—for? —the Navajo?

The next morning Candrew slept late, then went over to the motel office to get breakfast—a muffin, orange juice and, of course, strong coffee. Back in his room he showered and watched some travel programs on television until there was a knock on the door shortly after mid-day. His transport had arrived.

The taciturn guide set out to drive Candrew to the mine in his pickup truck. He spoke just enough English to explain that he was from Ecuador, but had worked in the tin mining industry in Bolivia. His halting descriptions were heavily accented.

They headed south out of town, and drove most of the way in silence. After about forty-five minutes on a deserted, two-lane tarmac country road, the Ecuadorian driver slowed and pulled off across a scrubby gravel depression. He headed along an indistinct trail that was little more than a couple of tire tracks where the weeds had been worn down. Eventually, he came to a stop and pointed to adjacent low hills with one prominent rock outcrop. "Mine," he said, pointing.

They jumped out of the truck and headed over to a partially-obscured mine opening. Candrew was surprised to see that it was closed by a heavy metal bar gate. It had a substantial padlock, but the Ecuadorian produced a key and unlocked it. He pushed, and the squeaking iron gate slowly swung open. Pointing into the mine, he said in his halting English, "Good minerals show. Line walls." He waved Candrew through the entrance.

Candrew stepped into the tunnel in the fading light and peered at the mineralized veins on the exposed mine walls.

"I get big light . . . in truck," the driver said.

But the truck driver didn't head for his vehicle. He stepped out into the sunlight, quickly swiveled around, and slammed the mine gate closed behind Candrew. As Candrew turned to face him, to see what was going on, the man snapped the big padlock shut and pocketed the key.

"What the hell are you doing?" Candrew yelled through the bars. But his captor ignored him, briskly jogged to the truck, clambered in, and drove away.

CHAPTER 12

CANDREW WATCHED IN ASTONISHMENT as the truck disappeared in a cloud of dust. This was an isolated area, and the locked gate with its sturdy metal bars faced away from the distant road. He could not see, or hear, any of the traffic on the far side of the mountain. When he shook the gate's metal bars furiously, they rattled, but showed no sign of coming loose. What was he going to do now?

He studied the gate in detail, paying particular attention to the padlock and the hinges, but couldn't find any weak points. In any case, he had no tools with him. Overwhelmed, he slid down onto a rock and sat in the gloom shocked and desolate. The eerie silence was broken only by water dripping in from melting snow.

After several minutes sitting in the stillness he realized that feeling sorry for himself would get him nowhere. He had to pull himself together, to be proactive. Candrew started by searching through his pockets to see what he had with him. There was little that might be helpful—only a ball-point pen, his field notebook, a Brunton compass, and luckily a granola bar and half-a-dozen candies. But no bottled water. However, he did have his cell phone. Candrew knew there would be no service in this area, but fortunately the phone was almost fully charged and could be used as a flashlight. The sun was low in the western sky, illuminating a few scattered clouds. Very little light penetrated the east-facing opening of the mine, and then only near the entrance. As his eyes adjusted to the low light, he continued evaluating his situation and stared back into the mine tunnel. In the murky distance he could see that the main track appeared to fork into two branches. He wondered if either led to another mine entrance.

Candrew snapped on his cell phone flashlight and set about exploring the tunnels. He was extremely careful to record the path he was following. He did this by picking up a pocketful of small colored stones from the piles littered along the base of the walls. Then he placed them at intervals along the route he was following—he certainly didn't want to get lost in what could become a maze.

When he reached the fork he hesitated, then carefully headed down the left-hand section of the tunnel. The passage there was only about six inches higher than he was tall, and it was less than five feet wide, with rough-hewn rock walls. He only glanced at the rocks. Any interest in collecting elegant minerals was a secondary concern compared with escaping, finding a way out of this labyrinth of tunnels.

After he'd made his way about forty feet along, the cone of cell phone light showed a shallow alcove to his right. It seemed to be blocked diagonally by a large wooden beam. He flashed his light up and down and saw that there was a large metal wheel overhead. It appeared to be a pulley. Hanging from it was a length of steel cable that disappeared into a hole in the ground that was several feet across. Candrew picked up a small pebble, tossed it down the shaft and watched it disappear. It was several seconds before he heard it hit bottom. He guessed this long shaft probably led down to a lower level of the mine. It was always possible, of course, that the lower level had a separate way out. But he had no interest in clambering down to follow it, at least not at the moment.

A bit further along the tunnel he was exploring, he came across an excavated side recess that was strewn with rubble. Perched on the lumps of broken rock, all about fist-sized, was a heavy, rusting iron cart. Candrew's immediate reaction was to wonder if he could roll that massive ore cart down, wheel it back to the mine entrance, and use it to ram and break open the locked gate. But when he examined it more closely, he saw one of the iron wheels was bent at an angle to its axle and certainly not functional. The cart was lying on the heap of rubble, apparently discarded. Another disappointment.

The tunnel extended into the dark distance beyond the power of his flashlight beam and he could see nothing significant. He made his way a little further along, brushing against the rough walls of the narrow passage, until he was faced with a huge rock fall that had cascaded in from the roof and sides. The broken rocks and rubble blocked the passageway and prevented any further progress. Turning around, he retraced his steps, following the row of colored pebbles he'd laid out. At the junction of the fork, he made his way down the other side wanting to know where that passageway would lead. He hadn't gone more than twenty yards when he discovered a stack of old mining machinery.

There was a large, corroded iron framework with a broken chain hanging inside it. Several metal wheels with cogs, bent pipes, and rods had once formed some sort of contraption. Now they were all rusted and corroded. When he used a broken off piece of rod to move one of the large metal panels there was a slight oily smell. Candrew shook a few of the other structures and a couple rattled, seeming loose. Without any experience in mining engineering, he had no idea what the machinery had been built for, but clearly this rusting equipment hadn't been used for many years. Candrew looked it over one more time, then continued on down the narrow tunnel.

The light in his cell phone was only marginally adequate, and he almost stumbled over a long object he hadn't seen, lying at the side of the tunnel, When he focused the flashlight on it he was shocked to see it was a human body. Lying face down was the corpse of a man.

Candrew sucked in a deep breath, his heart rate racing. The body was cold with no pulse. When he pushed and rolled it over, the body was stiff, but there was no sign of blood and no obvious sign of injury—the mouth was open, although the eyes were shut. Candrew was close to throwing up.

The dead man was wearing heavy, laced-up steel-toed boots, faded jeans, and a light leather jacket. He still had on an orange hard hat—but not the mining type with a built-in electric lamp. He seemed to have been prepared to enter the mine, although probably not as a worker. The man had a broad, worn leather belt with a geologist's hammer attached. There was also a large silver buckle.

Why was this man, dead and undiscovered, abandoned behind a locked gate? What had he been doing here? Collecting mineral samples? Did this mean he'd been alone in the mine? And Candrew worried that he himself was destined to suffer the same fate, since he'd been deliberately brought to this mine and locked in.

Wondering who the dead man was, Candrew searched through the man's leather jacket and trouser pockets. There was no driver's license, credit cards, or other form of identification, but he was still wearing a watch. Candrew was looking for a cell phone, though he was well aware there'd be no service. He was hoping that if he found one it might have enough charge for its flashlight to work. He did find a phone in an inside pocket, and was delighted that it still shone. He put it in his own pocket. As well as the cell phone, he also felt a folded piece of stiff card. He took it out, thinking he could roll it up and make a small megaphone. Then he could use that to call for help from the mine's front metal gate. Candrew looked at the man's hard-hat. Maybe he should take it to get protection from any falling rocks. But surprisingly, he found himself reluctant to remove the man's helmet—it seemed too much like stealing from the dead. Somehow, taking the cell phone wasn't so serious: he justified that as simply a loan. But he had no idea who he was borrowing from—even after his thorough search of the body, he'd found no ID.

Candrew left the cold body and headed back toward the gated entrance with his flashlight shining into the distance. Rattled by his discovery, and not paying sufficient attention, he tripped over something he didn't see. It was an obstacle about the size of a brick. When he bent down, he discovered a large flashlight. There was a moment's excitement. But further examination showed that it had been left with the switch in the 'On' position and the battery was dead. Useless for his purpose.

He continued back to the locked gate. From there he could barely see the outline of the countryside now that the sun had set, and the moon was not yet up. He took the piece of stiff card from his pocket and rolled it into a cone, then yelled through it like a megaphone. He didn't expect to attract any attention. This was more of a test— and a way of reassuring himself. For a while he sat silently evaluating his situation. He wondered why the body he'd found was not near the barred gate. Why wasn't the man attempting to get out, or trying to summon help? Did he know of an alternative exit? Was he on his way toward that? But the fact that he had no identification suggested these documents had been intentionally removed. And that, of course, meant he'd been deliberately left in the mine. He'd been murdered.

Candrew's adrenalin level had subsided, and he felt exhausted. He sat down to rest, ate his only granola bar, and dozed off. He woke a couple of hours later. His back muscles were aching from the uncomfortable position in which he'd fallen asleep. He stretched, trying to loosen up. A bright moon had risen and there was some light near the mine entrance.

He made his way back into the larger passageway to see if he could find anything else that would be useful. He was in no hurry, and along the way rested on a smoother than average piece of rock to think things over and evaluate his situation. Turning off the cell phone light to save the battery, he sat in utter darkness. Unlike typical nighttime outdoors, when he looked up there was, of course, not a single star. Apart from some dripping water, the only sound was his breath. As his eyes continued to adjust to the darkness he slowly became aware that there was a very dim, almost imperceptible light, near the roof. When he clicked on the flashlight to establish the direction, he noticed the dust particles stirred up into the air from his walking were very slowly drifting upward—there must be an air current, he realized. And that current was moving the dust motes toward where he thought he'd seen the very dim light. Candrew climbed over broken pieces of rock in the direction of the light, then scrambled up a short curving slope of mostly loose stones. Luckily, a few large boulders were keeping most of them in place. At the highest point he discovered a small hole just a few inches across. Through it he could see some outside light, since there was now an almost-full moon.

He pushed aside several loose rocks, but the opening where the light shined in was blocked by one of the larger boulders. He tried pushing it. While it did rock, Candrew could not move it enough to roll it out of the way. He attempted one more time with no better success. Discouraged, he sat in silence—such complete silence that he could hear his heart beating. After a rest, he tried again, this time setting his back against the wall and pushing the boulder with his legs. Still no luck. As he sat depressed, he decided that what he needed was something to lever the rock—but he had no tools. That was when he remembered the metal pipes he'd seen back with the defunct mining equipment.

He scrambled down the slope and set off back along the passage-way. But the cell phone flashlight was flickering, the beam fading with hardly enough light to get him back to the equipment. When he was only halfway along the tunnel, the light died altogether. Candrew was left standing in complete darkness and total silence. Moving along in the darkness was not an option, it was too danger-ous. He cursed. And stood still. But a moment later he thought of the phone he'd taken from the dead man. Pulling it out of his coat pocket he flooded his pathway with light and continued toward the old equipment. With relief, he soon saw the metal debris ahead. He sorted through it carefully, pulling on several of the substantial rods, bars and pipes until he was able to break one loose. He paused for a moment's rest and then set about breaking a second rod free for insurance. Candrew dragged both bars back to the rubble slope that led up to the blocked opening. He left one of them at the bottom and hauled the other up to the top.

There was just enough room for him to squeeze to one side of the big boulder and wedge the metal pipe under it. It took all his strength to make the rock move, but eventually he got it going and it bounced and rumbled down the rocky slope to the lower passageway. The noise in the small space deafened him for a moment. But he was revived, physically and mentally, by the bright opening in front of him.

The opening he'd discovered, however, wasn't big enough to climb through. So Candrew set about pulling some of the broken rock fragments out of the way and sent them rolling down the slope, crashing into the darkness. Others he pushed out through the gap, letting them tumble down the hill outside. Finally, exhausted but elated, he had a hole big enough to crawl through.

He had his escape route.

CHAPTER 13

CANDREW CRAWLED OUT THROUGH the narrow gap, tearing his jacket and getting multiple scratches along the way. For a moment he sat panting, his eyes adjusting to the bright light, gazing across the countryside. It was just after dawn and the distant hills were mere silhouettes. Usually he liked early morning, but not now, with the prospect of an unpredictable hike and the threat of a bleak day.

The hole that had provided his escape route from the mine was halfway up a fairly steep hillside. Candrew started to scramble down the scree, sending a cascade of pebbles, and a few larger rocks, rolling ahead of him. He was sliding most of the way, the dust making him cough. He wished he had the clambering skills of a mountain goat. Eventually he got to the bottom of the hill where the flat plain stretched away into the distance. He sat recovering, staring around, trying to decide which way to attempt a hike out. There were no well-defined trails among the boulders, so he made an arbitrary decision to go around the hill to his left, through the stunted bushes and gnarled junipers.

Candrew headed roughly south, the sun rising in a wash of golden light over his left shoulder, casting long shadows. It was bitterly cold and he turned up the collar of his thin jacket against the chill wind. There were no houses, roads, or other obvious signs of civilization, and he staggered along through the brush for at least an hour. Hungry and very thirsty, his tongue was swollen, and swallowing was difficult. He was shaking and 'running on empty'—except that he wasn't running, he was *staggering* along. He'd heard somewhere that you could survive seventy-two hours without water—not a pleasant seventy-two hours, to be sure.

Although not overweight or unfit, Candrew had never been much of an athlete. Now, tired and thirsty, he made his way with wobbling steps toward some large boulders at the base of a small cliff to rest and shelter from the wind. He wrapped his arms around his legs and drew his knees up to his chin trying to get warm. Eyes closed, he sat shivering for several minutes. He was stressed, and worried by the fact he hadn't seen anyone who might help him. As he crouched on the large boulder, he glanced down and noticed some whitish material in a shadowed crack among the rocks. He wasn't thinking too clearly, but it slowly dawned on him that it was ice—compacted snow. He picked up a large pebble and used it to break off a handful of ice slivers from the packed fissure and sucked them into his mouth. The frigid liquid trickled down his dry throat. Wonderful. He grabbed several more handfuls.

Much revived by his rest, and having had the melted snow to drink, he stamped his feet against the cold and continued south. Without gloves his hands were freezing, not helped by the lumps of ice he'd broken off. As he trudged along, he saw patches of color in the distance—early Spring flowers lit by the rising sun. But there was one spot of bright yellow that caught his eye because it was moving. He stood still and peered at it, then realized it was a district school bus. He made his way as fast as he could to where the bus was headed and waved. Relieved when he saw the bus stopping, he hurried toward it. Speaking hoarsely, he asked if he could be taken into town.

Unsmiling, the bus driver looked him over with suspicion. Candrew's clothes were dusty and ripped in several places, his shoes caked with mud, his face dirty, and his hair disheveled. He had no back pack.

"You're a long way from anywhere," the driver probed. "Your car break down?"

"No. I lost my way out here." Candrew was in no mood for a lengthy explanation and the driver apparently didn't have time for details.

The man behind the wheel continued carefully evaluating him. Finally, he said reluctantly, "Okay. Jump in." He clearly wanted to keep an eye on Candrew and told him, "Take one of the front seats."

Candrew scrambled up the metal steps, the school kids watching, first in silence, then with giggling laughter. He sat on one of the front seats, glad to relax—and be warm.

"Where do you want to be dropped off?" the driver turned and asked.

"Any one of the restaurants in town would be fine. I'm hungry, not fussy."

"There's a couple of eateries. I like the café down south."

"Okay. That'll be fine. Just let me off there."

The bus driver made several stops to pick up more kids, and they all eyed Candrew with curiosity as they struggled up the bus steps with their book-laden packs. After half an hour, most of the time with Candrew asleep, the school bus arrived in town and the driver pulled up in front of his favorite café. With Candrew still dozing, the driver woke him, "We've arrived."

"Thanks for the ride," Candrew blinked and said sincerely. "I really appreciate you saving me from that tricky situation."

"No problem. You going to be okay now?" he asked.

"Yeah. I'll be fine," He clambered down the steps, the children pushing forward, enthralled, watching him leave. One older boy pointed, mumbled something, and grinned. The little blonde girl beside him laughed, waved, and shouted, "Bye."

Apart from three elderly men in a corner booth, the restaurant was deserted. Candrew chose a seat at one of the tables by the window and picked up the menu. Before he had a chance to scan it, the waitress came over. Tall and slim with dark hair and glasses, she was twenty years old, give or take, and probably a student at the local Community College. "Coffee?" she asked.

"Sure. Water as well, please."

When she brought the drinks, Candrew ordered sausages, a couple of eggs over easy, hash browns, and toast. , He was ravenous and eager to eat. Tired and puzzled, he sat drinking his coffee and watched the scattered traffic out the window. When the food arrived, he set about it with enthusiasm, quickly emptying his plate. He broke open a small plastic container of berry jam and smeared it on his toast. The young woman returned and topped off his coffee cup. Satiated, he pushed back his chair, relaxed, and sipped the hot coffee.

Later, when the waitress brought his bill, she asked, "Anything else, sir?"

"Yeah. Can you tell me where the police station is?"

She seemed surprised he wanted to know that. "Well, the local office is about four blocks up the road," she said. "Go out our main door, and turn right."

"Thanks." Candrew paid the bill, tipped her generously, and set out toward the office.

Candrew found the police headquarters with no trouble. He went in and was greeted by an overweight woman with inappropriate long turquoise nails, tinted glasses and cropped brown hair. "What you need, hon?"

When he replied, "I want to report a murder, as well as an attempted murder," she was clearly unnerved by the seriousness of the request.

There was a short silence. "Hold on," she said, and disappeared into a back room.

After several minutes a uniformed officer appeared, straightening his tie and pushing back strands of unruly hair. "What can I do for you, sir?"

Candrew started to explain that he'd been deliberately locked in an abandoned mine where there was a dead body. The officer stared and raised his hand to stop him from talking. "Come on into my office," he said.

Inside, he moved a half empty coffee cup and a hunting magazine off the desk and gestured to the chair opposite. A police radio squawked on a side bench.

Candrew sat in front of the desk, starting to give more details. Before he got far with his descriptions, he was interrupted by the cop. Serious and officious, he wanted to know, "Why were you at that deserted mine? What were *you* doing there?"

Candrew outlined his interest in the mineral veins. "I was going to see if there were any big crystals and . . ."

"So, you a prospector?" He peered at Candrew's disheveled appearance which seemed to him to fit.

"No. I'm a geology professor."

The cop smiled. In college he'd seen more than one eccentric academic. He asked. "How did you get to that deserted old mine?"

"I got taken there by a guy in a pickup truck." He hesitated. "He didn't speak very good English. And he didn't talk much. He was from Ecuador."

The cop frowned. "Really? How did you know that?" Before Candrew could elaborate, he said, "Couldn't he have been from Peru, Columbia, or somewhere else in South America?"

"Well, he told me himself that he was from Ecuador, although he did say he'd worked in the tin mining industry in Bolivia."

"You get the license plate number for the truck he was driving?"

"No. Sorry. I think it might have had an Arizona plate."

The police officer slid open a desk drawer and pulled out a yellow legal pad. He searched around and grabbed a ball point pen, then clicked it open but didn't write anything down. "This body you say you found, it look like an accident?" he asked. "Any blood? Weapons?"

"No," Candrew said. "I didn't notice any injuries." He thought about that. "But you have to remember it was quite dark and I only had a cell phone flashlight. I couldn't do a detailed exam."

"You know the dead man?"

"I'd never seen him before. But again, I need to stress the lighting was pretty bad."

Candrew answered all the policeman's questions honestly and in detail. He explained how he happened to end up locked in the mine. Eventually, the policeman appeared to be convinced by his consistent account.

The cop got up and remained standing, shifting his weight from one foot to the other. "This mine you were trapped in, where was that? You know the location?"

"It was quite a way west of here. I was lucky to flag down the school bus and get a ride into town. I'm sure the driver could tell you where he picked me up. But I'd already hiked for a couple of hours before getting that ride. I'd guess that would be about four or five miles." Pausing for a moment, Candrew added, "I remember the early-morning sun being off to my left, so I must have been headed pretty much due south."

The officer went over to an old wooden file cabinet and from the bottom drawer took out a handful of folded maps. He sorted through them and pulled one out. Unfolding it on his desk, he smoothed it with his hands. "Here's our burg," he pointed. "And the road the school bus that picked you up would normally take is along here." He pointed again. Turning to Candrew, he said, "You remember where you got on, how long you spent on the bus?"

"No, not really. I was pretty tired, dozed most of the way. I guess somewhere around half hour, three-quarters maybe."

There was silence while the officer studied the map. "That would put you somewhere around here." He indicated an area on the map that had shading showing where there were hills or mountains. "I'm no expert on that part of the state, but I've been told there are some old mines out there. I've got a friend at church who collects minerals. He told me Search and Rescue has had to go out there more than once to rescue an amateur prospector or two who'd gotten lost." He studied the map. "That whole area is outside our jurisdiction. I'll need to have all your information. I'll get that over to the other office and those guys can follow up." He pushed the yellow pad across the desk and handed Candrew the ball point pen. "I'm sure they'll want an in-person interview. Hear all the details first hand. But they'll probably drive up to the university."

Candrew completed his contact information and presented his driver's license and university ID to confirm the numbers he'd written down.

"Thanks." The cop nodded. "Anything we can do for you right now, Dr. Nor?"

Candrew told him that he'd parked his car in downtown Albuquerque. "I need to get back there."

"Not a problem," the policeman said, now more cooperative. "If you can wait a while, I'll get Ken to give you a ride up to the Duke City. He has to go up there anyway."

"Thanks. That'll be great."

"You want coffee while you wait?"

"No. But I'd like some water." He was still feeling a bit dehydrated. "Oh, and can I get my cell phone charged?" As Candrew was asking that, he realized he had the dead man's phone in his pocket. He told the police officer, and handed it over. "I'm sure it'll give you some idea who he was."

"Great. That could be real helpful." He smiled. "Those cyberjocks in our central office are usually able to tease out an amazing amount of information."

A couple of hours later Candrew was dropped off at his Ford Explorer in the motel parking lot in Albuquerque. Tired but well fed, he sat in the SUV with the engine running and dozed for half an hour. Refreshed, he drove over to I-25 North and headed home. He passed the exit to Bernalillo, the northbound interstate narrowed to two lanes, and the traffic thinned.

As he got closer to Santa Fe, with the Sangre de Christos to the east and the Jemez Mountains to the west, he glanced over at the outlines of the Cerrillos Hills. He remembered Judy telling him that this had been an old mining area, mainly for lead. He also knew that the Ortiz Mountains behind them had produced some gold. But he'd never read anything about diamonds being found in either of those places.

Candrew had plenty of time to think about everything that had happened as he drove north. He wasn't quite sure what to do next, and wondered how the police would handle his entrapment and discovery of a dead body. The main issue was to identify the people responsible and, of course, identify the corpse he'd found—Who was he? How was he murdered? Why was he there? And how did he get trapped?

Now that he'd told the police about finding the dead man, he hoped they'd be able to resolve all these issues.

But Candrew was left with the questions that concerned him most—why was he deliberately locked in the mine? What was so special about him that they felt it important to do that? And was he trapped by the same group that shut in the dead man he'd stumbled on? And just what was the role of Raven, the Navajo, and the two students from his university. After all, they were the ones who'd suggested he go to the mine, and they knew the truck driver.

The light was fading as he turned into the driveway, happy to be home. His cat and dog were also happy to have him back. Candrew was more tired than hungry and didn't bother to cook an evening meal. He just stood in the kitchen eating a chunk of cheese with some crusty bread. He poured himself a generous scotch. Glad to be out of his ripped and dirty clothes, he showered, watched television for half an hour, then went to bed early.

CHAPTER 14

CANDREW SLEPT SOUNDLY AND got up late—too late. He quickly fed Chile and Pixel, downed some juice, and ate a banana. He had to hustle to get to the university on time for his Tuesday morning class. Once in his office, he reached over and grabbed the three-ring binder with the semester's course notes and rushed down to the classroom.

After class, two students who had followed him up from the lecture room came into his office. They had questions about topics he'd covered, and wanted more detailed explanations.

"It's all pretty well dealt with in your text," Candrew said, and flipped through his own copy, giving them the relevant page numbers. "Take a look at the two figures, and the graph on the following page." He pulled a journal from the issues on his bookshelf and handed it to one of them. "Here's another useful article you should read. And make sure I get it back."

The students left and Candrew slumped into his padded chair by the window. While students and teaching had demanded his immediate attention, his thoughts inevitably went back to being deliberately trapped in the mine, and how he'd managed to escape. But he also recalled that on the day he'd visited the diatreme he'd stumbled on an excavated cavity, one he was sure was a diamond mining operation. That reminded him that he had a chunk of that kimberlite in his car. He also had sand samples he'd collected from the arroyo to see if they contained indicator minerals.

Candrew hurried down to the parking lot and retrieved the backpack from his Ford Explorer. Heavy with the rock samples he'd collected, he hauled it to the lab for Judy. When he pushed open the door, she was seated at a desk working on the annual report to one of their funding agencies.

"You did such a good job separating diamond indicator minerals last time, I've brought you some more sand samples." Candrew laughed and she grimaced.

"Okay, but don't expect such a fast turnaround," she said. "I used up all the heavy liquid. You know, that foul-smelling iodine compound." She wrinkled up her nose at the memory. "We're going to have to order more."

"Not a problem," Candrew said. "I'll make sure we get a new supply, although it'll probably take a week or more to get here."

Judy poured coffee, and he gave her an abbreviated account of his eventful couple of days.

She shook her head finding it hard to believe what she'd just been told. "It looks as though diamonds around here have a sinister aspect."

Half an hour later, Candrew was back in his office. He phoned Renata and told her everything that had happened, including a quick description of the excavated space in the kimberlite pipe. After describing Raven, the Navajo, he told her that two university students had also turned up at the excavated passage. He said he'd followed Raven's advice to explore an old mine, but that was where he'd gotten trapped, and where he'd found the dead body.

"That's incredible," she said, clearly amazed. "You're lucky you were able to find a way out. Nobody had any idea you were there. You could have been left to die in that mine."

Candrew knew that had been a real possibility. "Come on over for dinner and I'll fill you in on all the details." He chuckled and said, "It'll be a pretty casual meal. No Cornish pasties."

"Don't worry," she said. "I'll bring a dessert."

Renata got to Candrew's house in late afternoon. They poured drinks and sat out on the patio. Although quite cool, it was warm enough sitting in direct sunlight. The Spring-time sun set early and a few clouds were blowing in from the west. They chatted for forty-five minutes, however, until it became too cold to be comfortable, then moved inside with Chile tagging along.

"You ready to eat?" Candrew asked.

Renata smiled. "Sure. Cold weather always makes me hungry."

Candrew retrieved a couple of frozen dinners from the freezer and slid them into the microwave oven. The particular East Indian dish was one of his bachelor favorites. He took two pieces of *nan* flat bread to go with the chicken tandoori he was heating, and got a jar of mango chutney out of the cupboard.

While Candrew was busy doing all this, Renata said, "You want to open another bottle of wine?"

"I think beer would go better with the Indian curry," he said. "There's half a dozen bottles in the fridge."

The microwave chirped, letting them know it had pumped energy into their frozen meals. Candrew and Renata loaded their plates and took them into the dining room. As they sat eating and drinking their beer, Chile lay expectantly under the table. He'd curled up with his head on Renata's foot and she stroked him behind the ears.

"So, why did you let them take you to the mine?" Renata asked. She pushed back her long hair and smiled sympathetically. "Part of your fascination with diamonds?"

"Indirectly." Candrew drank more beer, hesitated, then explained. "I was told that the old mine shaft had penetrated a kimberlite pipe. As well as looking for attractive crystals, I was planning to search for indicator minerals."

She frowned. "Those the diopsides and red garnets you told me about? Right?"

He grinned. "You've got a good memory."

"Well, did you find any of them in the mine?" she asked.

"I didn't even look." Candrew smiled ruefully, shaking his head. "I was much too busy trying to get myself out of there—and staying alive, not like the guy whose body I found."

When they'd been sitting on the patio, Candrew had told her most of the details of being trapped in the mine. He explained how lucky he'd been to find some old equipment and the way he'd used a rod to lever a big boulder out of the way. But he stressed that his most significant discovery had definitely been the body of the dead man.

"Remember my telling you about the body in the mine?" he said. "The one I searched to see if he had a working phone?"

"Yes, but you told me you didn't find anything else useful, except maybe that piece of card you were going to try and use as a megaphone."

"Right." Candrew got up and went over to the side table. "Here it is, the one hidden in the man's inside pocket." He handed Renata the stiff paper.

She peered at it, then turned the card over and studied it carefully. It was roughly deckled on three sides, but cleanly cut on the fourth. "This certainly appears to be an old map. Looks as though it's been sliced with a razor out of some manuscript volume," she said, examining it again. "I've heard of people cutting pages out of antique manuscripts, usually the illustrations, and then selling them to make a few bucks—or in some cases, a lot of bucks!" She perused the map in detail. "Since this guy still had the map in his pocket, it seems likely he intended to hang on to it," she said. "Which, of course, meant he was keeping it for its information content. Do you suppose he was interested in tracking down some rich mine location?"

"Possible, I guess, but unlikely. A rich mine would probably have been completely worked out by now. Nothing of value left."

There was silence for a moment while they ate, drank, and thought about that. Chile sat with his quizzical look, ever hopeful for a handout.

"How about those 'indicator minerals' that show diamonds might be present," Renata asked. "Could he have been looking for those?"

"Probably not. I didn't see any of the dark kimberlite rock in the mine, but then, I only had a chance for a superficial look. I made it through very few of the tunnels—I was pretty distracted finding a corpse, and then desperately trying to discover a way out."

"I don't know what minerals he may have been searching for," Candrew said. "Although he didn't have any rock samples with him when I searched the body. And there was no backpack. I guess whoever dumped him in the mineshaft could have taken them. It may well have been the motive for his murder. Again, pure speculation." He paused for a moment. "But I'm fairly certain his murder wasn't a simple robbery."

"What makes you think that?"

"Well, he was still wearing an expensive watch. Also, he had a large sand-cast, silver Navajo belt buckle. Both of those would have been easy to carry away and could be quite valuable."

"That's interesting. So he doesn't seem to have been an impoverished prospector."

"No. And the other thing he had was a cell phone," Candrew said. "It was really helpful for me as a flashlight."

"You were lucky with that."

"I certainly was. My own phone went dead, and I had to rely on his." He sipped his beer, thinking about how fortunate he'd been. "I left the phone with the police and their geeks are going to see what information they can recover."

"Really? It'll be intriguing to see what they find. Hopefully it'll let them figure out who the man was, and maybe why he was there."

After more beer and some silence, Candrew said, "One possibility is that the dead man had been a mineral collector. High quality specimens aren't common and they sell for a lot of money."

"Nothing new." Renata laughed. "Your human ancestors have been doing that for a hundred thousand years."

Candrew raised his eyebrows, puzzled. "They have?"

"A colleague of mine was at a conference and one of the speakers reported a cache of, quote, *non-utilitarian objects*. It was a group of mostly large calcite crystals with nice cleavage surfaces. That was in the Kalihari of southern Africa." She laughed. "Probably the World's first mineral collection."

Candrew nodded to confirm his interest, then paused while Renata used her *nan* bread to mop up the last of her tandoori. They both drank more beer.

Candrew suggested, "There's one more possibility for the mine victim."

"What's that?"

"He may have been a treasure hunter. You know, looking for some buried loot, some conquistador hoard."

"Interesting idea," Renata said. "There's certainly no shortage of rumors about lost treasure out in the desert southwest. Especially those Superstition Mountains in Arizona."

"And it doesn't have to be gold, or even silver doubloons. Spanish armor, or an antique musket, could sell for quite a bit."

"If some other searcher thought your dead man had found a lost hoard, they could have simply used the mine as an easy way to get rid of him. Just shut him in and left him to die."

"Maybe," Candrew speculated. "Though that seems unlikely from the way I found him, just lying there. But there's another, alternative scenario."

"There is?" He'd piqued Renata's interest.

"A rival group could have been involved and poisoned him somewhere else and then dumped his body in the mine." Candrew thought more about that. "They might have been hoping he'd never be found—just be written off as another prospector lost in the mountains. To be sure of that, they'd removed all identification."

"I guess that could have been what happened. I'm sure the police will have an autopsy done. That'll show any poison."

It was quiet for a few minutes as they thought through all the options. Then Candrew wondered aloud, "Why me? Why lock me in a deserted mine? I hadn't found any gold bullion—or even a rich mineral vein."

"Can't answer that one," Renata said. Then she suggested, "But you have become very knowledgeable about possible diamond locations out here in the West. You found that kimberlite mine which seems as if it's being explored for diamonds. From what you've said, it was worked surreptitiously. Maybe they didn't want any information getting out. That information could have been quite valuable—makes you a competitor."

She looked at the map again. "This does seem to be mostly topographic," she said. "You know, mountains and rivers rather than mine tunnels. Geographic. To me it appears more like a treasure hunter's map than a miner's underground directory."

Candrew sidled up, looked at it with her, and agreed.

She flipped it over, but the back was blank. "You need to take this to Bill Archuleta in the university library," she said. "He's pretty knowledgeable about these sorts of things."

"That's a good suggestion." Candrew gulped the last of his beer and finished his Indian tandoori. "It may even provide some clues as to who the dead man was, and what he was doing in the mine."

Together they brought their empty dinner plates to the kitchen, and Renata sliced the apricot pie that was her contribution to the meal.

"You want ice cream with that?" Candrew asked.

"Yeah, sure," she said, and he got the carton from the fridge.

"Don't eat too much," Renata joked. "Make sure you've got a good appetite for lunch tomorrow."

Candrew frowned and rocked his head to one side in a mute question.

"We're invited to lunch with the Pengellys. Remember?"

"No. I'd forgotten. Lucky, you've reminded me."

CHAPTER 15

Tenby Library, one of the original buildings on the University of Northern New Mexico campus, formed an entire side of the central plaza. The next morning Candrew went up its broad flight of stone steps and through the neo-Georgian entrance. He told the student manning the information desk that he had an appointment with one of the staff members, and she picked up the phone and called. After a few minutes Bill Archuleta, the university librarian for Special Collections, came down the stairway and introduced himself. He was of medium height, tubby with a shock of unruly dark hair, and rather formally dressed in a checked shirt and tie with a sport jacket. They went up to his spacious, carpeted office on the second floor, there a substantial antique mahogany desk had a large, high-tech computer monitor on one end.

'*Ancient and modern*' Candrew thought—and wondered which category his map would be in.

For a few minutes Bill silently studied the map Candrew gave him. Frowning, he said, "Since the edges are deckled, except for the one that's clean-cut, it looks as though it's been sliced out of a book with a razor."

"I'm no expert, but that's what it seemed to me," Candrew said. "Which is why I'm bringing it to you, to see if you might know where it was cut from."

"Where did you get it?" Bill asked. "You buy it?"

"No." Candrew hesitated, then gave an abbreviated version of his being trapped in an old mine and stumbling on the dead body.

"That's quite a story." Bill looked at the map again, then produced a small hand lens and studied it in detail. "To my knowledge this has not been reported stolen." He frowned, peering at the map again. "But libraries tend to keep quiet about theft and don't want word of their lax security to get out and deter potential donors from donating." He stroked his chin for a moment, thought about that, then said, "It's more likely that they're not aware a single page has been stolen from one of their manuscript volumes. We don't have anything like this in our collection. It's pretty specialized—and quite rare. I'm sorry it's been damaged. Such cultural theft is inexcusable."

Bill pushed his hands back though the bushy hair draping across his forehead. "You should check with *MINEx*, the Canadian mining company based in Calgary. Over the years they've acquired an extensive collection of old maps showing mining locations, as well as other historical aspects of the mining industry." He grinned, "It's become quite a hobby for their CEO, Dr. Chris Donnington. He'd certainly want to know if one of their manuscripts has been damaged, or part of it stolen. And I'm sure he'd like to see this map." He handed it back to Candrew. "He may even recognize it."

As Candrew got up to leave, Bill said, "If I were you, I'd contact Murray O'Connor. He's at the MINEx office in Calgary and coordinates their map holdings. Tell him I told you to call. I know him quite well." Bill hesitated, then added, "And if it's not part of their collection, he may know who had the original. Collectors of old mining maps are a rather close and exotic community. Most people know each other—and their holdings."

Candrew went back to his office and had spent twenty minutes on line Googling 'MINEx', which he found was *Mapleleaf International Exploration.*

His cell phone chirped. It was Renata letting him know she was down in the parking lot and ready to drive them to the Pengellys' for lunch. On the way, Candrew told her he'd just gotten back from visiting Archuleta in the library and how he'd been very helpful. "I really appreciate you suggesting I go see him. He recommended a map specialist at a company called MINEx in Canada. I can't wait to follow up and contact that guy."

Allison, Wilfred Pengelly's wife, met them at the door, welcomed them in, and took their coats. The Pengellys' home always had a warm and welcoming feel. A fire was burning in the main room, and there were large, modern windows with great views toward the mountains. A tiled floor and round beams—'vigas'—kept a western feel that was enhanced by Navajo rugs.

Wilfred came and greeted them, "Good to see you both. I hope you're ready for a social meal. I've invited a couple of students from the department. They're the only two women in our graduate program. Darlene is just finishing her Ph. D. with me. She's been invaluable in the lab." He introduced Darlene who was above average height, solidly built with auburn hair cut short. She smiled and shook hands with Candrew. "And Katie is starting a Masters degree," he said. She was shorter and blonde, and apparently less sure of herself. She just nodded.

They all moved into the living room and sat around the fireplace chatting while Allison was busy in the kitchen. After a while she let them know lunch was ready, calling out, "We're going to have fish."

Wilfred laughed, "But I bet you've never had fish served like this before."

There was an expectant silence as they moved into the dining room and pulled their chairs up to the table. Allison brought in the hot dish. It was a circular pastry with half a dozen fish heads sticking up through it, their glassy eyes looking toward the sky.

"*Stargazy pie*," she said, looking around and grinning at their surprised reaction.

"Wow. I've never seen anything like that," Renata said. "It's amazing."

"What do you all want to drink?" Wilfred asked. "Traditionally with this it would be shandy. That's a mix of half beer and what you Yanks call *Seven-Up*."

"Sounds good to me," Candrew said. The rest agreed and Wilfred disappeared into the kitchen.

Allison came back with dishes of mushy peas, mashed parsnips and boiled potatoes.

With shandies handed around the table, Wilfred said, "There's a bit of history here. A couple hundred years ago, around Christmas time, the weather off the Cornish coast was so bad the fishermen couldn't put to sea and people were starving. Then one brave sole did venture out, got a great haul, and saved the townsfolk. That's when stargazy pie was first made. The fish were pilchards, a sort of very big sardine."

"And the fishing port on the south coast was *Mousehole*," Allison said. "Although the locals pronounce it '*Mowsle*.'"

They all agreed that the fish pie—the *stargazy pie*—was excellent.

After the leisurely meal, Darleen helped Allison clear away the dishes. As she came back from the kitchen, she pointed to a painting on the side wall beside the window. "I really like that painting, especially its decorated metal frame."

"Yeah. The frame is tin," Allison said, smiling. "It fits well with our Cornish heritage, although they didn't do anything like this sort of work. This is Hispanic." She grinned, "The Cornish probably used most of their tin for cider tankards."

Allison went on to explain, "This particular piece is quite old. See, it has a matt gray color—that shows it's got lead in it. They stopped adding it to tin in the seventies and substituted zinc. That combination looks much more silvery."

Wilfred broke in, laughing. "We ought to have bronze statues around here as well. Historically—and I mean going back to the Phoenicians—a lot of tin mined in Cornwall ended up in Cyprus where it was mixed with copper to make bronze. And that bronze provided the material for Greek statues."

"That's interesting," Katie said. "I didn't know that."

"When the Cornish tin industry collapsed in the eighteen hundreds, the miners themselves went worldwide." He seemed pleased with the role that Cornwall had played in world history. "You know what they say—a mine is a hole in the ground with a Cornishman at the bottom."

Allison smiled politely. "That's the Cornishmen who didn't become smugglers or pirates." She disappeared into the kitchen and came back with a large hand-thrown ceramic platter loaded with scones. "Dessert. And another Cornish tradition," she said. "These scones go with jam and then you top it off with clotted cream."

Conversation rambled on, much of it centered on the university. Renata was aware there were only a couple of women in the graduate program. She was interested to know what opportunities a woman with a Ph. D. would have in the rather macho mining industry. She asked Darleen, "What are your plans after you graduate? You know what you're going to do?"

"I'd like to teach," she said. "But I'm sure that's a long shot. There aren't too many faculty positions and I don't have any industrial experience." She shook her head regretfully.

"And you, Katie," Candrew asked, "How did you get interested in ore minerals?"

"Well, my father is a geologist, but I was a political science major," she said. "I had to have a science elective and took freshman geology. Got hooked!" Katie chuckled.

Darleen turned to Allison and asked, "So, how do you spend your time when Dr. Pengelly's at the university teaching us all about mining?"

"Well, I run a house for one thing. That's time consuming—and an underrated chore. But I do occasionally find time to paint."

"Plein aire?"

"Sometimes. But I paint slowly, and outdoors the light keeps changing—especially if there are clouds blowing over—and so, I take photos to grab an instant in time. Actually, I take a whole series of photos and then use them indoors. Here, I'll show you."

She guided the two students down the passage to the back room that was her painting area. Renata, who'd talked to her about artwork on the last visit, followed along. In the studio Allison slipped on her reading glasses and showed them the painting she was working on. "I only paint in acrylics, and mainly do fairly realistic landscapes." She pointed to several paintings pinned up on the wall. "There's my last few efforts."

As the two graduate students looked at her latest efforts, Allison turned to Renata and said, "I feel so guilty. It was my last sketch, the one showing a new pile of mine debris, that persuaded Candrew to go back to the outcrops. And then he got tricked into the old mine."

"But he did escape." Renata said, trying to reassure her.

Wilfred and Candrew had stayed in the dining room chatting. Wilfred leaned over to Candrew "I was stunned when Allison told me about your bad luck in the mine."

"Amazing to discover a dead body, but then lucky to escape from the mine. I'm sure I haven't heard the last of all this. In fact, the police will be coming to interview me in the next few days." There was a moment's silence and Candrew said, "Something that might interest you, I found the dead man had a map in his inside pocket. Earlier today I showed it to Archuleta in our library. He was really helpful and gave me a contact in a company called MINEx in Canada."

"MINEx. Yeah, I'm familiar with them. There's several big copper projects of theirs active in Arizona. They've hired a few of our graduates. And a couple of their geologists have been guest lecturers in our seminar series."

"I'm hoping they can tell me about that map. It's clearly old and most likely stolen. It might help to figure out who the dead man was, and what he was doing underground."

"There was another rather peculiar aspect to my field trip," Candrew said. "I made it up to the top of one of the other kimberlite outcrops and collected samples. On the way down I discovered a narrow tunnel that led into a large excavated chamber. That, and the fresh debris pile outside, made me realize this was a working mine. And in a kimberlite pipe, that means one thing—diamonds."

"You're right. How interesting."

"But the really interesting thing was what greeted me when I came out. Standing at the entrance was a tall, dark-haired Navajo. He was quite aggressive, demanding to know what I was doing. But then came the surprise—Carlos, your Navajo student, and Brandon turned up."

"Really?" Wilfred said, surprised. "They were both at the Spring Break trip to the nearby kimberlite outcrop."

"Brandon explained to me that he was acting as a consultant for the Navajo."

"That's possible. He did some work with diamonds when he was on undergraduate at the University of Nevada. And he also spent a couple of years working for an exploration company before coming back to graduate school. So, he's had quite a bit of experience."

Candrew listened, not saying anything. It certainly explained why Brandon was older than most of the students in the mining department. Also, how he'd acquired his detailed knowledge of ore deposits.

"Is Brandon working for the Navajo just to get more experience?" Wilfred asked. "Or is he getting paid?"

"I've no idea," Candrew said.

"Well, he could certainly use the money. He's pretty hot on that Jessica Rylander and she's really well off."

CHAPTER 16

CANDREW'S WEEKS WERE STRUCTURED around his undergraduate classes. There was no flexibility as there was for research, writing, and his other academic activities. Today, Thursday, he was in the classroom a little before nine, talking to students, before lecturing. After the presentation he answered a few questions and then went back up to his office with the file of lecture notes and a pile of student assignments tucked under his arm.

A group of students milling around in the hallway outside Candrew's office quieted down and stepped aside to let two men through. The one wearing glasses was tall, lean and rather conventionally dressed in a brown suit. The other was shorter, overweight and in the uniform of a police officer. They checked the room number, and the shorter one leaned in and tapped on the open office door.

Candrew had been told that the homicide team investigating the body he'd found in the mine would be visiting the university to interview him. And they'd also want to ask questions about his entrapment.

"Welcome to campus, Gentlemen," he said. They shook hands in the doorway and the police presented their photo identifications. Candrew only glanced at them, not believing anyone would be appearing in his office impersonating a police officer.

The two men stepped into the office and sat down in the chairs facing Candrew's desk in front of the window. The one with glasses introduced himself as the detective assigned to the homicide case, and he introduced Officer Garcia who was working with him. "We're both part of the team carrying out the ongoing investigation to resolve the case of the corpse you discovered. We'll also be investigating your being locked in that same mine."

The rather serious and humorless detective started the questioning. "Can you please explain to us just what you were doing in that old mine? Why were you there?"

"As you know, I'm a geology professor," Candrew said. "so the chance to see a mine was exciting, even if it was no longer in operation. I had been told there were veins with large mineral crystals, as well as some unusual rock types." Candrew didn't say anything about the kimberlite that Raven had mentioned, although he did give them some additional background information.

"I take it then that you didn't know the dead man? You had no idea who he was?"

"That's right," Candrew said. "I'm sure I never met him while he was alive." He glanced at Officer Garcia who was sitting in silence. "Have you been able to identify the man?"

The question was left unanswered. "Tell us how you just happened to find a body, searched it, and took the cell phone." The detective stared at Candrew. "But you claim somebody had already taken everything else, like the driver's license, credit cards, and other personal items? What was your impression about that?"

Before he had time to answer, Officer Garcia said, "We only have your word that this is what actually happened."

"You accusing me of murder?" Candrew found that incredible.

Unsmiling, the uniformed policemen said, "Only checking the facts, sir, the possibilities."

"Well, when you get the time of death," Candrew said, "you'll find he died before I was locked in that mine. You can ask the people at the Duke City Motor Lodge where I stayed on Central Avenue. They'll give you the exact time when I left."

The detective nodded, then scribbled the name of the motel in his note book. "And after stumbling on the body," he probed, "in a mine with a barred and locked metal entrance, you just happened to find a way out? That right?"

"If I'd planned all this," Candrew snapped, "I certainly wouldn't have spent hours trudging across open country in freezing weather after I escaped. Ask the school-bus driver where he picked me up."

"We've already talked to him."

There was silence for a moment while the detective pondered the situation. Then he reached into his briefcase, pulled out a large manila envelope, and removed several photographs. He handed them to Candrew. All were nine-by-eleven glossy prints. "These were taken by the crime-scene techs," he said.

"Maybe the prints will jog your memory," the uniformed policeman said. "Help you recall some details."

The photos showed the man's body lying just as Candrew had found it. Several different camera angles had been used, and two of the images included a measuring tape for scale. Candrew looked up—the detective was watching his reaction. "The biggest difference," Candrew said, "is that I only had the dim light of an iPhone— and I didn't take any photos. But the body seems to be in the position I remember."

The crime-scene crew had obviously used a flash when they took the photos. It had brilliantly lit the walls of the mine as well as the area around the body. While Candrew's dim light had only shone on the ground and the lower part of the wall, now he could clearly see the rock wall from bottom to top. What grabbed his attention was a mineralized vein that cut diagonally across the wall.

He handed the photos back to the detective. "I don't have anything to add. The situation with the dead man looks pretty much the way I remember it."

"I see." The detective hesitated, then explained, "There was very little information on the body, but the cell phone you took from him will be helpful—now that we've gotten it back. Our technical people are still doing their thing. Identifying the body is a major aspect of our ongoing investigations."

Candrew had not mentioned the map he'd taken from the dead man's inner pocket. He'd kept that information to himself. *I probably should have turned it over to the police,* he thought. But he'd convinced himself they weren't likely to have experts on that sort of material. Better to wait and see if one of Bill Archuleta's MINEx friends with special knowledge had a chance to look at it. It did occur to him that keeping the map was withholding evidence—probably a crime of some sort. But he justified his action because he was doing it for a very good reason, one that might eventually help the police.

"How many days had the body been in the mine?" Candrew asked. "Any idea of the time of death?" He looked questioningly at the two men. "I suppose that will depend on finding out what caused his death. You any idea about that?"

Officer Garcia swiveled slightly in his chair and glared at Candrew, "We're the ones here to ask the questions. We interview *you.*"

"Okay." Candrew said, but asked, "You have a motive for the murder?"

"Motive?" The detective adjusted his tie and frowned. Leaning forward, he wanted to know, "Why would you be asking a question like that?"

"Remember, there was also an attempt on my life. I was locked up in that old mine. And with no food or water. You've got an attempted murder on your hands."

"Maybe." The detective was clearly not convinced. "For all we know, they could have come back and released you."

Candrew had to admit that was a possibility.

"As far as figuring out a motive for the homicide, we'll have to wait for all the information we're anticipating from the autopsy and get the Medical Examiner's final report," the detective said. "We're already following some leads." He didn't elaborate. "Also, we need the results of a detailed search of the mine. And, of course, the information from the iPhone."

Candrew realized that the detective and the police officer were doing a competent job in their questioning—irritating though it was. He hoped they would figure out that if he had any role in the homicide he certainly wouldn't have left the cell phone on the victim.

"I doubt the motive for murder was robbery," Candrew said. "When I found the body he was still wearing what looked like an expensive watch. And he still had his silver Navajo belt buckle. And the cell phone itself is not cheap. Anyway, I'm surprised whoever dumped his body there didn't take that, not to speak of all the information cached in it."

The detailed interrogation dragged on with a major emphasis on timing. They pressed Candrew to provide as much information as possible on the truck and its South American driver. The investigators were also interested in the man at the diatreme who had suggested Candrew visit the abandoned mine. The critical question was whether Raven knew the dead man and had any role in his murder.

The detective and the officer eventually decided that they'd gotten all the information they needed for the moment, but cautioned Candrew not to leave town.

"I'm not planning any long trips. If I do go, it'll only be for a day doing my field work research. I'll make sure the department secretary knows exactly where I will be."

"You just do that. We may have further questions."

Candrew escorted the two policemen to the door and watched them head down the passage to the elevator.

The few students still standing in the corridor seemed intrigued by police visiting one of their professors. They talked loudly enough to be sure Candrew would hear what they were saying.

Raising her voice, one student contended, "I've been told he was going to be arrested for giving way too many D grades, and not enough A's."

"And not to mention he assigned us term papers that took forever to write."

"He even makes us students, like, go out and collect our own rocks."

"The exams he gives expect far too much detail."

Candrew was amused. He always liked hearing students joking. But he did get up to close his door half-way. That was a compromise between having it sufficiently quiet to get some work done, and still being available to any student who genuinely needed him.

Candrew settled into his office and started to grade the pile of student papers that had been handed in. The office was a typical academic's lair with every horizontal surface cluttered with stacks of papers, folders, and books. And, of course, a few big chunks of rock. Although most professors liked to display their framed Ph. D. certificates, along with other degree information and awards from professional societies, Candrew was not that egotistical. The only thing hanging on the wall behind the crowded table was a framed map of the area where he'd done the field work for his doctorate.

His cell phone demanded attention and grading student assignments was interrupted. He hunted around and finally retrieved the phone from his briefcase under the table.

"Dr. Nor? This is Murray O'Connor with the *Mapleleaf International Exploration* company in Calgary. You probably know us better as *MINEx*. I got your message about the map you found."

"Thanks for returning my call."

"I checked with Chris Donnington, he's our CEO, and he says we could fly you up here. He'd like to see that map."

"Well, visiting certainly seems to be a good idea, though I will have to fit it in with my teaching schedule."

"We can work around that. As it turns out, one of our corporate jets will be coming up from Tucson on Monday. It's bringing some of our exploration people back to Calgary for a meeting. We can just detour into Santa Fe and pick you up—if that fits your schedule. And a return flight's not going to be a problem." After a moment's hesitation, he said. "I realize that this is all very short notice. I hope it won't complicate things for you."

"No. Not at all. I can make it on Monday. I don't have class that day." Candrew realized Wilfred Pengelly had some past dealings with MINEx in Arizona and would be intrigued to visit their company headquarters. Candrew asked, "Would it be possible to bring a colleague with me, another professor who's in the university's mining department?"

"I'm sure that won't be an issue." Murray was about to hang up, then said, "There is one more thing. You need to let us have your passport numbers."

"No problem," Candrew said. "I know mine is current. I'll check with Dr. Pengelly, who'll be coming with me." That was speculation on Candrew's part since he hadn't yet asked him.

"Make sure you have those documents with you when you arrive here in Calgary."

After dealing with a few more student papers, Candrew pushed back his chair and checked his watch: lunchtime. Hungry, and ready for a change of pace, he pulled on his jacket, and set out for the Faculty Lounge.

The usual crowd was ensconced at the corner table and, with their diverse viewpoints, were engaged in a typical heated discussion. Most likely either politics or sports, Candrew thought.

He sank into his chair and picked up the menu. The arguments at the far end of the table continued, but Ted Devereaux, sitting opposite him, leaned over and asked, "How's your diamond searching going? Find that big three-hundred carat, perfect gem yet?"

Before Candrew could say he'd not been that lucky, Arlan Dee broke in. "You need to concentrate in the area around Grants. Off Interstate Forty."

That seemed like strange advice. "Why Grants?"

"Because until recently they billed themselves as the carrot capital of the world." Joking, he was grinning broadly. "I know about carrots, but how much is a carat? I mean as a real weight, like ounces."

"Well, I don't know about ounces, but a carat is two hundred milligrams. Which means, of course, five carats is a gram."

"*Carat*? But that's a strange name for a weight," Ted said.

"*Ceratonia siliqua*," Lubie said laughing. He'd been listening to the conversation and joined in. "That's the biological name for the carob tree. It's common in the Middle East and the masses of individual seeds don't vary much. So they've been used as a weight reference for gems—a 'carat'—since the Middle Ages."

"Naming things is an intensely human activity," Candrew pointed out. "Not only do we name our kids, but also our boats, cars, even football teams."

Evelyn, the biology professor, had been drawn into the conversation. "Some names have been given as a put-down," she said. "Like when Sir Fred Hoyle called a competing theory for the origin of the universe '*The Big Bang*.' He intended that as a derogatory term, since Hoyle himself favored an unchanging, steady-state universe. But it's now the accepted term."

"And it's not just in science that happens," Ted said. "When Claude Monet first exhibited *Impression: Sunrise*, a critic branded him as an '*impressionist*,' not using that term as a compliment. And we all know how accepted that's become."

"*Gothic* is another example. It was used by the Italians as denigration of the northern architectural style, since in Italian it means *barbarian*."

After lunch, Candrew made his way back across the central plaza thinking about carats and other names. But before going up to his office, he decided he ought to visit Judy in the lab and see how much progress she was making with their research projects.

Judy was talking to one of the graduate students and showing him thin sections that had been sliced from some of the sandstones they were studying. "Cutting sections of rock that are only a fraction of a millimeter thick takes special equipment and skill," she'd told him. "We get ours cut professionally. Not cheap, but high quality." She glanced up as Candrew came into the lab.

The student briefly outlined his field project for Candrew, then left.

Judy laid out some of the maps showing areas where she had results. When they'd finished going over the data, Candrew got up to leave. On his way to the door, he told her he'd ordered the heavy liquid she was going to need for separating the indicator minerals from the sands he'd collected at the diatreme. "Should be here before too long," he told her. "It'll be enlightening to see what turns up with these new indicator minerals. See if we're close to a source of diamonds."

CHAPTER 17

EARLY FRIDAY MORNING CANDREW called Wilfred Pengelly and told him about the chance to fly up to the mining corporation in Calgary. Also, that the trip was tentatively set for Monday. Wilfred thought he could manage it, and after his contact with local MINEx geologists he was eager to visit their company's headquarters.

Candrew spent the rest of an uneventful day on campus grading papers, reading technical articles, and working on his manuscript. Late in the afternoon he drove home and put on clothes more appropriate for the Faculty Cocktail party scheduled for that evening. Suitably dressed, he drove over to Renata's.

She greeted him at the door with a hug, and, giggling, said, "Here, I've got a present for you."

Candrew didn't know what to expect and took the loosely-wrapped package from her. He stripped off the tissue paper and realized it was a T-shirt.

"I thought it would be appropriate," she said as he shook it out.

"Well, yes," Candrew said, grinning when he saw the image of a playing card—*The King of Diamonds!*

Candrew and Renata drove south from the university toward the home of the Vice-President for Academic Affairs. When Candrew told her about the police visit, she asked, joking, "They have enough evidence to lock you up?"

"No. But at one point in the interview it appeared as though they might be suspecting me of the murder."

"Really?" She sounded surprised.

"I could see their point," Candrew said. "I did find a man's body and claimed he was already dead. Then I'd searched the corpse saying all I found was an iPhone, even though his credit cards and other identifications were missing."

Renata turned toward him, listening, as he took the juniper-lined gravel side road that led to the Vice President's home.

"The detective questioned the fact that although I claimed to have been locked in the mine," he said, "I just happened to find a way out in a matter of hours."

"Well, that could certainly have given them a reason to become suspicious."

For several minutes they drove in silence as Candrew concentrated on avoiding the potholes in the twisting gravel road.

"One thing still puzzles me," he said. "That's the role of the people who locked me in the mine. It seems to me there are two possibilities. Either they didn't know there was a homicide victim in the mine, or, alternatively, they did know, but just planned to add me as other murder victim."

The Vice President lived in a contemporary house that sat on four acres—his 'ranch.' He hosted a faculty cocktail party once every semester, usually the week after Spring or Fall Break. As he explained, too many faculty were out of town during the semester break itself.

The VP was of medium height, had thinning grey hair, and wore glasses perched on a deeply-lined face. He greeted them, and the other guests, at the front door and ushered them all into the warmth of the house. "Plenty to eat and drink," he said, waving toward the tables loaded with food in the living and dining rooms. His wife was looking after those already there.

After years on the faculty, Candrew and Renata knew many of the people gathered for this social event. In the dining room, where there was a roaring log fire in the corner fireplace, they joined a group milling around the food and drinks. Renata poured herself some white wine and Candrew got a beer. They both nibbled the food.

Candrew always enjoyed the company of his academic colleagues with their unpredictable range of opinions. Hovering across the table was McKenzie-Burns from the astronomy department, one of the faculty members that Candrew knew. "Well, Candrew," he said peering over his glass of beer, "you have friends at NASA?"

"Why?" Candrew thought that a peculiar question.

"Because you need to get them to fly you to the 'ice planets.'"

"You mean Neptune and Uranus? Why would I want them to do that?"

"Then you could burrow down through the icy surface and dig up the diamonds." He laughed at Candrew's obvious confusion, since he clearly didn't understanding what he was getting at. "Experiments in Germany have shown that with the high pressures on those planets the carbon from methane gets converted into diamonds, big ones. Those scientists have estimated the crystals are about the size of a human. They're sinking down through the planet toward its core."

Candrew was intrigued. "Probably cost a hell of a lot more to go retrieve those diamonds than they'd be worth."

The physics prof standing beside them at the table, scotch in hand, had been listening to their conversation. "It would certainly be easier, and a lot cheaper, to make them in a lab here on earth. We wouldn't have to go to all the trouble of mining them." He was quick to point out

that most diamonds are already made synthetically. "But most are not of gem quality, of course," he said. "The majority are intended for use as abrasives."

While several of the faculty members knew about Candrew's current interest in diamonds, for most of those standing around with their plates of food, this was news.

An older overweight man, balding but with a fringe of white hair, quipped, "The one diamond I know anything about is the baseball diamond." He looked around the group, sipped his drink, and said, "A ticket to a game is the only thing associated with diamonds I can afford."

Beside him, a tall, slim man from the Music Department picked up on the conversation and chuckled. "Diamonds? That's my wife's interest," he said ruefully. Turning to Candrew he suggested, "You should take her along on your expeditions—she can spot a high-quality gem at fifty paces." Renata put her hands behind her back to hide her cubic zirconia ring.

A faculty member from the English department was cutting a slice of quiche. He paused the incision to tell Candrew he ought to read 'King Solomon's Mines.' "Might have some clues for you. After all, the explorer Quartermain, if I remember his name correctly, found diamonds the size of eggs." He drank some of his wine, then added a note of caution. "Be careful what sort of mining you get involved in. Stay away from any ores high in arsenic."

This was unexpected chemical information coming from a literature professor, and Candrew's face obviously showed his surprise.

The professor explained. "Vulcan, the god involved with mining and forging, is always shown as a cripple. That's because he'd been poisoned by arsenic in the ores he used. He suffered like many of the medieval miners down here on Earth."

"Good information," Candrew said. "I'll be careful."

Renata and Candrew refilled their glasses and moved into the adjacent living room where they chatted with colleagues. They were soon interrupted by the director of the Theater Department who loudly enthused about the coming Fall productions. Gushing, she told them about the stunning performances that were planned. Wildly extravert, she was overweight and busty with cropped dark brown hair. Candrew always thought she should be wearing a helmet with horns and singing in an opera—Brunhilde perhaps? Candrew and Renata were left with a wave of her hand as she headed to

refill her glass—not for the first time. Candrew smiled to himself—
It's not over 'til the fat lady sings.

As he turned back to the group, he was greeted by a member of
the Art Department who was also eager to let him know about an
upcoming show. This time, it was a sculpture opening.

"All modern materials, you know," he said, slurring slightly. "Res-
ins, Plexiglas, stainless steel, that sort of thing. Bent and sculpted
into novel and aesthetic forms."

Renata told him they usually went to Art Department openings
and would look forward to this new show. Even in the rather formal
setting of the VP's party the artist was wearing a black T-shirt and
paint-splattered jeans. He excused himself, saying, "I need a
smoke," and snuck out onto the back patio.

Renata left Candrew and went into the other room to talk to old
friends, and he headed to the bar to replenish his drink. He stood
next to the Dean of Arts and Sciences who was topping up his gin
with tonic, and dropping in ice cubes. The Dean was new to the university and Candrew had only met him once at a faculty committee
meeting. Candrew had heard that as a student he'd been an art history major before transferring to sociology. He seemed experienced
and competent, already becoming well respected.

"Dr. Nor. Right?"

"Yes. But 'Candrew' works just as well."

The Dean smiled at the informality. "I hear you're involved with
some geological research involving diamonds."

Candrew was surprised that he knew this. He was clearly tuned
in to the academic grapevine—a useful skill for an administrator.
"Yes, but mainly from a geological perspective." He grinned. "I'm
not planning to start mining."

The Dean nodded his understanding and sipped his gin-and-
tonic. "Aesthetically, I'm no fan of diamonds. Everything about
them is artificial."

Candrew was puzzled. He knew all the diamonds flashed around
in rings and earrings were natural, mined diamonds, not lab grown.

Seeing him perplexed, the Dean said, "What I mean by that, is they're not attractive when they're found in nature. They are all cut, faceted, polished, and nothing like the way they came out of the ground—not 'natural.' Personally, I much prefer natural minerals with their genuine crystal faces, the way they grew deep underground." He smiled. "And big."

Candrew was not quite sure what he meant.

"My hobby's collecting minerals," the Dean said. "So far that's been my main contact with your department. A couple of times I've been over to talk to Mark Kernfeld, the mineralogy prof. He's been helpful, though he's not a collector himself."

"Do you dig the minerals out yourself?" Candrew asked, thinking of the mine he'd been trapped in.

"Goodness, no." He laughed. "Both physically and technically, out of the question. I rely on the dealers."

Candrew believed him. Although not overweight, he was heavily built and clearly not athletic. Elegantly dressed, he wore thick horn-rimmed glasses and his hair was precisely cut. He didn't give the impression of an outdoorsy type.

"The highlight of my year is the Spring mineral show in Tucson," the Dean said. "That attracts dealers with minerals from every continent. To my knowledge, it's the biggest mineral, gem, and fossil show in the world." He sipped his gin-and-tonic again, apparently reminiscing. "You might want to talk to some of the dealers. Even if they're not in the diamond business, they would probably have useful information for you. A couple in particular come to mind."

The Den leaned against the drink table for a moment thinking about that. "Let's move to the food," he suggested, leading the way to the adjacent table. As he loaded his plate with carefully-selected items, he went back to the topic of dealers. "Up in southern Colorado there's a guy who trades mainly in Colorado minerals, but he's very well connected and knows what's going on. Has lots of associates and would be well worth a visit. You could drive up and back in a day." For a moment he munched on his bread roll with the smoked salmon and olives. "But the real star is Jay Wolverton in San Diego. Has some superb material—and prices to match! He's like the spider at the center of the web, he knows everything that's going on. He has a lot of prospectors working for him. They bring in some really incredible stuff." The Dean put down his plate, pulled out one of his business cards, and wrote contact information on the back. "I don't remember Wolverton's e-mail, but I'll send it to you."

Late that evening, after generous amounts of beer and wine, Candrew carefully drove Renata home. They sat in her kitchen drinking coffee and talking over the evening's events, especially the anecdotal stories of diamonds. He told her about the Dean's hobby as a mineral collector and the contacts he'd suggested.

Grinning, he said to Renata, "I hear this establishment serves a really special breakfast."

"True. Why do you ask?" She was smiling sweetly. "You do realize this is a *bed* and breakfast?"

"I certainly won't be working tomorrow, since it's Saturday. Staying overnight with you seems like a great way to start the weekend." He smiled at the thought.

They talked for a while, finished their coffee, then headed to the bedroom.

"And do you have a *Queen of Diamonds* sweat shirt?" he asked.

She leaned over and switched off the bedside lamp. "No. Just *Queen of Hearts*."

CHAPTER 18

EARLY MONDAY MORNING WAS quiet under a featureless, leaden-gray sky. It was cold with a few large snowflakes floating down. Candrew started his Ford *Explorer*, letting it warm up, while he went back into the house to get his down jacket and briefcase. He checked to see that he had a full tank of gas and drove to Wilfred Pengelly's house.

Wilfred threw his jacket onto the back seat of the car and clambered in. "I didn't expect weather like this until we got to Canada," he joked.

Candrew let the wipers sweep the wet snow off the windshield and then headed to Santa Fe for their flight to Calgary. They crossed the Rio Grande at Española.

A year earlier Candrew had gone to a History Department lecture on the New Mexico railroads. He glanced at Wilfred and asked, "You heard of the Chili Line?"

"Yeah, but I don't know much about it."

"It was a narrow gauge railroad that was supposed to haul people and freight from Antonito, Colorado to Santa Fe." For a moment he concentrated on driving. "But then because of a legal 'treaty,' the railway was stopped for ten years close to what is now Española. They finally got around to completing it to Santa Fe. That delay is why the town of Española developed here." Candrew laughed. "In the eighteen eighties a visitor described it as a 'raw and lawless place.'"

Candrew and Wilfred continued south out of Española and followed Route 285 to Santa Fe. At one spot Candrew pointed across the river to where the abandoned railroad bed of the *Chili Line* was still visible on the far side.

Fortunately, the weather had steadily improved, and in Santa Fe they took Airport Road west out to the airport. They drove past the crowded, temporary parking lot. The main terminal was a too-small pueblo revival building and was scheduled for a long overdue upgrade. Work had recently started.

A hundred yards further on, Candrew parked beside the "*Signature*" private aviation terminal. Inside, they let the woman behind the desk know they were expecting a plane coming in from Tucson. The efficient young woman, with short dark hair and long turquoise earrings, checked the computer. She told them, "It's on its way and estimated time of arrival is in thirty minutes."

Candrew told her his red Ford *Explorer* was outside and gave her the keys.

"We'll have it parked for you," she offered. "When do you expect to be returning?"

He said they were scheduled back late that evening.

"Tell the pilot to radio ahead and we'll have it waiting for you."

"Thanks."

The tiled waiting area had large, padded lounge chairs. Candrew and Wilfred poured coffee from the machine in the corner and settled down to wait. On schedule, the silver, twin jet *Challenger* with the *MINEx* logo on its tail landed, taxied and parked. The co-pilot came in to meet them.

As they walked out onto the concrete apron, Candrew was surprised to see Jessica Rylander, the student he'd met on the field trip to the diatreme. She was handing a bag and a small suitcase to one of the ground crew who loaded them into a twin-engine Beechcraft *King Air*. She noticed Candrew. "Hi professor," she said, smiling.

"I'm on my way out to San Diego. I didn't have time to go and see Mom and Dad at Spring Break." She smiled and nodded toward the aircraft. "Daddy's plane. At least I'll have some warm weather out there—and get to see the ocean. I miss that." Candrew wished her a safe flight as she turned, hurrying up the steps into the plane.

How the other half (half a percent?) lives, Candrew thought.

Wilfred and Candrew went up the steps and into the *Challenger*. As the co-pilot retracted the stairs and locked the door, he told them, "The weather forecast is good. We should have a smooth flight." Then he added, "A little over two hours. Make yourselves comfortable."

Candrew looked at the dozen wide-armed, generously-sized, leather seats and thought that shouldn't be a problem. He and Wilfred sat near the front on opposite sides of the aisle. Further back, a sofa on one side faced four seats around a table on the other. Two men and a woman were seated there. They raised their hands in greeting and the woman called out, "Welcome aboard."

The corporate jet taxied and took off to the south, banking west away from the Sangre de Christo mountains before heading north. Twenty minutes into the flight the woman from the back of the plane came up to get coffee. As she stirred creamer into the cup, she introduced herself, "I'm Marlene." Pointing to the two men at the back, she said, "Rex and Carl." She sipped her coffee, "We all work for MINEx. So what's bringing you up to the tundra?"

Candrew told her they were both professors at the University of Northern New Mexico. "I stumbled on an old map in an abandoned mine," he said. "When I talked to Murray O'Conner, he suggested I bring it up and show it to your CEO. Apparently, old maps are one of his interests."

"Yeah. Sure is."

"We're all geoscientists," Carl said. "We do all the high-tech stuff, but Donnington, our *jefé*, still has a soft spot for the old-time prospectors, their Indian legends—and their maps." "He seems convinced they might stumble onto something important," Rex explained. "But those guys deal in small stuff. Copper ore is our bread and butter in Arizona, and we move millions of tons. There's only a percent or two of copper and the minerals are hard to see—none of them spectacular or collectable."

"A colleague that collects minerals, told me several of the high-end dealers he met at the Tucson show rely on prospectors who poke around in old mines," Candrew said. Not for the first time, he wondered if the dead man he'd found at the mine had been involved in the trade in special minerals.

"You know who your friend talked to?" Carl asked.

"Well, there was one dealer up in Leadville, in Colorado." Marlene and the two men looked at each other, but they didn't seem to know who that might be. Candrew paused for a moment searching his memory. "And then there was someone out in San Diego called Jay Wolverton."

There was silence and Rex stared at Carl. "Stay away from him," he said. "And watch your back, he's pure trouble."

"I've never met him, or had business dealings," Carl said, "but his unsavory reputation is widely known. I heard he's cheated quite a few people." Grinning, he added, "And if I were you, I wouldn't be playing poker with him."

The rest of the flight to Calgary was uneventful and there was a limo waiting when they landed. The driver took them to a modern glass and steel building downtown, the office building that housed the headquarters of *MINEx*. He let them off at the front entrance and pointed inside to the bank of elevators in the lobby. "Take the one to floor seven," he instructed.

The elevator whisked them to the seventh floor where the doors slid smoothly open, leading onto a short hallway. It ended in frosted double glass doors. These bore the acronym "*MINEx*" and below that "*Mapleleaf InterNational Exploration*." Candrew and Wilfred entered into a plushly-furnished reception area where they were expected, and the secretary welcomed them.

"I'm afraid that at the last moment Doctor Donnington was called away to a meeting," she said. "He'll be back with you before too long." She peered over her glasses with an appropriately apologetic smile. "I've arranged for you to see Murray, our librarian—an expert on all things paper," she said smiling. "He's one floor down." A rather elegant young woman got up from a nearby desk and took them down to the library.

Murray was an easy-going Scot: tall, well-built, and bearded. "Welcome to my domain," he said, waving a hand at the impressive map library. As well as the drawers of maps, there were rows of filing cabinets full with old electric log profiles from exploration holes. A side table had a computer, printer, and a large, sophisticated video screen.

The far wall—it was more of a broad arch than a wall—showed an adjacent spacious room. Candrew could see a woman working at a computer keyboard. She looked up at him, smiled, and went back to peering at the image on the huge graphics screen above her terminal. Murray nodded toward the room. "It's where we keep all the mining records and technical publications," he said. "We've got one of the most extensive collections of mineral publications in the industry." Grinning, he added, "Chris Donnington, our CEO, is a bit of an academic. Likes to have all the available technical information at his fingertips."

"Okay," Murray said, "let's look at the map you brought." He spent quite a while examining it, then took a plastic ruler and got the dimensions—ten by twelve inches. "Give me a minute." He went over to the computer, typed in various bits of information and searched MINEx's data base. But as far as he could tell, the map remnant had not been stolen from any volume in their collection. "I'm sorry, but I don't recognize it. I'll call some colleagues, see what I can find out for you." He hesitated for a moment. "Anyway, show it to Chris Donnington." Then he turned and asked, "Mind if I scan it into our system?"

"Not at all," Candrew said. "Go ahead."

They waited a few minutes while the map was being scanned, and then returned upstairs.

The secretary was clearly not pleased having to tell them, "I'm sorry, but Doctor Donnington is still not back. He sends his apologies and said he'll be with you shortly. Let me take you to his office." She led Candrew and Wilfred down a carpeted passageway lined with framed photographs of various mining operations and several aerial photographs. "Would you care for coffee or a soft drink?" she asked.

They both settled for water.

The corner office had large glass windows with an expansive view across downtown Calgary. What drew Wilfred's attention were the superb mineral specimens on the window sills and on top of the sideboard. These weren't just rare minerals, but huge specimens, elegantly mounted.

The secretary had stressed the 'Doctor' and there it was, framed, on the wall—the certificate showing his name with *Ph. D. from Oxford University*. Framed beside it were his BS and MS diplomas, both from Colorado School of Mines. On the same wall were several framed antique maps, most showing western European countries, although there was one early map of the east coast of Canada.

Doctor Chris Donnington came in and apologized for keeping them waiting. "Hope you had an uneventful flight up." He made his way over and shook their hands. "But then to be certain of that, the company flies a Canadian plane—that *Bombardier Challenger 650* you came in." He pushed back his hair and said laughing, "Made in Canada."

Donnington was used to being in control and abruptly changed the subject. "Remember *The Graduate*, the film with Dustin Hoffman?" he said. "The career advice he gave was *Plastics*. If I was giving advice today it would be *Lithium*."

Candrew cocked his head to one side and smiled. "Really?"

"Sure. That stuff's going to be essential for all the batteries we'll need to run everything from cell phones to electric cars. And we don't have nearly enough." He stared at his visitors to be sure they were getting the point. "That's why I was late meeting you guys. Had to go to a conference with our lithium mining partners from Nevada. Made some crucial decisions, fast." He glanced around to be sure they realized the importance. "Some of us exploration geologists are going to have to go out and find a lot more of it."

"Can we recycle?" Wilfred asked.

"Not easily with the technology we have right now."

Wilfred nodded understanding, but then added, "Cobalt. That's just as important."

"Yeah, you're right. But there are good sources for that. Like the Congo—if they ever get away from artisanal mining and get the big boys to work. Of course, the Chinese have already moved in," he added thoughtfully. "And with copper, they've got the three C's—*Cobalt, Copper, Congo*." He laughed. "And I've been told about your interest in diamonds—you're after the four C's: *Carats, Color, Clarity, Cut*." He laughed again. "Well, maybe not '*cut*' in the exploration stage."

Candrew wondered where he'd gotten this information from.

"Anyway, since you've flown all the way up here, let me see the map you brought."

Candrew took the map out of his briefcase and handed it to Chris.

He looked at it in silence for several minutes. "Nice. With an obvious river, maybe only an arroyo, and mountain peaks drawn in, it should be possible to figure out the location." He stared at it a while longer. "Personally, I don't recognize the area, but I'm certain it's in the desert southwest. What did Murray say? Maybe one of our geologists in Arizona will know."

Wilfred Pengelly pointed out that the mountain illustrations were not generic. "See, hand-drawn illustrations with characteristic shapes. They should be recognizable to someone who knows that area." He looked at the map again. "Here in the margins are some sketches that seem quite specific. And there's a larger sketch at the bottom of the map. Appears to show caves with mineral veins."

"Murray, your map curator, made a copy, so perhaps he could e-mail it to your geologist out west," Candrew suggested.

"Consider it done," Chris said.

"I've had some contact with a few of your people in the field office in Globe," Wilfred said. "Dave Frandly came over to the university and gave a lecture in our seminar series."

"On company time?"

"That I don't know. I'm sure he treated it as public relations. And, anyway, your Arizona office actually did hire a couple of our graduates."

Chris nodded his head as though he thought that was a good thing. "Now, your interest in diamonds," he said, turning toward Candrew.

"Well, I'm not exactly in the mining business."

"Neither am I, not my bag. It's hard to imagine you can make a profit with one carat in a ton of rock. No way I'm going to crush, sieve, and separate that much material." Donnington sounded adamant. He looked at Candrew and Wilfred as if to be certain they appreciated the scale of mining operations. "Anyway, the prospectors have slogged up all the creeks in Canada sampling for indicator minerals. They've probably found—and staked claims on—all the kimberlite pipes that are potentially commercial."

That seemed to end any discussion of diamonds.

Late that afternoon the limo took Candrew and Wilfred back to the airport. Patches of snow were scattered over the ground beside the runway and they took off into a dark gray, featureless sky. Before long they broke through into sunlight. At forty thousand feet there was less turbulence and a great view of the setting sun.

This time, they had the plane to themselves. After takeoff the pilot came back and said, "Sorry Donnington hustled you up and back. He didn't get to take you out to dinner at one of Calgary's fashionable restaurants. You get good steaks there." He smiled sympathetically, but pointed to the galley up front. "We brewed you some fresh coffee and there's cold drinks in the refrigerator. And lots of candy bars in the top drawer—nothing healthy, but it all tastes good." He laughed and was turning toward the cockpit, but paused and said, "Should be in Santa Fe in just over two hours. We'll call ahead and have your vehicle waiting."

Later, Candrew leaned over and said quietly to Wilfred. "Donnington's office has his framed *Oxford Ph. D.* certificate."

"True. He certainly seemed proud of the title." He smiled. "Liked to be called 'doctor.'"

"Yes, but Oxford University doesn't give a *Ph. D.* degree."

"What? They don't?" Pengelly sounded surprised.

"Their doctorate is a *D. Phil.* So that nicely-framed piece of paper has to be a fake. Which makes you wonder, what else in MINEx is fake?"

CHAPTER 19

BACK AT THE UNIVERSITY, Tuesday started just like all the others for Candrew—teaching his freshmen geology class. And as usual, after the lecture, a group of students tracked him to his office. Although some of them were geology majors interested in understanding subtle geological details, there were also a couple of non-majors with questions. Candrew had a soft spot for all the philosophers, historians, and music majors who were forced to take a science course, and had chosen geology. He tried to make the earth and its rocks as fascinating as possible. The drama of drifting continents, predatory dinosaurs, erupting volcanoes, and destructive earthquakes made his task easier.

After answering the students' questions, Candrew was left alone. He put away his lecture notes and slumped back in his chair considering his tasks for the day. High on that mental list was a visit to the lab to see how his research assistant, Judy, was doing.

When Candrew took the stairs down to the ground floor and into the lab, Judy was seated at the computer, this time with a can of Diet Coke beside her, rather than her usual coffee. The big screen in front of her was showing several near-horizontal colored stripes of variable thickness that extended from one side of the screen to the other.

"My international traveler," she said, greeting Candrew with a smile. "How was your trip to Canada?"

"Couple of hours up, a three-hour meeting, couple of hours back. Done."

"You're turning into a jet-set geologist," she said laughing. "Well, was it worth it?"

"Enlightening to get the perspective of a large-scale mining corporation," Candrew said. "Quite different from our focused, academic approach to rocks."

"So, what is *their* focus?"

"Certainly no current interest in diamonds. Their emphasis is primarily on copper. At the moment they're mining mainly in Arizona and Canada, but with plans to expand. I did get the feeling they'd go after anything they could dig up and make money on." Candrew looked around for a pot of coffee and, disappointed, failed to spot one. "MINEx's CEO is interesting. Apart from his fascination with old maps—which he thinks might have exploration significance—he's also a mineral collector. Had some impressive crystals in his office. I'm certain he outclasses our Dean."

"Probably. I'm sure he has more money as well as more contacts."

"True," Candrew said. "So, what have you been doing in the last few days?"

"I've been going back through all the photos we took at our new site in southern Utah." Judy got up and pulled a folder off the shelf. "See here," she pointed at one of the printouts of an enlargement showing a rock face. "Very coarse-grained sand at the bottom but getting steadily finer-grained upwards. Classic turbidite sequence. Which means it was a single depositional event—laid down virtually instantaneously, well, on a geologic timescale. Maybe a thousand years." Candrew nodded his agreement.

"This got me thinking about sedimentation rates," Judy said. She slid her chair over in front of the computer screen. "Remember that commercial computer modelling package you bought and installed a while back?"

"*BasinMod*? Yeah, I remember."

She pointed at the computer screen. "Here's a plot using *Basin-Mod* to show how various strata in southern Utah have changed in thickness and depth through geologic time. The one we're working on is highlighted in yellow."

Candrew was impressed by the way this sandstone had been deeply buried in the past, and then more recently moved up closer to the surface—close enough that it was exposed so they could take photos and hammer off samples.

As he was leaving, Judy sipped her diet soda, then told him she'd gotten an e-mail from the chemical company letting them know that the heavy liquid supplies had been shipped and should be delivered by the end of the week. "I'll get around to separating your diamond indicator minerals as soon as I can," she said.

The previous day's storm had blown through, leaving a clear-blue sky with no clouds. But it was still quite chilly as Candrew left Judy in the lab and made his way across the central plaza to the Faculty Lounge for lunch.

Today the dominant topic of conversation for the 'lunch bunch' was basketball—'March Madness.' Candrew had never played basketball in high school and was not particularly interested in the game. But although he'd never played football either, he always enjoyed the televised gridiron battles. He settled into the last empty chair at the table and listened to the animated discussion. The different points of view were sparked by the previous night's college basketball games that had produced a couple of surprising upsets—as happened every year! While a few at the table were delighted by those outcomes, several were clearly dismayed.

"You bet on the games?" Arlan Dee asked Candrew.

"No, not my thing."

"Not going to risk one or two of the diamonds you find?" he said with a grin. "Not going to see if you can jack up your income?"

"That's all hypothetical since I haven't discovered any diamonds yet." Smiling, he added, "Typical professor—all theory, not actually involved with the real world."

Back in his office, Candrew rustled through the pile of notes on his desk and found the business card the Dean had given him at the VP's party. He dialed the number scrawled on the back.

"Yeah?" The voice was gravelly, but not unfriendly.

Candrew read the name off the back of the Dean's card. "I was calling for Conroy Elkerson."

"You got him."

"I was told you're a mineral dealer. I'm a geology professor and was thinking about driving up to Colorado and paying you a visit. Your name came from one of our faculty members who met you at the Tucson show."

Conroy recognized the Dean's name when he heard it. "That right? He's got a good eye, that man. Bought a couple of nice pieces." Candrew heard him cough. "Where're you driving from?"

When Candrew told him, the dealer was friendly and cooperative, agreeing that the coming weekend would be convenient. He suggested a time and gave detailed directions on how to get to his ranch.

After the call ended, Candrew pulled up the weather forecast on his computer. It appeared that the weekend was going to be fine. He called Wilfred. "I'm headed up to Colorado on Friday. Going to see a mineral dealer. You want to come along?"

"That sounds like fun, but I'm going to have to pass. We've got a Master's thesis defense scheduled for Friday afternoon and I need to be there."

"Too bad you can't make it. I'll see you soon." He hung up.

While Candrew was not averse to driving to Colorado alone, he felt it would be more appealing to have company. For a moment he considered asking Judy if she'd like to go along, but self-interest prevailed. He thought it better not to distract her from the computer modelling she was doing for their research project. That left the obvious choice—Renata. He dialed her number.

"You busy this weekend?" he probed.

"You just don't understand how we archaeologists work, do you? We sit in our padded armchairs, mug of hot tea in one hand, and think deep thoughts." Candrew heard her laugh. "Why would you want to interrupt that creative process?"

He told her about his planned Colorado trip and asked if she might like to ride along. "Tell you what, come over for dinner tonight and I'll give you all the details."

When she said she'd like that, he cautioned her it would be just pizza and beer. "No problem," she said. "I'll see you tonight."

While he'd been on the phone, his computer had chirped to let him know there was an incoming e-mail. The message was from the Dean giving him the address of the mineral dealer in San Diego. He typed in a quick reply thanking him for sending the information promptly, saying he'd let him know how things worked out. He wondered if the Dean had heard the rumors about Jay Wolverton's shady reputation.

———

Chile always liked it when someone came to dinner. He seemed well aware that it improved his chances of getting scraps of something more interesting than dog food. Pixel, on the other hand, was not so food oriented and the aging cat was curled up asleep in the big padded chair. When the doorbell rang, Chile was at the front door before Candrew. Renata came in, scratched the dog behind the ears, then gave Candrew a big hug and a kiss.

Candrew opened a couple of beers and they sat in the living room where he had a log fire blazing.

"So, you're going to bribe me with dinner and get me to drive you to Colorado." She sipped her beer, grinning.

"You don't have to drive. I'll be the chauffer."

"Anyway, why are you—or rather *we*—going?"

Before Candrew had a chance to explain, the doorbell rang. He knew it would be the food arriving. He paid for the pizza, took the box, and gave the young man a generous tip since he was sure he was a university student. They sliced the 'Ultimate Pizza' and took their portions into the dining room. Chile sat patiently at their feet.

"At the VP's party our dean had given me the names of a couple of mineral dealers," Candrew told her. "And one of them is in southern Colorado. I talked to the guy on the phone and arranged a visit for this coming Saturday." He glanced at Renata who seemed interested. "I thought it would be great if we made a fun trip out of the visit."

They talked about the logistics of the drive, and Renata was clearly happy to go along. They ate additional slices of pizza, and drank more beer. Chile finally got a reward.

As Candrew was tossing another pinon log on the fire, Renata asked, "Have the police figured out who the dead man was? The one in the mine where you were trapped?"

"If they have, they haven't told me." He smirked. "I'm not sure they will tell me. They'll need to find the next-of-kin first. I don't think they release that sort of information unless they have to."

"Or the media forces them to," Renata quipped.

CHAPTER 20

CANDREW PUT SOME CLOTHES, his camera, and a spiral-bound notebook into an overnight bag. He'd already arranged with 'Shell to feed Chile and Pixel, and had told Judy he'd be gone for a couple of days. He drove to Renata's home, loaded her travel grip into the *Explorer*, and they set out on the trip to Colorado.

Route 84 North took them through Chama and on to Pagosa Springs, across the Continental Divide, and into Alamosa. The weather was sunny, traffic was light, and the drive into Colorado very pleasant. They checked into a restored Victorian bed-and-breakfast where Candrew had made reservations. After registering, they ambled through the town, though many of the shops were closed. Candrew and Renata ate a leisurely dinner in a Chinese restaurant.

Their room for the night was on the second floor and there was no elevator. Warm, and comfortable, it was decorated with antique furniture. The typical Victorian bed was probably less than Queen-size and was high off the floor. But it did have a soft down mattress they both found comfortable, and they slept well.

The next morning began with an ample breakfast that was included in the room cost. Candrew and Renata ate eggs-over-easy, beans, mushrooms, tomatoes, and hash-brown potatoes with toast and coffee. They chatted with a couple at the adjacent table who said they were heading to Santa Fe and then on down to White Sands National Park. Candrew couldn't resist giving a mini-geology lecture, telling them that the sand there was gypsum, not the more typical silica sand.

Candrew and Renata left the bed-and-breakfast an hour later and detoured to see the wonders of Sand Dunes National Park. They parked outside the Visitors' Center. Renata had not been there before and was impressed by the dune field, some of the sand dunes over seven hundred feet high. For a while they watched a few hardy souls sliding down the face of a dune on their sand-boards.

"Sand. That's your thing, isn't it, Candrew?" Renata joked.

"Sort of. But this is 'proto-sandstone.'" He grinned. "I don't get excited until all the grains are stuck together to give a hard, real rock." He looked back at the dunes. "We sometimes bring students up here, so they can see the way sand moves around." Smiling, he explained, "We tell them that in geology: *The present is the key to the past.*"

Back on Route 285, Candrew drove as the road twisted through the mountains toward Leadville. There they followed the route west out of town to the rock dealer's ranch, and drove up, parking on the gravel. They walked across the flagstone patio to where Conroy Elkerson was waiting in the doorway at the top of stone steps. He was heavily built man with a shaggy dark beard and unruly long hair. He had on denim coveralls, a checked shirt, and wore circular, wire-rimmed glasses. The clasp on his bolo tie sported a big chunk of blue-green turquoise. Conroy seemed pleased to see them, shook hands with Candrew, and nodded, at Renata—with a smile that showed tobacco-stained teeth.

"Please, come on in," he said. "You mind if I smoke?" When they agreed that wasn't a problem, he struck a match on a chunk of rough rock. It flared, and he lit his cigarette.

Conroy ushered them into a long, wood-beamed room where he served them coffee—strong and bitter. They chatted about the drive up and life in the university. Candrew explained he was a geology professor there, and briefly outlined his interest in minerals. He talked about being drawn to diamonds, and their geological significance, as well as the role of indicator minerals.

"Lot of potential, I guess, but not something I get involved with," Conroy said. "More for the jewelers." For a moment he studied Candrew's face. "North of here, up on the Wyoming border, there used to be a diamond mine. Called it the Kelsey Lake Mine. That area had nine kimberlite pipes, but only two of them were open-pit mined. Not commercial anymore." He laughed. "Heard they were only getting about four carats per hundred tons."

With the discussion of diamonds having run its course, Renata told Conroy she was also a professor at the university—in archaeology.

"You work out here in the southwest?"

"No. My research is mainly in Guatemala. Mayan ruins."

Conroy glanced from one to the other and Candrew got the distinct impression that he and Renata were being evaluated.

"All through the West around here," Conroy said, "it's a mix of Federal land, Indian reservations, and, of course, interspersed patches of private land." He puffed on his cigarette. "The role of minerals on Indian land frequently isn't quite clear. But there are a few Indians who trade." The dealer smiled quietly as though he knew exactly who those Indians were, maybe he'd even gotten some of his mineral samples from them.

Renata looked around the room where there were several large clusters of perfect crystals, and asked, "How did you get involved with all these elegant minerals?"

Conroy gave a broad grin. "Started long, long ago. Way back in grade school. I saw my older brother sell some crystals he'd found to one of his friends. A light went on. I figured out you could make money selling rocks, and since we lived out in the country, there were plenty of them lying around." He stroked his beard and drew on his cigarette. "Slowly I got more and more involved, finally gotten into the business I'm in now." He puffed again on his cigarette, then stubbed it out in a stone ash tray cluttered with cigarette butts. "I think it's about time I gave you folks the tour. Let you see what you came all this way for."

Candrew and Renata followed him outside and along a gravel path that led to a large stone outbuilding. The heavy wooden door had two padlocks and an electronic key pad. Conroy pulled out keys for the padlocks, then punched in the numerical code. It was clear that with the high value of many mineral specimens, security was a major consideration. Inside he flicked the switches and fluorescent lights lit wooden shelves that stretched the length of the interior walls. There were no windows.

Two shelves along the wall to the left had irregular bundles of taped-up plastic bubble wrap, as well as some fabric-wrapped bundles. There was also a variety of cardboard boxes. Candrew assumed these held specimens brought back from mineral shows, or being readied for shipping.

The opposite wall was stunning. Candrew stood amazed. The shelves were loaded with crystals. Most were delicately colored, many huge, others in beautiful clusters, and the range of shapes was incredible. Conroy stood in silence, letting him take his time.

Candrew reached the far end of the room and Conroy said, half joking, "This is the quartz corner." He switched on some low spotlights that shone on large amethyst crystals, a group of smokey quartz crystals, and several clusters of clear quartz.

There were two ceramic bowls with small crystals that were pointed at both ends. "Diamonds," Conroy said.

He had Candrew's attention.

Laughing, Conroy pointed to the larger container. "*Herkimer Diamonds* from New York—they're actually quartz. These small, doubly-terminated quartz crystals are not worth a whole hell of a lot. I give most of them away to kids at the rock shows." Grinning, he claimed, "Get them addicted early."

As Candrew peered at the crystals, Conroy pushed the other bowl over. "Closer to home for you. From New Mexico. These are *Pecos Diamonds*, but again, actually just doubly-terminated quartz."

Mentioning diamonds, even if they were not the real thing, made Candrew recall the indicator minerals he'd been exploring for, the ones Judy had been separating, and his faculty colleague analyzing.

"You have garnets?" he asked. "Specifically pyrope, the red one."

"You're out of luck, my friend. I almost never have them. The only ones I see are usually pretty small," he said. "Maybe okay for making jewelry."

"How about green diopside?"

"Sorry. None."

Candrew worked his way along the middle shelf, carefully examining the awesome mineral specimens. He liked a large group of grey, interlocking cubes of galena from Cornwall in the U.K. He thought it a pity Wilfred couldn't be here. But it was the delicately colored, translucent minerals that he really admired. He asked the price of a large purple fluorite crystal that had a pale-yellow cubic shape visible in it's interior. The price for this unusual combination was high. He hesitated, but said he'd take it.

Renata wanted to know about the cost of a large topaz, and then some multicolored tourmalines. She shook her head at the prices: way beyond her budget.

At the far end of the long room was an alcove with a work bench. Candrew saw a drill press, band saw, and polishing wheels, as well as other tools. There were sheets of Plexiglas.

Conroy noticed him looking. "I sometimes make mounts for minerals, usually just the smaller ones. I've got a guy in Denver who does the big pieces for me. He's good at casting Plexi blocks and knows how to add lettering."

"You know the other dealers who handle the stuff that turns up at the Tucson show?" Candrew asked.

"Over the years, I've got to be friends, or at least business partners, with most of them. Of course, I see the foreign guys only once a year. Or maybe a couple of times if they're at other shows." He stared at Candrew, obviously judging his level of interest. "Since I deal with quite a few of the U.S. dealers, I got to know their holdings a hell of a lot better."

"You ever run across Jay Wolverton? He's based out in San Diego."

"Yeah, I know him." There was an uneasy pause while he ran his hands through his hair. "Not a great friend of mine. More of a competitor." When Candrew cocked his head to one side, questioning, he took his time explaining.

"Had a guy who worked with me, name of Alex. But he upped and left and went out to work for Jay, or so I was told."

"Why would he do that?" Renata asked.

Conroy shook his head and frowned. "Don't ask me. I don't know what Jay did to lure him to join his outfit. Some under-the-table deal, I'm sure. Anyway, perhaps the guy just liked California."

He lit another cigarette and puffed on it, thinking. "Hey, maybe when I said 'worked with,' that was a bit of an exaggeration. The guy was a loner, explored in the tradition of the old prospectors, typically all by himself. But he was okay working with others as well, especially if they were providing him information and money. And he did like to have a steady source of that—someone had to pay for his cigars and vodka. Give him credit, though, he turned up lots of neat mineral suites. I bought quite a few from him. The guy was from Czechoslovakia or Poland or someplace over there in eastern Europe. Had quite an accent—and an unpronounceable name." He laughed. "Everyone just called him *Alex*, though I have no idea what his real name was."

"You ever hear from him?"

"Not anymore. Must have found another market for his stuff."

The drive home was easy and relaxed with a dramatic western sky as the sun set under scattered clouds. Candrew and Renata talked about the mineral dealer.

"No sign of a wife to look after him," Renata said. "Conroy's overweight and smokes continuously. He's going to kill himself." Frowning, she said, "I wonder who's going to inherit all those beautiful minerals?"

Candrew had no answer.

Their return trip was interrupted only by a stop for a hamburger and fries. As they sat eating, Candrew mused, "Well, we've just met one more person who doesn't have much good to say about Jay Wolverton. Remember, he was the high-end mineral dealer out in San Diego." Candrew ate a few French fries and added, "On the flight up to Calgary, even the MINEx geologists on the plane had nothing good to say about Wolverton."

Candrew dropped Renata off at her house. "Hope you felt the trip was worthwhile."

"Oh, yes. Of course. The only problem was that I couldn't afford to buy any of the mineral specimens I really liked." She laughed, leaned across, kissed him, and went into the house.

He headed home with a tinge of guilt, wondering if he should have offered to buy her one of the crystal clusters she liked. At the house he was greeted by an enthusiastic dog. Pixel sat looking on at this unseemly display and appeared to be questioning: *Why did you leave us?*

Candrew tore the bubble wrap off the big fluorite crystals he'd bought from Conroy and placed the mineral cluster in the center of the kitchen counter. Certainly not their final resting place, but located where he could enjoy them right away. He stared at the crystals with satisfaction, even though he'd paid quite a bit more than he would have liked.

CHAPTER 21

BY MID-MORNING, CANDREW HAD strolled down the driveway, with Chile at his side, and gotten the Sunday newspaper. Back in the kitchen, he fried himself breakfast. As he sat eating, he looked at the comics, then read the front-page news. Working the Sudoku puzzle took most of his attention, but he did pause to savor the enticing aromas of bacon, toast, and coffee.

When he glanced up, the sunlight was catching his group of newly-acquired fluorite crystals. *Rather expensive*, he thought, but he was sure buying them had been the right thing to do.

Candrew spent most of the morning loading soiled clothes into the washing machine and reluctantly doing other long-overdue chores. But his thoughts kept drifting back to his visit with Conrad Elkerson in Colorado. He was curious to know why the European mineral hunter who'd worked with Conrad, the one everybody called *Alex*, had decided to leave and go and collaborate with Jay Wolverton in San Diego. What was the incentive? Thinking over the rumors he'd heard about Wolverton and his dubious reputation, Candrew wondered about this high-end dealer's alleged misdeeds—did any of these have a role in the business of diamond exploration? After all that he'd heard about Wolverton, he was intrigued by the possibly of meeting him face-to-face. The problem was, he didn't know how feasible a Californian trip would be during the semester.

The first thing Candrew did when he'd gotten into his office on Monday morning was to go online and check airline schedules to see if there were any flights to San Diego that would fit into his schedule.

As he sat at his computer and checked, it seemed possible to make the trip with a single overnight stay. However, he'd have to fly from Albuquerque pretty early in the morning. And returning the evening of the next day would get him home really late. Anyway, clearly, a visit was possible with merely tolerable inconvenience.

Candrew wondered if in fact a visit was a sensible thing to do. But he convinced himself he really had nothing to lose—and it could be an interesting trip. He called Jay Wolverton.

Jay himself answered the phone. "Yes?"

"I'm a geologist in New Mexico," Candrew explained. "I was curious to know whether it would be possible to visit."

"We're not running a supermarket here," Jay said rather bluntly. "I deal with most of our clients at the top shows. You're familiar, I'm sure, with the *Tucson Rock and Mineral Show*, and the *Denver Show*?"

Candrew said he was only superficially aware of them.

"You a collector, and I mean serious, you know, high quality stuff?" he snapped.

"No. I'm not a major collector," Candrew admitted. "Since I'm a geology professor, I do collect rocks and minerals as teaching material, but that's about all."

Jay didn't hesitate. "We're probably way out of your price range." There was a moment's pause and he demanded, "You got specimens to sell?"

"No, but . . ."

Before Candrew had a chance to explain, Jay butted in. "Then why do you want to come see me? Waste my time."

"I've recently got involved with diamonds. Right now, only from an exploration point of view. I've been looking at indicator minerals from kimberlites. You know, analyzing nearby eroded sands for garnets and diopsides. That sort of thing."

"Well, well. And you think we can help you with that?"

"I'm sure anyone with ore mineral experience across the West has the potential to help."

"You may be right." Jay seemed more interested, and Candrew wondered what was in it for him. "Okay," he said. "Why don't you drop by and we can talk. I don't have a lot of time, couple of hours max."

"You free this Thursday?" Candrew asked.

There was a pause, presumably while he consulted his schedule. They agreed on late Thursday morning.

So, a visit was scheduled. Candrew pulled up the airline website and made his reservations. Then he rocked back in his chair, his feet up on the partly-opened desk drawer, and thought about what to do next. He certainly wasn't in the mood for intense science.

He called Wilfred. "You busy over lunch today?"

"Nothing planned. I'm free."

"How about we go get something to eat, then."

"Sure. Though I'm not as big a fan of the Faculty Lounge as you are. How about the *Plan B*?" Wilfred was referring to a restaurant on the edge of campus that was popular with students—no white table clothes, no waiters, only self-service, but with acceptable food. It was frequently crowded, usually with a dynamic atmosphere. Candrew agreed and they settled on twelve-thirty.

Candrew had just put the receiver down, and picked up the technical magazine he was about to read, when the phone rang.

"Dr. Nor?"

"Yeah. Speaking."

"This is Detective Alvarez. I talked to you in your office early last week."

Candrew didn't remember the name. He held the phone tight to his ear and fished around in his desk drawer for the business cards the police had given him, but failed to find them. He assumed it was the detective who'd been on campus to interview him about the abandoned mine with the homicide victim. He did remember that a police officer had accompanied him.

The voice on the phone continued. "A week ago, Officer Garcia and I talked to you about the corpse you found in an old mine down in the south of the state. Yu know, the body you said you stumbled on by accident, the one you said you'd never seen before."

"That's right. I didn't recognize him."

"We're fortunate to have laboratory folks who are first rate. They've done a fantastic job and identified the human remains."

"That's wonderful. So, it'll let you wrap up the case?" Candrew said nothing more, giving Alvarez a chance to elaborate.

"A few things worked in their favor," he said. "First, they were able to get fingerprints, and not just get them, but identify them. We were lucky in our investigation because the homicide victim turned out to be a felon. He had a previous conviction."

"Really?" Candrew was surprised. "How did you know that? What was he found guilty of?"

"The fingerprints showed up in the FBI reference data base. He had a record because he'd been picked up by Customs a couple of years ago for trying to smuggle some dinosaur fossils into the country without an import permit."

"And found guilty?"

"Sure was. There was a fairly hefty fine, although he was released on probation. All of this, of course, meant we'd gotten a really good record on file," Alvarez said. "When you discovered the body it was still pretty fresh, and there was no doubt about how the photographs taken in that non-working mine matched the ones of our police records."

"So, you know who the guy is?"

"Sure do."

Candrew waited.

"He was a U.S. citizen now, but had been an immigrant who'd arrived here from Poland some years ago. He was called *Aleksy Pr* . . . , *Pby* . . . Hell, I grew up in New Mexico speaking Spanish. Can't pronounce these names that don't have no vowels in them."

"Can you spell it for me," Candrew asked.

"No problem. A-1 -e-k-s-y, P-r-z-y-b-y-1 -s-k-i." Candrew wrote it down. "But the records show he was usually called just 'Alex.'"

'Alex'—and eastern European! After everything he'd heard from Conroy, the dealer in Colorado, Candrew was amazed.

But the Detective broke into his train of thought. "The main reason I'm phoning, and telling you all this, is because I need to find out what you know about this dead man."

"Nothing," Candew said. "I'd never met him. But I did visit a mineral dealer in Colorado who said the Polish man had worked with him." Candrew hunted through the pile of papers on his desk, found Conrad's business card, and gave the phone number to Alvarez.

"Thanks. The other reason I'm calling is because we need you to come to Police Headquarters in Albuquerque. The body from the southern mine is in the morgue and you will have to make a confirming identification. We want to be certain the body is the one you discovered." Alvarez let that request sink in. "And we'd like you to make your visit as soon as possible."

Candrew stuttered. "Well, . . I, . . yes, . . I'm flying out of Albuquerque Sunport on Wednesday. I could probably be at your office by nine-thirty that morning."

"That would be excellent. I'd certainly appreciate it." Alvarez provided directions on how to get there.

"You made any progress in finding out who trapped me in the mine?" Candrew asked.

"Not yet. But it's still an ongoing investigation."

The phone call ended.

Stunned, Candrew sat with his elbows on the desk and his head in his hands. He stared into the distance. Aleksy—'Alex'—from Poland, so most probably with a very strong accent. This was almost certainly a characteristic of the colleague Conroy Elkerson had talked to them about, the one who'd left him to collaborate with Jay Wolverton in San Diego. And underlying it all was the fact that the

Pole had turned up dead in an unused mine—and he, Candrew, had been the one who found the body.

————

Candrew was seated at a corner table in the *Plan B Café*, glancing through a menu he was fairly familiar with, when Wilfred arrived.

"How did your Colorado mineral trip go?" Wilfred asked. "Sorry I couldn't come with you."

"Interesting dealer, but it was only marginally about minerals. The real dramatic information came this morning. I had a phone call from a detective with the State police in Albuquerque. They've identified the man whose body I found in the abandoned mine."

Wilfred put down his coffee cup and stared at Candrew.

"They told me he was a Polish immigrant who'd arrived in the States some years ago."

"What was his connection to the mine?"

"That I don't know. But what I do know is he'd been cooperating with the mineral dealer who Renata and I visited in Colorado. Conroy, that's the dealer, had told me a bit about him because they'd collaborated, and the Polish prospector had provided him with high quality mineral specimens. But then he'd suddenly moved to San Diego and gone to work with a different dealer, a man called Jay Wolverton."

"The plot thickens."

"It certainly does. Few people have good things to say about Wolverton. I talked to him on the phone earlier this morning." He grinned. "Didn't give me any reason to change that opinion."

Candrew ate a few mouthfuls of his sandwich. "The reason I called Wolverton was to set up a meeting. I'm going to fly out and get together with him this coming Thursday."

————

On his way back to the Geology Department in Kinblade Hall, Candrew went into the sedimentary lab to talk with Judy. He gave her a quick summary of the trip to the mineral dealer in Colorado and then told her that the police had identified the body he'd found in the mine. He let her know he planned to fly out to San Diego for two days.

Before he could say any more, she was grinning. "And you won't be back in time to teach your class on Thursday morning. Right?"

"Yeah, that's right."

"No problem. Just let me know what topic you're up to. I can take care of the lecture for you."

"Thanks. I really appreciate that," Candrew said. "I'll bring my lecture notes down and mark the page I've reached."

"As usual, there's plenty of work to do while you're gone," Judy said. "But it doesn't include separating those diamond tracer minerals you wanted. The heavy liquids I need still haven't arrived. Now they're saying delivery next week."

Disappointed, but not surprised, Candrew nodded.

CHAPTER 22

CANDREW WAS UP BEFORE the sun, grabbed some energy bars to eat on his way, and drove the dramatic route through the mountains, along the river, and down to Española. From there south to Albuquerque, the traffic was heavy but he made good time.

The State Police Center and its morgue were on the south side of town, and with Detective Alvarez's directions he found them with no difficulty. When he arrived, a secretary had him sign in. Then a technician in a white coverall, clipboard in hand, guided him to the cold room with its chilled human cadavers. The tech consulted his list, read the labels, and pulled out the relevant drawer. He uncovered a body. Candrew had briefly studied the man's face in the mine. But he'd only viewed the corpse for a few minutes in poor light under far from ideal conditions. From what he could remember, this was the body he'd seen. Strange, he thought, for an immigrant Pole to end up murdered and left in an old mineshaft in New Mexico.

Although he'd only had a very superficial view, there had seemed to be no trauma. Candrew asked the tech about the cause of death.

He consulted the pages on his clipboard. "The toxicology results aren't back yet," he said. "But we do expect them soon."

Glad to be out of the freezing morgue and back in the office, Candrew signed the several forms he was handed. In a subdued mood, he went out to his *Explorer* and drove to the airport, Albuquerque's International Sunport.

Parking in the garage, checking in at the airline desk, and clearing TSA's scrutiny was tedious but routine. He'd chosen a window seat for the flight to San Diego since he liked to look out and study the terrain he was flying over. Doing geology at ground level often got to be personal and very localized, but from thirty-five thousand feet the sheer scale of the science he studied was obvious. He watched as the braided river valleys and rugged mountains, bare above tree line, slid under the flight path. It occurred to him just how very small diamonds are in the scheme of things, and just how much impact such a tiny piece of rock could actually have. Diamonds command huge prices. And not only do they satisfy the egos of the wealthy, but 'blood diamonds' provide funds for some terrorist groups in Africa. This philosophical musing ended when he fell asleep—it had been an early morning and a hectic day.

The thump of landing woke him. He rubbed his eyes and waited for the plane to taxi to the gate. He had no checked luggage, only his bulky briefcase. Quickly he made his way through the busy terminal and got a cab that took him to the hotel where he had his reservation.

In the warm, sunny California morning, Candrew walked along the hotel's cactus-lined, sinuous garden path and into the half-empty restaurant. He was looking around for a table when a man over by the far wall rose and motioned.

"Professor Nor?" he queried as Candrew walked toward him. He was short, well-muscled, with thick curly, dark brown hair that was starting to show streaks of gray. Smiling, he waved Candrew to a chair opposite him. "Hi. I'm Sergie," he said, sitting with his back to the wall. "Mr. Wolverton sent me here to meet you. I checked your university department online and recognized you from your photo."

Sergie had clearly done his homework. Candrew wondered what else he'd managed to find out. They chatted casually before he suggested Candrew go ahead and order breakfast. He appeared to be in no hurry to leave. Sipping his coffee while Candrew ate, at one point he checked his iPhone. He seemed to be carefully evaluating Candrew—and his briefcase.

Candrew had almost finished his meal, and was spreading marmalade on his toast, when Sergie began to probe. "You're a collector then? You specialize in specific minerals? Or are you one of those guys who just collect from a particular country?"

"As I told Jay Wolverton on the phone, I'm a geology professor, so I collect rocks and minerals mainly for use in teaching." He bit into his toast, sipped his coffee, and explained what actually happens. "Students scratch the minerals to establish hardness, and they also make a 'streak pattern' to get the color of powdered rock. That's often quite different from the lump of rock itself. After a while, with twenty or more students, they actively use up all the samples we have."

"And as a senior geology professor, do you provide advice on exceptional minerals to other people who might be interested in building a collection?"

"No. That's not something I ever do." Candrew smiled at this low-key interrogation.

"So, you're acquiring personal specimens for science rather than aesthetics?"

"Yeah. You're right about that."

"What brings you here then? We specialize in unique pieces for discriminating collectors." He smirked, implying: *and they're not cheap*.

"I realize that. But I wanted to talk to Mr. Wolverton about some diamond exploration techniques."

"Okay, then." He checked the time on his iPhone and got up. "Let's go do it."

Candrew followed Sergie to the parking lot, to his blue BMW X5. He drove north-east out of town toward the mountains for about forty-five minutes. A cautious driver, he talked very little, concentrating on the morning traffic. At one point he did ask, "You been in San Diego before?"

"Only once," Candrew said. "I came to a scientific conference some years ago. I didn't see much of the city, although I did get to the zoo."

"Yeah. That's impressive."

Candrew had gotten the distinct impression that he'd been vetted over breakfast, and only after passing that evaluation was he being taken to see the elusive Jay Wolverton. What was it with these mineral dealers? Conway Elkerson in Colorado had checked him and Renata out before letting them see the minerals he had for sale. And now Wolverton. What were the dealers suspicious of?

After leaving the main road, they drove a secondary route and then followed a gravel track that led through an open gate in a tall metal fence. There was no sign. They pulled over and parked beside two trucks in front of a ranch-style house. The red *Lincoln Navigator* was immaculate. But the *Ram* with oversized tires had several large dents and was covered in dirt.

"Journey's end," Sergie said, getting out of the car and motioning Candrew toward the front door.

They entered a broad passageway brightly lit by skylights. A tall, lean man was hurrying toward them and Sergie introduced him as 'Skip.'

Skip smiled, shook Candrew's hand and apologized. "Sorry. Have to run off. Jay just got an urgent message. Got to check out a dealer from Mongollia." He was grinning. "The whole surface of the world is covered with rocks and minerals, but damn few of them are worth much." He raised a hand in a farewell gesture and hurried out the door.

Skip had sun-bleached hair tied back into a pony-tail and sun-tanned skin the color of café-au-lait: the look of a typical California surfer. But Candrew had grown up far from the coast and saw him more as a hippie. As Sergie escorted Candrew into the main room, Candrew glanced out through the prominent glass windows—fortified with substantial vertical iron bars—and saw Skip drive away in the battered, dusty Ram pickup truck.

Jay Wolverton was seated at the far end of a large, high-beamed room. Slowly he got up from his padded armchair. Jay was average height and slightly overweight with thinning blond hair and a lush mustache. He wore tinted glasses. His pallor implied that he rarely made it out into the sunlight to track down minerals. Clearly, he left that chore to other people. Candrew wondered what Skip's role was.

Sergie said, "Here's Professor Nor. He made it in last night . . ."

" . . . from New Mexico," Jay said, finishing the sentence for him.

Sergie nodded to Jay, turned, and left.

Jay shook hands and smiled insincerely, well aware that Candrew was not here to buy any of his expensive specimens. Only reluctantly was Jay sharing his time. He sat down and gestured to the hard-backed chair on the opposite side of the low coffee table.

"So, you're going after diamonds." He phrased it almost as an accusation. Jay was getting straight to business, there were no introductory pleasantries. "Your interest is purely in research?" he wanted to know. "Or do you need to boost a measly university salary?"

Candrew ignored the implications. "As a geologist, I'd like to understand what diamonds can tell us about the deep earth. Let us figure out what's going on at depths that are way too deep to drill."

"So, research. How altruistic," he said sarcastically. "Where have you been searching?"

"Well, mainly New Mexico, of course. There are several kimberlite pipes there, and some over the state line in Arizona."

"On Indian reservations? Navajo?" Jay asked.

"Some."

"Are the Indians involved? You exploring with them?"

"No. I haven't worked with any," Candrew said, although his thoughts ran back to the tall man, almost certainly Navajo, he'd run into at the excavated cavern in the diatreme. He, of course, was the person who'd persuaded Candrew to visit the abandoned mine where he'd been locked in. That diatreme had been one of the locations where he'd collected kimberlite samples—the samples which Judy was now waiting to separate indicator minerals. "My guess is, they just sell the minerals they find," he said. "Frankly, I doubt the Indians on the reservations have the resources, or interest, to go after diamonds. Why do you ask?"

"Because it takes specialized skill and experience to identify the few kimberlite pipes that actually have diamonds in them." He stared at Candrew, smiling. "And after that it would still need substantial capital to exploit them. I suppose they could always collaborate with investors. Even work with one of the international mining corporations."

That made Candrew think of MINEx. But he was well aware that commercial explorers rarely share their site information. In contrast, if academics can get their information published, and establish priority, they're more than happy to tell colleagues what they've discovered. He himself had site data, but no actual diamonds to provide proof.

Jay's phone rang. He leaned over, grabbed it off the low table and glanced at the number. "Excuse me," he said, and got up. He stood with the phone cradled to his ear, looking out the window, his back to Candrew.

Candrew looked around. There were two large contemporary paintings on the side wall. Under them, broad, polished wood shelves carefully displayed absolutely gorgeous, mineral clusters. Some were impressively large, many beautifully colored. A central table had more specimens, and these included two interlocking fluorite crystals about the same size and color as the ones he'd bought from the dealer in Colorado. Although Wolverton's fluorites didn't appear to be of noticeably higher quality, the professionally-printed label indicated they were fifty-percent more expensive.

The main room widened at the end, with double doors, both open. There, a lone woman was seated at a work bench. She had light brown, almost blonde hair of medium length and bangs. She wore a white tee-shirt over a three-quarter length faded denim skirt, and sneakers. Her hazel eyes were partially hidden behind glasses with frames that had some sort of flecks making them sparkle as she turned to look at Candrew.

She pulled out her earbuds. "Welcome to where the workers toil," she quipped, laughing and waving at the bank of technical equipment. At the end was a rack with some photographic gear, and beside it was what Candrew recognized as a spectrometer. A heavy cabinet at the end of the bench had a radioactivity icon on it. There was a strong smell of organic solvents.

"Lots of people bring you samples?" Candrew asked.

"They do indeed. It's my job to get them prepped for sale."

Candrew peered at the group of big crystals lying beside a small diamond saw. "Looks like you're doing a great job."

She took the compliment with a smile.

"You ever deal with that European who's got a thick accent? Alex?" Candrew asked.

"You mean the Russian guy?"

"Actually, Polish."

"Bit of a loner," she said. "We haven't heard from him for quite a while. The last time he turned up here he brought some great crystals. Had a few really unusual combinations."

"Is he scheduled to come back and bring more minerals?"

"That I don't know."

She seemed unaware that Alex had been murdered. Candrew was curious to find out if Jay knew anything about Alex's demise.

Jay had finished his phone call and had been watching him carefully. He came across the room to join them. "Frieda," he said gesturing to introduce the blonde. "I'm sure she took good care of you while I was on the phone. Sorry about that. Some things just won't wait"

The two men went back to the far end of the large, main room.

Candrew pulled out his cell phone. "Mind if I take some photos," he asked.

"No." The reply was blunt, clearly not negotiable. "The high-end mineral business is too competitive to have our wares exposed."

"They'd only be for my personal reference. Certainly nothing commercial."

"I said no."

There was an awkward silence, then Jay proposed, "Why don't you go east with your explorations, instead of west? Go over to Arkansas. They've got some well-documented occurrences of diamonds there."

"That's right. I've read about the Crater of Diamonds State Park. Visitors can dig their own gems."

"Not trivial. Over thirty thousand diamonds have been found—and hauled away: finders, keepers." He shook his head at the thought as if he regretted not getting there before it went commercial. "The biggest one was over eight and a half carats. That'll cover a bit more than the entrance fee." Jay smirked.

"At several sites I've been to, I collected kimberlites, then got the indicator minerals separated," Candrew said. "Looked at a lot of different minerals, like ilmenite, but concentrated mainly on garnets and diopside."

"You analyze the pyrope garnets for chromium?" Jay wanted to know.

Diopsides, garnets and their chromium concentrations. Candrew was surprised he knew that much about the technical aspects of prospecting for diamonds—which he'd claimed was not his business. "You're up to speed on diamond exploration techniques," he said.

Jay frowned, looked down, and after a moment said, "You hear a lot listening to other collectors." He appeared to force a grin.

"There are some closer diamonds," Candrew said. "Not long ago I visited a dealer in Colorado and he told me about the Kelsey Lake Mine on the Wyoming border."

"Conrad Elkerson?"

"Yeah, that's the one. Said he'd worked with a prospector called Alex, and then the guy left him and came to collaborate with you." Candrew pursued the issue. "Elkerson didn't seem too happy about that."

"Right, but not my doing. Alex, a tough European, made his own choice. He was, of course, quite an asset, although not for diamonds," he noted skeptically. "He's brought me some excellent material. But none recently. I heard he'd cleaned out one or two mining locations. Anyway, I haven't seen him for a couple of months, but that's not unusual."

Candrew waited, but Jay volunteered nothing more. Either he didn't know of—or was covering up—Alex's death and his own abandonment in the mine.

Later, Sergie drove Candrew back to the airport. After tolerating the check-in process one more time, Candrew had almost a three-hour wait. He spent the first part of the delay eating a hamburger and onion rings in one of the fast-food restaurants. As he sipped his diet coke and watched the frazzled travelers dashing to their airline gates, he thought over the day's visit: *Had it been worth his time and effort?*

Candrew had again chosen a window seat for the flight. Soon after takeoff they crossed the coastal range and he sat looking down at the folded mountains. With few big trees, they had the appearance of crumpled textiles. Soon, however, the sun set among scattered clouds in the west and as the flight continued east to Albuquerque the pale moonlight didn't give enough light for him to make out details of the terrain below. Only a few lights were visible on the ground. For a while Candrew stared into the darkness, then pulled down his starboard-side window shade. He had plenty of time to think about Jay Wolverton's operation and pondered the work that Frieda, the woman in his workshop, was doing. Why was there was so much high-tech equipment? All he knew was that classic mineral clusters needed a thorough cleaning and then an appropriate mount, usually in stainless steel or Plexiglas.

After the flight arrived in Albuquerque, only fifteen minutes late, Candrew retrieved his Ford *Explorer* from the parking garage and headed north on Interstate 25. The drive home took well over three hours, even though there was little traffic. He arrived at the house drained and went straight to bed.

CHAPTER 23

CANDREW WOKE LATE TO bright sunshine, his bedroom in disarray. He clambered out of bed. The aging cat Pixel was curled up asleep in the disheveled shirt he'd tossed on the floor as he'd crept into bed late the previous night. Hungry, Candrew made his way into the kitchen followed, as always, by Chile.

It was pleasantly warm at the sunny end of the patio, and after a hearty breakfast he sat there drinking his coffee and reading the newspaper, Chile at his feet.

He thought over the previous day's visit to Jay Wolverton. Diamonds were a fairly new research area for him. As a tenured professor with an endowed chair, he could pick and choose the research projects that excited him. But becoming expert in any topic—and building a scientific reputation—took intense study and usually the need to develop expertise in a narrow field. He was already well known for his geological research on sandstones. Candrew enjoyed teaching geology and was gratified when the graduate students he supervised succeeded. But he no longer had the focused enthusiasm he had when he was in graduate school. Although not exactly jaded, his activities had become more routine. Certainly, as he accumulated data, new concepts emerged, though somehow there seemed to be an inevitability about them. The insight and flash of excitement—the proverbial light going on—was no longer there. Diamonds were different. His recent studies of these amazing gems had rekindled some of his earlier fervor. The whole field was new to him, and the technical papers he read opened up a novel, fascinating area of research. His recent field trips had been planned with enthusiasm and full of eager anticipation—though certainly some had consequences he'd not expected!

———

It was mid-morning before he drove to campus. Candrew parked on the gravel in his usual spot behind Kinblade Hall and went directly to the lab to see Judy.

As he let himself into the lab, he asked, "How did yesterday's *Introductory Geology* class go?" He settled onto the tall stool at the end of the worktable, resting his elbows on the bench.

"Fine." She pushed a box with two remaining glazed donuts toward him. "The students said it was awesome to have an instructor who explained the earth sciences in a way they could understand." Giggling, she peered at Candrew.

Fortunately, he knew she was kidding—or hoped she was. Candrew poured himself a mug of coffee and took one of the donuts.

"There were quite a few questions at the end of my lecture," she said. "You seem to have a group that's gotten really interested in geologic esoterica."

"Maybe some of them will change their major to geology. We always like to have a few more students."

"I do have some other good news for you." Judy pointed to several substantial cardboard boxes at the end of the lab. "About an hour ago the shipping company delivered the heavy liquids we'd ordered. I'll be able to start separating the last batch of your indicator minerals." Laughing, she added, "I'm bracing for that terrible smell again. I guess that's why I didn't become a chemistry major—and became a geologist."

"I'm looking forward to seeing what you find in this new batch of sand samples," he said. "You did a great job last time."

"Processing those sands is going to be a fair amount of work. And I've got all our other projects as well." She looked at Candrew seriously. "I hope you don't mind, but I asked Kate Montoya, one of your graduate students, to help me separate all those potential indicator minerals from your samples. I told her we could pay her for the time she worked. I know she needs the money."

"Like most graduate students. And she probably has student loans to pay off." Candrew grinned. "No problem. One of the nice things about my having an endowed chair is that it's endowed." Smiling, he explained, "I've got discretionary money I can use. You made a good choice with Kate. She's smart, and very conscientious."

"She's got class this morning, but we planned to get started on your sands after lunch," Judy said. "I've already done some of the preliminary magnetic separations."

"Let me know when you get results," he said.

Candrew thanked her for giving his Thursday lecture, taking care of the lab, and getting everything organized. He then picked up his lecture notes and left.

He took the stairs up to his office. After checking e-mails, the first thing he did was send Jay Wolverton an e-mail to thank him for taking the time to talk about diamond exploration techniques. He didn't expect a reply, and in fact never got one.

As he sat thinking over the previous day's visit to California, he realized he'd learned more about Wolverton's business than he had about diamonds. And he'd obtained very little information about possible locations of kimberlite diatremes—just two possible sites. He'd learned nothing concerning 'Alex' who had allegedly been working with him.

Candrew went over to his bookshelf and pulled out a three-ring binder. It was the one he was using to keep all his notes on diamonds, and he added a page summarizing what little he'd learned from his San Diego visit. As he was doing this, the phone rang and he picked it up. It was Renata.

"How did your fact-finding trip to the west coast go?" she asked. "Those Californians have all the answers?"

"If they do, they didn't share them with me."

"Nothing at all?" She sounded surprised.

"Well, a few snippets of information."

"Come and have dinner, and you can tell me all about the mining secrets you learned."

"Best offer I've had all day. Happy to accept," he said, and meant it.

A student had been hovering outside his office door and Candrew waved him in. He was one of the graduate students doing his Master's degree research on a western sandstone outcrop. He had new results. Candrew spent almost an hour helping him evaluate the data.

Late morning, Candrew made his way over to the Faculty Lounge. It was a pleasant day as he walked across campus, breezy, with a clear-blue sky. Students were scattered in groups, some throwing Frisbees, most in groups chattering, and some with textbooks actually studying.

Coming toward him across the Central Plaza was Claudette from the French Department whom he'd gotten to know fairly well from several academic committee meetings. With her was the college Dean, the professor he'd talked to about minerals at the faculty party a couple of weeks ago. They stopped and chatted.

After the usual campus gossip and trivia, Candrew told the Dean he'd gone to see the two mineral dealers he'd told him about. "In fact, I got back yesterday from visiting Jay Wolverton in San Diego."

"What did you think? Was it worth the long trip?"

Candrew was a bit cautious in what he said, not knowing the Dean's relationship with Wolverton. "He had a wide range of spectacular minerals for sale."

"Yeah, I'm sure he did." The Dean said. "I hope you didn't buy any."

Candrew raised his eyebrows, looking puzzled.

"One of my mineral-collecting friends gave me some background information on Wolverton. I was told that several of the crystal clusters he'd bought were not what they appeared to be. They'd been put together from disparate sources, sort of assembled from different minerals."

"I wondered about that," Candrew said. "I was surprised to see a wide range of technical equipment at Wolverton's place. Not what you'd expect for someone who just buys and sells minerals."

"No, it isn't." The Dean nodded with understanding. "My friend had the big crystal group he'd bought examined under ultraviolet light. You could see where transparent acrylic glue had been used to cement the different mineral crystals together."

"And I wouldn't be surprised if he didn't irradiate some crystals to enhance their color," Candrew said. "There was a radioactive source in their work area."

The mineral topic ran its course with Claudette seeming to have little interest. She asked Candrew how his semester was going. They talked about life in the university for a little longer, then went their separate ways.

Candrew continued on to the Faculty Club. As he rode the elevator, he thought about his lunchtime colleagues. He always learned a lot from this 'lunch bunch' with their wide variety of backgrounds in the humanities and business, as well as in other scientific disciplines. Their views, often quite different from his—and enthusiastically expressed—got him thinking in novel directions.

At the lunch table he was greeted in the usual friendly fashion, but no one asked him about his activities with diamonds. He was relieved. Groups seated around the table were mainly involved in defending their political positions, enthusing about the prowess of their sports teams, or touting their favorite fishing locations. While Candrew waited for the Reuben sandwich he'd ordered, he realized that this bunch almost never talked about university affairs. Like him, they regarded lunch time as a chance to relax and get away from campus problems—sort of neutral territory.

Back in his office after lunch, he spent half an hour going through the most recent technical journals. It was always an ongoing battle to keep up with relevant publications. Candrew was aware that science continuously develops as more data are acquired and new theories evolve. Professionally, of course, he needed to remain up to date, and he also felt a strong obligation to keep his lectures current. Inspired by this thinking, he took the opportunity to flip through the course notes he'd got back from Judy, and made a few revisions and additions to the material for next week's class.

The rest of the afternoon was taken up working on his current manuscript that had now become more urgent. The editor of the publication that would include Candrew's contribution had imposed a revised deadline for submissions. *Too short a time frame,* he thought, but he could live with it. He spent a couple of hours struggling to find the best way to present his novel ideas, with all the scientific data to support them, as well as wrestling to produce grammatically-correct English. He finally gave up for the day.

Dinner with Renata seemed to promise a relaxed evening, and he drove to her house a little after six. On the way he thought about his enthusiasm for scientific research, including his recent interest in diamonds, Although he enjoyed teaching and working with students, it was his technical activities that occupied most of his waking hours. But it was Renata, though, who filled the gaps in the personal aspects of his life. She met him at the door with her usual big hug.

They sat in the comfort of her living room, drinking margaritas and talking for a while, before moving into the dining room. Renata had cooked spaghetti with clams. As they sat eating, she asked, "Does Conroy Elkerson know you've been out to San Diego to see Jay Wolverton?"

Candrew twisted spaghetti onto his fork and speared a clam. "I haven't told him. Not only does he not know, I'm sure he doesn't care." Their visit to Conroy in Colorado had been instructive, although Candrew hadn't considered calling to let him know that the Polish mineral searcher—the one who'd deserted him to go and work with Wolverton—had been found dead. It was always possible that Conroy might have some ideas about that murder. Candrew made a mental note to phone him in the morning. He'd already told Detective Alvarez about Alex's relationship with Conroy.

A long moment passed. "Tell me more about your California jaunt. Was it worth going all that way?" Renata asked. "What did you learn? What business does this Wolverton do?"

"On paper, he acquires and sells exceptional minerals specimens."

"And in reality?" She raised her eyebrows.

"I've gotten the impression he acquires not-so-perfect minerals, doctors them so they look exceptional, and sells them for exorbitant prices."

"So, he's into a sort of mineralogical faking?" Renata said. "Clearly not to be trusted. Money the driving force?"

"Isn't it always in business?" he said, grinning. "I also suspect he's involved in some mineral exploration projects. He seemed quite interested in what I was doing with diamond indicator minerals. And he was surprisingly knowledgeable about exploration methods. I got the impression he had more than a casual interest in exploring for diamonds, although he denied that. I didn't get any clear idea of what his role might be."

Candrew pushed his empty wine glass across the table and Renata filled it. "I did get to meet a few of the people who worked for Wolverton."

"Collaborators, or paid help?"

"I'm sure most were just paid help. But there was one exception, a guy called Skip. He looked like a California surf bum and drove a battered off-road pickup truck. He seemed to know what he was doing in mineral exploration. Unfortunately, I only had a very brief conversation with him."

As they sat eating the blueberries and ice cream Renata served for dessert, Candrew speculated on what Wolverton actually knew about the Polish man's death. "I find it hard to believe that that San Diego dealer had no idea what was going on," Candrew said. "They were collaborators, for heaven's sake." He ate some berries and thought for a moment. "I talked to the woman doing technical work," he said. "She didn't seem to know anything about the death of the Pole."

"Do the police have any idea who killed him?" she asked.

"No. Or if they do, they've been tight-lipped about letting me in on their homicide investigations. I haven't heard how he was killed. I assume it was poison, since he didn't seem to have any obvious physical injuries. However, that's still just an assumption."

For a moment Candrew sat quietly staring at his dessert. "There's still the question of who killed him, and who dumped his body in the mine. And what was their motive? That Pole, Alex, didn't die by accident. He was murdered for a reason."

CHAPTER 24

JUDY KNEW CANDREW WAS eager to find out what his recently collected sand samples would show. She'd gotten Kate, a geology graduate student, to help her get the project done quickly. She'd come to the lab on Friday afternoon after class, ready to work. Tall and athletic, she was dressed in jeans and a university *'Yellowlander'* tee shirt.

Judy explained the process. "I've already ground up the samples and sieved them. Now we're going to drop those grains into the liquid methylene iodide, that's the foul-smelling, 'heavy' liquid." She grinned. "The name comes from its very high density. So high, in fact, that many of the common minerals actually float in it. Only the dense ones sink, and they include the garnet and diopside minerals we're after. They're the ones Dr. Nor is sure can show association with diamonds."

"Didn't they sometimes find diamonds when they were panning for gold?" Kate asked.

"Same idea," Judy said. "When you're panning, you swirl the water around and the lighter minerals get swept off the pan and the heavier ones—gold and diamonds if you're lucky—accumulate at the bottom. We're sort of doing the same thing using heavy liquids and letting the denser minerals sink and get separated."

Kate immediately understood what they had to do, and together they worked diligently on separating the indicator minerals. Although they made good progress, they weren't able to finish that afternoon. They agreed to get back to the task on Saturday morning. Kate was quite enthusiastic—and the fact that she could earn some extra cash was an added incentive.

———

Mid-morning on Saturday, Candrew sat at home listening to a Carl Nielson symphony on his stereo system, drinking hot tea, eating cookies, and reading a novel. But all this made him feel guilty—everyone else seemed to be working, and he was just relaxing. To assuage his guilt, he took out the trash and loaded the dishwasher with accumulated dirty dishes. Then he watered a few garden plants that seemed to be wilting.

Candrew went back and slumped into his padded chair and picked up his novel—but guilt still dominated. Since he'd been out of town for a couple of days earlier in the week, there were several things he felt needed doing. He found a dog treat and tossed it to Chile, then grabbed his briefcase and drove to the university,

The campus had a deserted feel on this Saturday morning, with few students around. In his office he pulled his chair up to the computer and checked the recent e-mails. He was surprised by one from Murray O'Connor, the map librarian at the MINEx mining company. The e-mail had come in late the previous night. He sat back in his chair and read it.

Dr. Nor:

I've gotten some information for you concerning the map you brought up to our MINEx office in Calgary. It's the one that Chris Donnington, our CEO, was interested in seeing.

You may recall that there were a couple of geologists on the plane when you flew up here. One of them was Carl Denby, and he's good friends with a company geologist in Arizona who thinks he might know the location that the map is showing. Carl wants to talk to you about that, but doesn't have any contact information. I'll give you his phone number and e-mail so you can find out what he wants to tell you.

Hope everything is going well for you down there in your Lower Forty-Eight.

Thanks again for bringing up the map you found on that dead man and letting me copy it—although I have still not figured out what manuscript it had been cut out of.

Sincerely, Murray O'Connor.

Interesting, Candrew thought. He read the e-mail again and jotted down the contact numbers. So, someone might actually know about the area shown on Alex's old map. Maybe that information could help show why the immigrant Pole had been murdered—and perhaps provide a clue to the motive.

Candrew was less excited by the other e-mails, especially the one from his department chairman scheduling a departmental faculty meeting for two o'clock on Monday afternoon. He wondered what this time-consuming gathering would be about.

The next couple of hours passed quickly while he worked through most of his remaining projects. Later that afternoon, as he drove home, his thoughts centered on the message from Murray. In particular he wondered what Carl, the MINEx geologist who'd been on the plane, wanted to tell him. He looked forward to Monday's phone call.

Candrew and Chile ambled down the driveway and retrieved the Sunday newspaper. He poured coffee and had just settled down to attempt the weekend Sudoku challenge when the phone rang.

"Sorry to disturb your Sunday peace." It was Judy. "I hope I'm not calling too early, but I know you're eager to get results for the latest group of indicator minerals."

"You're right about that," Candrew said. "And, no, you're not calling too early."

"Well anyway, yesterday Kate and I finished separating out the garnets and diopsides you're interested in. They appeared to be especially abundant in one of the sandstone groups. The group you'd labelled 'R.'"

Candrew tried to recall just where that was. With the phone pressed up against his ear he went to the living room and got his field notebook from his bag. He flipped through the pages.

"I know you don't pay overtime for weekend work," she joked, "How about hazard pay for all that foul-smelling liquid you made us use?"

"Sorry. Not a chance."

"I was thinking of taking the separated mineral concentrates over to Kernfeld's lab," Judy said. "You know, get the chromium data you want. He's such a workaholic and I'm certain he'll be there, even though it's Sunday. And that new post-doc who works with him is just as bad—or is it *just as good*? He's certainly enthusiastic about their research."

"Excellent idea," Candrew said. "I know they're busy, but it'll be good to get into their schedule. I'm really excited about seeing what results they get. Especially for my Group R."

On Monday morning when Candrew climbed the stairs and arrived at his office he was met by a couple of students.

"You got time for a quick question, professor?" asked the one with a baseball cap on backwards wearing well-worn jeans.

"Sure. Not a problem." Candrew unlocked his door and ushered them in.

It turned out not to be a 'quick question.' It took him nearly thirty minutes to explain the intricacies, and he pulled out a couple of textbooks and provided them with Internet references. "Come back if you have any problems with the material," he told them.

The students left, obviously not too sure about the extra amount of work this would involve.

Typical week, Candrew thought, staring at his list of things to do. Student interactions, of course, were an on-going part of being a professor, and he accepted that.

His first chore today was to phone Conroy, the mineral dealer in Colorado. After several rings, the call was answered by a woman. "Sorry, he's not here right now," she said. "Can I help you?"

"When do you expect him back?"

"I'm not sure." There was a long pause. "Maybe late this afternoon. He's out with clients."

Candrew thought about leaving a message. Should he let Conroy know about Alex's murder? Or would it be better to take him by surprise and get an off-the-cuff, knee-jerk response—a reply possibly closer to the truth?

"I'll call back later," he told the woman on the phone

"You want to leave a message?"

"No. But you can tell him Candrew Nor called."

"I'll do that," she said.

Next on Candrew's list was to phone Carl Denby, the geologist in Calgary that Murray O'Connor said wanted to talk to him.

Candrew couldn't remember if Calgary was in the same time zone, but if not, there'd only be an hour's difference. That shouldn't matter. He called.

"Yeah? Carl here," he answered briskly.

"This is Candrew Nor in New Mexico. I got an e-mail from Murray saying you wanted to talk to me. Remember, I was on the flight with you going from Santa Fe to Calgary."

"Right. Good to hear from you." There was a moment's silence as if he was clearly considering what he wanted to say. "When you came up to MINEx you brought an old map. At the time, nobody here was certain if it showed a specific location. And if it was an actual area, where it would be? The consensus then was that it probably showed somewhere in the desert southwest."

"It certainly looked like that to me," Candrew agreed.

"Well, that's part of the world where MINEx is active. Got a lot of copper mining going on down there in Arizona. And quite a few experienced geologists working our leases. One of them, a friend of mine, knows the area real well. I got Murray to send him a copy of your map and he thought he knew where it was. He spends a lot of his spare time hiking, and does some free-lance prospecting as a hobby."

"Where?" Candrew asked, intrigued. "Just in Arizona?"

"As far as I know he rambles farther afield than that. But, in fact, he thought your map showed an area right at the eastern Arizona border with New Mexico. So, it's close to your territory."

"I wonder if he's learned anything about the abandoned mine where I was trapped—where I found Alex, the murdered Pole?"

"I don't know anything about that. You could call him and ask him."

"What did he think the map was showing?" Candrew asked.

"I'm not sure how much time he actually spent exploring the buttes and arroyos, but what he told me was that it was probably a kimberlite pipe."

Diamonds was Candrew's immediate thought—but he didn't say anything. Did the kimberlite intrusive provide a reason for Alex being out there?

"Will MINEx pursue this?" Candrew asked.

"Donnington got where he is today not by being nice but by being devious," he mumbled. "Hold on a second. Let me close my office door." Candrew heard it being shut, then Carl was back on the phone. "Our chief has worked a few dubious deals on Indian land in the past. Which is interesting because Bert—that's my friend—is actually part American Indian. For many years his father worked as a medic on the Navajo reservation and then married a Navajo woman. I think growing up on the rez, with all those dramatic rock formations, is what got him interested in geology. As far as I know he still spends some time out there."

"Does he speak Navajo?" Candrew asked.

"That I don't know," Carl said. "I'll give him a call and see if he'll talk to you. Like me, he's curious to know why the page of an old map you found was on the body of a dead man—a murdered man."

CHAPTER 25

AFTER CARL DENBY'S INFORMATIVE Monday morning phone call, and the afternoon's time-consuming department meeting, Candrew's week settled into an uneventful academic routine. On Tuesday, he taught his undergraduate class, dealt with student problems, and worked on his research with Judy. The only pleasant surprise was an invitation to lunch with the Pengellys the following day. But lunch today would be with his usual colleagues in the Faculty Lounge.

A little before noon on Wednesday, Renata picked Candrew up and drove to the Pengelly's house east of campus. On the way, she told him about the current status of her research program. "I just got an e-mail from my research colleague in Guatemala," she said. "There's quite a bit of semester left, of course, but I'm already starting to plan my ongoing digs at the usual Mayan location."

Candrew knew that for several years her research program had centered on a Mayan archaeological site, and that she still had a career's worth of work remaining there. He also knew that spending summers in Central America provided a chance to visit her parents in Costa Rica, and she always looked forward to that. It gave her a break from the scholarly excavations.

He glanced across at her. She looked particularly attractive wearing a rich blue cotton blouse with light grey linen slacks. Candrew was well aware that he'd have to endure a couple of summer months without her.

"There's a surprising amount of stuff that needs to get shipped to the excavation site," Renata said, "as well as getting people scheduled."

For a moment there was silence as she turned off onto the rural road toward the foothills.

"We have to plan way ahead and get everything organized. We can't just turn students loose and let them start digging. They need to be supervised. There's always the chance they could dig up an artifact that may be worth a lot of money on the black market. That would be a real temptation for students who generally don't have much money anyway. And, of course, we could lose major artifacts, as well as all manner of important insights they might give us."

"It's bad enough that you have to deal with the grave robbers," Candrew said.

"Yeah. That's almost part of the local culture. It's been going on for centuries."

She swung the car into the Pengelly's driveway and parked.

Wilfred greeted them at the door. His wife, Allison, was out on the back patio, and they went through to join her in the shade under the portál.

Wilfred pulled his chair up beside Candrew. "How's your semester going?" This seemed to be the opening question among academics.

"Pretty much the same as usual," he replied. "But as always, I'm amazed how fast time slips by. I'm already thinking about questions for the final exam."

"Then all you'll have to do is grade it," Wilfred said, grinning. "My main task is to run one more field trip. I feel it's important to keep showing students the real world."

"Where're you taking them this time?" Candrew asked, wondering if it would be somewhere he'd be interested in visiting. He knew the old cliché: *the best geologists are the ones who've seen the most rocks.*

"Up to Questa," Wilfred clarified.

"That old molybdenum mine? You going to have Brandon go with you this time?"

"No. He said he couldn't make it, he had some sort of conflict. That's a shame. He knows a lot of geology, and is a good monitor, and the students like him."

"I'm sure you can handle it," Candrew said, being supportive.

Allison leaned over. "Don't you guys ever talk about anything but work, and science?" she said joking, but with a grain of truth in her question. "Anyway, it's time to eat," she told them, changing the emphasis.

They went into the dining room, picked up plates, and served themselves from an enticing selection of dishes—all traditional American food this time with no Cornish delicacies. They carried their loaded plates back to the patio and sat eating, drinking, and chatting in the warm sunlight.

"Are you still painting?" Renata asked Allison.

"Yeah. Mostly in the studio, but also sometimes outdoors. It's that time of year when it's warm enough to lure me out into the wilderness. So, I paint some of my landscapes *en plein air*."

Later, when they'd finished eating, Allison took Renata back into the studio to show her the partly finished landscape she was working on.

The men sat drinking their coffee. Candrew had already told Wilfred that the Dean was a mineral collector and had given him information about a couple of dealers. "I've visited both of them," he said."

"You told me about the one in Colorado. *You* becoming a mineral collector?" Wilfred said grinning.

"Well, not with the high-end items these two peddle. Although I did buy a nice fluorite from the guy in Colorado," Candrew said. "But the California dealer is way out of my league. Beautiful stuff, but expensive." He considered how much to tell Wilfred. "However, I'm beginning to hear rumors that some of his proffered minerals may have been tampered with to make them look a lot more attractive—and a lot more expensive."

They talked for another ten minutes or so, then Wilfred said,

"Come and see the painting Allison's working on. A landscape." As he pushed back his chair and got up, he added, "I'm no aesthete, but I do like her artwork. I guess I'm more into realism than into abstracts."

They headed to the studio at the back of the house, going along a passageway lined with local artwork, but also with some photographs and a hanging Navajo carpet.

Allison was pleased to show Candrew her partly finished painting. "It's still a work in progress," she said smiling. "I had to stop when the wind got too bad. A three-foot square canvas on an easel behaves just like a sail. If you're not careful it'll go flying off." She laughed, clearly tolerant of the challenges of painting outdoors.

"On my last trip, when the wind picked up, I *packed* up." She grinned. "That's when I rely on the photos I take so I can finish the painting back here in the studio. Thank God for iPhone cameras."

Allison got more serious. "But wind wasn't the only nuisance we had to put up with. My friend and I had been painting for about an hour when a tall, rough-looking character came and sort of hassled us. Told us in no uncertain terms that we were on the Navajo reservation. He was curious to know what we were doing. I would have thought that was pretty obvious, but he did look carefully at the paint boxes and our paintings. He wanted to know why we were taking photographs—and when we were leaving. Anyway, we finally convinced him we were harmless women and he left us alone."

Candrew asked where she'd been painting. "It's an area Wilf suggested," she said. "He thought it had an interesting and colorful mix of arroyos, hills, and mountains."

The location she described was a bit south of the area that Candrew had gone to on the field trip with Wilfred and his mining students. He remembered the visit to the kimberlite diatreme.

"Lots of exposed rocks. Naked geology," she said smiling. Since Candrew seemed interested in the area, she told him, "Hold on, let me go and get my cell phone." She disappeared into the kitchen and came back holding the phone in one hand, flicking through the images with the other. "Ah, here we are. This is close to the place where we had our easels."

Candrew looked at the photo and was interested to see what appeared to be a fresh pile of rock debris spilling down the edge of one of the hillsides. He pulled out his own cell phone, searched though the photos, and showed her some locations close to where she'd been painting.

He realized one of his shots was taken from an almost identical position to hers. He put the cell phones side-by-side. "Look at these two images. See, that butte is the same in both of them. And the outlines of the distant mountains are identical." He glanced up at her. "Even that group of dark bushes is the same in both photos."

Allison, looking over his shoulder, agreed.

But what struck Candrew immediately was that his view, photographed several weeks ago, had no broken rock talus pile. He stood in silence, amazed. This meant that the scattered debris of broken rock was recent. Clearly, it was new, and had been dumped down across that rock face in just the last week or so. The implication was obvious: someone was currently mining there. And what would they be mining in a kimberlite pipe? He had no doubt.

Although somewhat distracted by his thoughts of the recent appearance of the broken rock talus, he did join the others in looking at Allison's recent work. He liked the intense colors she'd used for the hillsides and mountains, and the contrasting deep-colored juniper trees. Wilfred discussed the chance of one of the Santa Fe galleries showing her paintings.

Later, as they got ready to leave, Renata said, "Next time, lunch is on us. Even if I'm sure I can't match your culinary skills." Laughing, she said, "Maybe I'll cook some Costa Rican food. Then you won't know what it should really taste like."

On the drive back to campus, Renata was eager to talk about

Allison's artwork and also the splendid food they'd been served. Candrew, however, was wrapped up in thoughts of the fresh talus pile in the area where Allison and her friend had been painting.

Renata dropped Candrew off at Kinblade Hall, since he planned to go to his office and wrap up a few things before heading home.

He had taken care of the essentials, and was just about to shut his office door and leave for the day, when the cell phone in his jacket pocket chirped. Mark Kernfeld greeted him with the welcome news that he had some analytical data.

"Not for all your samples," Kernfeld explained. "Judy, that Research Associate of yours, had prioritized some of the separated minerals. We've only had time to analyze less than half your rocks, so we started with the ones she thought would be of most interest. The ones you'd put in the 'R' group."

"That's fantastic. I appreciate your getting the compositional data so quickly."

"Glad to be able to help. And the values are intriguing. I looked back at the numbers we have on file for the last batch of samples we analyzed. Then you were interested in the chromium concentrations in the pyrope garnets, and they were quite high. But this new set have even higher values."

"Really? Wow."

"I just wanted to let you know that I've e-mailed all the numbers we have so far."

After some academic pleasantries the phone call ended and Candrew was eager to get back to his desk and pull up the computer screen with the data.

What he saw was a table showing the analytical values for about half the minerals Judy had separated. He looked at the column with the 'R' sand numbers, his highest priority group.

Kernfeld was right—those garnet chromium values were abnormally high. Candrew got his sketch map showing the places where he'd collected the samples. The high-priority 'R' sands were from an inside bend of the twisting arroyo. When water is flowing fast, it drags along eroded minerals, but where the current slows down on the bend, the heavy minerals drop out. Here's where the dense indicator minerals should be present in the highest concentration—and they were. And not only were there lots of them, but the high chromium content strongly suggested an association with diamonds.

Candrew printed out the file, stuffed it in his pocket, and hustled down the stairs to his lab. But the door was locked and Judy had obviously already left. He went out to his parked car, mulling over this suite of data.

From Kernfeld's analytical data for the indicator minerals, and Allison's cell phone image of the new talus pile, he had no doubt he needed to go back and explore that whole area in more detail. As he unlocked his Ford *Explorer*, clambered in, and drove home, he plotted a trip. If he left after class tomorrow, Thursday, he'd have Friday and the weekend clear. And there'd be no university commitments until class on the following Tuesday. Plenty of time.

CHAPTER 26

AFTER EXPLAINING THE SUBTLETIES and drama of geology to his Thursday morning undergraduate class, Candrew went back up to his office and called Renata. "I've definitely decided to take another look at the kimberlite pipes out on the Arizona border," he told her. "I'm going to drive to the area later today."

"Can't stay away from that debris pile? Just have to know what they're digging up?" He heard her laugh.

"Well, that's true, but there's another factor. After you dropped me off on campus yesterday, I got a call from Mark Kernfeld. Remember him? He's the guy who does the detailed chemical analyses of the minerals I collect. He'd gotten preliminary compositional data for a group of the indicator minerals. Some of those garnets had really high concentrations of chromium, and that's a well-known indicator of proximity to diamonds. So, I'm planning to go back and take another look at the kimberlite pipes I sampled earlier."

"And last time, that's where you got tricked into being locked up in an old mine."

"Well . . . yes." That was something Candrew had deliberately not dwelled on.

"Take care this time," she said. "I'll see you when you get back with a pocketful of gems."

Candrew drove home, ate a quick lunch, and packed—watched by a suspicious dog. That reminded him to call 'Shell, the graduate student who fed his pets and walked Chile when he was out of town. Fortunately, she answered her cell phone right away and said she'd have no problem coming to the house and taking care of the animals.

In the early afternoon, after stopping at the gas station to fill up and get a can of cold soda, he drove west on Route 64. This took him out to San Juan County, through Bloomfield, and on to where he could see Shiprock dominating the skyline. Candrew remembered that when he was here with Wilfred and the 'Major Miners', the Navajo student in the group explained the Diné myth of how the mountain got to be called *The Rock with Wings*. That student was Carlos Nez. Usually Candrew didn't have a particularly good memory for names, but this combination of the Spanish *Carlos* with the Navajo *Nez* had stuck.

An hour later, Candrew checked into one of the few motels on this section of the road. While not fancy, at least the spartan room was clean, and had a comfortable bed. He got up early the next morning, ate an energy bar he'd brought with him, and drank the motel's coffee.

It was a bright sunny morning as Candrew continued south on the highway for about forty-five minutes. He parked close to the kimberlite diatreme he'd been to with Wilfred. Candrew pulled on his broad-brimmed hat and put on sunglasses. The rocky area was pretty much as he remembered it, and he spent an hour trudging up the poorly marked, gravel footpath to the side of the kimberlite intrusion. Pushing his sunglasses up into his hair, he went into the excavated tunnel he'd discovered on his last trip.

He snapped on the flashlight he'd brought. This time he could see more than on his previous visit, when he'd only had the marginal illumination of a cell phone. He did notice a slight chemical odor and thought it might be from explosives, but he was no expert. Although he could see the light reflecting off the rough chiseled walls in more detail, as far as he could tell, nothing had changed since his earlier visit.

The hillside and surrounding areas were deserted with no sign of activity. He collected a few rock samples, took photos, and staggered back down the rocky path to his car.

Candrew drove along the road toward another of the diatremes marked on his geologic map. This one was close to where he thought the recent debris pile was located. He parked, pulled out his binoculars, and scanned the landscape to the west. It didn't take him long to spot the talus-covered slope, prominent as it was with its fresh, un-weathered, light-colored debris. Slowly, Candrew drove another mile down the road, paying careful attention to the topography. Closer to the talus pile, where there was a flat gravel area at the side of the road, he pulled off.

Looking around, he eventually saw a poorly defined, irregular path to the south side of the talus. Stumbling on the rough gravel, and pushing past the low bushes, he followed it up. Half way toward the top he stopped to rest and drink some water. Then he made his way over the cobbles and broken rock fragments to the talus slope. Several lumps went rolling down ahead of him and set others in motion. He was certain this pile was new and there hadn't been time for it to stabilize. Candrew sat on one of the larger boulders and pulled out his hand lens, eager to identify the rock type. None of the pieces he examined were kimberlites. Engrossed in his study, he suddenly got the feeling he was being watched. Slowly he stood up, turned, and looked around.

About forty yards further up the trail were two men standing silently, staring down at him.

Then the taller one shouted, demanded, "What the hell do you think you're doing?"

"I'm a geologist, looking at the rocks," Candrew yelled back.

"On the Navajo reservation? Without permission? You got a permit?"

"There's no fence, no warning signs," Candrew said defensively. He picked up his back pack and made his way up the trail to confront the men. They watched him approach.

When he got closer he recognized both of them. The dark-haired, younger man, was the student who'd been on the university field trip, the one who'd described the myth of Shiprock. He remembered him as Carlos.

The taller man had his long dark-hair corralled into a pony tail, and wore faded jeans and cowboy boots. His bulky backpack lay on the ground beside him. He'd been at the excavation in the other kimberlite pipe when Candrew was last out in this geologically interesting area. This man, of course, had suggested Candrew ought to go and see the old mine, the one where he'd been locked in and abandoned. Now, suspicious and very nervous, Candrew glanced around. The surrounding hills with their scrubby bushes were deserted. He was here alone with these two Navajos.

Candrew was hesitant, but direct. "So, you're here exploring for diamonds?"

"Maybe." The taller man's reply was reluctant. "But if we find any, we intend to keep them," he said bluntly. "We Navajos are used to being plundered. But not anymore. We learned our lesson from the tons of uranium stolen from our lands—and look at all the chaos that mining left behind."

"Right," Carlos agreed. "Dozens of abandoned uranium mines littered across Diné. And lots of radioactive trash piles. The Government's not exactly rushing to fund uranium clean up. Best they can do is call it a *Superfund Site*. They claim there'll be jobs for tribal citizens, though we haven't seen too many of those yet." He paused and glared at Candrew as though it was his fault. "And it's not only the surface that's been screwed up, our ground water's contaminated as well. Anyway, many of our people don't have running water. Or electricity. And that's in spite of the value of all our uranium that was dug up and hauled away."

There was silence for a moment, then the older man said, "At least we've made some progress with the Fed folks. Mining uranium on the reservation is now banned." He nodded as if to show his agreement with this new policy. Reminding Candrew his name was Raven, he added, "And, by the way, I'm Diné." He stared at Candrew who thought it appropriate he was wearing a black sweatshirt. "And you're . . . ?"

Candrew told him.

"And you are a science professor, right?" He looked Candrew over. "Problem with modern science—western science—is that it ignores anything sacred. Leaves out the spiritual. That's part of the reason so much of our land has been screwed up by you outsiders."

"We weren't given control of our own reservation," Carlos said. "Had to take orders from the Bureau of Indian Affairs."

Raven agreed. "This time we'll get it right. Do things our way. In harmony with Nature."

"And this time it's diamonds. Correct?" Candrew asked.

Raven gave him a suspicious look. There was a lengthy pause. "And why are you so interested in what we're doing?" he demanded to know. "You spying for the BIA?"

"No. Not at all."

Candrew stood evaluating this tall Navajo he'd met at the other diatreme, trying to decide whether he should pursue the question uppermost in his mind. Finally, he did. "So why did you send me to get locked up in a disused mine with a dead man?"

"I didn't," Raven snapped emphatically. "You'd convinced me you were an academic interested in minerals. I knew about a group that studied old mines looking for crystals they could sell. All I did was put you two together. I didn't even know where the mine was. And all I wanted was to get you off the reservation." He stared at Candrew as if to convince him he was telling the truth. "And I certainly knew nothing about a corpse being there. When I heard about that, it was incredible news for me. A big surprise."

"The victim was a Pole, and he had a strong accent. Everyone called him Alex," Candrew said. "Did you ever meet him?"

"No. Or if I did, I don't remember," he said, glancing down at the ground.

"That guy had been murdered," Candrew stressed. "If you've got any information about the people who worked the mine you should let the police know. They have an active homicide case going and need all the cooperation they can get."

"Yeah. I guess." The Navajo man seemed uncomfortable, and Candrew got the impression he was reluctant to deal with authorities.

Candrew was intrigued to hear Raven's explanations, although they seemed a little too well rehearsed, too well thought out. He wasn't sure whether to believe what he was being told. But his thoughts were interrupted by another man toiling up a trail that snaked across the back side of the butte. This was another person he recognized—Brandon.

Panting, Brandon reached the rim, came over to the trio, and dropped his pack. "Greetings," he said. He turned to Candrew, "I didn't expect to see you here."

"And I didn't expect to see you, either," Candrew replied.

Raven broke in, explaining. "We needed a geologist with knowledge of mining to help us." He nodded toward Brandon. "We'll have to file a mining claim, and have to have someone with expertise in doing that."

"But first we want to get enough information to be able to justify filing such a claim," Brandon said.

"I see you've already dug out quite a lot of rock," Candrew said, thinking of the talus pile beside the trail he'd hiked up. "But none of that looked like kimberlite."

Brandon grinned at Candrew's lack of knowledge of the mining process. "We excavated a vertical shaft beside the kimberlite pipe," he said. "That's where all the broken rock you saw came from, and you're right, it's not kimberlite. Now we can go down that shaft and tunnel horizontally into the pipe, haul away the rock, and separate the diamonds."

Candrew knew that there was usually only a carat or two in a ton of kimberlite. "You'll have to move a lot of rock."

"True."

"So, how you going to do that?" Candrew asked.

"Truck it out." Raven pointed toward the back trail Brandon had come up.

Candrew went over to the edge and looked down into the valley. At the bottom was a dirt road that led north and out onto the main highway. Multiple tire tracks suggested it had been used recently.

"But this is only our first step. Just an evaluation," Raven said. "We've got a long way to go."

Brandon explained their plan. "We want to have enough information about the diamond content of these kimberlite pipes to file a mining claim—and persuade investors to kick in some real money."

This comment made Candrew think of MINEx, the exploration company he'd visited in Calgary. They already had major mining operations active in Arizona. And they were just the sort of well-funded outfit that had money and mining experience—and they had a CEO who wouldn't care about a project being on Indian land.

CHAPTER 27

THE SUN'S LAST LIGHT was a faint orange glow over the western hills as Candrew drove toward home. Tired, lethargic, and emotionally drained, he felt it made sense to spend the night in a motel. Then, refreshed, he could complete his journey the next morning. Ironically, the motel he was approaching was the one he'd stayed in last night—not the most appealing, and now he was going to stay there for the second time in two days.

He pulled up, checked in, and parked outside the unit labelled B5. The dismal room with its threadbare carpet was already getting cold, but there was a corner gas heater. Candrew found a box of matches and lit it. The vintage television, resting on an old wooden chest of drawers, offered only a limited number of channels. He had no interest in the game shows, and little concern for the political arguments. He settled for one of the two sports channels. Long before the game ended, he was asleep.

After breakfast of an apple, motel muffins and coffee, Candrew sat in his *Explorer* SUV and called Renata. He gave her a brief outline of what had happened on the previous day at the potential diamond site. "I'll be back early afternoon," he said. "Let's get together for dinner this evening."

"I know it's your turn to cook," she joked. "But you've been busy, so I'll dream up some culinary surprise."

Candrew was ready to be surprised. "I'll be there around six."

After an uneventful drive, Candrew got back to campus at one thirty and, of course, went straight to his office. Even though he'd been gone only a couple of days there was the usual lengthy list of e-mails, and he promptly deleted much of the spam.

The most interesting e-mail was from Mark Kernfeld since it included additional mineral data. The covering note said that the lab had obtained analyses of trace elements in more of his minerals, particularly chromium in the pyrope garnets. Candrew printed out the attached file with the table listing the new data. Several of the sand samples he'd collected had very few indicator minerals, and Kernfeld's analyses showed they had low quantities of the critical chromium. One group looked a little more promising, however nothing spectacular. Two other groups that Judy had separated had not been analyzed yet, and he'd have to wait patiently for those numbers.

Candrew looked through the data again. Nothing was in the high range he'd gotten for his 'R' group minerals. That group included the sands eroded from the kimberlite pipe where he'd just met Brandon with the two Navajos, Raven and Carlos. He was starting to get a consistent picture of a possible commercial diamond site. He pushed back his chair, ran fingers through his hair, and thought about the implications of a diamond mine on the Navajo reservation.

The list of e-mails on his computer screen included one with an address he didn't recognize. He opened the message and found an unexpected e-mail from the police:

Dear Professor Nor:

Recently I visited you in your office at the university with Officer Garcia. We are part of the State Police team investigating a homicide. We interviewed you because you were the person who found the victim's body in an old mine. The deceased man had no identification and noth-

ing in his pockets. The only exceptions were the cell phone you took and the buttoned-up patch pockets in his working pants. These contained several lumps of rock. Since you are a tenured senior geology Professor with an endowed chair . . .

Candrew smiled to himself. The detective had certainly done his homework.

. . . and you are also the person who discovered the body, you are already involved in our procedures. We want to know if you would be prepared to examine these stones and let us know what they are. There is always the possibility that this information might provide another piece of evidence that could be helpful in our ongoing investigations. I can bring them to the university anytime next week that fits your schedule. Please e-mail me a time that would be most convenient for you.

I assume that the stones will be from the US, but that may not be the case. You already have been advised that the homicide victim was originally from Poland, but had become a U.S. citizen. In pursuing our contacts with Federal Agencies, they had information in their files that in the past he had worked for Alrosa. Alsosa is a Russian diamond company and I'm told it is one of the biggest in the world. The agency had no information about when he terminated his position with them and whether he still had a role in their exploration program. This raises the possibility that he was acting as a source of confidential information for them, letting them know about any likely diamond mines in the US. Or diamond mining planned by American companies. I will talk to you more when we get together.

Sincerely, Detective Ortega, New Mexico State Police.

Candrew was stunned to learn that Alex may have been a Russian spy. He was quite eager to see what mineral specimens would have been in his trouser pockets. He promptly replied to the police e-mail suggesting they bring the rocks to campus on Monday afternoon and he'd take a look at them.

Candrew was in no mood to work, and drove home to an excited dog and a merely tolerant cat. They both followed him out onto the patio where he slumped into the only padded chair, and drank a can of fruit juice.

He sat thinking about the new kimberlite pipe he'd climbed and the three people he encountered there. Uppermost in his mind was Raven's assertion that he knew almost nothing about those responsible for locking him in the mine, only the name of the mineral group—and their truck driver. All three claimed they had no knowledge of Alex's Polish background, or his current role in accumulating diamond information.

Candrew wondered whether the Pole's activities with diamond exploration was the reason he'd been murdered. But by whom? And was the same group who'd murdered Alex also responsible for locking him in the abandoned mine? Candrew was still not sure about Brandon. Why was he cooperating with the Navajos, and what role did he have in their proposed mining project?

He walked out into the garden, following a scrubby footpath winding among the junipers and pinon trees. Sitting out there on an old wooden bench, seemed to be the ideal place for thinking deep thoughts.

Thirty minutes later Candrew made his way back to the house and phoned Wilfred. "Tell me about Brandon," he said, "and his girlfriend."

"Bright student," Wilfred said, "but then he's older than most of his peers and had finished his degrees several years ago. After graduation, he worked for a couple of exploration companies, so has had quite a bit of real-world experience. What did you want to know?"

"Does he have any experience or special knowledge about diamond exploration?"

"That I don't know," Wilfred said. "But, now you mention it, I think maybe he did do a project on diamonds s part of his graduate degree."

"How about his collaboration with the Navajo?" Candrew asked.

"Again, I have no direct knowledge," Wilfred said. There was a moment's pause. "But now that I think about it, he does seem to be close friends with Carlos Nez, and he's Navajo."

Candrew changed his topic. "How about Jessica Rylander. She still his girlfriend?"

"I'm not privy to any of the details, so I don't know about that. They still seem to be good friends."

Late in the afternoon, Candrew showered, shaved, and managed to find a clean shirt: it was still hanging in a plastic sleeve from the dry-cleaners. With his distracting thoughts, he hardly paid attention to the route as he drove over to Renata's for dinner.

As always, she greeted him with a big hug and a kiss. They got wine and sat in the living room. He told her about climbing up two of the western diatremes. "I thought all the excitement was going to be with the kimberlite pipes," he said.

"Out in the wilderness where you geologists thrive. Right?" she quipped.

"Not entirely. I had an especially interesting e-mail from the state police when I got back to campus."

"You stealing gems?"

"No. I'm finding dead Russian spies in abandoned mines."

"Really?" She raised her eyebrows, looking puzzled. "That's a new twist." She was interested. "Tell me what the police told you about their homicide investigations."

"From detective Ortega's e-mail, it seems that the dead man had ties to a huge Russian diamond corporation. Called *Alrosa*. May have been an informant for them, telling them about North American diamond exploration projects," Candrew said. "Makes me wonder if this was why he was murdered."

"And raises the question of who was responsible."

"That's an intriguing question. I don't know how much the police have actually discovered about Alex's background. Or how much the FBI and CIA have told our local cops."

"Well, we know Alex worked for the mineral collector we went to see in Colorado," Renata said.

"Yes, that's right. Although I don't think Conrad Elkerson dealt in diamonds, or even had any intention of getting involved in that business." For a moment Candrew ate and thought about the possibility. "But then, Alex did collaborate with him before he left to go work with Jay Wolverton in San Diego. And Wolverton's certainly someone who could have had plans to explore for diamonds."

"And from what you told me after your trip to California, he'd probably have the sort of mining contacts with sufficient funds and experience to do that," Renata said.

"We don't have definite proof Alex was involved with diamond exploration, of course, but I suppose it's certainly a possibility."

"He definitely seems to have had wide knowledge of what was going on in the mineral business."

For a few moments they both ate in silence, thinking over different facets of this complicated situation.

Candrew sipped his wine. "Diamond mining involves moving vast quantities of rock. The gems are only a trivial percentage of the total rock mass. This means you need a pretty big company to economically mine those gems. It's not the sort of thing an old-fashioned prospector with a mule and a shovel could do."

"So, this limits the likely companies?" she asked.

"Yes, it does. I keep thinking of the Canadian company MINEx. They're already active in Arizona and have staff geologists scouring the area. It was one of their geologists who figured out what area that old map was showing. I haven't had a chance to go and check out that specific location myself, so I don't know if there's any kimberlite pipes. It's always possible that a company geologist has gone and looked at the rocks."

Renata realized where the conversation was heading. Grinning, she said, "So how long before *you* head to that area?"

"No plans," he said, grinning. "But speaking of the competition by big companies, there's always the Australians. They're already major producers—and aggressive in exploration and development."

"What about South Africa? That's what you always hear when people talk about diamonds."

"'*De Beers*.'" Candrew said. "A pioneering diamond company and another active explorer. They're already involved in dozens of countries. I guess they have to be a possibility."

"This is getting quite international. Apart from the usual suspects, you've even got the Navajo Nation involved."

"Yeah, that's right. But I'd be surprised if the big players, such as Russia, Australia and, of course, South Africa, would be threatened by minor outfits like those in the U.S.," Candrew said. "Although, I can't help feeling that the Canadian company, MINEx, is a real competitor."

"I suppose if you're in the business, it's prudent to keep an eye on all your potential competitors."

"And I'm sure Donnington, their CEO, is keeping an eye on everything."

They talked until after eleven, but failed to solve the world's diamond exploration problems. Renata went into the kitchen and made hot cocoa. They talked about interesting topics that didn't involve mining for a while, and Candrew stayed overnight.

When he woke, he was alone in the bed. Renata had gotten up early, and now Candrew dressed, savoring the inviting smell of coffee and the aroma of frying bacon and sausages. Renata took a jug of orange juice and a platter of toast to the sunlit table on the patio. They carried out their fried breakfasts and coffee.

Candrew drank his juice looking across at the mountains. It was a still morning but warm enough. He missed watching Chile poking around and exploring for evidence of nocturnal visitors. "You need to get yourself a dog," he told Renata.

"I always thought of you as my pet." She grinned mischievously.

"Great Dane or Pekinese?" he asked.

She laughed, poured their coffee, and said, "I'll take the fifth."

CHAPTER 28

CANDREW'S WEEK STARTED WITH a typical Monday morning. He spent the time grading student papers, revising lecture notes, talking with students, and working on his manuscript. But what dominated his thoughts were the memories of both his visit to the diatremes, and the police e-mail telling him that Alex may have been working for a Russian diamond company. He was eagerly anticipating Detective Ortega's afternoon visit that would give him a chance to examine the rocks Alex had collected.

He gave up the attempt to do anything more productive, and left for an early lunch at the Faculty Lounge. When he got to the Lounge, only three of the usual group were there. One of them, Lubie, promptly quizzed Candrew, "Did you read this morning's paper?"

"Only the comics, sports page, and a glance at the headlines. Why?"

"Well, since you're our diamond magnate, you probably should know about the Australians moving in."

"Really?"

"You ever hear of *DiamonEx?*" Lubie asked. He didn't wait for an answer, "It's an Australian company, and they've just acquired diamond leases north of here, up on the Colorado-Wyoming boundary. It's known as the State Line area, and if I recall correctly, there's a *Sloan 1* and *Sloan 2* mine. In the past they've been worked for diamonds."

Candrew raised his eyebrows in interest. "I've read about the

Sloan mines, but didn't think they were still producing. I guess the Australians are planning some sophisticated new technology." But Candrew was thinking that this diamond exploration area was, of course, just up the road from the mineral dealer Conroy Elkerson. That raised the question of whether he had any role in this exploration. Or was it Alex who'd been involved? He'd worked with Conroy, and Candrew had just learned that he apparently had some sort of relationship with the diamond-savvy Russians.

Ted Devereaux from the Business Office leaned over and offered advice. "If you're going to end up a diamond billionaire, you'd better get your diamond prospects leased fast. Get in before the competition."

Candrew's interest in diamonds was strictly academic, and he had no intention of going commercial. Arlan Dee didn't know that, and gave additional advice. "You might want to take Cecil Rhodes as a role model. In the late eighteen hundreds he founded *De Beers*, the company in South Africa that dominated the world-wide diamond trade for years. Made enough money to fund the Rhodes Scholarships at Oxford University in England." He grinned. "And he was politically astute enough to have a country named after him—*Rhodesia*."

"Well, Professor Nor," Ted said, "I'm sorry to have to tell you that '*NOR-WAY*' is already taken."

Candrew grinned, amused by his colleagues' suggestions.

Evelyn, the biologist, came over and pulled up a chair. "You still trying to figure out how to make a fortune mining diamonds?" she asked Candrew.

"Ah, but '*A diamond is forever*'," Ted said.

"You mean it has tenure?" she quipped.

Candrew walked back to his office still pondering the new State Line diamond project. Could Conrad Elkerson or Alex really have been involved?

———

An hour later, police detective Ortega arrived at Candrew's office on schedule. Candrew greeted him and motioned him to the empty chair in front of his desk. Tall and lean with dark glasses, Ortega gave the impression of being serious and humorless.

"Thanks for taking the time to evaluate these lumps of stone," Ortega said.

He had brought with him a large, zipped-up, black carrier bag. He reached in and pulled out a clear plastic box that he handed to Candrew.

Candrew pried off the snap-on lid and found the contents wrapped in newspaper. Altogether there were three pieces of rock about the size of sugar cubes, and several smaller fragments. The larger lumps felt heavy in his hand. All had dark coloration with a bluish tinge.

The detective stood in silence watching Candrew as he pulled open his desk drawer and reached for his hand lens.

Each of the rock samples had large irregular crystals embedded in a fine-grained matrix. The biggest crystals were a few millimeters across—"phenocrysts" was how Candrew described them. He identified the green minerals as olivines, and also found some garnets—but no diamonds. Each of Alex's rocks appeared to be a classic kimberlite. He gave that information to Detective Ortega and explained its relationship to diamonds.

"So, this is consistent with the information the CIA gave us. That Alex could have been working for *Alrosa*, that Russian diamond company," the detective said.

After a moment's deliberation, Ortega seemed to be pondering to himself as he asked, "Do you think there's any chance the homicide victim could have had diamonds in his pants packet? That that could have been a motive for murder? You know, it was essentially just a robbery?"

"I doubt it," Candrew said. "He'd have had to move and process a huge amount of rock to separate any diamonds from their host kimberlite. That would have taken a lot of equipment."

"I see."

Candrew picked up the chunks of rock. "Can I keep the samples?" he asked, hoping to get Mark Kernfeld to analyze them and provide chemical compositions.

"'Fraid not. They're evidence in our ongoing investigations. They'll have to stay in our evidence room until the investigation is completed. That could take years."

"To bad." He looked at the detective. "How about photographing them?"

Detective Ortega glanced at the rocks laid out on Candrew's desk and paused before saying, "I guess that won't pose a legal problem."

When Candrew finished snapping images with his iPhone, Ortega said, "What I would like you to do, is write a brief report on what you've found. What you've just told me about these chunks of rock. Something geological with a fancy name we can put in our file for the record." As an afterthought, he added, "And include the photographs you've just taken."

Candrew was happy to cooperate. But he had several questions. "How is your homicide investigation progressing? Do you have a suspect for the murder?"

"No suspect yet. We're making a lot of progress, but the Federal agencies complicate issues. The fact that in the past the victim, Alex, had eastern European connections has made things more difficult. We're waiting to see what the CIA finds—and, of course, what they're prepared to tell us."

"I assume the homicide was a poisoning. Have they identified what poison was used?" Candrew asked.

Ortega hesitated, but then said, "Well, yes. It was a fast-acting neurotoxin."

Just the sort of thing the Russians had used in other assassinations, Candrew knew. He probed further. "What was the time of death?"

"Probably only half a day before you stumbled on the corpse," Ortega said.

"All this raises the question of why I wasn't treated the same way as Alex. Why did they just leave me abandoned? And there's still the issue of who wanted me locked up in the mine. And why?"

"Yes. These are important questions. Hopefully we'll have a better idea when our investigations progress."

The detective rewrapped the kimberlite samples and put them back in the plastic container—much to Candrew's disappointment. Ortega thanked him for his cooperation. "The police department will keep you informed." He turned to leave, then added, "We appreciate your expert help in the State Police's homicide investigation."

Candrew accompanied him to the office door and thanked him for bringing the rock samples. He turned back to his desk thinking about what he'd just learned. The fact that Alex had several pieces of kimberlite in his pockets certainly seemed to tie him to diamond exploration. But why did his killers leave them on the body? And why did they leave the old map, and especially the cell-phone? Candrew thought all this suggested that the murder had been carried out by an amateurish group, certainly not by professional assassins. But was that right? They'd used a neurotoxin—a sophisticated poison not generally available.

Late in the day Candrew stuffed some of his work papers in his briefcase, locked the office, and went down to the basement lab. Judy was seated at a work bench talking to Katie Montoya.

Candrew pulled another wooden stool out from under the bench and perched on it. "I want to thank you both so much for separating those heavy indicator minerals. And for getting it done quickly."

"It was fun to be involved in some frontier research," Katie said. "Do we get to see the results?"

"Sure. I can do that. I think you know high chromium in pyrope garnets shows proximity to a diamond-bearing kimberlite. That's exactly what turned up in the 'R' series sands you separated." He grimaced, "But unfortunately, not in the other samples that have been analyzed so far."

Katie smiled and said, "You've gotten me interested in diamonds. I needed a topic for my term paper in the Mineral Economics class. I decided to go with diamonds."

"You in that class with Jessica Rylander?"

"Right. Sure am," she said. "But Jessica's a bit of a snob. Seems to think Daddy's money makes her, like, superior to everyone else." Katie looked around the lab for a moment, then said, "One good thing about the class, apart from Professor Pengelly, is the Teaching Assistant. That's Brandon." She smiled at the thought. "He's awesome, real helpful, and knows an awful lot about the geology of this area—and the culture too. He's friendly with several Navajos, and some Hopis. He seems to have learned a lot from them."

"Well, let me know if I can help you with your diamond term paper, and if you need any references."

Candrew talked to Katie and Judy about the economics of diamond recovery for a while, and then left.

———

At the house, Candrew was greeted by his enthusiastic pets. He fed both of them in the kitchen. Then he retrieved a frozen dinner, glanced at the cooking instructions, and slid it into the microwave. As he waited for it to pump energy into his frozen meal, he poured himself a beer, and sat on a bar stool.

The large fluorite crystals he'd bought from Conrad Elkerson in Colorado were standing in the center of the kitchen counter. They were glowing, catching the last of the sunlight. After what he'd heard at lunch, he wondered whether Conrad, or even Alex, had been involved with the Australian company in the new State Line diamond mining project.

CHAPTER 29

ON THE WEST WALL of the large room where Candrew gave his undergraduate lectures hung a big, framed, geologic map of the world. He glanced up at the areas in South Africa, Russia and Australia that were major diamond producers. Quite a geographic range, he thought. The map also showed tectonic plates, mountain ranges, and undersea ridges. After the previous day's strong quake in Chile, Candrew could point to it and ask the class, "Is this where you'd expect a big earthquake?"

Several students realized it was, and in the ensuing discussion referred to the converging tectonic plates. Candrew was pleased they'd understood—and remembered—material from previous lectures.

Back in his office after the morning class, he shelved the three-ringed binder of lecture notes, and called Renata.

"I know it's my turn to cook dinner," he told her, "but I've found a way to avoid doing that."

"You're going to get *me* to cook again?" He heard her laugh.

"No, not this time. I've decided to take you out to dinner. How does the *Casa del Rio* sound?"

"It sounds great. What a pleasant surprise." She chuckled, "I'm sure they can match your culinary skills."

They agreed on a time for dinner, and after hanging up he called the restaurant and made a reservation. The restaurant was widely recognized as one of the best around campus. Not inexpensive, it attracted more faculty than students. He looked forward to the dinner—and a break from his usual microwaved meals.

Candrew sat thinking about what to do next, and decided to write the brief report Detective Ortega had requested. It seemed a straightforward task. He set up a new file on the computer and started a draft of the text describing the type of rocks that Alex still had in his pockets, even after being murdered. Without cutting thin-sections, and doing a microscopic study using polarized light, he had reached a conclusion. He was certain they were all essentially the same rock type—all kimberlites. Briefly, he outlined the implications of finding this diamond-bearing rock type on a corpse. He read and revised the summary, then printed out a copy. All that was left was to transfer the photos from his cell phone to the e-mail. Candrew added a note thanking the detective for letting him see the rocks. He told him that he'd send a hard copy in a few days, since he thought the investigators might like to see the e-mail report right away.

That job done, he rocked back in his chair. Candrew was concerned about the dead Pole's possible role in diamond exploration in the American Southwest and wondered who he was collaborating with. The phone rang before he reached a conclusion. He grabbed the receiver.

"Dr. Nor?"

"Yes."

"This is Carl Denby from MINEx in Calgary. We met briefly on the company plane when you were flying up to see Chris Donnington, our CEO. You were bringing him part of an old map."

"Right, I remember. We also talked briefly a week ago when you told me one of your company geologists, a friend of yours, thought he knew the site the map was probably showing."

"Yeah, Bert Yankovitz. Since then, he's done more detailed scouting around that part of the world and he's changed his mind. Now he claims he's pinned down the map site and is certain of its location."

"Really? So where is it?"

"That question puts me in an awkward position. You see, I was at a meeting with our CEO, a confidential meeting. That's when he said he was planning to follow up on Yankovitz's data to decide whether the kimberlite pipes he'd located, based on the map, were suitable for development. As Donnington put it: *'We're already mining in Arizona. A few more holes there won't matter.'* Not surprisingly, he's ignoring any legal complications about it being on Indian land."

"I'm sure Yankovitz is a competent field geologist—does he have past experience exploring for diamonds?" Candrew paused to consider. "Did he work with Alex, the Polish geologist?"

"That I don't know." Carl said. "Look, as soon as I have any relevant info I'll give you a call." He hung up.

Candrew was fascinated by what he'd just been told. So, MINEx could be planning to get involved with diamond mining in Arizona. He wondered where his own analyses of indicator minerals would fit in. And how Alex was involved—if at all. Was he a competitor? Was that the reason he was eliminated?

But Candrew immediately realized that would implicate MINEx—and Chris Donnington—in murder. Even with the potentially large sums of money involved, this seemed a bit far-fetched. But *somebody* killed Alex.

Curious to know if his other separated minerals had been analyzed, Candrew visited Mark Kernfeld's laboratory on his way to lunch. The lab door was ajar; he knocked and went in. The Post Doc working with Kernfeld was seated at a high-end computer typing in data. He glanced at the screen, then turned to Candrew and said, smiling, "I know why you're here, but I don't have any good news for you. We haven't had time to get the chromium data for your remaining samples."

"No problem," Candrew said. "I'm not expecting anything particularly dramatic from that last group of minerals you got."

Nodding, the Post-Doc said, "I was the one who actually did the analytical work on your earlier samples." He grinned, implying: *But that was okay, it was Mark's lab. He funds everything.*

The afternoon was a boring prelude to what Candrew was sure would be a pleasant evening. After going home and changing, he picked Renata up and they drove to *Casa del Rio* north of the university campus.

The restaurant was in an old adobe with thick walls, heavy beams, and small windows. Some years ago, an engineering faculty member at the university had failed to make tenure and given up on academia. He and his wife bought the old building, remodeled it, and developed the premier restaurant in the area. Personable and outgoing, the owner recognized Candrew and welcomed them as they came through the heavy pine door. He shepherded them to their table. Even at mid-week the room was quite crowded.

As Candrew settled in with Renata, he looked around and recognized one or two of the other diners, though none were close friends. But seated at the table in front of the window was the Dean who'd told him about the mineral dealers. Being sociable, Candrew went over and said 'Hi.' The Dean introduced the young man seated with him and said he was being interviewed for a faculty position in sociology. They chatted for a few minutes.

When Candrew returned to the table, Renata was scanning the menu. Choosing selections was a challenge since all the choices looked tempting. They ordered drinks from the hovering waiter.

"I suppose when you're a wealthy diamond producer we'll be eating here all the time," she joked.

"Well, it seems other people might be trying to cash in on the diamond business." Candrew told her about the Australian Mining company and their new diamond leases in northern Colorado. "Those leased areas are in close proximity to Conroy Elkerson," he said. "Of course, that's not proof he's involved, but it does make you wonder."

"Certainly does. He seemed to me to be the sort of person who'd

get involved in lots of projects. Anything he could make money on."
Renata stared at Candrew. "Why are you smiling?"

"The north-west corner of Colorado is famous—infamous—for another diamond project. Known as the *Great Diamond Hoax of 1872*, the area was 'seeded' with real diamonds. This was so potential investors would assume it was a productive area and get involved. They ended up losing a lot of money."

"A cautionary tale," she quipped, smiling pointedly at him.

"There's been another development in the diamond world," he said.

Renata put down her drink and paid attention.

"This afternoon I got a call from one of the MINEx geologists. He told me that the old map I found on the murdered man showed the location of a group of kimberlite pipes. He didn't have any actual information about whether they were diamond-bearing or not."

"Really? That's interesting, so it does have to be a possibility."

"But the most interesting thing is that the Canadian mining company may be going to develop those kimberlites."

"There are other groups involved with diamonds. How about the Navajos you met?" Renata asked. "And that student of ours, Brandon. From what you've told me, he seems to be involved with them. Does he figure in all this? Are these Native Americans serious contenders?"

"Good question. I'll talk to Wilfred and see if he knows anything." Candrew sipped his wine. "But we'll have to wait and see how these various possibilities work out."

CHAPTER 30

WHEN CANDREW GOT BACK to his office after teaching Thursday's class, he checked the latest crop of e-mails. Although the one from Mark Kernfeld had new data, the more intriguing message came from Detective Ortega asking him to call. Candrew picked up his phone and dialed the number he'd been given. A secretary answered and transferred him to Ortega.

"Thanks for calling, professor. You were very helpful in identifying the rocks our homicide victim had on him. I got your e-mail report. Thank you for that."

"You're welcome."

"Now I'd like to ask for your help with another matter. Our cyber experts have worked with the cell phone you found on the corpse. They've retrieved all the messages in the phone memory, even a few the victim thought he'd deleted. I'd like help in identifying people whose names he gave as contacts. We want to know more about them, and in particular how they related to the dead Pole. That information could be real helpful in pinning down the perp responsible for the homicide. And it might also be significant in trying to establish who was responsible for locking you in that mine."

"Right," Candrew said. "Of course, I'll be happy to help in any way I can." There was silence for a moment and he could hear papers rustling.

"Here's the list," Ortega said. "Most names came with a short message, just a sentence or two." He started to read off names. "Jimmy Overstein?"

"Don't recognize him."

"Marcia Gonzalez?"

"Nor her name."

Ortega continued down the list, but Candrew wasn't familiar with any of the names. "You have to realize," he said, "that Alex, your victim, was a mineral dealer and a lot of the people he contacted were probably clients. You know, people who bought minerals from him, but had no other relationship. I'm sure the texts on the cell phone will probably make that clear."

Ortega said he was aware of that. He continued down the list until he got to the name 'Skip.' There was no surname. Although that name sounded familiar, for a moment Candrew couldn't quite place it. "Hold on a second," he said while he thought back. "That sounds like someone I've heard of." Then he remembered—it was the surfer (hippie?) who had driven the off-road, Ram truck when he was out at Jay Wolverton's place. "Yes, I met him briefly in San Diego," he told the detective. As if by confirmation, the next of Alex's cell-phone messages had been sent to Wolverton himself. The message gave only a meeting time but no location.

Candrew briefly outlined what he knew about Skip and Wolverton, and described his California visit. He told the detective how he'd been impressed by the scale and sophistication of Wolverton's operation. "What was the message?" he asked.

Ortega hesitated, but seemed to realize Candrew might have insights that he'd not get in any other way. He read the content:

Hi Jay: You were right with your guess that the Epsilon Project we discussed might be a great possibility. It involves some pretty good looking kimberlites. I hacked off several pieces of rock while I was there. We can get them analyzed and see if they are likely to have diamonds. I'll bring them next time I come. For your information, there was another rock hound poking around while I was out there. I don't think he saw me since I was just about to leave.

See you at the site at high noon. Take care. Alex.

"That's interesting information," Candrew said. "It certainly seems Alex and Jay were collaborating on a project that was more than just collecting attractive mineral specimens for resale."

For Candrew, the reference to diamonds implied a mining operation. He was curious about the specifics of the 'Epsilon Project' that had been mentioned. Clearly they had been working together, but what exactly was their relationship? And there was the comment that another geologist appeared to be exploring the area. Could it have been Bert Jankovitz from MINEx?

Several of the iPhone messages the tech guys had tracked down had been sent by Alex to Conrad Elkerson in Colorado. Candrew thought these must have been made some time ago when they were collaborating.

"Do your cyberjocks have the dates when the phone messages were sent?" he asked Ortega.

"Yeah, we've got all that information." He gave the dates and times, then went on to read the relevant text messages. They referenced a mine with a name Candrew didn't recognize, and it was in an unspecified area. Although they did describe minerals Conrad had found, this time there was no reference to kimberlites or diamonds.

The rest of the list the detective read through didn't have names that Candrew recognized. He asked for a printout of the people Alex had contacted and said he'd check with a couple of his university colleagues. Ortega agreed that was a good idea and the phone call ended. Candrew decided to wait until Ortega's list arrived before pursuing the issue.

For several minutes Candrew sat tilted back in his chair with his hands behind his head thinking things over. So, Alex and Jay were working together on a mineral project that seemed to be more than just finding high-quality crystals for sale to collectors at a mineral show. And that joint project involved diamonds. But now Alex was dead, murdered, and there was still the question of who killed him—and why?

A student from Candrew's morning class was hovering outside

his office door. He ushered her in and answered several geological questions. As she left, Candrew pulled up the e-mail from Mark Kernfeld. It listed data for the final suite of Candrew's indicator minerals separated by Judy and Katie. There was nothing exceptional, nothing that would suggest proximity to a source of diamonds. Disappointed, but not surprised, he carefully examined the numbers. He was about to e-mail a reply, but then decided he'd stop in at Kernfeld's lab on his way to lunch.

When he knocked and went into the lab, Mark Kernfeld was talking to his Post Doc. "Thanks for the recent e-mail with the final analytical data," Candrew said to them.

"No problem," Mark said. "Glad we could help. I actually learned a few things," he was grinning. "I now know all about indicator minerals and high chromium pyrope garnets in exploring for diamonds." He nodded toward his Post Doc and said to Candrew, "You had a first-rate analyst. It's a pity the chromium concentrations were low on that last batch of garnets. At least the 'R' series we analyzed for you earlier did show really high values. Do we get a share in the profits from the diamonds you find?" He laughed.

"Well, first we have to develop a productive mine." Candrew grinned. He thanked them again. "Judy'll come by later and pick up the left-over sample material."

Candrew walked across the main plaza on his way to the Faculty Lounge. He was thinking over the results Kernfeld had gotten, and how they showed one location was potentially rich, although all the others were unlikely to be prospective. The question in his mind was whether the mine location was the one Bert Jankovitz had identified from the old map. And he wondered if Bert knew anything about the other mine—where he'd been trapped and stumbled on Alex's body.

Candrew joined the group at the lunch table in the lounge where ongoing arguments were stressing the skills of individual athletes playing for different sports teams. Candrew pulled up his chair and sat listening. As always, he was amazed by the arcane knowledge his colleagues had of individual players, and the surprising allegiances they had for particular professional and college teams.

As Maria took his lunch order, Arlan Dee turned to him and asked about the progress with diamond exploration.

"Diamond mining needs big projects, needs a large company. It's not a trivial operation. And it's not cheap—you have to move a lot of rock," Candrew said.

"But isn't that what miners do?"

Candrew recalled Wilfred Pengelly's quip that *a mine was a hole in the ground with a Cornishman at the bottom*. He said, "Don't knock it. In the past, miners have made some spectacular inventions."

"Like the wheel," Lubie broke in to say. "And that was in my part of the world." He chuckled and looked around at the quiet group. "It's been suggested that eastern Europe's Carpathian Mountains is where copper miners started using wheeled carts for the first time. And they did it to move ore almost five thousand years ago."

The archaeologist at the end of the table joined the conversation. "In the Americas they had wheeled toys but never made wheeled carts. The usual explanation is that they didn't have any draft animals."

"But the old copper miners in eastern Europe didn't use animals," Lubie said. "All the evidence suggests they hauled the carts themselves."

"I read that we can also credit miners with inventing our alphabet," Evelyn noted.

"Really. How come?"

"While they were digging turquoise for the ancient Egyptians, the uneducated mine workers simplified complex hieroglyphics. They made plain glyphs, like the 'A' we've still got in our alphabet."

Discussion of the role of miners in advancing civilization seemed to have run its brief course. Candrew ate lunch listening to his colleagues' heated views on topics that ranged from theater productions to fishing lures.

Candrew knew Renata rarely ate lunch, and if she did it was usually only a piece of fruit. Since the chances were good that she'd be in her office, he dropped by after leaving the 'lunch bunch.'

"My *King of Diamonds*." Chuckling, she greeted him, put down her diet Pepsi, and looked up from the stack of papers she was grading.

"I got a call from the detective working on the homicide case," he told her. "He said their lab people had ferreted out a lot of information from Alex's iPhone." Candrew settled into the only chair not piled with books and papers. "Jay Wolverton, out in San Diego, was on the list, and so was the man named 'Skip' that I also met when I was out there. Ortega ran a lot of other names past me, but I didn't recognized very many. I've been promised a printout."

"You said the Dean had contact with quite a lot of mineral dealers," Renata said. "Would he recognize any of the names?"

"I don't know, but it's a good suggestion. I'll take the list over to him when I get it."

"There's still the question of who killed Alex, as well as finding out who dumped his body in the abandoned mine?" Renata said. "Did the detective say they'd made any real progress?"

"No. But maybe we can eliminate Jay Wolverton as a suspect since the phone records showed the two of them were apparently cooperating." Candrew thought about that, then said, "Or maybe not. There would have been an incentive to eliminate someone who was going to get a cut of the profits from a joint project."

"And where do you fit into all this?" Renata asked. "After all, someone arranged for you to be taken out to a deserted old mine and locked in. And that was a mine where they'd already dumped one body."

"I've wondered about that," he said. "And who told the truck driver from Ecuador to pick me up at the motel and then drive me out to that mine?"

"Do the police have any information about that truck driver?"

"None that Ortega's told me. But then he can be a bit evasive. I'm sure he's limited in what he can divulge, even though I was a victim."

CHAPTER 31

CANDREW'S THURSDAY AFTERNOON FOLLOWED the usual routine of answering student questions, reading scientific journals, and revising his manuscript—until the phone rang.

"Hi. This is Bert Yankovitz," the caller said. "I'm a colleague and friend of Carl Denby. He told me about your old map, and how you found it. Sent me a copy. Also said the police had identified the map owner as a Polish mining engineer everyone calls Alex."

"That's right," Candrew said. "Thanks for calling. Carl told me you're very familiar with the mining geology of the southwest."

"Sure am. I've had years of experience working in the West. Actually grew up there. The mountain outlines on the map are pretty characteristic, and I'm quite certain I know where those mountains are," Bert said. "Chris Donnington, our CEO, was intrigued by that map and wanted me to check it out. If the evaluation holds up, and I'm any judge of character, he'll have MINEx mining right away. I don't think he knew that Pole, Alex, or anything about him."

Candrew waited patiently for site information.

"Don't worry, the mine's not too far from where you live. It's in Arizona, but it's on the east side. I've only had time for one superficial visit."

"Did you have a chance to see whether Alex's map included a kimberlite pipe?" Candrew asked.

"Judging from the notes he'd scribbled in the margins of the map, it's quite possible. But to be sure, we need to take a field trip out to the location and check it in more detail." He paused for a moment. "Could you meet me in Chinle sometime?"

"I do have teaching commitments," Candrew pointed out. "But the weekend would be okay. How about this Saturday? Could you make that?"

"No problem." Bert gave Candrew the name of a filling station in the northern Arizona town of Chinle. He described his truck, and suggested a time to meet.

Candrew had kept the map in his desk drawer, and when the phone call ended he pulled it out. He carefully studied the drawings and checked the handwritten comments on the margins once more. It would take a site visit to really be sure about the geology. With luck he would have Alex's mine details by the weekend. But would he have any information about *why* Alex was murdered?

Later in the afternoon Candrew went down to his sandstone research lab to talk to Judy. He needed to get up-to-date on the progress of their funded research projects in the Four Corners area. He knew it was important to have well-documented studies that would lead to significant technical publications. These would be critical in helping Judy develop an impressive resumé that could lead to a permanent faculty position at a prominent university.

"Everything is going well," she explained, "although not nearly as quickly as I'd like." Smiling, she said, "Everything seems to take two or three times longer than I expected."

She went over to the desk. "Here's what I've gotten so far." She pulled out several maps showing their project areas, and laid graphs on them that showed data for rocks they'd sampled from specific locations.

"You may think you're working slowly," Candrew said, "but you've done a tremendous amount." He grinned, "Even with digressions into separating diamond indicator minerals."

"You still planning to continue your diamond explorations?" she asked.

"I am. And I'm probably headed out to a potential site in Arizona this weekend." He saw her questioning look. "Don't worry, I plan to be back in plenty of time to teach my class on Tuesday."

Judy laughed. "And while you're out there are you going to get more sands for Katie and me to work on?"

"You did such a good job with the last lot, I thought I'd get you some more."

She grimaced, but then smiled and said, "I'm sure Katie can use the extra money—even if I don't get paid overtime."

Back home, Candrew fed his dog and cat, put soup on to heat for dinner, and sliced his sourdough loaf.

He phoned Renata. "A lot has happened since we talked at lunchtime," he said.

"Don't tell me you're going to take a sabbatical and visit the diamond mines in South Africa."

Candrew laughed. "No. But travel is involved, although only as far as Arizona." He told her about the planned weekend trip to Chinle, out near Canyon de Chelly, where he was going to meet one of the geologists from the MINEx company. "He thinks he knows the location of the mine shown on that old map I found on the homicide victim."

"Well, make sure you don't get locked in a dark mine this time."

———

Candrew left home early on Saturday morning and drove through Española and Santa Fe to Albuquerque where he turned onto Interstate 40. He drove west, glancing at the flat-topped sandstone mesas to the north, as well as the parched desert in front of them that stretched to the highway. He reached Gallup, the town just before the Arizona border, and turned north through the Navajo capital of Window Rock, in Arizona, and on through Ganado. He followed route 191 to Chinle. With little traffic it was a pleasant drive under a cloudless, bright blue sky dotted with occasional soaring turkey vultures.

As he approached the town he thought about Raven, the Navajo, who'd said he had grown up in Chinle. Was he familiar with the mines in the area? He certainly seemed to have more than a casual interest in mines now, especially those involving kimberlites.

As Candrew drove up to the filling station, he saw Bert Jankovitz leaning against his truck reading the local newspaper. He recognized him from the description he'd been given on the phone. Bert was of medium height and stocky. He wore a multi-pocketed khaki shirt and a wide-brimmed, battered cowboy hat. Candrew parked in the open space to the far side, got out, and went over to him.

They chatted for a while, Bert with a slow drawl. Then Candrew transferred his gear into the black, but dusty, F-250 Ford truck. Bert said, "I've brought a copy of the old map with me." He pulled it out. "It's going to take us about forty-five minutes to get to the map location."

He drove most of the way on the main road before turning onto a dirt track. Eventually he pulled to the side and parked in the shade of a high sandstone cliff near a large pile of recently excavated rock debris.

Bert clambered out. Heavily built, he walked with a slight limp. His leather trousers and worn boots had seen many miles of backcountry. He settled a pair of sunglasses over his nose, and they gave a dark contrast to his white beard and unruly white hair sticking out from under his hat.

Candrew spent the next hour with Bert evaluating the area's geology, and then they investigated two mine shafts. Bert had brought a couple of powerful flashlights that were invaluable as they explored the narrow passages. One of the mine tunnels seemed to have been worked recently, showing fresh tool marks. Both Candrew and Bert took cell phone photos.

After their geological investigations there was no doubt about this being a large kimberlite pipe—and the obvious implication was that the commercial target would be diamonds. Candrew collected sand samples in plastic bags, labelled them, and dropped them into his backpack.

They sat outside in the shade to rest, drink water, and talk through their findings. A lizard skittered past, and a pair of crows complained about their presence. Bert pulled out his field notebook and started recording his observations and conclusions. For a while they sat in silence.

Candrew had been impressed by the stark ochre sandstone rocks with their smooth vertical faces, such dramatic structures that towered above them. Cliffs like these were his academic specialty—but now, distracted, was not the time for a detailed study.

Candrew's interest in diamonds was purely academic. He knew these gem minerals—and especially their inclusions and imperfections—had the potential to provide information about the deep earth that couldn't be obtained in any other way. But the economics of mining diamonds presented a very different issue. An open pit mine, with its tailings, toxic chemicals and heavy machinery, would destroy this landscape. From his reading, he knew that the Orapa diamond kimberlite pipe in Botswana was the biggest in the world, although it only had an area less than three hundred acres. A combination of open cast surface mining, underground tunnels, and access roads, however, could still cause a lot of environmental damage. Candrew had mixed feelings about seeing any area on the Navajo reservation being developed like this.

Suddenly there was an unexpected sound of nearby truck engines. "Look." Bert pointed at two vehicles pulling up and parking further down the trail. "Seems we're not the only ones interested in this mine," he remarked.

They watched as several men clambered out of a tan-colored truck with a king-cab. The shortest one looked vaguely familiar. With his large bushy moustache and dark hair, Candrew realized it was the Ecuadorian who'd driven the truck that had taken him to the old mine, and locked him in. What was he doing here?

When the door on the other truck swung open, the driver

climbing out was Skip—the 'surfer' from San Diego, the man he'd met briefly when he was visiting California.

To see these two men was stunning. It implied that the driver from Ecuador and Wolverton's group had some sort of working relationship. But it prompted the question of whether that relationship involved Alex.

Skip glanced in their direction and stopped, seemingly surprised when he saw Bert's parked truck.

"The Wolverton group," Bert mumbled to Candrew as he raised his hand in greeting. They got up and went toward these new arrivals. Bert obviously knew Skip. As they got closer to the parked trucks, Candrew carefully assessed the truck driver. He showed no sign of recognizing Candrew and continued talking to his colleague in Spanish. This raised the important issue of who gave this driver instructions to lock him in that mine. Also, Candrew wondered, was this Ecuadorian the one who dumped Alex's body in the same mine? And in response to whose instructions?

Skip seemed aware of Candrew's scrutiny, but said nothing. He turned to Bert and nodded toward the mine entrances. "Great minds think alike," he joked. "You planning to get Donnington's outfit into the diamond business?"

"That's his decision," Bert replied unsmiling. "I just give him the information."

"And what info is that?" Skip asked sharply.

Bert ignored the question. "So, what are you doing here?"

"Only showing our working colleagues in the truck the mine location, and how to get here."

"A mine that Alex, that engineering geologist, had scoped out?" Bert asked.

"Right." Skip looked down and kicked a few pebbles with toe of his boot. "He did a good job evaluating the potential." It was said almost reluctantly. "Anyway, let me bring these guys up to speed."

Skip ambled over to the men leaning against their truck. He talked to them in Spanish for several minutes before going back to his own vehicle to get a cardboard folder that he handed to them. After further conversation, the three men climbed back into their Chevy truck and it reversed out.

Candrew made a mental note of the type of vehicle they were driving and the Arizona license plate number.

Skip rejoined Bert and Candrew.

"You headed back to Chinle?" Bert asked.

Puzzled by the question, Skip said he was.

"Well, I'm planning to head north, but needed to drive Candrew into town where his car's parked. Could you drop him off?"

"Yeah. I can do that. No problem."

They talked about the local American Indians and the geology of the area in general terms, then got into their trucks. Skip's vehicle was not the tidiest. He leaned in and scooped piles of maps, water bottles, empty food cartons and candy wrappers off the passenger seat and dumped them into the back. Even after throwing in rain gear, a flashlight and a rock hammer, there was still stuff left on the floor. When Candrew climbed in, he barely had enough room for his feet.

Bert followed Skip along the dirt track for a couple of miles, driving in a cloud of dust, before reaching the main road. There they set off in their opposite directions.

Skip drove into the Chinle filling station where Candrew's Ford *Explorer* was parked and pulled up to one of the gas pumps. He got out, flipped up the gas cap, and stuck in the hose. As Candrew opened his side door, Skip leaned across and asked, "You want a taco? The ones here are great. I can recommend them."

Candrew declined, planning to eat later when he got to Gallup. But he did realize Skip seemed familiar with the place. He'd obviously been here more than once. As Candrew leaned back into the truck to get his pack, the cell phone fell out of his shirt packet, bounced off the seat, and landed on the passenger-side floor. When he leaned in to get it, he noticed a white cardboard box under the seat. It seemed to have a medical label. He pulled the box out and flipped open the lid. Inside were two hypodermic syringes and a vial of clear liquid. Glancing outside, he saw that Skip was still in the store ordering his tacos. He hesitated only a moment before sliding the white box into his backpack. He zipped it shut and carried it over to his SUV.

Coming back to the truck, he saw Skip was now munching on his taco and watching the fuel gauge on the gas pump. Candrew thanked him for the ride, went across to his *Explorer*, and left to drive back to Gallup, Interstate-40, and home.

CHAPTER 32

IT WAS DARK BY the time Candrew reached Gallup. Hungry, he pulled into a truck stop with its brightly-lit diner. Few people were eating there, and he sat in a booth by the far wall. Food choices were standard fare and he ordered a chicken-fried steak with all the trimmings.

While he waited for the waitress to bring his meal, he had plenty of time to think over all that had transpired on his visit with Bert Yankovitz. The recently worked mine tunnels certainly suggested some group was actively evaluating commercial possibilities. Since Skip had shown up, it was presumably the Wolverton group—or was it? Bert knew all about the potential mine, so MINEx also had to be a possibility.

What amazed Candrew most was seeing the truck driver who had taken him to the old mine and locked him in. How could he have casually trapped someone in a deserted mine like that—essentially condemning them to death—and then not even remember it? Or was that just a ruse? Did that driver know there was already a dead body in the mine?

Candrew thought of the hypodermics and the medical vial he'd found in Skip's truck—items now in his own backpack. If the drug could be identified, and shown to be the same as the one used to kill Alex, he felt sure it would be a critical element in helping identify those responsible for the homicide. This long day's trip to Arizona could really pay off.

After finishing his meal, he got a cup of black coffee to go and drove down to merge onto Interstate 40. With little traffic on a Saturday night, he headed to Albuquerque, turned north to Santa Fe, and on to Tierra Amarillo and home. To keep himself alert, he sipped his coffee and turned up the radio volume. It was well past midnight when he finally swung into his driveway.

Early on Sunday morning a loud crashing sound startled Candrew awake. Sleepy, and not sure what caused it, he stretched, and with hands behind his head, laid listening. Then a bright lightning flash lit the dull, leaden sky, followed by a crash of thunder. He dragged himself out of bed as the rumbling thunderstorm approached.

Chile didn't seem perturbed by the loud, echoing thunder. He was more concerned with making up for his master's recent absence by following him around the house. Candrew was tolerant, and tossed him treats. Then he took his own simple breakfast out onto the patio and sat under the overhang, watching the torrential rain. *Just what the garden plants need*, he thought. The gusting wind was blowing early blossoms out across the gravel path. But the rain and mist hid the panoramic view of the mountains he was used to seeing.

He went in to the kitchen to replenish his coffee and turned on the television to watch the weather forecast and the morning news with Chile sitting by his feet. He'd almost gotten caught up on the latest international political crises, when he was interrupted by the ringing phone.

"You okay?" It was Renata. "I thought I'd call and check that you made it home safely."

"I'm safe. Didn't get trapped in any mine this time. Right now, I'm sitting in front of the kitchen TV, drinking coffee, and petting my dog." He scratched Chile behind the ears.

Candrew told her about his discovery of the drugs. "I was thinking about taking them down to Detective Ortega tomorrow. Let his lab boys analyze them. It would be great if they could confirm that the drug I'd gotten from Skip's truck is the same type as the one the Medical Examiner found had killed Alex." He paused to let Renata absorb the importance of what he'd discovered.

"That's amazing," she said. "It could really move the investigation forward."

"I don't have class on Monday, so I'll probably drive down to Santa Fe," he said. "You want to come along? I'll take you to dinner in one of those fancy upscale restaurants."

"Well, that seems to be a better option than sitting here reading about Mayan ruins." She laughed. "Especially if it's undergraduate students who've done the writing. I'm happy to accept."

"I do have to check with the police officer in the morning, but I hope to leave right after lunch."

Monday morning was bright and sunny. The storm had blown over and only a few crisp-edged, white cumulus clouds towered over the western hills. Candrew called Detective Ortega, gave him details of his trip to Chinle, and described the mine location.

"But the important thing about that mine visit," he said, "was that we weren't the only ones there. Two other trucks showed up. One was driven by a mineral dealer I met briefly in California. I recognized him as the man called Skip. You may recall that name, it was one of those on the list retrieved from the homicide victim's phone."

"That could be an important association," the detective said.

"The driver of the other truck was the guy who'd taken me to the abandoned mine and locked me in. Remember, I told you he was from Ecuador. Interestingly, he didn't appear to show any sign of recognizing me, or if he did, effectively covered it up."

"The truck was a tan colored Chevy Silverado with a king-cab, oversized tires, and a jacked-up suspension. It had Arizona plates. I'm pretty sure about their three letters, but not so sure of the numbers." Candrew provided Ortega with his best recollection.

"That's helpful," Ortega said. "I'll get our records people checking it pronto. It'll help let us narrow down the vehicle used in your abduction."

Candrew continued telling the detective about the Arizona mine visit. "It was obvious that the Ecuadorian driver and the Californian dealer were working together. I had some luck because Skip, the dealer, gave me a ride back to Chinle where I'd left my vehicle. While he was in the store getting something to eat, I came across a box of hypodermics and drugs under the passenger seat in his truck. He didn't see me take them over to my SUV. I'm planning to drive down to Santa Fe later today, and thought I'd drop them off at the police forensic lab. I'm sure they'll be able to do the scientific studies needed to identify the drug. It would be critical to know whether the drug is the same as the one used to murder the homicide victim."

"Yes it would." For a moment Ortega said nothing. "Okay. I'm in Albuquerque, but I'll call the Santa Fe laboratory and tell them you're coming to bring some samples. When you get there ask for Dr. Ebbinghaus. He'll check your materials in, and arrange for analyses. Make sure you get a receipt."

After briefly swinging by home to put on a clean checked shirt and pick up his sport coat, he drove around campus to Renata's. He only had to wait fifteen minutes for her to finish getting ready, and they set off for Santa Fe.

Candrew had no trouble finding the lab in Santa Fe. The New Mexico Public Safety Forensic Laboratory was an impressive new building at the dead end of Galisteo Street. They got there late in the afternoon and the receptionist called Dr. Ebbinghaus.

The staff member, tall and balding, arrived after a few minutes and introduced himself. "So, Detective Ortega tells me you have some drugs that might give him information that could be important for one of his current homicide cases."

"That's right." Candrew handed him the cardboard box he'd gotten from Skip's truck. He'd sealed it in a Ziploc bag.

"Have the contents been kept refrigerated?" Ebbinghaus asked as he unzipped the plastic bag, flipped open the box, and peered at the contents.

"No. But it had been under the seat of the truck for who knows how long before I found it. I didn't think I needed to keep it cool."

"Probably not. Depends on exactly what it is. Anyway, we should be able to get some useful information."

Dr. Ebbinghaus explained he was an analytical chemist. He gave more information about their instrumental capabilities than Candrew needed to know. "A liquid like this shouldn't be too much of a problem," he said. "We'll probably have chemical results for Detective Ortega before too long."

Candrew thanked him for his help and said he'd be eager to hear what results they'd find.

He went out to his *Explorer* where Renata was waiting, sitting in the shade of a large globe willow, reading.

"How did it go?" she asked.

"Fine. The man I talked to, one of the forensic chemists, was helpful and appeared very competent. It'll be interesting to see what he comes up with."

Candrew glanced at his watch. "It's still a little early for dinner. You want to drop by one of the book stores. There's a great used-book store on Cerrillos Road." He thought for a moment, "And a used paperback outlet on Osage."

They chose the paperback store, and after more than half an hour's searching through the extensive stacks, both of them left with several books. Candrew had gotten all murder mysteries—pure escapism. Renata had bought primarily travel books, although she did get a volume of Thai recipes.

Candrew drove out along Old Pecos Trail to *Harry's Road House* on the eastern edge of town. *Harry's* had no white linen table cloths with well-dressed waiters bringing 'foodie' specials. The selections were mainly locally inspired and carefully prepared. It was a favorite of Santa Fe natives as well as many knowledgeable visitors—which meant it was often crowded.

Luckily, Harry's wasn't too busy when they arrived. They only needed to wait in the entry passageway a few minutes before being taken to a table by a window that looked out onto the back garden. The waitress brought menus, and they both ordered house margaritas.

"From what you said, the researcher at the forensics lab seemed really cooperative."

"He didn't think they'd have any difficulty analyzing the liquid I found in Skip's truck." Candrew sipped his margarita. "This could be a real breakthrough in pinning down the people who wanted Alex dead."

"We still need a motive," Renata said.

"True. But if mineral leases are involved, especially for diamonds, there could be a lot of money at stake." He grinned. "And big egos won't want to share it."

The waitress hovering at the table asked, "Are you ready to order?"

Renata took a moment to look at the menu and then made her selection, picking the Moroccan stew. Candrew had been to Harry's Restaurant several times, and only glanced at the choices before ordering. "A smothered burrito, beef, green. Please." Green was his choice of chile.

As the waitress left, Candrew thought back to the truck with its Arizona plates. "At least we know what vehicle the miner from Ecuador was driving. I'm sure that truck must have been the one he used to take me to the mine, even though I don't remember all the details."

"You've certainly turned into a persistent investigator." She smiled and took a long slow sip of her drink. "Competition for Detective Ortega?"

"I know. I know. You're expecting me to tell you again that geologists are like detectives—they look at what's here right now, and then figure out how things got that way in the past."

The waitress brought their meals, and they ate, glancing around at the other diners. Locals tended to be dressed fairly conservatively, but out-of-town visitors were really getting into the spirit of the West. One woman was wearing a squash-blossom necklace and silver earrings, while her friend had on a concho belt and a turquoise necklace. Both husbands wore cowboy boots, jeans, and bolo ties. The man at the next table was still sporting his cowboy hat.

Candrew looked out the window at the stone path twisting through the tall grasses, native pinon trees, and the non-native Russian olives. The setting sun was giving the tops of the tall trees an orange glow. Quite a pleasant setting.

They finished their main course and decided not to have dessert—until the waitress brought the menu. It didn't take much temptation to change their minds. Renata ordered cherry pie, Candrew got chocolate cake, and they both drank coffee.

"This trip to the police forensics lab could really provide them with some key evidence," Candrew said as they walked out to their car for the drive home. "I'm anxious to hear what results they get. I hope Ortega lets me know promptly."

CHAPTER 33

SHORTLY BEFORE CANDREW'S CLASS was scheduled to start on Thursday morning, his office phone rang.

"Good morning, Professor. This is Detective Ortega. Dr. Ebbinghaus at the Forensics Lab in Santa Fe e-mailed me the results of their analysis for the sample you took down to them."

"That's great. They certainly didn't take long." Candrew was excited to hear what they'd found. He grabbed a pen and notepad and settled into his chair.

"Apparently the chemical analysis was quite straightforward, no problems. The liquid you recovered was *lixisentide*. A large peptide molecule." Ortega was clearly reading from the e-mail message he'd gotten.

Candrew had had chemistry courses as an undergraduate. But that was many years ago, and he didn't recall ever hearing of this compound. Clearly, quite a specialized molecule. "Is this the same medication that was used to kill Alex, the Polish mining engineer?" he asked. "That neurotoxin?"

"No. Not at all. This particular medication is very different. Dr. Ebbinghaus said it's widely prescribed as a treatment for Type 2 diabetes."

"Diabetes?" Candrew was amazed. He took an involuntary deep breath and ran his fingers through his hair. This was not what he'd hoped for. "So, nothing like the neurotoxin that killed Alex."

"That's correct," Ortega said. "This drug can be prescribed as a daily injection. I'm sure that's why there were a couple of hypodermic syringes in the box. Here in the U.S. it's marketed with the name *Adlyxin*."

Candrew thought over this new information. There was obvious disappointment in his voice as he said, "Then this just means Skip probably suffers from diabetes, and the drug I found didn't have anything to do with Alex's death."

"That seems to be a correct conclusion." The seconds ticked past and Ortega said nothing more for several moments. "You do realize that your taking the box of medications from the truck without the owner's permission was theft?"

Candrew hadn't thought about it that way. He'd been more concerned with trying to get information that would lead to convicting whoever killed Alex. "That didn't occur to me," he said. "I was treating the acquisition as gathering evidence, certainly not as theft."

"Maybe not," Ortega said. "But I'm sure you understand the legal problems if this ever went to trial. The defense attorneys would jump all over the chain of possession issues for the liquid we had analyzed. There would be no legal proof of where it came from, or where it had been."

Candrew felt a little foolish about the way he'd behaved—but what if the analyzed medication had tied Skip to the murder?

"The issue's moot," Ortega said. "We don't intend to prosecute you for theft."

Candrew imagined the cop grinning as he said it. But would Skip sue him for theft? And, of course, he'd been left without his daily medications. Candrew shook his head, sighed, looked out the window. So, his unpremeditated theft had apparently led only to a dead end. He thanked Ortega for the information and hung up.

Candrew's undergraduate geology class started in two minutes. He grabbed the binder with his lecture notes, and rushed down to the lecture room. Fortunately, he was quite familiar with that day's particular topic, which was lucky for the students since he felt he was giving a rather distracted presentation.

In his office an hour later, Candrew slumped into his chair and rocked back. As he sat thinking again about the significance of what Ortega had told him, there was a soft tap on his office door.

"You open for visitors?" It was Renata.

"Of course. I have an open-door policy," he quipped. Candrew was pleased to see her, even if he didn't have good news. He always found Renata perceptive and intelligent, often approaching problems with a different perspective from his own.

"Just before class, Detective Ortega called," Candrew told her. "He'd gotten the analysis for the drug sample we took down to Santa Fe. That scientist in the forensic lab, Dr. Ebbinghaus, had obtained the results pretty quickly. Unfortunately, not what I wanted to hear."

"They had a hard time figuring out what that liquid was?"

"No. They were able to work out exactly what it was—a treatment for Type 2 diabetes." He paused, still trying to come to grips with that new information. "Something called *Adlyxin*. It's nothing like the neurotoxin used to murder Alex."

She pushed back her hair and thought about that. "But most people who have diabetes, and get treated, lead fairly normal lives. Just because Skip's a diabetic doesn't mean he couldn't have been involved in the murder."

"I guess that's right," Candrew said, smiling at her insight. "But what I thought was going to be a major piece of evidence tying him to the crime has turned out to be useless." He smiled. "And I'm the criminal—committing a crime by stealing his medications."

"Don't worry. I'll visit you in prison," she laughed. "And I'll look after Chile and Pixel."

Candrew grimaced.

They chatted amiably for a while and then Candrew said, "How about lunch? I'll treat you to the elegant cuisine of the Faculty Lounge."

Renata rarely ate lunch and almost never went to the Faculty Lounge, but this time she did agree. They strolled across campus, most of the way in silence as they thought about Detective Ortega's news.

"But after your visit to the Arizona mine with the geologist from MINEx, you know now that Skip, and probably Wolverton's group, are somehow involved with the man who locked you in the abandoned mine," Renata said.

"True." He pondered that. "I've often wondered why they picked that particular mine. Whether there's anything special about it. Maybe just a convenient place to get rid of bodies."

There was no real answer to that question, and they rode the elevator up to the lounge on the top floor of the Student Union.

In the lounge they joined the social group of faculty and staff members. Renata ordered a salad, but Candrew's selection was more substantial. For him, lunch was often the main meal of the day, which meant, of course, he wouldn't have to cook at home in the evening.

Renata sat beside Evelyn, whom she'd known from several faculty committee meetings. Candrew was still rather subdued, but eating his enchilada when it arrived cheered him up. He was pleased when the conversation veered away from diamonds and the related murder.

———

After a pleasant and social lunch, Candrew and Renata headed back to their departments, intent on pushing back the frontiers of knowledge in their respective disciplines. On the way, Candrew detoured to his basement lab to talk to Judy and see how the research was going.

"I don't have much new data," Judy said. "And Katie's been too busy with course work to help separate your latest crop of sands and their indicator minerals." She shook her head regretfully. "The only useful thing I've achieved is working on the draft of our final report to the funding agency."

At least somebody's making progress, Candrew thought.

After they had talked for a while, he left and slowly climbed the stairs to his third-floor office. Unenthusiastic about doing anything creative, he spent half an hour perusing some scientific journals before deciding to call Wilfred Pengelly.

"Hi Wilfred. How are things going in the mining world?"

"Oh, you know, the usual conflict with administrators and the environmentalists." Candrew heard him laugh. At least he'd learned to cope with those challenges.

"Well, I spent part of the weekend at a kimberlite pipe mine in northern Arizona, out past Chinle." Candrew said. "Got taken there by one of the MINEx geologists, a guy called Bert Jankovitz. Seemed pretty knowledgeable about that area, and claimed that this was what was plotted on that old map we took up to Calgary to show Chris Donnington."

"So, he finally tracked down a real mine from that map. Not a gold mine, I gather."

"I'm not sure it's producing anything, but most likely it'll be diamonds."

"That'll get Donnington's attention," Wilfred said. "I wonder how he's going to handle the competition?"

"Good question."

For a few minutes they talked about Skip and the Ecuadorian driver being at the Arizona mine site, and their possible role in developing a commercial operation. Then out of pure interest Candrew asked how classes were going, and about Brandon and Jessica Rylander.

"Jessica's Jessica—still thinks the world revolves around her. You know, for most students it's the usual ups and downs. Actually, Brandon is going to be away this weekend at his university's reunion. That'll be in Reno, at the University of Nevada where he went to school. It's one of the mining department's periodic alumni get-togethers."

University of Nevada. So that's where Brandon got his degree. For Candrew this was prompting some half-remembered but stirring memories.

CHAPTER 34

CANDREW HAD NEVER BEEN to the University of Nevada in Reno, but was well aware of its reputation for having a first-rate mining program. That's where Brandon had gone to school. Out of interest he pulled his chair up to the computer and Googled: *University of Nevada*.

He learned that Nevada was called the "Silver State" for having the first major discovery of silver ore in the U.S., as well as for its history of silver production. He also read that John Mackay had come to the U.S. from a poor family in Ireland, but with mining projects in Nevada had become wealthy and a prominent philanthropist. Appropriately, mining geology at the university is now taught in the Mackay School of Earth Sciences. Candrew continued reading the details of the high-quality mineral department with its well-respected economic geology program.

He phoned Wilfred. "Sorry to pester you again, but by any chance do you know when Brandon attended school in Reno?"

"Not off-hand, I don't. He worked with a mining company for a few years before coming here to graduate school. I'm sure the dates you want will be in his personnel file. Anyway, why do you need to know that?"

Candrew explained. "When you mentioned that Brandon was an alum from the University of Nevada, it jogged my memory. Skip Engelmann, the guy now working with Jay Wolverton, also went to school there, and also in mining. Since they appear to be about the same age. I wondered if they overlapped in college, if by any chance they'd gotten to know each other. It seems to me that could be significant now that they're both involved in mineral exploration in the southwest. The key question is whether they are collaborators or competitors."

"Brandon hasn't talked much about his time at the university," Wilfred said. "Although he occasionally enthuses about the university's football team—the *Wolf Pack*. I don't think Brandon ever played football himself, but now he seems to be an ardent fan."

There was silence for a moment, then Wilfred said, "While you're checking up on the history of silver and the Comstock Lode in Nevada, remember there was an important role for all the 'Cousin Jacks'—those Cornish miners."

"I'll bear that in mind." Candrew laughed. "Mining is certainly an international activity."

"Including the Navajo Nation."

Candrew flipped through one of the piles of paper on the table beside his desk and searched for Detective Ortega's personal phone number. He eventually found it and called him. If Brandon and Skip had actually attended the U of N at the same time, they'd be of similar age—give or take a year or two. One way of getting age information was from a driver's license.

"Detective Ortega? This is Professor Nor." He explained his idea to the detective. "Would it be possible for you to contact California motor records and get this information for me?"

"Yes, I would be able to get that information because we're conducting an ongoing investigation. But no, I wouldn't be able to release it to you. It's confidential and can't be given out." There was a long pause. "First you steal a box with drugs, now you want me to make an illegal release of confidential information. Are you turning to a life of crime, Professor?"

Candrew groaned. "Quite the opposite. I was hoping to solve a crime." He was at a loss to explain what he intended. "I thought that

if I could confirm that Brandon Rawlins and Skip Engelmann had
been contemporaries, and knew each other, it would give a whole
new way of looking at your homicide case. Especially since we've
seen that Skip obviously works with the truck driver who locked me
in the mine."

"I suppose that could be of importance."

Ortega was not willing, or able, to cooperate in getting information on Skip's birth date. Good idea, Candrew thought, but with a
lousy outcome.

That evening Candrew was on the patio eating a dinner of microwaved clam chowder and a chunk of sourdough bread when the cell
phone chirped. Chile raised his furry head for a moment, looked up
at Candrew, then laid his chin back on his extended paws.

The call was from Renata. "I know you're stressed with everything that's been happening, so I'm suggesting you start tomorrow
on a positive note. And by that, I mean eating a genuine New Mexican breakfast."

"I could handle that."

"How does the *Conquistador's Chile Shack* sound? You don't have
class tomorrow, so would nine o'clock be a good time?"

"That sounds great to me. I'll be there at nine."

The *Chile Shack* was a little over a mile north of campus. The next
morning Candrew got there only ten minutes late, and swung into
the gravel parking area. Renata had arrived earlier and was already
in the café where she'd claimed a round table by the window. It over-
looked a shallow, dry arroyo with grubby bushes and stunted trees.

"This was a great idea of yours," Candrew said as he took the
menu from the waitress. "It certainly beats my usual granola, or
more often just a piece of toast." He smiled, "Of course when I stay
overnight with you, I'm always treated to a sumptuous breakfast."

With its wood floors, soft Spanish music, the enticing smell of
cooking, and an aroma of coffee, the restaurant had a cheerful

ambiance. It was nearly full, mostly with men in working gear who were probably local ranchers or truck drivers. Candrew and Renata both ordered huevos rancheros and sat drinking coffee, chatting while waiting for their food.

Renata rarely wore jeans, but today had on a neatly-pressed pair held in place with a silver concho belt. She noticed Candrew's glance and chuckling said, "Genuinely American—the land of red, white, and blue jeans."

He laughed.

"Mister Prospector, you've got some diamond competitors," Renata teased him.

"I have?"

"Yeah. In South Africa they've just found a three thousand carat diamond." She grinned. "It's black, however, although it's expected to sell for several million."

"I'm planning to stick with colorless gems," Candrew said, joking, "But I do know the 'Enigma' black diamond from Central Africa was over five hundred and fifty carats and sold for one-point-seven million." He smiled. "And if that doesn't pique your interest, the largest rough diamond ever found came from Brazil in the eighteen hundreds. It was over three thousand carats. That one sold for more than four million dollars."

Renata got more serious. "So, what makes some diamonds black while others are colored? Time for your lecture, Professor."

Although mineralogy was not Candrew's geologic specialty, he'd been reading a lot about diamonds. "Well, several different reasons for color."

Before he got to elaborate, the dark-haired waitress with faded jeans, a turquoise tee-shirt and large swinging earrings, brought their eggs and tortillas. She gave each of them a knife and fork wrapped in a paper napkin.

As he unwrapped his cutlery, Candrew explained, "Color is due to impurities. What the jewelry industry calls 'Type II diamonds' are rare and mostly colorless gems. The Koh-i-nor and the Cullinan are in this category. They're pure carbon with no other elements. But 'Type I diamonds' have nitrogen contaminants." He paused to take another bite of his huevos rancheros, obviously pleased with their taste and texture. He glanced at Renata, who still seemed interested in what he was saying. Candrew sipped his coffee and continued. "The famous Hope diamond, that's now in the Smithsonian, is blue because it contains boron. And it's thought to have formed much deeper than most diamonds. Violet diamonds have hydrogen as the impurity."

"Fascinating. Is there going to be a quiz?"

They were interrupted by the waitress who topped off both their coffee mugs. Candrew asked for a cinnamon roll, and looked questioningly toward Renata who declined.

She grinned. "I'll just steal a corner off yours."

Inevitably conversation drifted back to what was happening at the university.

An hour later, satiated and pleasantly relaxed, Candrew was back in his office ready to work, when the phone rang.

"Hi Candrew. Carl Denby with MINEx. Chris Donnington, asked me to give you a call and see if you had a chance to get together with Bert Yankovitz."

"Yeah, I did. I think Bert was right about the area he's identified as being the one sketched on that old map. Last weekend Bert and I went out to the site and took a detailed look at the geology. It seemed to match up pretty well." He hesitated. "I'm sure that whoever drafted the original map—and that was a long time ago—was mainly interested in gold. Possibly silver, maybe lead, zinc, even copper, but certainly not diamonds."

"But what you and Bert evaluated was a kimberlite pipe, right?" Carl asked.

"Yes, definitely. No doubt about that. And there were already a couple of tunnels excavated into it," Candrew said. "Your CEO might be interested to know other people seem to be looking at that kimberlite, presumably for diamonds,"

"Really?"

"One of them I'd met before. A guy from California who works with Jay Wolverton in San Diego."

"Know his name?" Carl asked.

"Yeah, Skip Engelmann"

"Small world! Funny the way things work out. A few years ago I was with him in a mining company out of Butte, Montana. He was strongly focused, an intense geologist. A real outdoors type. He was quite experienced, but very willing to learn new things."

It seemed a longshot, but Candrew asked anyway. "You didn't by any chance know a Brandon Rawlins?"

"Why sure. As it happened, Brandon was working for the same company in Butte. If I recall correctly, he was fresh out of university and new to mineral exploration. But he wanted to acquire some real-world experience before going back to school to get an advanced degree."

"So, he was there quite a while?"

"Yeah. All of us mining geologists used to go out and eat beef chow mein every Friday night. And drink a few beers." He laughed. "Used to eat at the *Pekin Noodle Parlor*. Famous—it's the oldest Chinese restaurant in the country."

"Interesting. I didn't know that."

"Opened in 1911 in a two-story brick building on Main Street. Now it's about the only thing left of the old Chinatown. Lots of Chinese came to Butte in the late eighteen hundreds to work in copper mining, but there was a lot of prejudice. That's when the restaurant opened—with opium and illegal gambling—but I wouldn't know anything about that!"

They talked more about the location in Arizona that seemed to be the one shown on Alex's old map. The comments scrawled on the back also appeared pertinent. "If I were you," Carl said, "I'd get some satellite imagery of the area. Tie it to GPS coordinates." He seemed to be thinking it over and then suggested, "If you like, I can get our tech people to ferret out that information for you."

"That's a good suggestion, and I'd certainly appreciate your help." Candrew thanked Carl for what he'd proposed. They talked amiably for a while, and the phone call ended.

Candrew was amazed at what he'd learned. There was now no doubt in his mind that Skip and Brandon knew each other, and had even worked together. But what was the importance of that for current diamond exploration in the southwest? And would it have any role in resolving the case of Alex's murder?

The next morning, Saturday, Candrew sat on his patio drinking coffee and eating a breakfast of toast and marmalade. He would much rather have been with Renata at the *Chile Shack* eating huevos rancheros. But Chile, on the other hand, had a considerably more resigned attitude and sat on his haunches, with the crumbled ear down, waiting patiently for any scraps thrown his way. He was not disappointed.

Candrew leaned back in his chair pondering whether Brandon and Skip had ever worked on a joint project. He'd never seen the two of them together, so had no sense of their relationship. He thought about that, and tossed Chile the last corner of his toast. But he did remember that Brandon seemed to have some sort of interaction with Raven, the Navajo. Were these two groups actually part of a larger effort? The Ecuadorian truck driver was presumably working with Wolverton—and his group certainly included Skip. This meant the driver could have been involved with Brandon, Raven, or even Carlos Nez, the mining student, who like Raven, was Navajo.

Candrew realized there were far too many possible relationships. But then he recalled it had been Raven who'd arranged for him to be taken to the abandoned mine on the pretext he'd see spectacular minerals. There he'd been locked in—trapped in a mine that had already been used to get rid of one dead body. He also remembered Raven claiming that the driver, and the company he worked for, were merely casual acquaintances based on their mutual interest in naturally occurring minerals.

Candrew sipped his coffee, glancing at the garden plants thriving after the heavy rain from the recent storm. He ran his fingers through his hair. Did Conroy Elkerson in Colorado have any role? It seemed unlikely, although Alex had worked with him, and some diamond prospects in his area recently sold, even if they were bought by an Australian company. Thinking of international mining outfits, reminded him of MINEx in Canada. That company, of course, was already active mining in Arizona, even if it was for copper rather than diamonds. It was their CEO who'd expressed interest in the old map and sent Bert Yankovitz searching for the actual location.

This line of thought was leading Candrew nowhere. He considered going into the university to catch up on some of his research. But there were plenty of things that needed catching up on at home. Reluctantly, he washed the dishes that had accumulated in the kitchen sink, and then took a pile of dirty clothes to the washing machine. He separated out the ones destined for the dry cleaners and threw the rest in the machine. All this, with tidying and cleaning house, took the rest of the morning.

With the stereo system playing a favorite concerto, Candrew ate a lunch of cheese and crackers with an apple. It still nagged at him that he had little idea of how the people involved in southwest mineral exploration related to one another. And how, if at all, they were involved in Alex's death. He was looking for his half-read novel when he got a call from Wilfred.

"You managing to relax and think about anything other than diamond mining?" Wilfred chided.

"Well, I have to admit, cleaning house and washing dishes has been a distraction."

"The reason I'm calling on a Saturday," Wilfred said, "is that I was with some of our students in the rock identification lab yesterday and Carlos Nez was describing his Spring Break. He talked about having gone to some potential mine locations with a prospector called Bert Yankovitz. Not someone I know. Apparently, the reason

Bert wanted him along was that all the prospects were on the Navajo reservation, and, of course, Carlos is Navajo."

"Did he say what sort of mineralization?"

"He only mentioned silver and copper," Wilfred said. "I know what you're thinking—no diamonds." There was a pause. "Carlos did mention they'd briefly run across a man he didn't know, a man with a foreign accent who seemed very familiar with the local geology."

I bet that was Alex, Candrew thought. There may have been a diamond connection after all. But Alex being there was triggering a different thought—timing. Candrew had not given much attention to exactly when the Pole had been poisoned and dumped in the old mine. The body had certainly been fresh when Candrew had stumbled on it. And from what Carlos was saying, he'd definitely been alive during the early part of Spring Break. Had Detective Ortega gotten time of death from the autopsy? The next step would be to find out where each of the suspects had been at that time.

Candrew started his work week by going to the basement sedimentology lab to check with Judy. She was an early riser, always on campus before he was.

"Everything's ticking along nicely," she told him. "Katie and I even got your indicator minerals separated from the sands. I've taken them over to the analytical lab. They say they'll get the data as soon as possible. They know how important those results are for you."

Candrew was pleasantly surprised, and thanked her. They spent half an hour going over the progress with their sandstone research projects before he went up to his office.

It was a little early for lunch. Only half the 'lunch bunch' were at their usual corner table in front of the large picture window. Its impressive view of the mountains always impressed Candrew.

"Haven't seen you for a week," Arlan Dee said. "You been out spending those ill-gotten diamond gains?"

"I wish that was an option," Candrew said grinning, as he pulled his chair up to the table. "I'm still an impoverished professor."

"You need to change your focus," Arlan said. "You need to make a more serious effort to get rich." It was not too surprising a suggestion coming from someone in the business office. "You're a geologist and there's lots of valuable stuff lying around just waiting to be discovered. Gold for example. You just have to get out there and start panning for those nuggets."

This prompted Lubie to suggest, "Maybe you should take some of your colleagues and try to find the Lost Dutchman Mine, you know, down there in the Superstition Mountains. Legend says it's got a treasure trove of gold."

"I'm sure that's nothing more than a myth that's been rehashed around campfires for years," Candrew said. "Anyway, the Superstitions cover several hundred square miles."

"And it's not that simple," Evelyn the biologist claimed. "When we were down there doing some field work a year ago, the rangers told us that there'd been a big earthquake in 1887. That probably cascaded a lot of rock down the hillsides. It could have covered up the entrance to any mine, making it impossible to find now."

"You all make it sound incredibly difficult," Candrew said. "I think I'll just stick with diamonds."

CHAPTER 35

WITH NOTHING PRESSING ON his afternoon schedule, Candrew strolled back across campus enjoying the sunny, warm weather. He nodded to a couple of fellow faculty members as they passed. Students were lounging in groups: most chattering, a few eating takeout, and some actually reading textbooks. A pair of students from his freshman course waved and shouted, "Hi, Professor Nor." He waved back. This is the next generation, he thought. How well we train them is going to impact our future.

As he climbed the stairs to his office, he thought about that morning's phone call from Wilfred Pengelly. The news that Carlos Nez, the Navajo student, had accompanied Bert Yankovitz to some mining locations on the Diné reservation was particularly intriguing.

When he got to his office, he phoned Wilfred. "I've been thinking about what you told me, that your student Carlos had gone to some mining locations on the Navajo reservation, acting as a sort of guide for a prospector."

"Yeah, interesting. He didn't actually give much detail, his comments were pretty general. You know, no specific mine locations."

"I'd like to talk to him," Candrew said, "if that's possible. Any idea when he would be available?"

"Well, he'll be in the mineral economics class for the first part of this afternoon, but he'll probably be around after that."

"Okay. If you see him, would you tell him I'd like to talk to him?"

"Sure, no problem. I'll let him know you're coming over."

Candrew checked his university handbook to see what time Carlos' class would end.

Later that afternoon he went across campus to the Mining Department. There, Carlos was with a group of students, all male, jostling in the hallway. He stepped away from them. "Dr. Pengelly said you wanted to talk to me."

"Right. Is now a good time?"

"Sure. Good as any. I don't have class."

They went and sat on a wooden bench under a window at the end of the passageway.

"What," Carlos asked, "do you need to know?" His tone was defensive.

"I heard that a prospector, a man called Bert Yankovitz, asked you to go with him to some mining locations during your Spring Break. He was especially interested in visiting possible mines on the Navajo reservation."

"Yeah, that's right. He'd heard I'm Din." No more information was volunteered.

Candrew probed. "When did you go out there with him?"

"Middle of Spring Break. Thursday."

"And while you were out there did you meet up with another prospector? A man with a foreign accent?"

"Yeah, that's right. I think Yankovitz called him *Alex*." Carlos seemed to becoming more helpful. "We were just coming out of one of the new mines. Yankovitz was pretty friendly with him, appeared to know the guy well. I stood there drinking my bottled water and they ignored me. They had a real long discussion."

"Concerning the mines?"

"You got it. They talked about the shaft we'd just come out of. I distinctly remember Yankovitz saying that it wasn't in the same league as the 'Utopia' mineral prospect." He paused, ran his fingers through his hair, glanced away, then said, "I think I've gotten the name right." After a moment he explained, "I was standing quietly to the side. They were still ignoring me, forgot I was even there."

Several students walking past along the department passageway appeared surprised to see Carlos sitting, talking to a professor.

"So, did Alex leave?" Candrew asked.

"Well, yeah," Carlos said. "But first they talked more about information they had on that Utopia mine. I distinctly remember hearing Yankovitz asking whether he could really be sure about all the data. The foreign guy got quite annoyed, glared at him. He yelled that he was a professional, and you could trust his information. That's when he pulled out his field notebook and waved it at Yankovitz, shouting: *Here, take a look if you don't believe me.*"

"And did he?" Candrew said.

"He sure did. But it led to a rather heated discussion," Carlos looked away for a moment. "I wouldn't actually call it, like, an argument," he said, "but it ended. Then that Alex guy went over to his truck and left."

"You remember what color his truck was?"

Carlos raised his eyebrows in surprise at the question, but answered. "Like, sort of grey or perhaps tan."

"Anything else you want to tell me?"

"Not really. I think I've covered just about everything you'd want to know."

"You in favor of mining?" Candrew asked.

Carlos took a moment to think about that. "Have sort of mixed feelings, after all it is my planned career." He grinned. "It depends on what you're going to be mining, and where exactly. But I don't make those decisions." There was silence for a few seconds. "My father is in favor of mining because he thinks it'll create lots of jobs. We need them on the reservation."

Their meeting seemed to be over, but then Carlos said, "One little thing. That Alex guy had his field notebook with him, the one he showed to Yankovitz, and it was bright yellow!" Chuckling, he added, "Who on earth would have one that color? You get your hands real grubby doing field work, and something that light color would get super filthy."

Candrew, amused by Carlos' observation, didn't say anything. He just thanked him for all the information and got up off the bench and left.

Candrew had accepted Renata's invitation to dinner. When he arrived, she told him it would be quite casual, nothing exotic. As she was inside fixing drinks, Candrew sat on the patio watching dark shadows creep up across the rugged eastern mountains, the colors fading with the setting sun. Noisy house finches were squabbling over prime nesting real estate under the eaves on the far wall.

Renata brought out gin and tonics and a tray of cheese and crackers. He asked how her week was going.

"Typical academia," she told him, grinning. "A lot of infighting among faculty members in the department. They all have different ideas about how things should be done. I just let them get on with it. I've got my own problems getting everything organized for this summer's excavation in Guatemala."

Candrew told her about his talk with Carlos Nez.

"Seems everybody knew Alex." She sipped her drink and smiled. "They've all worked with him at some point."

"Yes, but who had a reason to kill him? We still don't have a motive."

"I would think it has to be related to some rich mine," Renata said. "You know, something of high value, like a diamond locality."

"Certainly a possibility."

They had drunk in silence for several moments, when Candrew said, "Well, I know from talking to Carlos Nez that Alex was alive on the Thursday, and he was certainly dead when I found him on the following Sunday. That narrows down the time of the murder. I'm sure the Medical Examiner has established a much tighter estimate of the probable time of death, though the police detective hasn't shared that information with me."

"There's still the question of where Alex was when he was injected with the poison that killed him," Renata said. "And that leaves the whole issue of how, and when, he was taken to the old mine."

"Dumping him there wouldn't have been a simple thing to do. Dragging an inert body into that dark mine would have been a major effort—probably more than a single person could manage. Which must mean there had to be at least one accomplice." Candrew paused, sipping his gin and tonic. "That implies, of course, that the killer was familiar with the mine. We know the Ecuadorian truck driver who took me there knew it. I wonder if he could have been the helper?"

"I guess that's possible," Renata said. "But there's still the question of what sort of vehicle Alex had been driving in the past, and where it is now."

Candrew considered that. "I know from talking to Carlos that he did drive a truck, and that it was grey in color."

"A lot of people have worked with Alex," Renata pointed out. "It shouldn't be too difficult to find out what model he had—and perhaps even where it is presently."

"Good point. Maybe the police can find it. That might give some useful information in pinning down the sequence of events."

For a few moments they sipped their drinks and nibbled cheese and crackers in silence. Then conversation turned to more pleasant topics. Renata was a more enthusiastic gardener than Candrew and couldn't resist giving him instructions as to what he should be doing with his overgrown garden.

CHAPTER 36

CANDREW SAT IN HIS office staring out the window. He'd given his Tuesday lecture and answered all the questions from students. As usual, his office door was open—students were welcome whenever they needed help. But it was not science, it was murder that was on Candrew's mind. After last night's dinner with Renata he wondered why no one seemed to be checking on Alex's vehicle. It might provide important information for the homicide investigation—but what could he do about it? He decided he should try to find out what sort of truck Alex owned and where it was now.

He thought through his mental list of people who might have known about this—Conrad Elkerson in Colorado, Jay Wolverton and Skip in San Diego, Bert Yankovitz, and possibly even Brandon.

Candrew knew Alex had worked with Conrad, and started by calling him. "I'm trying to find out what sort of car or truck Alex, the Polish engineer, drove," he said. "And where it is now."

"That was so sad about Alex," Conrad said. Candrew heard him take a deep breath. "Who'd do a thing like that?" There was a lengthy pause. "As for the truck he used, I don't have any details. All I remember, is that it was small, old, and beat-up. Toyota, Chevy maybe, I'm not sure."

"You remember the color?"

"No. But pretty nondescript. Nothing fancy. No bright red or yellow. And almost certainly not white or black."

"Well, thanks for that information. Do you have any idea where the truck is, now that he's no longer alive? You know what happened to it?"

"Can't help you with that," Conrad said. "The police making any progress in finding who killed Alex?" he asked. "I sure hope they get that bastard. I got on pretty well with Alex, though we did have our differences. I was none too happy when he quit working with me and went out to California, to that Jay Wolverton dealer. That Polish guy had no loyalty."

After a few more general comments—with Conrad explaining he was no longer buying high-end minerals—the call ended.

Next on Candrew's mental list was Bert Yankovitz. It was clear from what Carlos Nez had told him that Bert knew Alex quite well. They even seemed to have been collaborating on some major mineral prospect. Candrew wondered if it was an equal partnership— and if not, who dominated.

Bert answered his cell phone, saying he was in his truck heading out west.

"I'm trying to find what sort of vehicle Alex had," Candrew said. "You worked with him, what did he drive?"

"Nothing fancy. Just a mid-size Ford or Chevy. I didn't pay much attention. Wasn't something that would stand out in the pack. When you're hauling rocks in the back country, the main thing is that every time you turn the key it starts." Candrew heard him chuckle. "Reliability is what you need. Don't matter whether it's Japanese or German, or built here in the good 'ole U.S. of A."

The call ended without Bert giving additional information.

Candrew was hesitant to call Skip. He'd not had any contact with him since he'd taken—stolen—his diabetes medication. But he felt he had nothing to lose and picked up the phone.

Before he had a chance to dial, Maria, the department secretary, appeared in his office doorway. "Dr. Rosenberg wants all the faculty together for a meeting first thing in the morning," she told him. As chairman, Rosenberg had the challenging job of herding the faculty 'cats'—a role he often overstepped.

"What's the urgency?"

"Apparently there was an accident in one of the chemistry labs," she said. "So, there's going to be a university-wide evaluation of all equipment that has any potential to cause injuries. A thorough safety review."

"Okay. I guess I'll be there. What time?"

"Ten o'clock." She turned to leave, but then told him the room number.

When she left, Candrew thought about his own laboratory. There was very little analytical equipment, and none of it potentially dangerous. There were some poisonous liquids, of course, the ones Judy and Katie were using to separate the diamond indicator minerals. That made him wonder how Kernfeld and his colleagues were progressing in analyzing his most recent batch of minerals. But he'd checked with them only a short time ago. It didn't seem fair to keep pestering Kernfeld, especially since he was doing the chromium analyses as a favor.

Candrew glanced down at Skip Engelmann's phone number scrawled across the slip of paper on his desk. He phoned, but only got a recorded message.

Apart from his undergraduate lecture, nothing geologically significant had been accomplished during the morning. Candrew gave up and went to lunch at the Faculty Lounge. The usual crowd greeted him.

"What are you going to name that huge multi-carat diamond when you find it," Arlen Dee wanted to know. "All the big ones have names: the *Cullinan, Hope, Koh-i-Noor*."

"Right," Lubie said. "It seems to be human nature to want to name everything. And not just our kids and our pets. We have a *'George Bush'* aircraft carrier, and an *'Apollo'* spacecraft."

"We even give names to hurricanes and wildfires," someone observed.

"And don't forget all our cars—the *Mustang, Corvette, Cayenne*, and on and on."

Laughing, Arlen said, "You're forgetting the most important names—*FortyNiners, Colts, Cowboys, Broncos,* and all the other football teams."

"But you have to be careful. You can't pick a team name from an American Indian tribe anymore."

"We still have the *Chiefs,*" Lubie said.

"True."

The sociology prof at the far side of the table asked Candrew, "So, have you decided what you'll call your big diamond when you find it?"

Before Candrew had a chance to answer, Evelyn broke in to say, "If you're smart, you'll name it after Renata." She gave Candrew a cheeky smile.

"You mean, I should call it *The Queen of Diamonds?*" he said, laughing.

Back in his office, he phoned Skip again. This time the call was answered promptly.

"Well, well. The drug thief," Skip said.

Embarrassed, Candrew waited in silence, apprehensive about where this would go.

"Don't worry," Skip continued, "I'm not going to hold it against you. I'm well aware of your reason for doing it. I know how you must have felt, stumbling on Alex's body—and being trapped in the mine yourself."

"Yeah, I'm sorry about taking your medication. Hope it didn't cause a problem." Candrew pressed the phone close to his ear, propping it against his shoulder, and swiveled his chair. "Alex is why I'm calling you," he said. "The police are still trying to resolve the homicide. I'm wondering what happened to Alex's truck. Do you have any idea where it is now? What model he drove?"

"Whatever make it was, it wasn't reliable, but then it was old. Probably early-nineties. He was always taking it to a mechanic to get something fixed."

"Any idea who worked on it for him?"

"Not the details. I know he talked about an outfit on the far side of Flagstaff."

"Anything else you can tell me?"

"Not really. His truck was unimpressive, sort of drab color. The only thing exceptional was the jacked-up suspension. He always said he had to have that for all the off-road field work he needed to do."

"Did you do much mineral exploration with him?" Candrew said.

"We checked out several locations together. Alex had done some detailed geology and had a lot of data. One or two places seemed real promising."

"For diamonds?"

"Maybe. Alex was going to file mining claims."

"Jointly with you?" Candrew was curious to know the details.

There was a moment's silence before Skip replied. "That was something we needed to work out between us. He could be very demanding, very self-centered. He didn't like to compromise—or share. Alex was often real irritating, keeping data to himself. Anyway, are the police making progress?"

Candrew told him that as far as he was aware the homicide case was still active. But he didn't know how much progress they'd made.

After the call to Skip ended, and he'd learned the location of Alex's possible repair shops, Candrew Googled auto repair garages in the Flagstaff area. There were two on the west side of town, and either of them could have been where Alex got his truck worked on.

He sat staring at the computer screen, and it was then that he decided he ought to drive out to Flagstaff.

CHAPTER 37

GLAD THAT WEDNESDAY'S TEDIOUS faculty meeting about the risks of lab equipment and toxic chemicals had finally ended, Candrew went to his laboratory. There he told Judy the new safety rules.

"Most of those don't apply to us," she said. "We don't have any fancy, million-dollar pieces of equipment that run at thousands of volts and use poisonous chemicals."

"But you do have that toxic methylene bromide you've been using to separate the diamond indicator minerals."

"Yeah, you're right," she said. "Okay, I'll be careful to follow any of the new rules that apply."

"And make sure Katie knows what those rules are."

"Speaking of indicator minerals," Judy said, "Mark Kernfeld called and told me he's gotten the results from your last batch of samples. The chromium values for the pyrope garnets were very low." She'd worked often enough getting Candrew's samples analyzed to know the significance of this. "It suggests, of course, that this sand was unlikely to have come from a diamond-prone kimberlite."

Candrew was disappointed by the results for the sands he'd collected on the trip with Bert Yankovitz. He wondered what Bert's reaction would be to this information. But after hearing about his visit to several Navajo sites with Carlos Nez, and also that they'd met Alex there, maybe Bert had other more promising locations to explore.

On the way back to his office, Candrew went into the department office, checked his mail, and poured himself a cup of coffee. Once back at his desk, he dumped all the safety information pamphlets on to a side table, slumped into his chair and phoned Renata. He bitched to her about the time wasted in the safety meeting, which had little relevance to what he did. Then he said, "Remember, we talked about Alex's vehicle, and where it is now?"

"You found it?"

"Not exactly, but I may have some leads on possible mechanics who worked on his truck." He told Renata what he'd heard. "I've decided to drive out to Flagstaff after class tomorrow, and I'm planning to visit a couple of auto shops there and talk to the mechanics."

"Then you'd better come to dinner tonight, so you'll be well fed in preparation for such an arduous assignment," she said laughing. "I'm well aware your bachelor food is nutritionally marginal. Your idea of *haut cuisine* is ten minutes in the microwave."

"Well, yes. But I'm sure your excellent cuisine will bolster my trip. I'm happy to accept."

After teaching his class on Thursday, Candrew went home to collect a few things and put down food for his cat and dog. He then drove to Flagstaff. This took several hours and he arrived late in the afternoon. After checking into one of the chain motels, he ate a fast-food meal and spent the rest of the evening watching television.

Early the next morning he ate a complimentary breakfast of yogurt, a couple of donuts, and orange juice before pouring himself a to-go cup of coffee. He drove to the closest of the two auto sites he'd identified, just over a mile west of Flagstaff. The mechanic in that automobile workshop had no clue about Alex's old truck. Although the garage manager was cooperative, he too didn't know anything about an old truck driven by someone with a foreign accent. "Sorry I can't help," he said. "You might try the place down the road." He gave Candrew an address that was one of the two he'd already found online.

When Candrew pulled into the second garage and talked to the manager, he remembered the old truck and the couple of guys who had brought it in.

"We'd worked on that vehicle quite a few times over the years," he said. "As usual, that truck of his needed our tender loving care," he joked. "His attitude seemed to be: *'If it's working, don't mess with it.'* Didn't care a hill of beans about the way it looked—all the dents and scratches. Said he spent a lot of time off-road, so it was always getting banged up."

The manager wiped his hands on an oily rag. "Come on outside. It's quieter there, and I need a smoke." They sat on a low wall and he lit his cigarette. There was silence while he adjusted his baseball cap with its Red Sox emblem.

"To be honest, we give good service at a reasonable price. Keeps them customers coming back. But once in a while we do get some people driving through on *Forty* that have a problem." He kept talking about the business, telling Candrew more than he needed to know.

"So, you never did any repairs for Alex, that foreign guy?" Candrew finally asked.

"Not for dents and scratches." He laughed. He threw his cigarette butt down and ground it out with the heel of his boot.

"Come on into the office."

Candrew followed him past a car raised on a mechanical lift, and into a side space that served as an office. Disorganized and dusty, with a few retro ornaments, it did have a desk and an old filing cabinet. Candrew sat on the canvas chair the manager pointed to.

"The guy you're interested in was always having mechanical difficulties. We worked on those problems for him. Easy, that old truck. Don't have no computers, and not a fancy electric EV. Last time he came, he brought his own beat-up truck for us to work on. Then went off with a friend who'd come with him in his own truck. They left together."

"You remember what that friend was driving?"

"Why sure, automobiles are our life," he grinned. "He had a Ram Charger. Red. I guess it was about four years old."

"The friend, a bearded, heavy-set guy?"

"You got it. That describes him pretty well."

The truck and the man's description left Candrew in no doubt that it was Bert Yankovitz who'd been with Alex.

"While that foreign guy, Alex, was telling the mechanic about his most recent engine problem, the bearded hombre talked to me. Said, in confidence, that as soon as the truck was running well, the foreigner was probably going to sell it."

"I let Alex know—politely of course—that a junk yard might give him a good price." He laughed. "As it happened, we got a call later the next day asking if we could deliver the truck to a used car dealer down on the north side of Phoenix."

"Was it Alex, the man with the accent, who called you?" Candrew asked.

The manager thought about that for a moment. "Now that you ask, it wasn't the truck owner with the accent, it was the other guy."

Interesting, Candrew thought. So, Yankovitz arranged for Alex's working truck to be sold. "You have the address of the used car dealer in Phoenix?"

"Sure do."

Candrew drove the short distance east along I-40 and then took I-17 down toward Phoenix. North of town, he had no trouble seeing a large field of decrepit automobiles. He followed a gravel track in and headed to the office that was beside a parking lot full of used cars, all decorated with streamers and strings of balloons.

As he got out, he was approached by a large woman with silvered hair parted down the middle, and heavy-framed glasses perched on her nose.

Sporting a broad grin, she asked, "What can I do for you?" She glanced at his parked, almost new, Ford *Explorer*. "Looks like you already have a nice set of wheels."

"Thanks. Yes. I'm trying to track down an old truck that was recently delivered here."

"Oh yeah? The one from Flagstaff?" She answered her own question. "I remember that Toyota truck." Turning, the woman pointed to the side lot. "You need a second truck to haul stuff?"

Candrew decided not to tell her that the owner had been found murdered. "A friend of mine . . ." *a bit of an exaggeration*, he thought, *for someone he'd never actually met*, " . . . died suddenly, and I wondered what stuff was left in his truck."

"Sorry to hear that. Usually, we check everything damned carefully when the automobile's hauled in. We've just gotten this one, so it hasn't been worked over yet." Glancing at Candrew, and over at the Toyota truck, she lapsed into sales talk. "With that jacked up suspension it would be great in rugged country. And those big tires look almost new, still have plenty of heavy tread, lots of miles left. Be a good buy."

Candrew listened patiently until she said, "Let's go take a look at that vehicle."

Alex's truck was not locked and when the driver's side door swung open there was an unmistakable smell from a heavy smoker. The central ash tray was full of cigarette butts. Candrew noted the five-speed shift, and she said, "Probably mid-nineties." He stretched across and flipped open the glove box. It was empty.

"No car papers," the sales woman said. Grinning, she explained, "Not unusual. A lot of the vehicles we get are probably stolen or being junked. We don't ask no questions. Just fork over the money and send happy sellers on their way."

She leaned over and opened a rear door. Candrew peered under the back seats of the extended cab. Only an empty cigarette package—no diabetes medication, he smiled to himself. The pocket on the back of the driver's seat had nothing in it, but the one on the passenger side was rewarding. He pulled out a folded geological map and half a dozen sheets of paper with hand-written notes.

"Mind if I take these?" he asked. "Just my friend's notes. Sort of sentimental."

She stared at him for a moment as if trying to work out whether he was telling the truth. In the end she believed him. "Okay," she said. "Go right ahead. Less junk for us to have to deal with. We'd just toss 'em in the trash."

Candrew climbed out from the rear seats and looked into the open cargo space. There were a couple of cardboard boxes. He leaned in and pulled over the nearest one, which was quite heavy. Folding back the lid, he saw that most of the contents were dark-colored rock samples. Probably kimberlites, he speculated.

Candrew turned to the woman showing him the truck. "Okay if I take these chunks of rock?"

"They valuable?"

"No, not really. Some rock hound might be interested in taking a chunk or two. That's all."

"What on Earth are they? What do you want them for? You planning a rock garden?" Before Candrew had a chance to reply, she said, "Anyway, go right ahead. Of course, we'll be happy to get rid of those heavy lumps."

He went over and started his *Explorer*, backed it up to Alex's Toyota, and loaded the boxes of rock samples.

Candrew thanked her for all the help, then fished out one of his business cards. "If you stumble across anything else that might seem unusual, would you let me know?"

"Will do." She peered at his card. "So, you're a professor?"

"Yeah. A geologist."

She smiled. "I see why you wanted to take those rocks. You sure you're not in the market for one of our exceptional autos? Don't you need a nice truck with four-wheel drive to haul all them rocks you collect?"

"Not this time," Candrew said.

Candrew pulled onto Interstate 17 and headed back toward Flag-staff. Although he paid adequate attention to the traffic, his mind was focused on the papers he'd taken from Alex's truck. At the first rest stop, he pulled off the highway, drank some of the remaining cold coffee, and sorted through the hand-written notes. They were a revealing bunch.

CHAPTER 38

CANDREW REALIZED THAT HE'D been frequently arriving home late at night. Chile seemed to agree and met him barking at the front door when the driveway lights flicked on. Candrew fed both his pets, got himself a late-night snack, uncapped a beer and drank half of it. Then he went to bed, satisfied by his productive trip to Flagstaff.

Next morning Candrew strolled down the driveway with Chile bounding alongside, and retrieved the Saturday newspaper. Back on the patio, he ate croissants with butter and marmalade, drank his black coffee, and set about solving the Sudoku puzzle. Having succeeded, he turned to the front page and the current world crises, but only felt more relaxed when he'd read the sports page.

Leaning back with his hands clasped behind his head, and looking out across his yard, Candrew felt lucky to live in such a pleasant spot—with a friendly dog and a tolerant cat! Quite a contrast to the used car dealership where he'd located Alex's old truck in a lot with rusting cars, scrubby vegetation, and weedy gravel.

Back inside the house at mid-morning, he fumbled through his backpack and jacket pockets, but failed to find his cell phone. He eventually located it where he'd left it in his car. He called Renata.

"I finally tracked down Alex's truck," he told her, "in a used car lot outside Phoenix. How it got there is an interesting story."

"I can't wait to hear the details."

"But the really important thing was finding that it still had some of the rocks he'd collected. And it also had his maps and notes. They're intriguing."

"Come on over for lunch," she said. "You can tell me about your trip and show me what you've got."

Candrew was happy to accept the invitation.

An hour later Candrew drove to Renata's house where he was greeted with the usual big hug and a kiss. Pleased to see her, as always, he brought in the folder that contained Alex's papers. He was eager to let her see what they showed, and to make space for these items, she pushed back her own books and papers that were spread across the dining table.

"Let's start with the map," Candrew said. He pulled out the folded segment that had obviously been torn from a larger map, and spread it across the table, smoothing it with his hands. Several map locations had been ringed with a red, felt-tipped marker, and two were ringed in green. All of them had been identified with pairs of handwritten letters.

"What's the area covered by the map?" Renata asked.

"It's the southwestern part of New Mexico, up against the Arizona border."

"So, that makes it close to the abandoned mine where you stumbled on Alex's body."

"That's right. Good point."

Candrew pulled out the papers with Alex's scrawled notes. "See, his comments are coded to the letters on the map. All of them have information on the local geology, as well as on the minerals he collected." He pointed to one of the red spots on the map that for some reason had been labelled 'BD.' Smiling, Candrew flipped through the papers and took out the notes for BD. The letters were emphasized with triple explanation marks.

"Clearly, Alex's views on the BD location are enthusiastic," he said, "although there are several enigmatic notations I don't understand. And even a few phrases that are probably in Polish. But the gist of all this is clear—he'd found an exceptionally rich area with the potential for high diamond content."

"This is stunning," Renata said. "There's so much data for what's presumably a diamond-rich site. There's a pile of information—information that could certainly have been a reason for murder by a rival. For someone who wanted to cash in, it could've provided an obvious reason for homicide," she said.

"I'm sure you're right. It appears as though we've finally established a motive."

"Which just leaves us to figure out the motive for the second planned murder."

"It does? Sorry, I don't understand."

"*You*." She peered at him, laughing at his puzzled look. "Why were *you* left locked in a mine with no chance of rescue? Who had a reason to get rid of a geology professor?" She grinned, "Apart from a bunch of students you were giving F-grades to."

Candrew hadn't given this a lot of thought. "Well, I did have some information about mine sites backed up by analyses of diamond indicator minerals. You know, the high chromium values for garnets." He raked back his hair and thought more about the situation.

"So, you think you could have been considered a rival?"

"Possible, I suppose," he said. "Except I have no intention of getting into the diamond mining business, and I certainly don't have any acreage leased. I wouldn't have been a competitor. But I suppose they wouldn't know that—whoever '*they*' are."

Renata pushed aside some of the maps and went into the kitchen to get the plates of food for lunch. They both broke off chunks of the sourdough bread and ate it with ham, cheese and olives. Merlot washed it down.

After eating in silence for a few moments, Renata asked, "What are you going to do with the rocks from Alex's truck?"

"Separate diamond indicator minerals, of course." He laughed.

"Judy, with Katie's help, is getting really proficient at separating them. And Mark Kernfeld has been very generous with his research time. But this group of rocks is really important, although I'll just follow my usual procedure and get the chromium content measured." He sipped his red wine. "What I'm really anxious to see is how these mineral analyses tie in with the map locations and his site descriptions. *BD*, of course, looks especially critical. High chromium values for the pyrope garnets would certainly confirm Alex's field studies."

"And would strengthen the motive for homicide," she said.

They pondered that implication quietly for a while, and then Renata asked, "Have you told the police detective about finding the truck Alex used?"

It was obvious from Candrew's blank stare that this was something he hadn't considered doing. "No," he said. "But then he always treats me as though forensic amateurs shouldn't be competing with the professionals." After a moment's hesitation he said, "I'll give him a call in the morning. I'm sure he'll appreciate getting the information."

They took their wine out onto the patio and Renata talked about her Mayan research program in Guatemala. She was especially excited about some of the glyphs one of her students had been able to decipher. "I'm really looking forward to being back at the site this summer," she said. "Field work is always an exciting contrast to classroom teaching."

Candrew grinned and nodded.

Cheeky magpies were calling and Renata threw them some chunks of bread.

On Monday morning, Candrew's week started in the laboratory, talking to Judy. He described his trip to Flagstaff and told her how he'd heard that Alex's truck had been sold to a used car lot in Phoenix. But the important thing was that in the back of the truck there were still some of the rocks he'd collected. "The car dealers would just throw the 'lumps' away, so I rescued them."

"More rocks," she said, grinning. "And my guess is they're kimberlites, right?"

"Right. And I'm sure you've already figured out I need the indicator minerals separated. The ones labelled with *BD* numbers are particularly critical."

"Okay. We'll do those first. I don't think Katie has a class on Monday, so we might be able to get them done pretty quickly, maybe even later today." She hesitated, then said, "The supply of that noxious heavy liquid we use in the separations is running low. There's probably enough for these rocks, but that'll be about it."

"I don't plan to get any more kimberlites worked on, so let it ride for the time being." Candrew was impressed by Judy's organization and efficiency. "Give me a call when the garnets and augites are separated and over at Kernfeld's lab," he said. "This time I plan to go and get the results from him myself."

Back in his office he called Detective Ortiz and told him about finding Alex's Toyota truck. He gave him the location of the used car dealer.

"You have a description, and the license plate number?" Ortiz asked bluntly.

"Yes, I've got that." *You'll be asking for the VIN number next,* Candrew thought. He described the truck and gave the plate number. He did not mention the rocks or the map and corresponding notes that he'd taken.

Ortiz reluctantly thanked him for the information, but before the call ended Candrew said, "Let me know what you find out."

Judy was close in her estimate of how long it would take to separate the diamond indicators. She came up to Candrew's office early on Tuesday morning and told him that they'd separated the high priority garnets. "I know Kernfeld is a workaholic, and sure enough, he was in the lab late on Monday night when I went over there.

Candrew was pleased to hear that his samples would be analyzed so quickly. He put down the manuscript he was revising and was thanking her profusely, when the phone rang. It was Detective Ortiz.

"Our Arizona colleagues checked out that used car location you told us about," he said without any introduction. "The truck you described wasn't there."

"What?" Candrew was amazed. "They have the right place on I-17?"

"Certainly did," Ortiz replied. "The people at the car lot knew it had been brought in, but claimed it had already been sold."

Candrew was surprised that Alex's old truck was such a popular commodity. "They know who bought it?" he asked. "And where he was going with it?"

Detective Ortiz hesitated, but then said the used-car folks had only taken the buyer's money and didn't get personal details.

"Well, you do have the license plate number," Candrew said, "if it wasn't changed after the truck sold. I'm sure you'll be able to track it down if you need to. You've got the resources." He thanked Ortiz for the update and the call ended.

Late on Wednesday afternoon he left the office and went to Mark Kernfeld's laboratory. When he went in, the Post-Doc greeted him, joking. "You're becoming one of our very best customers."

"That's what happens when you're in academia, not just out in the real world," Candrew quipped in reply. "And the zero rate you're charging me to do all these analyses is such a good deal."

Grinning, the Post-Doc replied, "I'll get Mark," and disappeared down the passageway.

Candrew sat looking at the surrounding high-tech equipment. The antiseptic space was humming with the sound of vacuum pumps, and filled with racks of electronic gear and their flashing lights and video screens. A printer surprised him as it clicked on and spewed out half a dozen pages covered with rows of numbers.

He didn't wait long before Mark bustled out of his office and into the lab holding a sheaf of computer printouts.

"Hi Candrew. Here are the results we got for your latest batch of samples—at least the high-priority ones."

"Thanks. It's really great to get these results so quickly. I think this will probably be the last batch, and I want to thank you personally for all the analyses you've done in the last few weeks." He took the folder from Mark, flipped it open, and perused the summary sheet. One group of chromium values, including those for *BD* and nearby samples, were really high.

Mark watched him, and said, "Those are some of the highest values we've ever gotten for you."

Candrew glanced down through the other chromium concentrations, then looked up at Mark and said, "But things are getting more serious. This batch of mineral samples was collected by a man who was later murdered. They may give the police important evidence that could help with their homicide investigation."

Mark leaned his head to one side and frowned. "This is getting a bit dramatic. You'd gotten me all psyched up about finding a diamond mine—but now murder? That opens up a whole new prospect." Grimacing, he asked, "Will I have to testify in court?"

Candrew went back to his office cradling the printouts Mark had given him. He was delighted with the results for the rocks from Alex's truck. When he unlocked the door, he saw the light on his phone was flashing. He listened to the message, and got a woman's recorded voice. It said she was phoning from the used-car lot in Arizona, the one he'd visited a few days earlier. There was a name and phone number.

The request was simple—"call me." Candrew did, and she answered on the second ring.

"You wanted me to phone you if anything unusual happened," she said. "Well, there's been not one thing, but two. First of all, that truck you were looking at sold, and was driven away. We don't have it no more. Then police turned up looking for it. I had to tell them I didn't know who the buyer was, he paid cash."

Candrew was surprised. "That old truck sold fast," he said. But from what he'd told Ortiz he knew the police showing up was to be expected.

"However," she said, 'the buyer was a good-looking, tall blond guy, sort of athletic—my type." He heard her snigger. "He wanted a fill-up, and happened to say he'd be driving the truck to California."

The description was a good fit for Skip. Candrew felt pretty sure the truck was headed to Jay Wolverton's outfit in San Diego. They'd cooperated with Alex for several years and would have known what sort of vehicle he drove. But why did they want it?

He sat thinking through the possibilities, but reached no conclusions.

CHAPTER 39

RENATA KNOCKED ON THE open office door and walked in, surprising Candrew. "Thought I'd pay my faculty colleague a visit," she joked.

He stopped peering at his computer screen and looked up. "Well, much appreciated. Anyway, what brings you to this part of campus?"

"I'm on my way back from the Chemistry Department."

"Really? What were you doing over there?"

Renata slumped into the chair in front of Candrew's desk and explained. "Mercury."

Candrew's eyebrows raised. "The element or the planet? But then I guess if you were at the Chemistry Department it would have to be the element, quicksilver."

"Right. I read a recently published study that showed many Mayan sites, just like the one I'm working on, are riddled with mercury pollution." She shook her head in regret. "You're a geologist, you know what 'cinnabar' is?"

Candrew smirked. "Sure, the main mercury ore, mercury sulfide. A hydrothermal mineral."

"Yeah, and I'm sure you know its bright scarlet. And with the ancient Mayans, bright red was associated with blood and was sacred. Cinnabar was widely used for centuries as a pigment and in ceremonies. The Mayans ended up with a toxic environmental legacy, widespread mercury poisoning. Of course, they didn't know that."

"So why were you talking to the chemists?"

"I wanted to get soil samples from my site analyzed to see if we should be cautious about our excavations. I need to find out whether mercury could be a real hazard for us archaeologists digging things up. After all, I'm responsible for the grad students. I need to be sure they're working safely," Renata explained. "When I went to see Mark Kernfeld, he said they didn't do that sort of analysis. But he suggested I go and talk to the chemists because they have an environmental research unit that does have the capability. I went over and talked to them, and they said they'd be able to analyze soil samples for me. They were really interested in cooperating. Quite a friendly group. I even asked one of them if they did any work with diamonds."

Candrew perked up, this was a new thought for him. "And did they?" he asked.

"The guy I was talking to said the only thing he knew about diamonds he'd learned from his wife. But then he did say one of his past graduate students had gone to work for a company with specialized high pressure/high temperature equipment they used for making synthetic diamonds."

"Interesting. I wonder if Alex—as well as Yankovitz, and Skip, even Wolverton—were threatened by competition from that source."

"The impression I got was that natural and artificial diamonds don't compete." She laughed, "*A diamond is forever*—not made last year in a lab."

"It certainly seems that Alex was hunting for the real thing, and wasn't concerned at all with synthetics."

There was a brief interruption by a young woman student wanting a reference. Candrew always had time for students and he provided the textbook title and page numbers. She jotted the information in her note book, thanked him, and left.

"I've been thinking a lot about Alex, now that his truck has turned up—but then sold so rapidly," Candrew said.

"I've been thinking about him too," Renata said. "We still don't know much about his background. Even what relatives he had. Maybe the police have tracked down the next of kin."

"He's certainly the center of everything. I'm still wondering why two exploration groups were involved with his truck—one trying to get rid of it, and the other acquiring it."

"You think Yankovitz got what he wanted, but then Skip didn't know that he had it?"

Candrew smiled. "I certainly got what I wanted—rocks and an important map."

"But it's clear Alex had something the two different groups were after. And my guess is it was information."

"Like the location of a potentially prolific diamond mine?"

"Yeah. It could mean one group got all they were after," Renata said, "then killed Alex so information about the location of the diamond site wouldn't get spread around."

"You're suggesting Alex got caught up in a conflict between rivals?" Candrew said. "That's an interesting take. I guess what we're hypothesizing is that one group is associated with Skip, probably backed by Jay Wolverton, while the other has Bert Yankovitz, who may well be supported by Donnington and MINEx in Calgary. Both of those groups have had lots of mining experience."

Candrew pushed his chair back from his desk and, frowning, stared off into space.

"What are you thinking?" Renata asked.

"There may be a third group."

"Really? And who would that be?"

"Remember, when I went back alone to the diatreme where Wilf Pengelly had taken his mining students—the 'Major Miners'—at Spring Break, I ran into two Navajos—Raven and Carlos Nez. They were the ones who suggested I visit the old abandoned mine where I was trapped, and where I found Alex's body. And, of course, Carlos was the one who guided Yankovitz to some of the mining locations on the Navajo reservation. It's clear the Navajo are interested in developing their own resources."

"Then it's possible Carlos could be a link between two of the groups."

"Right. I think I need to pay him another visit."

Wilfred answered Candrew's call and said Carlos would probably be in his room on the top floor of the department.

"I'll be right over," Candrew said.

He met Wilfred in his office and they went up the stairs to the row of student work rooms. On the way, Candrew gave Wilfred a concise account of tracking down Alex's truck. He described how it had been shipped to a used car lot by Yankovitz, but then subsequently acquired by Skip who was with the Californian mineral group.

Four students shared an office with Carlos on the third floor. It was a typical student hangout. Posters hung on the wall, a couple for technical conferences, but others for rock groups, as well as photos of travel locations. A couple of backpacks had been dumped on the floor in one corner, while a pair of skis and a fishing pole leaned incongruously in the other one. Desks were pushed up against the walls. A cheap particleboard book case was crammed with notes, textbooks, a few rocks, and CD's. A CD player perched on top was playing too loudly and Carlos turned the volume down and ushered them in. The only other student, tapping on his laptop at the far desk, tactfully got up and left.

A little surprised at having two faculty members appearing in his office, Carlos put down his cell phone and nodded acknowledgement. "What are you here to talk to me about?"

"I'm still trying to figure out who murdered Alex, the Polish mineral expert," Candrew said. "You met him out on the reservation at Spring Break when you were there with Bert Yankovitz, looking at kimberlite pipes."

Carlos looked down at the floor and nodded.

"Last time we talked, you told me Bert and Alex seemed to be friends, on good terms."

"Well, I'm not sure about friends, but they certainly knew each other. They stood chatting a long time, drinking bottles of soda." He hesitated for several moments. "Actually, they did get into an argument. I think it was about when they were going to get together at some other exploration spot. They seemed to be arguing about a particular day or two. But they did finally agree on a Friday."

"Anything else that seemed to be out of the ordinary?" Candrew asked.

"No. Not that I remember. I'd never met that guy before, and he didn't talk to me out on the rez."

"How about Raven, your fellow Navajo. Did he know Alex?"

It was quite a while before he answered, and Candrew let the silence drag on. "I don't think so, but I'm not sure."

Candrew let that go, then asked, "How did Raven know about the old, abandoned mine where I was taken the day after I met him. Did he know the South American who drove the truck?"

"Again, I don't know anything about that. You'll have to ask Raven."

Wilfred had been standing in silence. Now he said, "How about Brandon. Was he doing mineral exploration with Raven?"

"I think they might have been cooperating, but I'm not really sure." He looked from Wilfred to Candrew. "You have to know I'm only a student. I'm trying to find out as much as I can about mineral exploration, and maybe processing. I'm not actually working with any of these people you're interested in. I'm only here to study, trying to get my degree."

Candrew said he understood that. He thanked him for his time, added that he'd been very helpful, and left with Wilfred.

"You didn't seem to get much information," Wilfred said as they went down the stairs.

"Not quite true. Carlos said Yankovitz and Alex agreed to get together, and he had heard when that would be." Candrew stopped in the stairwell and looked at Wilfred. "And that was the day before I found Alex's body—so it must have been the day he was murdered."

CHAPTER 40

CANDREW AND WILFRED CHATTED for a while, standing in the hallway, mainly gossiping about people in the mining department, although they did range over sports and some personal issues. Wilfred talked about his wife Allison, and how well her painting was going. He was obviously proud of her artistic efforts and had clearly become a fan, saying he liked her more realistic landscapes.

But Candrew's thoughts were drifting away, focusing on what he'd recently learned from Carlos and its relevance to the timing of Alex's murder. He left Wilfred, and set out on his way back toward Kinblade Hall, the geology building. This took him across campus and past the Archaeology Department where he hesitated only a moment before going in and heading up the stairs to Renata's office.

"It's my turn to pay a colleague a visit," he quipped as he went in.

"Well, good to have you here," she said smiling. "To what do I owe this sudden return visit?" She put down her pen, and Candrew sank in to the sole padded chair in her office.

"I've just been talking to that Navajo student, Carlos, again. I wanted to see if I could learn anything more about his field work with Bert Yankovitz on the reservation, you know, when they were together out there at Spring Break. I was particularly interested that they'd met Alex."

"And did you find out anything new?"

"Sure did. Carlos remembered hearing Bert and Alex talk about getting together at another mineral exploration site. And the day they agreed to meet was a Friday. Remember, I found Alex's body on Saturday, so that Friday must have been the day he was murdered."

"Wow. That's a critical piece of information." She looked at him, smiling, clearly impressed by what he'd deduced. "Didn't that detective tell you the autopsy showed Alex had been poisoned? That would take some planning, and maybe even help from an accomplice. It's not like shooting someone when you merely pull the trigger."

"That's true. The only thing I can think of is that maybe while they were having a few drinks, one of those drinks had a sedative in it. The fatal dose could have been injected when he became unconscious. Then they got rid of the body by hauling it off to the mine."

"My, you'd make a good criminal." She laughed. "I hesitate to offer you a drink." She leaned toward a group of water bottles and cans of soda on a side shelf. Candrew nodded, accepted one, and snapped the tab on a can of diet Pepsi. He drank several mouthfuls. "Tastes normal to me," he said grinning, gulping more.

"Of course, we're assuming it was Yankovitz who carried out the murder," Candrew said. "But maybe someone else drugged Alex and then administered that fatal dose. Possibly one of the other rival groups you suggested. Skip perhaps."

"So, you're suggesting that as far as Bert Yankovitz was aware, Alex simply failed to turn up for their meeting? That Bert had nothing to do with the homicide."

Candrew nodded. "Well, that certainly has to be a possibility."

"Interesting you mention Skip. You certainly found drugs in his truck, even if they were only for diabetes. But he must have had dealings with some pharmacist."

"Which makes you wonder why he was so eager to get Alex's truck. Could he have been looking for drugs? Possibly to remove them as evidence. Or perhaps he just wanted to see if there were any mineral maps he could use." Candrew paused for a moment.

"But that doesn't seem likely since the maps were still in Alex's truck when I searched it."

Renata smiled, "I can see you've given this a lot of thought."

"Of course, the other thing that has to be explained is how the Ecuadorian driver fits in," Candrew said. "He drove me to the old mine, but was he merely an innocent paid helper? We don't know if he had any role with Yankovitz. He certainly knew Skip. I saw them talking when Yankovitz and I were out at the kimberlite pipe north of Chinle. But Bert and that South American didn't talk to each other. It wasn't clear they even knew each other."

Candrew sat for a moment in silence thinking about Skip. "Carl Denby, one of the MINEx geologists, had worked with Skip in Butte, Montana, and said he'd left to get more real-world experience in Mexico. But Carl had heard it didn't work out, and after a few months he'd moved down to South America. I don't know the details—Peru maybe. Now I think about it, maybe that's where he got to know the guy from Ecuador."

"Pure speculation—although an intriguing possibility," Renata said sympathetically. "You said that even though he drove you to the mine and locked you in, later he showed no sign of recognizing you. So, he could be quite capable of playing dumb when he needed to."

"Yeah, that's true," Candrew said. "There's lots of loose ends. Maybe Bert Yankovitz drove the drugged Alex to the mine. After all, he did end up with Alex's truck and then left it in Flagstaff before sending it to the used car lot in Phoenix."

"But would Bert have had a key to that heavy metal door at the mine entrance?"

"Good point. Also, Alex was pretty solidly built. It would probably have been a challenge for just one person to drag him down a dark mine tunnel. And that, of course, implies a helper of some sort."

"Look, I'd like to keep talking so we can solve this homicide," Renata said. "But the University insists I teach once in a while— and the next time is in five minutes." Smiling, she got up from her neatly-organized desk and picked up lecture notes from the side bookshelf.

"Okay, I'll let you go give another stellar lecture," Candrew said as they left her office and she closed the door behind them.

At the end of the hallway, a tall, lean, sandy-haired young man with a bulky folder under one arm was coming toward them. As he greeted Renata, she said "Look, Aaron I've got my class in a couple of minutes." She turned to Candrew, "I think you two met at the faculty Spring party." She turned and hurried down toward the lecture room.

"You're the geologist, right?" Aaron said. "I remember talking to you about doing some exploration out West. You probably realize that as a new faculty member I have to get my research program underway. I'm doing some preliminary excavations on the remains of pre-pueblo cultures in abandoned sites, and even a few caves. I could certainly use some geologic insights."

"Sounds like you've already got a range of intriguing projects going."

"I don't teach on a Friday," Aaron said, "and was going out to one of my closer sites to take some photographs. You want to come along? I'd appreciate your geologic input." He described the site location, and said that to his untutored eye it seemed to be mainly sandstone.

"Yeah, that's possible," Candrew said. "Sandstones are my geologic specialty, and I'm always glad to go look at another outcrop."

"I should warn you," Aaron said, grinning, "I'll be leaving pretty early in the morning. Right at six o'clock. It'll be daylight by then."

"Not a problem."

Candrew left Aaron and the Archaeology Building and followed the gravel pathways across campus toward his own office, walking in and out of the shadows of the trees. On the way he thought over his discussion with Renata about the possibility of Yankovitz and Skip's groups being rivals. He realized, however, that Brandon had also shown an interest in diamond exploration and had been involved with Raven. He remembered Wilfred speculating that Brandon might want to get rich in the diamond business, so that he could have a better chance as a suitor for Jessica Rylander. Would that be a strong enough reason to eliminate a competitor like Alex? And it was obvious that his colleague, Raven, knew about the old abandoned mine, where Alex's body had been dumped.

Candrew looked forward to getting out into nature, especially since he would be able to visit a sandstone outcrop he knew little about. There was always the anticipation of what he might find. At six the next morning he was back at the Archaeology Building to meet Aaron. What he didn't expect was that their transport to the old pueblo site would be a bright yellow Chevy Corvette. Candrew scrambled in.

Aaron drove fast, but as he explained to Candrew, "I felt deprived as a high-school kid. My friends all had cars. I didn't—had to bum rides and that made dating damn difficult." He laughed. "So, when I finally landed my first well-paid job here on the faculty, I got myself a 'babe magnet.'" He concentrated on driving a twisting section of the road for a few minutes, then glanced over at Candrew. "I know what you're thinking—that this is hardly the right automobile for our New Mexico dirt roads. Not right for gravel."

"Well, yes," Candrew agreed.

"That's why we're not going to be driving all the way to the work site."

"We have a long hike?"

"No. I've got a guy with a high clearance, four-wheel drive pickup truck that's going to take us along the roughest part of the way," Aaron explained.

An hour and a half later they pulled off the main road and parked on a flat area beside a tan-colored, pickup. Its roof rack was lined with headlights, and to Candrew it was vaguely familiar.

The truck driver greeted Aaron, but ignored Candrew. Candrew was surprised. He had no doubt this was the driver and the pickup that had taken him to the mine where he'd been locked in and stumbled on Alex's body.

The driver turned away and quickly scrambled into his truck. Aaron climbed in beside him, and Candrew got into the back seat of the extended cab. Rocking along the poorly maintained, pot-holed track, they drove in silence toward the archaeological site.

When they arrived at the sandstone cliff face with its several cave entrances, they unloaded their gear. The driver didn't get out, and didn't offer help but sat in the cab reading a newspaper.

Aaron had not been told about Candrew's previous contacts with the driver, and now Candrew drew him aside. "How did you get linked up with this guy?"

"He's called Fernando. From Ecuador." Aaron glanced back at the pick-up truck. "He's been doing hauling chores for several mineral exploration groups working out here in the southwest. I've heard it was a guy from a group in San Diego who first ran across him in South America. I seem to remember he went by the name of 'Skip'."

Candrew asked again, "How did *you* find out about him?"

"Pure chance," Aaron said. "I got into a basketball pickup game with some of the mining graduate students. One of the older students, called Brandon, told me about Fernando. Said he'd heard about him from that San Diego exploration group. And it was Skip who'd apparently run across Fernando when he was working for a mining company down in Peru." Smirking, he said, "I got the strong impression that Fernando was an illegal alien, although I didn't know any of the details."

Candrew thought about that as they hiked over to the archaeo-logical site. It would certainly fit with all he'd seen and heard.

"I've had him carry stuff for me a couple of times," Aaron said. Dressed in a denim shirt and blue jeans, he pulled on his well-worn, wide-brimmed hat. Then, picking up his pack and a big flashlight, he headed toward the nearest cave, dark behind the remains of a low adobe wall at the front.

"Since we did such a good job of driving all the Native Americans away from their ancestral lands, there's been no one left to look after their religious artifacts. No more cultural caretakers." Sadly, Aaron shook his head. "That's left it open to the grave robbers. And over the years, there's been lots of them. I'm here to see what they left—what they failed to find."

He started his evaluation of the adobe remains, and Candrew began studying the sandstones, working his way along the cliff face. He chipped off numerous samples, took lots of photographs, and made copious descriptions in his field note book. This could provide a potential research project for one of his graduate students, he thought.

After a couple of hours Aaron shouted, "You ready for a break?" Candrew, about fifty yards away from the adobe ruin, struggled back with his pack loaded with rock samples. Fernando appeared to have no interest in what they were doing, although he did bring bottles of water out of the truck, and tossed them some power bars. They sat on rocks resting as they ate and drank.

Candrew stuffed the wrapper from the bar in his pocket and took a long drink of water. He looked over at Fernando, sitting by himself in silence—*time for confrontation*, he thought.

Candrew got up and took a few steps toward Fernando. "Remember me?" he asked, keeping his anger under control. He got a blank look and no reply.

Candrew sat on a flat rock about six feet from Fernando. "Let me jog your memory. You picked me up at a Route 66 motel in Albuquerque and drove me to an abandoned mine in the south of the state." Fernando sat unmoving, looking down at the gravel. "That's where you locked me in with no way to escape. Then you drove off."

There was still no response.

"Who paid you to do that? Who were you working for?"

There was silence. "Do you understand English?" Again, no answer.

Aaron joined them, "I know you work for other archaeologists and for several mining groups," he said. "Like the man from California, or the one from Arizona. Right?"

Fernando looked up and answered reluctantly. "Si. Yes."

"Who was it that wanted to drag a dead body into that old mine? Who did you help do that?" Candrew asked.

"No remember."

This questioning was getting nowhere. He glanced across at Aaron. Candrew was irritated and realized he'd find out nothing if he didn't take a tougher approach. and, though not certain, surmised, "You're here illegally, right?"

Fernando's faced morphed from featureless disinterest to serious concern. It left no doubt that he knew only too well the potential consequences of his alien status.

"You worked some sort of deal in Peru with an exploration geologist called Skip Engelmann. That right? He was going to get you into this country. Through Nogales perhaps?" Candrew stared at him. "But you must know that as an illegal alien you can just as easily be shipped back."

Candrew had clearly struck a nerve.

"I work hard. I do right thing. Help everyone." Fernando struggled with the English language, but speaking quickly explained. "I send money to Quito. Have wife. Two little ones, girls. They need me, need my good money." He took a deep breath. There was an interminable silence.

"Look, I'm not going to call in ICE," Candrew said, sympathetic to Fernando's situation. "But I do need information. You have to tell me who got you to drive your pickup to the old mine. Once with a dead body, once with me, right?"

Fernando sat quietly, breathing deeply, clearly feeling trapped.

"You've been involved as an accomplice in a murder, and probably in an attempted murder," Candrew said. "You have critical evidence. Who gave you the key to the mine?"

Again, there was a reluctance to talk. Then Fernando said, "The man I carried rocks for in my truck. He called me on cell phone.

Said friend asked me take you to old mine." After a long pause he added, "And lock you in. Said he pay me."

"And you had no scruples about doing that?" Candrew asked, but quickly realized Fernando probably wouldn't understand the word 'scruples.' He changed the subject. "Who got you to take a dead body to the deserted mine? Did you help someone drag it in? And who was that?"

Fernando was stubborn, clearly not going to say anything more. He threw his empty water bottle into the back of his truck, ignored Candrew, and walked over to where Aaron was retrieving his photographic gear. "I help you?"

Aaron looked across at Candrew, a look that implied, *I don't think you're going to get much more out of this guy.* All three of them cooperated in loading rock samples, artifacts and backpacks into the pickup truck.

They drove back to where Aaron's yellow Corvette was parked and their items were offloaded and transferred. Candrew gave Fernando his business card and said, "If you think of anything I need to know, call me. It would be good for you to provide all the information you have." Fernando glanced at the card, then stuck it in his pocket. He climbed into his pickup and drove off without comment.

Candrew watched him pull away in a cloud of dust. He turned to Aaron, "Win some, lose some."

"And what did you win?"

"Well, I learned that Raven, the Navajo, and Brandon, the Teaching Assistant in Mining, had some sort of relationship with Skip and the San Diego group. And that they all used Fernando to haul heavy stuff."

"I guess that helps you sort things out. What did you lose?"

"I learned nothing at all about who planned to dump the dead man in the old mine. Or, for that matter, who murdered him."

CHAPTER 41

CANDREW AND AARON DROVE back to the university in the Corvette—Candrew's feet jammed up against his loaded backpack in the well. Aaron noticed and laughed.

"I haven't found space to be a problem when the top's up," he said, "though I have to admit when it's folded down it can take up a bunch of the space." He concentrated on the road for a while, then, smiling, said, "Of course, I can always get Fernando with his pickup to transport any bulky items for me."

"Assuming he's going to be around," Candrew noted. "I'm fairly certain he's an illegal alien and knows a hell of a lot more than he's letting on."

Aaron nodded. "I'm sure you're right, but the few times he's transported stuff for me, he's talked very little. I got his phone number from Brandon. We might ask him how much Fernando knows about the people he's worked for."

"Good idea. I'll call him."

Saturday evening was warm and still, with the few scattered clouds tinted orange as they caught the last light from the setting sun. Candrew and Renata sat on her patio, drinks in hand, watching a small flock of birds settling in for the night.

"I envy you," Renata said. "You can just dash off to another sandstone outcrop—or tempting diamond location—anytime you want. You don't have to pack up your stuff, get permits, and ship it all off to Guatemala."

The reference to Central America reminded Candrew that Renata had grown up in Costa Rica and spoke fluent Spanish. He'd already told her about Friday's trip to Aaron's research area, and his own chance to study a new sandstone outcrop. But the main surprise had been meeting face-to-face with Fernando, the driver from Ecuador. Now he wondered whether Fernando would be more forthcoming if he was questioned in Spanish. He suggested this to Renata.

"Well, I'm quite happy to talk to him," she said, "and be the interrogator. But first you're going to have to get the two of us together."

"I'll phone Brandon. He seems to know how to contact Fernando. Maybe Brandon can trick him into coming to campus if we tell him we've got a load of rock samples that need to be transported someplace. I'm sure he needs the extra money"

For a while they sat quietly sipping their drinks, thinking about this idea. Then Renata said, "That other student in mining, Carlos, the one from the Navajo reservation, told you he'd heard Alex and Bert Yankovitz planning to get together at some mine, possibly a diamond mine, on the day Alex was murdered."

"Yes, that's right. And Fernando seems to have been involved, although it's not clear how. We know Alex's truck was left in Flagstaff, but Bert had his own truck and gave Alex a ride. This raises the question of whose vehicle was used to get Alex's body to the old mine."

"I would think it's probably Fernando who drove." She sipped her drink. "You said he seemed quite familiar with the route to that abandoned mine."

"Which raises an interesting dilemma," Candrew said. "Fernando would know the murderer—but the killer would be able to threaten Fernando with deportation, since he's an illegal alien. A sort of standoff might have developed."

Having no solution to this problem, they drank more wine, gossiped about university affairs, and then moved inside to eat the meal Renata had cooked.

Just after dawn the next morning, Candrew rolled out of bed and left Renata sleeping. Quietly he made his way into her kitchen, filled the coffee machine and set it percolating, then retrieved the Sunday newspaper from the driveway. After reading the comics, he got halfway through the political arguments from politicians who, regardless of party affiliation, all claimed to have the ultimate solutions for current problems.

Renata, yawning, wandered into the kitchen. "I'm just following the aroma of coffee," she said. "So, what are you going to cook for our breakfast?"

Candrew smirked, "You know me well enough—when it comes to food, I'm a consumer, not a preparer. And anyway, there's not a snowball's chance in hell that I could compete with your culinary skills."

"Excuses, excuses."

Candrew continued reading the newspaper, and Renata went and showered.

An hour later they finished what Renata called an 'international breakfast'—British. "It's what Queen Elizabeth often ate," she explained.

Candrew had enjoyed the unusual royal meal of scrambled eggs garnished with orange zest and a sprinkle of nutmeg. He sipped the hot coffee—his contribution to their breakfast. "I've been thinking about you talking to Fernando in Spanish," he said, setting down his coffee mug. "I'm planning to get him to campus. I'm going to phone Aaron, or Carlos, and have them lure him here with the pretext of needing to transport some heavy items."

"Devious," Renata said laughing. "I'll be happy to cooperate any way I can."

An hour later Candrew drove home from Renata's to be greeted by two lonely pets who did their best to make him feel guilty for abandoning them. He spent some time fussing with his dog and cat, and both appreciated the treats they were given.

Candrew went into his home office where it took him a while to track down Aaron's home phone number. His call was promptly answered. "Look, I need a favor," he said. "Renata Alcantara is a close friend of mine and she's fluent in Spanish. I thought it would be a good idea if she talked to Fernando, your truck driver, in his native language. Hopefully, he would be more likely to answer our questions about the groups that hired him to dump a body—and me—in an old mine."

"Happy to help. But do you think Fernando will be receptive to interrogation by a woman?"

"That's a risk worth taking. Maybe he'll treat her as a motherly figure."

"Whatever. I'll give Fernando a call and see how soon we can get him here on campus."

"Thanks. I appreciate that. Let me know what you arrange."

Candrew considered calling Carlos, but decided that would be overkill. He made tea, slotted a favorite classical CD into the player, and lunched on cheese and crackers.

It was mid-afternoon when his phone rang. Aaron told him that Fernando was not busy and they'd arranged for him to be at the Archaeology Department after lunch the next day. Candrew was pleased by Aaron's prompt reply and Fernando's availability. He called Renata to give her the details. "You've got several hours to learn all about mining geology so you can ask those pertinent questions in Spanish."

"Sure. I was sitting here with nothing to do," she said sarcastically.

Lying in bed the next morning, Candrew pondered what Renata should ask Fernando. What questions was he most likely to answer honestly? What did he know about Alex's murder? And would he provide any information about diamond prospects and the people exploring them? But Candrew had graduate students to mentor, undergraduates to teach, a funded research program to supervise, and technical papers to publish. As he lay in bed the shadows from the low morning sun crept across the wooden vigas of the bedroom ceiling. Too much going on, he thought. Reluctantly he pried himself out of bed to face this Monday morning.

By ten o'clock Candrew had fed himself, his cat and his dog, driven to campus, and parked in his usual space behind Kinblade Hall.

Judy was examining rock thin-sections with a high-powered, polarizing microscope when he went into the sedimentology lab. She pushed her stool away from the work bench, and put her glasses back on. "Still piling up the data," she explained.

"I'm glad to hear that," Candrew said smiling. "I'll need those numbers to add conviction to our research proposal, the one we'll be sending to the National Science Foundation. The deadline is only three weeks away."

They discussed the current status of their ongoing sandstone project for the next hour, and then Candrew went up to his office.

He talked to a couple of students waiting for him and helped resolve their technical problems and questions about turbidites. In his office, he pushed aside some of the scattered papers on his desk, clearing an area big enough to sit on. He perched there, picked up the phone, and called Detective Ortiz. Candrew was eager to know how the police investigations were proceeding and what, if anything, they had discovered about Alex's murder—at least what the detective would be prepared to tell him. He also felt an obligation to give Ortiz the information he'd acquired. But the phone rang several times and switched to an answering machine. He declined to leave a message.

With hands clasped behind his head, Candrew sat slumped in his desk chair, looking out the window. This office was his personal space. He alone had selected all the books and journals on the shelves. The scattered photographs were memories of people and past events he considered significant. The lumps of rock brought back thoughts of significant field work, and the maps he'd chosen to hang on the wall illustrated those areas. The few mineral clusters on the window sill reflected his personal aesthetics. In this modest office area he had complete control—unlike the outside world where his control was marginal at best.

Candrew sat thinking over the afternoon's planned meeting with Fernando. He was sure Renata would ask relevant questions, and he hoped she would be able to pry out useful information.

He spent a distracted hour and a half working on the research proposal intended for the NSF, but then gave up and went to have a late lunch at the Faculty Lounge. The typical group was ensconced at their corner table on the top floor. They greeted Candrew in the usual friendly manner as he pulled up the last empty chair. Arlan Dee put down his iced tea and asked how the diamond efforts were progressing.

"Actually, I've been studying a new sandstone outcrop." He grinned, "At least new to me. It has nothing to do with diamonds, it's more like the ongoing research projects with Judy, my research associate."

"So, you've given up on becoming a billionaire? Quit searching for diamonds?"

"Well, no. I've always been intrigued by the scientific information that can be gleaned from those gems coming up from deep below the Earth's surface. But I've gotten more interested in the people involved in diamond exploration." He glanced around the group. "And especially the one who got murdered. I'd like to know the reason he was killed, and who did it."

"So, you turning into a detective?"

"Only in a very amateurish way. I wish I could be more effective." Candrew thought about the meeting with Fernando scheduled for that afternoon and hoped it would be productive. He also wondered if the professionals, like Ortiz, were making any headway.

The talk around the table drifted to other topics, and he listened to the latest campus rumors, ate his sandwich, and drank icy diet coke.

Lunch over, Candrew headed to the Archaeology Department to

meet Renata and Aaron. They were both in Aaron's office, which was disorganized and seemed as though it could use Fernando's efforts to haul away some of his heavy-looking cardboard boxes.

Renata smiled at Candrew. "Buenos Dias."

"Come on in," Aaron said, moving a pile of books and papers from one of the high-backed chairs. "We've got fifteen minutes before Fernando's supposed to arrive—but then he's often likely to treat a given time as a mere suggestion, rather than a definite commitment," he said as he settled into his desk chair.

"Does he know where your office is?" Renata asked.

"I'm sure he'll remember. The other time Fernando hauled stuff for me he helped carry it up to my work space, the room just next to this office."

Renata nodded in understanding. "What do you know about him? I mean personal things."

"Not a lot," Aaron said. He looked at Candrew, and then told her, "From what I've heard, I'm sure he is an illegal alien. He's a conscientious worker and I know he's good-hearted. He's sending money back to his wife, and their two young daughters, in Quito, Ecuador."

That information made Renata more sympathetic to this man she'd never met.

Renata and Aaron were both archaeology professors, and as they waited for Fernando their conversation inevitably involved the excavation problems they faced, as well as other technical issues.

Candrew was only half listening, thinking about the information he hoped Fernando would be prepared to give them. He thought again of Fernando's illegal status, and how it might provide a way to put some pressure on him. But mainly he wondered how he would respond to being questioned in Spanish.

Only ten minutes after the scheduled time they heard a loud voice, with a Spanish accent, asking one of the students in the hallway where Aaron's office was. A moment later Fernando came in, nodded to Aaron, and to Candrew whom he recognized from the field trip.

But he was clearly surprised by the presence of a woman.

CHAPTER 42

FERNANDO HESITATED, THEN STEPPED into Aaron's office. Of medium height, he had on well-worn jeans with a wide leather belt, a black sweatshirt, and a baseball cap. Clearly uncomfortable in this setting, he reluctantly lowered himself onto the seat Aaron pointed to.

"Good to see you again, Fernando. Glad you could get here today," Aaron said smiling, trying to make the situation a little less threatening. He rocked back in his chair and put his feet up on a wooden crate intended for artifacts, further trying to create a casual atmosphere. "We wanted to talk to you about some of the jobs you've done."

Fernando nodded, uncertain, and said nothing, looking at the other two.

"This is Candrew Nor, you met him when we were out at the archaeological site last week," Aaron said. He had dispensed with formal titles—Doctor, Professor—keeping everything low key.

Again, Fernando nodded, still saying nothing. He didn't smile.

"And this is Renata Alcantara. She's also an archaeologist here at the university."

Renata leaned toward him, smiled and said, in Spanish, *"Nice to have you here helping. I've heard you're from Ecuador."* She paused, watching for his reaction. *"I'm from Costa Rica."*

He was obviously surprised at being greeted in his native tongue, and by someone from Central America, especially a woman. He seemed to relax somewhat.

"You been in the States long?" she asked.

He answered in Spanish. "Si. Now almost five years."

"You like it here?"

"People are friendly. I'm doing a good job. Helping a lot of people."

"But your family is in Ecuador, in Quito."

He was clearly surprised she knew that.

"Yes. That is true. But it is not good." He pursed his lips, his voice cracked. This was clearly a major concern. "I wish we were all together. My wife, my daughters."

"Maybe that will be possible if things here work out well." Renata had cast the bait.

Candrew and Aaron sat in silence, not able to follow the Spanish dialog. Then Candrew asked, "You've been trucking stuff mainly in Arizona and New Mexico. Right?"

Fernando replied to the question in English. "Si. Yes. There has been much work in two states. Keep me very busy."

"Mainly with people in mineral exploration? Ones who want you to carry equipment and haul rocks?" Aaron said. "Do they pay you well?"

"I work hard and help them. I do good work. I earn that money."

Renata smiled and switched the conversation back to Spanish. "Do you send some of the dollars you earn back to your family in Quito?"

He looked at her suspiciously, but answered. "Yes. They rely on me."

"The people who pay you well, do you remember their names?"

"They pay in cash. Give me dollars. No names needed."

"Then how do you contact them?"

"I have their cell phone numbers so I can call. And they have my number. They can reach me if they want me to bring my truck. To help them."

Renata turned to Aaron and Candrew, briefly summarizing what had been said.

"It's true," Aaron said. "I have his cell phone number. That's how I've contacted him."

Candrew was pleased that Fernando seemed to be telling the

truth, He asked him if he remembered anything special about the men he'd worked for. "Were they tall, short; fat, skinny, you know, balding or bearded, wearing glasses?" he asked. "What town were they from? What sort of cars did they drive?"

"They were like all you Norte Americanos," was Fernando's non-comital answer.

"Oh, come on. You can do better than that," Candrew said. "Tell me one thing about one man."

Fernando did not reply and sat in silence.

Renata broke in, speaking to him, again in Spanish. *"I'm sure you are honest and hard-working, but you are paid in cash. Have you ever paid taxes on that income?"* Fernando looked down at the floor, reddening slightly. She continued, *"In America, not to have paid taxes is a federal crime. And it's also a crime in the states where you worked."* There was silence. *"You could be arrested and made to pay all your back taxes."* She let the impact of that register.

With Fernando under pressure, Renata changed the topic back to the people he'd worked for. She spoke in English. "Tell us about some of the people you hauled material for. What were they like? Who were they?"

Fernando appeared to realize he was in an awkward situation—the people in this office seemed to have too much damning evidence about him. But he apparently felt he'd not lose anything by going along with this request of Renata's.

"I work for one group from California. The town San Diego, I think. They wanted me to move large pieces of rock. Came from new mines. Mines in this state."

"You remember any names?"

"No. The man who did arranging, called me on the phone, was tall. Had long blond hair. He seemed to be very strong, good shape. He knew a lot about rocks. Sometimes he drove his own truck."

Candrew had no doubt he was describing Skip. "Anything else you want to tell us about this man," he asked.

There was a long hesitation and Fernando looked around the

group as if trying to decide what he should say. He lapsed into Spanish. *"At one mine in Arizona the blond man brought out a lot of big crystals, very beautiful crystals. Told me to wrap them carefully. Protect them. He made me promise not to tell anyone where they came from. I think it had to be kept a secret from other people who found and sold minerals, other dealers."* Again, he quietly looked around, apparently wondering why they wanted to know all this. *"From what I heard him say to the men working with him, that mine was on government property. Maybe a state park, or something. They shouldn't be taking the rocks out of there. Taking those minerals would be breaking the laws."*

Renata translated. So, Candrew thought, Fernando had information about these rockhounds' illegal activities. And he could possibly use that to offset his own tax evasion situation if it became an issue with the IRS.

Fernando, still obviously nervous, again looked around, apparently trying to figure out the reason for their interest. For the first time, he initiated a conversation. "Why you get me here this afternoon?" Turning to Aaron, he asked, "You have boxes for me to load? Where are boxes now?"

Aaron slid his feet off the wooden crate and leaned toward Fernando. "Today we just wanted to talk to you. In the future I'll have plenty of jobs for you. Lots of work. Well paid work."

"Before we get to that, let me ask you one or two more questions," Candrew said. "How well did you know Alex? The man who was found dead in the old mine you took me to."

"Very sad." Fernando said it quietly. "I only met him once, two times, before."

"And where was that?" Candrew continued his interrogation.

Fernando was in no hurry to answer. Eventually he said, "It must have been when we loaded rocks from one of the excavations. You know, minerals. Stuff, out of mine shaft."

"But the next time you saw the man called Alex he was just a dead body, right? Did you drive his remains to the mine?"

Fernando said nothing.

"Before you answer my questions," Candrew said, let me ask, "do you have United States citizenship?" He paused, but there was no reply from the startled Ecuadorian. "You here on a Green Card? You have a visa?" For several moments there was an icy silence in Aaron's office.

Candrew knew the answers to his questions, and he knew that this information could be used to put pressure on Fernando. Hopefully it would get him to talk about Alex's body in the old mine, and who put it there. "You realize that as an illegal alien you can be deported by ICE. No more jobs. You can't be too careful. No more money. How would you tell that to your wife?"

Fernando looked down in silence, the bill of his cap hiding his face. It was clear he felt trapped. Candrew let the silence run on. Eventually Fernando looked up, breathing deeply, his face pale. He started to speak—in Spanish.

"Many weeks ago I worked for a man from Canada."

"You remember his name?" Renata asked.

"I'm not sure, I think it was something like Yovich, maybe other name was Bart. He was a geologist. He called me by phone and told me where to meet him. At a motel in Socorro." He looked around the three of them listening silently. *"When I got to the motel, he said he had a little problem. There was another man in his room, that man was Alex. But he was slumped in a chair, seemed unconscious. Bart told me he'd probably had a stroke. He wanted me to help move the man into the truck—my truck. I always followed instructions from people I worked for. Do the best I can to help them. We moved the body into my truck, onto the back seat. There was nobody in the parking lot, nobody saw us doing that. Then Bart gave me directions and I drove for maybe an hour to the mine you know about."*

Renata took a moment to translate the main points of what Fernando had clearly explained in Spanish. She stressed the involvement of a mining geologist.

This was obviously Bert Yankovitz. Candrew was stunned: Yankovitz! He thought back to their joint visit to the new mine near Chinle in Arizona. Bert had seemed a very reasonable guy, not a murderer. And at that time Bert hadn't talked to Fernando at all. It was Skip who'd talked to this Ecuadorian driver. On the other hand, Yankovitz was the one who'd later tried to get rid of Alex's truck in the Phoenix used-car lot. "Get Fernando to keep talking," he said to Renata.

She turned back to Fernando. *"What happened when you got to the mine?"*

"It was getting dark and that area was deserted. I helped him carry the body into the mine shaft. We propped him against a wall and Bart told me to leave them. I had my own light and made my way out. About ten minutes later Bart came out, locked the mine gate, and tossed me the key."

"Anything else you want to tell me?"

"No." He turned away from Renata and stared at Candrew and Aaron. *"I say too much already,"*

"And then you both drove back to the motel?" Renata probed.

"Yes. Most of the way not talking. At one point he threatened me—if I ever said a word about this to anybody, I'd be on my way back to South America the next morning."

Smart, Candrew thought when Renata translated. Fernando had the key to the mine, it was his truck that was used, and Bert Yankovitz had a hold over him as an accomplice. "Did you ever see Bert again?" Candrew said.

"Once or three," Fernando said in English. "For him I no do work. I found out the man Alex had been murdered in two weeks."

"Let's get to the next question. Why did you take me to that same mine, the one that wasn't being worked anymore, and lock me in? Who wanted you to do that? Was it Bert again? Did he pay you?"

Fernando looked down and said nothing.

CHAPTER 43

RENATA TOOK OFF HER glasses, wiped them with a tissue, and laid them on Aaron's desk. She sat in silence with Candrew and Aaron, waiting for Fernando to answer Candrew's question about his being taken to the mine and trapped. Candrew wondered whether the delay was giving Fernando time to conjure up a convincing lie, or was it just letting him decide if he should implicate other people.

Candrew pushed his chair back and looked around. As a new faculty member, Aaron had been fortunate to be assigned quite a large office. But he had not been in academia long enough to have acquired all the years of academic journals that would fill his bookshelves. He had not yet accumulated many technical books of his own, and most of the volumes on the shelves had library tags. There was, however, a nicely bound version of his dissertation. But there were no rows of theses and dissertations from successfully-advised graduate students. Side tables did have piles of student notes and drafts of manuscripts he was working on. There were a couple of rather fine American Indian patterned, ceramic bowls on the half empty book shelf beside his field notebooks. But Candrew's knowledge of pueblo pottery was superficial, and he had no idea where those pots had been made.

Renata glanced at him, then turned to Fernando. She encouraged him in Spanish. *"You need to tell us the truth about who wanted you to take Candrew to the mine and lock him in. If we don't know that, the police will assume it was solely your decision."* She pointed her finger at him for emphasis. *"That'll put you in a very awkward situation. May even get you jailed in the U.S. for attempted murder. Most likely the authorities would have you deported from this country and sent back to Ecuador."*

Frowning, Fernando looked around the group and slowly nodded, apparently realizing his dilemma.

"I don't know name of the man," he said quietly in English, turning toward Candrew. "He was from big Indian reservation, you know, Navajo." There was a moment's pause. "He told me to pick you up at motel in Albuquerque. Said where to drive with you." There was another hesitation. "When he asked me, I told him I had key to mine."

Candrew stared at him. That made sense, since it was Raven who'd suggested it would be worth his time to go to the now-abandoned mine and take a look at the remaining minerals.

"I did not know who you were," Fernando said. "I never seen you before. I did only what I was asked. I got paid. Got money in advance."

"You certain he was Navajo?" Candrew probed.

"Yes. I am sure. I had hauled rocks for him and comrades two times." There was another long pause. Fernando seemed to be trying to decide how much he should tell them—but he apparently realized his chance to remain in the U.S. might be at stake. "That man, Indian man, often had younger guy with him. A student. Also Navajo. Sometimes there was other student, he not Indian."

"Tall? Blond? And quite athletic?"

"Yeah. You are right."

Candrew was getting a clearer picture of Raven, Carlos, and Brandon's involvement. They were the group he'd seen together several times, most recently at the new mining location on the eastern edge of the Navajo reservation. He'd collected samples near there, and Mark Kernfeld had analyzed them. He'd shown their high chromium contents were consistent with a diamond-rich location. Raven seemed to have been the leader—and was the one responsible for sending him to the mine with Fernando. But why was Raven interested in locking a geology professor in an old mine? And did he know about Alex's dead body being there?

There appeared to be little more that Fernando would be able to tell them, but Candrew had one last question. "Did the Californian group of mineral prospectors you'd worked with in the past have anything to do with me being taken to the mine?"

"No." It was said with conviction.

Candrew believed him. But he felt it was imperative that he talk to Brandon and the two Navajos.

An hour later Candrew was sitting at his own office desk, still pondering the information he'd gotten from Fernando. What should he tell detective Ortiz? Fernando's account was, of course, only word of mouth. How should he approach Brandon and Carlos? They were, after all, students in his university. And what about Raven? Should the Bureau of Indian Affairs, the BIA, be brought in?

Candrew rocked back in his chair, hands behind his head, wondering what to do next. He decided that calling Detective Ortiz would only involve a simple—although dramatic—update with the information he'd just gotten from Fernando. Nothing more would be needed. He phoned the detective.

"This is Dr. Nor. I have some information that could help in your homicide investigation," Candrew said. "I wanted to let you know I've found out who drove me to the mine. And that, of course, was the driver who locked me in.'

"How did you find who it was?" Ortiz sounded skeptical.

"Well, he'd worked for some of the archaeologists and also for several people involved in mineral exploration. I happened to meet him through an archaeology professor here at the university."

"And why would he want to tell you about his role in trapping you?"

"In part, because he realized I recognized him. But mainly because he's an illegal alien and wants to cooperate. He's hoping that would give him a better chance of being allowed to stay here in the U.S."

"I see."

"The main issue though is that he admitted driving with a Canadian geologist when they took Alex's body to the mine where I found it. He said the man was unconscious, apparently drugged, as they drove him to the abandoned mine."

"That's interesting. Quite an amazing confession. Were there other witnesses?"

"Only the three of us," Candrew said walking across his office to the window with the cell phone pressed to his ear. It was taking Ortiz a while to comment on this information.

"So, what you're telling me is all hearsay evidence—nothing that would stand up in a murder trial. But you should know that the toxicology report from the autopsy did show the presence of two drugs. One was a sedative." There was a pause, and then he said, "The other drug was fatal and almost certainly the cause of death. This, of course, supports your story, actually the alien's story."

Candrew heard Ortiz shuffled papers, and then he told him, "The sedative was something called *Flunitrazepam*. We know it better as *Rohypnol*, the date rape drug."

Candrew was impressed by the details of the chemical analysis, and was pleased to hear it was consistent with Fernando's account of what happened. He told Ortiz that Aaron had Fernando's cell phone number. "And I also have his truck license plate number. You shouldn't have any trouble tracking him down."

"So this illegal alien, this Fernando, is admitting to being an accessory to murder?" Ortiz confirmed.

"I guess that's right. But from what Fernando said it seems to me it was actually an explorationist called Bert Yankovitz who carried out the murder. The unconscious man was at Yankovtz's motel room where they met."

"Really? Hold on a moment." There was silence for a while and Candrew heard more papers being rustled. Then Ortiz said, "One of the things our report shows is that on the homicide victim's cell phone there was a conversation with the man you called 'Yankovitz.'

He was asking for information on a mine location, and wanted details of mineral content and economic prospects."

"I'm sure you remember that Yankovitz was the one who ended up with Alex's truck and sent it to the used-car lot outside Phoenix," Candrew said. "He's Canadian—you might have an international incident on your hands. Especially since he seems to have been working for one of the big Canadian mineral exploration companies, an outfit called MINEx. It's headquartered in Calgary."

"We'll find him. We have a good working relationship with our police neighbors to the north."

After a few final comments and some clarifications, the call ended.

For several minutes Candrew stood at the window watching students milling around outside the department, then he went back and slumped into his desk chair. He phoned Wilfred Pengelly.

"Hi Wilfred, Candrew here. There've been some significant developments in the murder case the police are working on. The one where I found a body in the abandoned mine." Candrew elaborated on what he'd heard from Fernando that afternoon. "I'm going to need to set up another meeting with Carlos and Brandon. We should talk to them as soon as possible."

"Okay. I'll try to get us all together first thing in the morning," Wilfred said. "That be okay?"

"That would be great." Candrew put the phone down, stared into the distance for a moment thinking. Then he immediately picked it back up, dialed Renata, and invited himself to dinner.

It was early evening when Candrew drove up to Renata's house.

"Quite a session we had with Fernando," she said, greeting him.

"Yeah. And I think your talking to him in Spanish was really important. It made him feel less of an outsider. More cooperative."

They went through to the living room and Renata brought in some cheese and crackers, and the inevitable glasses and bottle of wine. As Candrew poured the wine, she said, "You'd better fill up on cheese since I didn't have time to cook an exotic meal."

"Not a problem," he said, grinning.

"But I have ordered some Chinese take-out, so we won't starve."

Inevitably, conversation drifted back to the afternoon's session with Fernando. "I got the impression he's basically honest," Renata said, "that we can trust what he's telling us. Although there's no proof—and he does have an agenda to try and stay in the U.S."

"True. But we're certainly getting a consistent story. However, I do want to question Brandon and the Navajos in more detail." Candrew told her that Wilfred was going to set up a meeting for the next morning.

"And what do you expect to get from them?" Faced with Candrew's uncertain silence, she answered her own question. "You expect them to confirm their role in having you locked in a dark mine?" When he nodded, she went on to say, "What I don't understand is the motive for locking you up. We still don't know why they would want to do that."

CHAPTER 44

CANDREW'S PHONE CALL TO Wilfred Pengelly the previous afternoon had led to an early morning meeting in the Economic Minerals Department. Carlos and Brandon arrived together and on time. The college Dean had also been asked to attend the meeting so there would be an independent witness, and now the five of them sat in Wilfred's office.

Wilfred leaned back in his office chair, patted his ample midsection, and made a sweeping hand gesture toward Candrew, clearly letting him know: *this is your meeting*.

For a moment there was silence as the two students, both casually dressed in jeans and tee shirts, sat motionless and frowning. Obviously wondering why they were here to be questioned, the presence of the Dean made them particularly nervous.

Candrew spoke first. "You were both with Raven when I met you at the site of the new diamond mine that was going to be developed in a kimberlite pipe. You heard him suggest I go and look at some minerals in an old abandoned mine. Apparently, Raven was the one who arranged to have me taken there, and presumably he was the one responsible for having me locked up."

Neither student moved. The Dean clicked open his fountain pen and jotted notes in his leather-bound notebook.

Candrew stared at the two students. "Being locked in a deserted mine where there's no way to escape is attempted murder. We're talking about a very serious crime here: homicide." Candrew glanced from one to the other. "I want to know what role you both had."

"No role." It was Brandon who answered bluntly. "I was just there helping to evaluate the economics of the potential new mine site. I had nothing to do with sending you to that old mine."

Candrew nodded and turned to Carlos. "And you? What was Raven's reason for wanting to have me locked up? You know why he did that? This could have been a death sentence—murder."

"No. Not murder. That wasn't the reason," Carlos quickly replied.

"Then what was the reason?"

He leaned forward in his chair. "Navajo people have been very badly treated over the years," he said. "There are few paved roads, and right now forty percent of our people don't even have running water. Raven was well aware of this. He was really angry about it, and sensitive to Diné's awful treatment in the past. Especially, you know, like uranium mining and the toxic legacy it left." Carlos turned to Brandon as if for confirmation. The Dean looked up, then continued writing in his notebook. "Raven was determined not to see anything like that happen again. He thought of diamonds as a possible important commodity for Diné. This time he was determined not to let a valuable resource fall into non-Navajo hands." He stared at Candrew. "He saw you as a serious competitor."

"Really? So he was going to murder me to remove some competition?" Candrew was stunned.

"No. No. You've got it all wrong." Now it was Brandon talking. "Raven planned to let you out of the mine in a couple of days."

"What was the point of that?" Candrew was puzzled.

"Locking you up was only intended as a warning," Carlos explained. "He wanted to give you a very clear message that you should stay away from diamond exploration on the reservation. And not meddle in searching for diamonds. And not steal from us Indians." Carlos looked across at the Dean who had his head down writing. "Raven was a real strong supporter of all things Navajo, particularly our culture. He was inflexible in his insistence that we not be swamped by Anglo ways of doing things. Raven was single-minded about that."

This explanation definitely had a certain logic to it, Candrew thought. But he wanted to know, "Where is Raven now?"

"By now he's most likely back in Diné, on the reservation."

The Dean asked, "Do you have his cell phone number? I'm sure the police will want to contact him and they're going to need that."

"Cell phones don't work in most parts of Diné," Brandon said. "Just one more way the Navajo have been neglected."

There seemed to be little more to be said. After a few moments silence, Carlos asked, "Are we done here?"

"No. Not quite through yet."

"Well, you see, I've got class in ten minutes."

"Okay. We can let you go." Candrew thanked Carlos and Brandon for coming and for providing important information. The meeting broke up.

Candrew had a scheduled Tuesday class later that morning and hurried back toward Kinblade Hall to teach. As he made his way across the main plaza he thought over Carlos and Brandon's remarks. He was relieved that being locked in the mine was apparently not an attempt to murder him, but it was instead a serious warning. It seemed Raven had been determined to make sure a non-Indian stayed out of the diamond exploration business on Navajo land.

Through his morning's undergraduate lecture, Candrew was challenged to keep his thoughts from wandering and stay focused on geology. He was glad when he made it through all fifty minutes to the end.

Back in his office he phoned detective Ortiz. "Sorry to interrupt you again," he said, "but you'll want to hear what I've just found out." Candrew summarized everything Carlos and Brandon had told him about Navajo diamond mining and Raven's participation. "So you see, my being stuck in the old mine wasn't an attempted murder. It was intended as a warning for me not to get involved in mineral exploration on the Indian reservation."

Not surprisingly, Ortiz repeated what he'd said on the previous phone call—that this was only hearsay evidence. "Our staff and attorneys are going to have to sort it all out," he said. "I'm sure, however, your additional evidence will be important. I'm pleased you had your Dean there." He thanked Candrew for the new information.

Candrew was relieved that both Alex's murder and his being trapped had been essentially resolved, even if some of the details still needed to be clarified.

Relaxing, he phoned Renata and told her, "Well, I now know the reason I was locked up in a deserted mine,"

"You do? Why?"

"It was meant as a warning from the Navajo, and intended to force me to stay out of the diamond business on their reservation."

"You must be relieved to know there isn't someone out there who wants you killed." There was a short pause. "Dinner tonight?"

"Of course."

———

Candrew glanced at his watch—lunchtime. He logged out of his computer and headed down the stairs on his way to the faculty lounge. There he joined the usual 'lunch bunch.' Even though the campus grapevine was surprisingly efficient, news of that morning's interview with the students in Wilfred's office had not yet made the rounds.

"So, you still beavering away looking for diamonds?" Arlan Dee from the Business Office asked as Candrew pulled an empty chair up to the table.

The professor sitting opposite, the one with the tinted glasses and pony tail, said, "If you are, this time you'd better be careful not to get trapped underground and left to die."

Candrew explained that being trapped seemed to have been just a warning, not an attempted homicide. He sipped his diet coke. "Anyway, I'm ready to abandon the mineral exploration business. I'm going back to concentrate on my sandstone research."

"Sandstones make good garden walls," Arlan said, chuckling. "So you'll always have a steady market. But they're not quite in the same price range as diamonds."

"And I'm sure Renata will be disappointed you're not going to shower her with costly gems," the man opposite Candrew quipped.

Evelyn Snowparski, the biology professor at the end of the table, said, "Diamonds may be a *girl's* best friend—but obviously not a *guy's* best friend." She grinned. "From what you've told us, you seem to have been lucky to have survived with just a warning. That other diamond prospector wasn't so lucky, he got murdered."

"Alex? Yes, you're right. But that was by a different group," Candrew said. "A group with a very different agenda."

"Maybe you should stay in the diamond exploration business but move outside the U.S., go international," Evelyn said. "Get away from the locals." She reminded him to read '*King Solomon's Mines*,' the Ryder Haggard classic. "In that novel, exploration in Africa led to a cathedral-sized cavern with diamonds as big as eggs, even fist sized."

Candrew laughed. "I'll keep that in mind."

THE END

Glossary

This murder mystery is set in the southwest of the U.S. where some words are of Spanish origin and may be unfamiliar or pronounced differently. So, here's a very short glossary:

Adobe: Sun-dried earthen bricks; also, a house made of adobe bricks.

Arroyo: A natural stream channel. Typically dry most of the year, except during flash floods.

Banco: A solid bench built at the base of a wall. Usually made from adobe.

BIA: Bureau of Indian Affairs

Butte: Steep-sided, flat-topped hill. (Similar to a mesa, but smaller).

Canales: Water drain spouts extending out from the parapet of a flat roof and designed to protect adobe walls from falling rain-water.

Diopside: A green, silicate mineral.

Chile: The usual New Mexican spelling for "chili"

Chinle: Pronounced "*Chin-lee*"

Diatreme: A breccia-filled volcanic pipe formed by a gaseous explosion. Typically miles deep and a mile or more in diameter.

Duke City: Albuquerque. A town misnamed for the Spanish "Duke of Alburquerque" [*sic*].

Indicator minerals: Minerals associated with diamond-rich kimberlites, especially garnets that are chromium rich.

Jefe: Chief, boss.

Kimberlite: The rock type that is commonly the host for diamonds. (It is named after the town of Kimberly in diamond-rich South Africa).

Kimberlite pipe: *see* 'Diatreme'

Latillas: (pronounced with the Hispanic 'y' for the 'll'). Juniper or alder branches installed between vigas on ceilings.

Mesa: See 'butte." The word is Spanish for 'table'

Pahana: Hopi term for an Anglo—a white man.

Portál: Quite different from a *portal.* This is a covered porch that has a beamed roof over an outside patio and usually runs along the side of a house.

Posole: Corn and meat stew, traditionally with pork, spiced with red or green chile.

Talus: A loose rock pile, generally a slope on a hillside.

UNM: University of New Mexico (located in Albuquerque).

UNNM: University of Northern New Mexico (fictitious).

Vigas: Beams made from debarked tree trunks that are exposed in a ceiling where they hold up the roof.

Yellowlanders: The nickname for the fictitious University's sports teams. The University is close to the town of Tierra Amarillo—which translates as 'yellow land'